THE ODYSSEY
OF THE
BLUE SWAN

——————— by ———————

ALWYN A. CARDER

Sponsored and Edited By
Carolyn S. Partlow
Illustrated by author

authorHOUSE®

AuthorHouse™
1663 Liberty Drive
Bloomington, IN 47403
www.authorhouse.com
Phone: 1-800-839-8640

First published by AuthorHouse   6/24/2009

ISBN: 978-1-4259-4025-6 (sc)

Printed in the United States of America
Bloomington, Indiana

This book is printed on acid-free paper.

Credits and Acknowledgements

I WISH TO EXPRESS my gratitude to all the librarians, especially in the research departments; archivists all up and down western Ohio from Toledo to Cincinnati; and all the resource persons in the canal towns in between.

A great amount of credit is owed to stories and memories of Daisy Gast Peters, and the stories from her mother, Leanna Keller Gast. The barge canal experiences of George Gast, father of both Josephine and Daisy Gast, were equally important.

Many humorous incidents were handed down to the Gast Family, and to the author, who is related to this Old Brementown family by marriage. Other humorous events were also related through other old families. Many tales came from the Schweitermann, Kattmann, Keller, Osanbrook, Kitsinger, Pepplemann, and the Backhaus and Watermann families. Many stories came directly from the endless supply of Lulu Gast Morgan - stories that she picked up along the way and never forgot.

The author has placed the setting many years before the life spans of Josie and Lulu, the Josie and Lou-Lou of the novel, but he has tried to maintain the spirit and outlook of the later Gast descendants as though they were living in those early days of the old canal. That sense of humor has prevailed in many of the descendants of the Gast family here in America. The others, who were left behind in old Alsace near the German border, did not fare so well. Germany overran Alsace-Lorraine in the Franco-Prussian War of the 1870's and annexed these provinces. However, after World War I Germany was compelled to relinquish its claim of conquest. French language was again permitted. The same fate befell these brave people with the Nazi onslaught of the 1930's, but found liberation again in 1945. Their indominatable spirit lives on. Gast genealogists in America have been successful in establishing connections and ties with the Gast descendants in the area of Ligsdorf, Haut-Rhine and in Alsace in France in recent years.

Dedication

This book, *The Odyssey of the Blue Swan*, is dedicated to the memory the author has of Josephine Gast Current and her cousin Lulu Gast Morgan, those two intrepid wayfarers on life's towpath. They found the going not always easy, but they somehow managed to inspire us, the younger generations, with their humorous memories, endless anecdotes, and wisdom about life along the towpaths of their childhood in old "Brementown."

The Odyssey of the Blue Swan
Setting

The setting for this anthology of many stories is along the towpaths of the Miami and Erie Canal in western Ohio near the Indiana border in general, but in New Bremen, "Old Brementown," in particular. The beautiful <u>Blue Swan</u> packet show barge from the canals of Europe was the property of the unusual Gast family whose forebears had come to Western Ohio from Alsace near old Strasbourg. The Swan barge changed the lives of many of the staid and conservative local towpath people in Brementown, but it definitely changed the lives of the Gast and Kattmann families and nearly all the people its voyages touched.

CHAPTER I

THERE WAS GREAT EXCITEMENT at the gate of Lock 1 in New Bremen as the grain flotilla made ready to get underway for the long trip down the canal to the Maumee River, and on to Toledo on Lake Erie.

The Gast brothers, owners of the huge grain depot there, were taking a line of grain barges loaded with wheat and other grain to the larger grain elevators at Maumee and Toledo. From there the grain would be loaded onto lake steamers, shipped across Lake Erie, and on to other ports.

Louise Gast was overjoyed that she had been given permission by her overly cautious mother to join her cousin Josie, and the other Gasts, on this long trip. Even though her father, Hermann Gast, would accompany his brother, Ben, on the voyage to assist at the rudder tiller, Lou-Lou's mother had misgivings.

Bertha and Ben Gast welcomed Lou-Lou and her brother, Benjie, to their group as if they were part of their immediate family. Josie and her brothers, Charley and Lou, raced with Lou-Lou and Benjie onto the dock at Lock 1. They were reprimanded to stop, and then commanded to get aboard the barge. Otherwise, they would be left on the dock.

Louise, or Lou-Lou, as most called her, and Josie were rather reluctant to leave all their friends behind, especially their close girlfriends: Milly, Dort, and Gerta. They were also thirteen years of age - the same as they. Likewise, the boys, Charley, Lou, and Ben knew they would miss their friends who were the same age as they were. It would only be a few days, but it seemed like a long time to the young boys and girls. It was unusual, but there was some sort of special comradeship between the boys and girls, brothers and sisters included. The boys of the family were close to Schani, Jakey, Alby, and Fritzy. For some reason, they had permitted their sisters, Lou-Lou and Josie, along with their close girl friends, to share in their everyday conversations, pranks, and leisure hours.

The elders viewed it with good humor. The girls were not necessarily "tomboys" and the boys were not usually rude or demanding. They just all played, romped, and sang together in a spirit of good fun and comradeship.

Now came the moment of departure. Ben and Hermann Gast instructed Ian MacPherson, the lockmaster, to climb out on the lower lock gate downstream, the way the water flow went, and open the small wicket sluice in the bottom of the gate. He turned the long metal lever that allowed the slats of the louvered wicket to open. The impounded water immediately began sloshing out through the sluice into the canal beyond.

The rate of descent with an opened wicket was usually about one foot per minute inside the lock, and the heavy grain laden barge started to settle lower inside the lock with the receding water. In a short time, the barge was lower than the gates in front, and still the water rushed out through the wicket sluice in a great cataract. The lock gates did not dare to be opened before the bottom had been reached and the momentum of the impounded water was slackened to a minimum, because the barge inside could be thrown forcibly against the opened gate or the wall of the lock. Both barge and lock could be damaged, especially wooden locks.

When the water in the lock inside the lock gates reached the same level as the canal on the lower level beyond the lower gate, it was safe to open the great heavy lock gates to let the canal boat leave the lock and depart on downstream.

Ian MacPherson operated the balance beam on the right side while his lock helpers, the lock tenders, operated the beam on the left side. They slowly opened the massive gates inward so that they folded into their niche inside the lock. The gates were made to come together, not horizontally, but at an angle, so that their meeting produced an apex always pointing upstream. The wedge shaped slant made the gate stronger against the tons of water lodged against it, and this angle always was headed upstream. The water in the canal was constantly flowing, even if very slowly, from the source of the dams or reservoirs to the lowest level where it passed into a weir, or stream at the end of its destination.

Milly, Gerta and Dort gave shrill screams of laughter and farewell as the grain barge glided gracefully out of the lock into the canal. The polemen had nudged her gently out of the slip into the canal proper below the lock and now the drivers, or "haw-gee" men, attached the towline to the tow post a few feet back of the bow. The three waiting horses took up the slack slowly on the long line as their drivers urged them to start. The pull at first was slow and hard, but as the frictionless barge picked up speed, the tow seemed effort-less and the horses settled into their accustomed towpath gait.

Jakey, Alby, Schani, and Fritzy ran along the towpath calling last minute messages to Charley, Lou, and Benjie. Just beyond First Street, the barge passed Josie's home, which fronted a side view on the canal. The canal started to angle to the right(east) on its way to Lock 2 at New Paris - just a couple of miles before it straightened its course and started due north through eleven locks in its eight-mile course to St. Marys.

The canal would fall gently with the terrain as it went north through Auglaize County into the drainage watershed of the St. Marys River and all of its creeks and tributaries. After cutting through a mile or more of high moraine at Deep Cut, the canal once again went lower into the watershed valley of the Auglaize River on its way to the large Maumee at old Fort Defiance.

The boys kept up their banter; those on the barge hurling broken corncobs at their tormentors on the towpath, who were trying to sting them with hard beans and actual lead shot from their elderberry rod peashooters.

The barge with the Gast family, followed by another loaded grain barge, had no sooner crossed under the bridge at First Street when hysterical frantic cries from back up the canal, even beyond Lock 1, caught everyone's attention. People stopped in the streets because they thought there was a fire or some terrible accident. The deep, almost bass voice of the huge pie shop woman, Grünwalda Peppleman, called down the canal to the barge in her broken English, half-German, argot vernacular.

"Stop! Ger-stop! Mein Gott, vee forgot der pies. Ben Gast, Hermann Gast, hove to, stop der barges ein minute! Der special pies I bake for Bertha and all of you are ready."

The huge woman's face was flushed from using her oven on the hot June summer morning. She tried to run along the towpath while tugging a huge market basket that held the pies. Ben and Hermann sent the boys back on the towpath to help Grünwalda, as they slacked speed to stop the barge. The barge behind them also slowed down. Bertha Gast came out on the top deck of the barge from her makeshift kitchen cabin at the front to inquire about the screaming and to see why they were stopping so soon. When she learned what the cause of the commotion was, she turned on her daughter, Josie, and her sons, Charley and Lou.

"I forgot about the pies. You boys were supposed to go to Grünwalda's kitchen and get them early this morning."

"Ma, she didn't have them ready. I think she must have had two dozen pies out on her table and cupboard that were ready to bake this morning."

"Well Ben," she told her husband, "it's a good thing you heard her and stopped. She would be crushed if we went off and forgot her pies that she worked so hard to bake for us. She just has too much to do."

"Heard her, Bertha?" Ben teased, "Und how could anyone not hear all that caterwauling and squalling? Vy the whole town is turning out as if for a fire brigade of buckets." Ben Gast lapsed only occasionally into a few German words as did his brother, Hermann. Frau Kattmann's family used more German words sprinkled between their English words when they were in her presence. She was a dominating German Prussian mother who was called "Frau Kattmann" by everyone. Augusta Kattmann, in her arrogant self-importance, never bothered to learn either correct German or correct English when she came to the American States as a young girl. She was too busy and too interested in her important projects to bother with academic syntax. In addition, she usually translated her German with worse broken English. Then Augusta rushed on to the pressing demands of her busy life.

Jakey, Schani, and Fritzy ran back to the puffing Grünwalda and relieved her of the heavy basket full of pies.

The boys carried them carefully under Grünwalda's constant barrage of admonition as she trudged along behind them. The pies were handed over the gunwale to the hands of Ben Gast, who took them to the kitchen cabin door where Bertha took them from him. The townspeople gathered along the towpath in amusement.

"Mein Gott in Himmel - iss there a fire?" Gerta Hemel called down from her upstairs window above her husband's blacksmith forge.

"Not likely, woman," the gruff voice of the heavy muscled blacksmith, Jake Hemel, called up to her. "Now don't stir up one and you won't miss nuthin'," he warned in a gruff voice.

"Hey there Ben, Hermann," Henry Backhaus called down from an upper window of his flour mill on the canal "We thought you were hauling grain to Lake Erie. Are you starting a delicatessen too?"

Grünwalda scowled up at Henry and commanded him to get back to his "making dair flours" so that she would have some fresh supplies for her pie shop. She growled in her deep bass voice that "all dair men in dis town are loafers . . . und my Charley is the biggest loafer of dem all."

Marta Schweitermann's high cheerful laughter rang out over that end of town as she came down a side street and up onto the towpath with a huge basket of white clothes that she was delivering to some of her customers. She and Henry exchanged their usual pleasantries and private jokes in German. Ludwig Waterman and Leo Wiemeyer joined in the laughter from the doors of their establishments, which lined the towpath. All three mills used waterpower from the canal where it fell over the sluice dam at the lock, then into a basin of mill wheels, and back again into the canal at the lower level.

After more goodbyes, the flotilla of barges moved on down the canal past Langhorst's huge tile works and the dry dock toward New Paris.

As the canal barges neared St. Marys after descending the many locks down the Loramie summit toward the north, they paused a while to "lock through" at Fledderjohn's sawmill at Lock 6. Josie Gast and her cousin Louise, called Lou-Lou affectionately by family members, were almost as interested in the working of the water-powered sawmill as her brothers and Louise's brother, Benjie. They liked to watch the logs that were fed slowly from their carriers into the huge slow, but powerful vertical saws that sawed steadily up and down, hour after hour, by the swivel-crank wheel. The crank wheel was powered by the main over-shot water wheel.

Surplus water flowed over the cataract of the overflow sluice when the lock gates were closed or when they were in the operation of locking through. The state who owned the canal and land of the right of way of the towpath and berm permitted landowners to erect water mills at these sites. They used the power from the impounded water that fell a distance of ten or eleven feet at each lock of the descending canal gradient.

The horses breathed easier after a few minutes of rest at the lock. To keep his sons out of mischief and away from the saws in the sawmill, Ben Gast put his boys to work bringing wooden buckets of water from the canal below the lock to water the horses of both barges.

Nothing could suppress the excited energy of the young adolescents. They were only a few miles away from home and yet everything took on a special meaning to them. It felt like a holiday with a new freedom. This was the sixth lock they had descended or locked through since number one in New Bremen. However, each time they were fascinated with the working of the sluice wickets and the lowering and opening of the gates. It was more special if the younger boys were permitted to assist the lockmaster with the huge balance beams that were attached to the gates.

Lou-Lou and Josie seemed to enjoy running up and down the lock incline from the lower level towpath, up the graveled hill lock to the upper level, and then running back down again to see how far their momentum would carry them down the lower towpath. A small water battle was started when the boys, Charley, Lou, and Ben, flipped water out of their horse water buckets onto the girls.

The play was soon stopped when the two barges were ready to resume the short trip of four miles into St. Marys. The barges would travel through six more locks in that short distance. At each lock, they frolicked. Sometimes they raced on the smooth wooden dock planks of the wood locks, and sometimes they waited for bullfrogs to surface after the turbulence of the rushing water from the lock gates.

Ben and Herman Gast, owners of the barges and the grain depot in New Bremen, exchanged news with each lockmaster, (lock tenders) or barge captain. When they met another barge coming up the canal from the south, the men carefully supervised the handling of the towlines to prevent tangled lines. The barge coming upstream and on the right side had the right of way. The barge standing over usually let their lines go limp and rest on the bottom of the canal so that the barge with the right of way could pass smoothly over it, keeping the towline taut and under strain. They met such a barge at Lock 10, which had just been lifted up the lock and laid over to give it the right of way, and then entered the slip of the canal to be lowered, using the same coffer full of water that had brought the other barge to their level.

The men hastened to get by the oncoming barge that was pulled by the flat scow oxen led by their owner, Uriah Hornback. He was the barefoot preacher who preached the gospel of Swedenborg all along the canal to anyone who would stop and listen. Although he was dedicated to his faith and meant well, he was a nuisance to the more hurried barge captains who were in a hurry to get through the locks and on to their destinations to unload or take on more cargo.

Although the Gasts tried to be civil and hurry on, there was no stopping Uriah from starting to visit with them. He knew everyone in this short section of the canal from Junction on south to fabled Lockington of the six locks to the south of "Brementown."

They managed to get by him and on through the other locks to the high aqueduct over the St. Marys River just south of the town. Where the great large reservoir feeder joined the canal, Ben and Hermann attempted to point out to the children as well as Bertha Gast, how the two-mile long feeder was supplied water from the great reservoir, which was impounded behind the levee dikes several miles long. They explained to their listeners that the reservoir was the largest artificial body of water in the United States, and for all they knew, perhaps in the world. The boys began asking their fathers why they could not make a large sailboat, bring it up, and try it on the artificial lake. The reservoir was dangerous for such boats, their fathers explained, because when the state took over the 17,600 acres, or nearly 29 square miles of this Black Swamp forest land needed for the reservoir, most of the trees were left standing. There was no time to clear them out and the cost would have been prohibitive. The important thing was to get the reservoir built for the water supply needed to feed the canal from Lock 11 just south of the feeder, down to Junction, and on to the Maumee River in Defiance (over fifty miles north).

Beaver Creek and all its tributary creeks had been dammed at the western levee at Celina to create the huge lake. An overflow weir at the western levee carried wastewater back into the creek, which was a tributary of the Wabash River to the west. Even though the Wabash was claimed by Indiana as its nostalgic and storied river of the sycamores, it rose here in western Ohio's Darke County, south of old Fort Recovery of Revolutionary days.

It was dangerous to use anything but small boats on the reservoir because of the fallen trees, but more so because of the submerged snags and stumps left just below the waterline when the rotted trees blew over into the water. The state public works, along with the federal government, had declared the right of eminent domain and had acquired not only the canal right of way, but also this vast tract of woods and swampy creek bottom land for the reservoir.

The reservoir was shallow, averaging only five or six feet of water in most places, but having a depth of over ten feet in some of the former lowlands and swamp sloughs. There had been some opposition fifteen years earlier when the reservoir was constructed. Many people considered standing bodies of water, especially with trees left standing in them, as health hazards causing swamp miasma, malaria, cholera, and "bad night air." In the end, the canal hysteria won out in the race for progress and for an outlet for commercial produce to markets. Ohio people as well as Indiana people, who were champions of the canal systems, derided the uninformed peasant hooligans as "ignorant hill jacks." They learned that masked bands of marauders in southern Indiana's Clay County had cut the dams and tried to drain the reservoirs because of the shallow ponds with "trees standing." They were worried about the reservoirs causing unhealthful air.

The canals were the only answer for progress and financial prosperity in these new states where only woodland trails and muddy ox roads prevailed. There was no access to markets.

Ben Gast and his brother Hermann told the boys that a sailboat was out of the question because of the hidden underwater danger.

Bertha Gast smiled to herself as she sat on the open top deck of the front barge shelling garden peas for the noon meal. It was not easy for her to corral Josie and Lou-Lou into helping with the chore because they were just as high-spirited as the boys were, and they were afraid they would miss something along the towpath. The traffic was picking up as they neared St. Marys, and it would continue to do so all the way to the Maumee River at Defiance. Bertha smiled when she heard her husband, Ben, talking with his brother, Hermann, about the danger of boating on the grand reservoir. She knew they wanted to go boating on the reservoir in spite of the danger. She knew that they talked not only of a sailing boat, but they had heard stories of steam propelled barges on the lower canal south of the central state town of Loramie Summit; on down around Dayton and in the more cosmopolitan area of Cincinnati. They were like schoolboys when they sat on rainy days in Jake Hemel's blacksmith shop or Elihu Sanders' tinker repair shop and talked "steam engines" and steam propulsion with the other men of the town.

In a short distance, perhaps a half-mile or so, the barges left Lock 11 and Feeder's Junction and approached the covered aqueduct over the St. Marys River. This aqueduct was longer than the one they were more used to south of New Bremen at Fort Loramie. There the aqueduct carried the canal over Loramie Creek in a wooden trough, or flume.

"Now why do they put a roof over these things when they are already wet with water flowing through them?" Lou-Lou asked her aunt. It was for some sort of protection to the timbers, but no one outside of the canal engineers knew the answer. Perhaps it was to protect the exposed timber of the flume or the wooden towpath. It was like a covered bridge inside of the aqueduct. The sound of the horse's hooves on the wooden flooring of the towpath inside the aqueduct caused a few of the twittering swallows to leave their nests on the ledges up near the roof. They would swoop down ahead of the barge, and then swoop down low over the canal to catch insects. Bertha ducked her head when some of the trusting birds swept too near her.

In a few minutes, they left the cool shade of the aqueduct roof and glided out into the sunlit canal. Josie and Lou-Lou looked down into the deep ravine of the St. Marys River in the brief moment allotted to them before the barge moved on into the canal and their view was shut off. The canal grade was rising higher here because of the low ground that sloped down into the little ravine valley of the river. The canal kept its grade between locks. It was imperative to do so, or the water would find a low place and start a disastrous overflow. It would wash out the berm or towpath bank and cause a breach down into the surrounding fields or woods. At each lock, the grade was lowered as the canal descended the general lowering slope of the land, and as it followed the topography of the land. Canal engineers had surveyed the land before they dug the canal. There had to be a source of water supply on the top of each summit in order for the canal barges to be lifted or lowered, for water could not be forced uphill.

In little less than half a mile, they entered St. Marys. They stopped in the large basin just off Spring Street at Lock 12.

Mrs. McKeeters, who lived in an upstairs flat above the basin, was sitting out in the sun on her balcony tending her flowers in the pots and flower boxes on the porch railing. She missed but little that passed on the canal or the basin below. As the Gasts were locking through, she saw them and came tripping down her wooden stairs to the barge at the lock. She was an old friend from New Bremen, but she was also a close friend of Gerta Hemel, the wife of the blacksmith. She was also a friend of Marybelle MacPherson, wife of the lockmaster at Lock 1 as well as a friend of Clara Nell Sanders of the tinker shop.

She visited chattily with Bertha Gast as the barge was being lowered. She was pleasant at first, but she soon launched into her favorite subject, that of her tormentor, the old Irish codger. O'Hooligan was a rough mouthed drunkard who loved to insult all the women. He especially enjoyed insulting old women along the canal whom he suspected of promoting all the gossip there was about him and his curious cargo, all up and down the canal. He had been through the lock that very morning going up toward Junction. When she referred to the direction of north, she said, "Up," although the canal people said "Down north" since the canal was descending down to the Maumee River valley at the north. Bertha sympathized with her but advised her to leave her porch balcony when she saw him coming. One could always hear him coming because of the ribald song he sang over and over again just to antagonize bystanders and other canalers on the towpath.

Mrs. Sarah McKeeters was well known for her famous cheese. Some of the German people relished it, but many other townspeople thought it was a runny, brown, evil-smelling mess, unfit for human consumption. Many thought her ingredients were suspect. There was gossip about the cheese because many had seen her carrying small baskets of rabbit manure and others kinds of manure up her stairs. She explained that it was mulch for all her flower boxes, which had to be replenished with fertilizer from time to time. The women neighbors knew how the cheese was made and thought nothing of it. Maybe it was more violent than limburger, but it had more character and a deeper, richer taste. The men were not so charitable. They had started the rumor about the evil-smelling cheese.

"Now Josie," Lou-Lou began, "if she gives Aunt Bertha any of that rotten stuff, we can't stay on board and take that stuff into the city of Toledo with us."

"We'll chuck it overboard when Ma isn't looking," Charley insisted.

"Oh no," Hermann Gast said from his seat at the rudder tiller.

"Some of that would taste mighty great. *Ja, Ist gut*," he told the girls. "Some of that cheese for dinner with sauerkraut and sausages would be wonderful! *Ja, ist gut*."

"Oh, Papa," Lou-Lou cried, wrinkling her nose.

"Now sh-h, be quiet, *mein Liebchens*. Mrs. McKeeters will hear you and she would be offended," Hermann told the girls.

The conversation with Mrs. McKeeters switched to the traffic that was all going north to Junction. She told them of a carnival or fair of some sort that was going on there along the canal, and in the adjoining fields and lots beside the canal. The two canals joined there but went on into Toledo as one. Junction City had sprung up there almost overnight when the Indiana Canal, the Wabash and Erie, was joined at last by the Miami extension of the Miami and Erie canal after much foot dragging by the Ohio legislature. It was said that Ohio was tardy because the Federal Government had given Indiana unheard of federal land grants of land to build her canals. Ohio wanted that sort of land grant and money to build the extension of the Miami Canal. Indiana had the ticklish job of building the canal in Ohio all the way into Toledo. The difference was resolved many years later.

After waiting their turn through Lock 13 on Spring Street, the Gasts made the turn to the north through town. After meeting oncoming barges cautiously, they soon left the city limits and followed the canal down the valley of the St. Marys River toward Kossuth. They passed under many bridges where country roads crossed over the canal. Soon they crossed the aqueduct over a small creek, through another lock, curved past wharfs and docks in Kossuth, and then approached the village of Deep Cut where the canal was to pass through the deep cut and the St. Marys clay moraine. This ridge of clay extended for a mile and a quarter. It was left there by the last great glacier as a moraine that divided the watershed of the St. Marys River from that of the Auglaize River at Lock 14. There was a small settlement of houses and shops.

The young boys as well as Josie and Lou-Lou, had heard of this Deep Cut nearly all of their lives and wondered just what it was. It sounded so dangerous and exciting.

Canal engineers had worked with a crew of five hundred men for four years to dig this trench through the moraine with only picks, shovels, horse carts, and a few horse drawn drag scoops. Now here, it was a trench of over fifty feet deep - from the height of the Moraine's Summit that ran for over a mile, and the towpath was notched out of the steep hillside above it. There was a bordering carpet of yellow summer flowers through the entire length of the deep cut, but they strangely disappeared once the canal was out on level ground and in the open sunlight. Most people called these weeds. However, Lou-Lou and Josie teased Charley and Lou about skipping off the barge and running ahead to gather some of the daisy-like flowers.

Soon they were at the lock in Spencerville, had descended it, and headed on north for Delphos. Beyond the Delphos lock, there were white geese and ducks in the wide canal that paid but little attention to the barges. They bobbed in the water for water bugs or dived among the reeds and weeds at the edge of the canal for other insects.

As they left Delphos, they passed under an arch of tall cottonwood trees that overhung the canal. It would soon be time for an early noon meal, and

Bertha Gast gave the girls tasks to do to help her get the food ready. With their help, she could get the plates ready to be served to the men in the barge that was behind them at the next lock. They would not lose any time stopping to pass the food back, but would eat while underway or during the locking through process.

"How much better ham, garden peas, fried potatoes, and ordinary boiled cabbage tastes when you're out in the open," Lou-Lou said over her plate up on the top cabin deck.

"Things that you are used to always taste better away from home," Bertha Gast told her. "It's the change of scenery."

"It's jes that ye've got up a big appetite from scampering all over the decks and running along the docks and towpath," her brother told her. "Ye're jes excited over the fair up at Junction that Mrs. McKeeters told us about."

"Wonder if we'll see Hogback Mary and her animal acts this year," Charley said as he ate his hot biscuit with homemade butter.

"You shouldn't call the poor woman that," Bertha Gast admonished. "Her name is Mary Hogan, a kindly old Irish soul who loves those animals, even her donkeys, dearly. She sleeps with them".

The towns of Ottoville, and Mondale passed. When they approached the larger aqueduct over the wide Little Auglaize River just south of Melrose, they knew they were only eight or nine miles from Junction. Next, just beyond Melrose, they crossed the Blue Creek aqueduct. These aqueducts were made of wood, but some of the smaller culverts were made of stone where a brook or run was taken beneath the canal bed for drainage. There were a few made of logs, but that practice held grave dangers. Rotting could take place and permit a collapse of the canal bed above it. The result of such a collapse had caused disasters along the upper canal. The bed of the canal grade was washed out by the water flow of the small runlet beneath it where the logs had rotted. As the wash grew larger, the canal bed above gave way and permitted the canal to start a wash down into the hole. Soon the hole became a raging torrent when the whole flow of the canal tore out the bed and side berms and raced down into the land below the grade. It drained that section of the canal between the locks.

At length, the barge flotilla neared the double stone locks beyond the Blue Creek Aqueduct. At this lock, two barges going the same way could be locked through, or even locked through in opposite directions at the same time. It was necessary here because of the short distance to the junction of the two canals. The canal traffic was doubled here. Therefore, the double locks helped to prevent bottleneck delays.

After leaving the double stone lock, the barges descended to the lower level and proceeded to the aqueduct over Flat Rock Creek. It was less than a couple of miles on north into Junction City. As they drew nearer to the town, the traffic increased. There were rigs, wagons, and carriages stirring up dust on the road that paralleled the canal. Everyone was going to the fair.

The afternoon had passed into early evening. They had traveled at the usual speed of five miles per hour, resting the horses at the locks. Every ten miles they changed the horses with a fresh trio for the tow hitch. The horses were carried in the grain barge that followed. The front barge was equipped with small and cramped living quarters, while the hold was filled with sacks of wheat for the market in Toledo and Manhattan. The second barge had small sleeping quarters for the polemen, linemen, and drivers. The horse compartments, or stables, were in the middle.

Lou-Lou, Josie and the boys crowded to the front of the top cabin deck on the lead barge as they neared Junction City. They could see the crowds, and the hitch racks were full of horses with carriages and wagons. Out in the field there were tents for various displays and animal stalls. The young people up on that top deck could hear the beating of a bass drum and a brass band. Their excitement grew when they began to hear the steam calliope on one of the showboats tied up either along the docks of the towpath or in the basin.

The girls knew that simple melody, having heard it many times up and down the canal when that small showboat had gone through New Bremen on its way south to Berlin (Ft. Loramie), and to the fair at Lockington Village.

As the calliope skirled out its rather off-key melody, the girls sang with it.

"Sing cal-li-o-pee-e; hear that mel-o-dy; how you sing to me-e." After the barges had found berthing space on down the canal through the congestion of the juncture and the village, the polemen and drivers tied them up, and started taking care of the unhitched horses. The horses were watered and fed. Afterward, the horses grazed on the green grass just off the towpath down the berm.

The crewmembers took turns at staying on the decks of the barges so that the Gast families could go to the fair and carnival shows. Bertha walked with the girls along the towpath when there was room, but they soon descended from it and walked in the road over in the grassy lots where the bazaars and display tents were.

Charley, Lou, and Ben came running to tell Lou-Lou and Josie that they had found Hogback Mary and her animal, dog and pony show. They led the girls to her show and watched her pet each one before she put it through its act. One little dog would sit up with its paws in front while sitting on the back of the trotting pony. Later in the evening after her show, the girls saw Mary going to the canal with her wooden buckets, fill them and carry them on the wooden bow across her shoulders to water her ponies and donkeys. They looked at that sturdy wood crossbow over her shoulders with a heavy bucket of water suspended by a small rope from each end. No wonder they called her "hogback." She hunched over, arching her broad back and shoulders to resemble a fattened shoat. Nevertheless, Mary Hog an smiled at everyone, puffing her corncob pipe, shuffling along with her load, crunching the gravel with her leather heeled, wide brogan shoes.

After making the complete round of the fairgrounds and towpath show barges, Josie and Lou-Lou found that they were fascinated most by the rather dressy Spanish Gypsy showboat. The male and female dancers, as well as members of the orchestra, seemed to be of a much higher grade than the usual lot of carnival people. They all looked more like a light opera company from Toledo or Cincinnati. Maybe they were from the fabled Erie Canal in New York, or perhaps they were a New York City troupe traveling the back hinterland for the summer.

People began buying tickets for the Spanish showboat and going up the gangplank to the cabin auditorium. The orchestra and dancers put on a small show up on the top deck so that they could draw customers.

Chapter 2

Faster and faster the Spanish dancer whirled, and her lace mantilla floated from the high-jeweled combs in her black hair. Booted heels clicked furiously as the male *flamenco* dancers accompanied the whirling señorita with the stomping of their booted heels upon the planks of the wide canal dock.

The music grew faster; the castanets clicked. Men, women, and children drew in closer from the canal banks and the streets of the little village. The outside world had come to Western Ohio of the 1850's bringing a breath of romantic excitement into the back country rustic village. Farmers, townspeople, canal travelers, barge captains and crewmen crowded in to get a better view of the colorful dance, and to hear the wild Spanish *Gitano flamenco* music from the chorus of guitars on the canal showboat.

Josie Gast and her cousin Louise stood open-eyed and drank in the graceful dramatic spectacle in front of them. Mrs. Gast watched from the deck of the canal boat a few yards down the canal from the moored showboat.

There was a call of "fight" down the dock and Josie's brothers Charley and Lou, along with Louise's brother Ben, had run down the towpath to see the excitement. Some Irish crewmembers of a tied-up cargo boat had gotten into a brawl with some other Irishmen from another cargo barge. The other barge crewmembers were from another country in the "auld sod," and that was cause enough for fisticuffs and "donnybrook."

Hermann and August Ben Gast hurried through the crowd after their sons and brought them back in front of their moored barge. The Spanish dance whirled on and on, and then with a shout of "Olé," it came to a furious but sudden end. The barker started hustling the crowd to sell tickets for the show aboard the moored showboat. People rushed the ticket man and shoved their way across the gangplank into the showboat to get the best front seats.

With misgiving, Bertha Gast allowed herself to be wheedled into going to the show with the girls. Hermann and August Ben Gast took the boys and strolled on down past the other barges of the traveling carnival moored along the docks and in the basin of the small village of Junction.

Buggies and wagons crowded the hitch racks in the hitch yards. Amish spring wagons and buckboards stood in lines along the dimly lit streets. It was summer and the first of the traveling circuses, carnivals, and showboats were beginning to ply the small towns along the canal's 266 some odd miles from Toledo to Cincinnati.

To the amazement of the boys, huge elephants suddenly appeared on the towpath. After being hitched to one of the great long showboats, the elephants began to tow it farther up the canal where it was moored in the wider basin. Crowds were waiting to go aboard to see the circus animals in the huge cages. Charley and Ben were game enough to try to touch the huge animals when Hermann Gast called them back sharply.

Next, Charley and Lou went with their father, August Ben, to try their luck with hurling wooden balls at straw dolls for prizes. Hermann Gast took his son, young Ben, to see the farm animals at the pavilion over in the town's grove where a sort of a small fair was going on.

There was more excitement on the canal bank docks when the steam calliope started to play its off-key show tunes to get the crowd to come to a musical variety show in one of the long showboats. The excited boys ran ahead of their fathers to see the caravan of camels perform across the canal on the flat meadow at the end of the basin. Colored flares lighted the caravan as their turbaned drivers put them through their paces, and then caused them to lie down. When the camels were prodded into getting to their feet again, they made the strangest groans of protest the boys had ever heard.

Up in town there was a light commotion as town constables hurried through the throng toward the canal towpath with their nightsticks raised in threatening positions. There was a stir of excitement as a rumor spread that there was trouble - something about an old Irishman, a regular nuisance to both man and beast on the entire length of the canal, who had traded insults with some foreigners on a passing log raft. He had received a rock in the head for his bad manners. His crewmembers had fished him out of the canal. The dark swarthy foreigners stood silent on their raft farther upstream. They waited for the lawmen, and waited to face whatever consequences might come from their self-defense.

The night wore on, and tomorrow was a day to be started early, for there was a long haul ahead to Toledo. It was time to go aboard their barge and get to bed, Ben Gast advised.

There was so much more to see and the night was still young, but with their parents insisting firmly, the younger ones in the family had been reluctantly led back into the darker shadows of the canal towpath to their own cargo barge tied up away from the boisterous showboats.

Louise Gast, usually tempestuous, and second, in high spirits, was unusually so. She ran ahead of the rest of them, whirling as she ran laughing and singing. She snapped her fingers to imitate the Spanish dancer's castanets as she called back, "I'm a dancing señorita from romantic old Madreed-a." The boys joined hands with Josie and all of them were running in a straight line down the cobbled towpath. They began to play "whip cracker." Then they circled Louise.

"Lou-Lou, you're no Spanish dancer. Your legs are too chubby!" her brother Ben teased her. She passed him and poked him in the ribs, then continued pirouetting down the towpath.

"Ja, Lou-Lou's a little Dutch sausage," Charley called. In a game of mock tag, Lou-Lou took out running after her cousin. In the dark, she almost collided with a swarthy gypsy man with large earrings who flashed white teeth and called out something in the foreign tongue of Romany.

Louise wheeled on her toes and raced back toward her elders, muttering to Josie, "Ach! Mein Kleine Josie. No spiken da Onglisch!"

The girls shrieked with laughter at Louise's blunder, when Bertha Gast called out, "You children stop clowning. You'll fool around and fall into the canal, and then I'll take a paddle and dry you good!"

The Gasts herded the capricious youngsters aboard the barge. They were too full of life, and the tempo of the carnival, to think about bed. After some refreshment of cookies and milk, the lamps were turned out and the barge was prepared for the night. The horses were checked; the lanterns were turned low at both bow and stern.

The boys were permitted to sleep on the top deck with their blankets since it was a warm night. After all, the crewmembers were sleeping on deck on the stern of the barge. It would be safe even with gypsies on the roam and a line of circus show boats tied up at the docks.

Sleep would not come to Josie and Lou-Lou. They whispered and giggled far into the night. They tried to picture what the bustling miles of wharfs and docks would look like at Toledo at the Lake Erie port, and at Manhattan. What exciting things would they see, and what would the stylish ladies of society be wearing at the depots as they boarded the lake steamers, or the canal boats, from their coaches that dropped them at the wharf?

What would the new boat look like? This was the uppermost thing in all of their minds, for they were to pick up their new passenger boat and take it back down the canal to their home, to Old Brementown. They knew that they would be the envy of the county as well as of the other barge people on the canal. However, not one of them had seen it - only Grandma Kattmann who had bargained for the boat up in the New York State somewhere along the Erie, knew what it would be like. It might be a drab black "snub nose," an ark, or it might be a trim, sleek packet.

Finally, sleep stole over them. Distant boat horns sounded up and down the canal as late barges passed in the night.

Daybreak of that next morning in early June came cool and damp. A light blanket of fog spread over the surface of the canal water and the surrounding countryside. All the carnival barges were quiet and closed up. Off to one side cattle were bawling in the meadow whose low places were filled with wisps of white mist. Ben and Hermann Gast were up before daylight to get their tow horses fed, curried, and harnessed so that they could get their barge underway before other barge captains did. There were several barges tied up for the night, there in the widened basin at Junction where the long canal from Indiana joined the Miami and Ohio Canal on its way northeast to Maumee and Toledo on Lake Erie. Ben and Hermann wanted to be first through the weigh locks, toll stations, and above all, the locks. They wanted to make Toledo before dark that evening, and they had fifty miles or more to go. Fast packets for passengers might make 80 or 100 miles a day, but 50 or 60 miles was a good day for a medium sized freight cargo barge traveling at only 4 or 5 miles an hour.

"Breakfast will be ready by the time you men are," Bertha Gast said to her husband from the small kitchen cabin in the bow. She would let the children sleep; they could eat later when they were underway. She hurried at her small cook stove preparing ham, eggs, and bacon with some hot cakes and syrup.

"Bertha, feed the crewmen first, especially the drivers. Hermann and I can take turns and eat underway. We want to get an early start ahead of all the rest of these," Ben Gast answered. To save time, Hermann Gast helped the crewmen curry the horses that were being fed near the stern of the barge.

"Lower your voices, you two. They will all be awake and get ahead of us," Hermann cautioned the joking driver hoggees, or "haw-gees," as some called them.

The drivers and pole men dipped up some cold water from the canal and washed for breakfast. They sat at a makeshift table, which consisted of boards over a barrel, and ate their breakfast with relish, as rapidly as Bertha Gast could serve it. The barge was crowded with cargo so that there were only cramped living quarters, but nevertheless, it was a great and exciting holiday to the Gast children. They finally were able to take a long trip on the canal.

Tumbling from their shelf-like tiers of bunk beds in the small sleeping quarters just off the kitchen cabin, were Charley, Lou and their cousin, young Ben Gast. There was too much excitement going on, and they did not want to miss any of it by lying in their bunks, when they could hear all the commotion of getting ready to shove off and travel up the canal.

"Now you youngin's get out from under foot. If it were any other time, I'd have to pull you out of bed. Scat now! Your father's in a hurry to get started," Bertha admonished her brood.

"Gee, Ma! We have to help. We're crew too, you know."

"No you're not. Not up here in all this mess of cargo and traffic," Bertha replied as she took a huge copper pot of coffee up on deck to the crewmen.

"We have to eat too, Ma. We got to help ride, heave fenders, and pole off," Charley and Lou began, "And besides..." However, they didn't get their words finished before their mother was coming back down the steps into the kitchen cabin. She took up her pancake turner and gave both boys a swat across the seats of their britches, and hurried them back into the sleeping quarters. There was a hint of a smile around her mouth, but she tried to be serious.

"Help ride? Indeed, you are not. That's why we brought crewmen on this trip. There's no place for *hoggee* boys in this congestion." All three boys managed to sneak back out and stood with hunched shoulders around the warm kitchen range well out of the reach of Bertha Gast.

"You would confuse *haw* with *gee*."

"Ah, Ma, that's half the fun! Wait until we get back and tell the other boys. . . "

"There'll be enough to tell as it is. You got to ride yesterday afternoon, and that was dangerous enough what with passing all those slow barges through Deep Cut."

"All those slow barges, *Ach in Himmel*. I don't know what your father and Uncle Hermann meant. They are as bad as you boys."

The boys knew that she was beginning to be irritated when she lurched into half-English and half-German phrases, and they became leery of her pancake turner or wooden ladle.

"Now, if nothing else will do you but to be up and underfoot, get your jackets on and clear out of here," she said. "*Mein Liebchens,* it's cold and chilly up there in the morning mist."

Charley and Lou, with their cousin, young Ben, hurried up onto the deck. In the morning fog, they could make out the high mule bridge that spanned the canal so that drivers could cross from one side to another where the two canals met. Then they went on north as one. It appeared higher than it was, but Charley bet the others that the bridge was at least as high as a medium barn. It looked narrow and rather rickety. The boys wondered how horses, and especially mules, could cross that high above the water without blinders on their bridles.

Hermann Gast kept the shivering boys busy. They carried up water from the canal in wooden buckets to water the horses. The water level was too low from the berm or towpath to let them drink themselves.

"Man alive," Young Ben gasped, as he tugged the heavy wooden bucket up the gangplank, "that big old white Ned can walk up the towpath." The drivers had finished their quick breakfast. The poleman was ready on the bow. Another crewman took the tiller when the horses were hitched and the towline was fastened in the cleat on the bow. Just as Ben and Hermann were ready to unfasten the lines from the snubbing posts on the dock pilings, a small-bonneted figure came sprinting up the gangplank and called into the kitchen cabin with a high, cheerful voice.

"Miz Gast, Wal I do declare. I never did know you to be a line-boat wife!" She laughed out in a cackling voice.

"Elvira Brenner. Wherever on earth did you come from?" Bertha Gast asked her visitor. "We didn't see your *Wabash Loon* tied up here with the other barges when we turned in for the night."

"Law, no! We jist snuck in from Indianny on the Wabash and Erie," she said as she motioned in the foggy darkness to the Indiana canal to the west, "and a plumb foolish thing to do, it was. However, there's no telling Joel Brenner anything. Why we came nigh bumpin' a time or two with other barges tied up in the fog, and that would'er bin a fine mess!"

"Are you going on up to the lake this trip, Elvira?" Bertha asked.

"Satan's drawers! I'd hope to say not. We just delivered a load of brick from the kilns at Ft. Loramie to Fort Wayne. They want another twenty, er meebe fifty-thousand, as soon as we kin git 'em up to 'em fer some buildin' or other, and Joel can feel them dollars in his hand, so we travel and work night and day, haulin' eighty ton a load. Got to git it while the gettin's good," she cackled as she raced on, "We're tying up for vittles!"

Hermann and August Ben were impatient to get underway, and without appearing to be rude, gave Bertha a gentle hint that they were all ready. They ask her to get loose things tied down. Elvira saw their impatience, and tying her bonnet strings tightly under her chin, she gave Bertha Gast one last piece of advice: "Now you're not used to this, dearie. Now that you're gittin' up where the traffic is heavier, and more and more cities, don't leave your cabin door unlocked a minute when you're docked. Better to see that someone is on board all the time. Your girls along?" Bertha nodded that they were, but that they had not been called for breakfast yet.

"Better keep them close inside when you pass some of these loadin' docks, and stuff cotton in their ears. Taint fittin'! Law!" Bertha nodded her head while Elvira continued; "Now them Dutch or 'Doitsch' ain't quite so bad, but them dumb foul mouth Irish barge men and dock rowdies, law! There's one old devil of a codger, an old scoundrel. They call him O'Hooligan. Now there's trouble fer ye. He is allus drunk and squalls some song."

"I know only too well who <u>he</u> is. He passes our place singing that same old Irish Jig ditty, and carrying on," Bertha admitted. Ben Gast cleared his throat with impatience. Elvira raced on, anxious to warn Bertha, but at the same time anxious to pass on some canal gossip.

"Allus fightin' and cussin' all the ole wimmen he sees. Well, most any grown woman, fer that matter. Got it in fer mostly ole wimmen. He thinks they are evil and cause all the troubles in this world. They say no one ever sees his cargo in the hold. All outside deck stuff is all covered up or in closed boxes or barrels. Some say he's handlin' stolen goods between Toledo and Cincinnati. Some yell at him that all he has is boxes of manure - just to get him mad."

"Elvira. . . why on earth. . .?" Bertha tried to interrupt. Elvira lowered her voice, and stepping closer, she almost whispered:

"There's them what say he is transportin' bad wimmen between Irish work crews for a few coins. Some say they are kidnapped white slaves, and then some say its poor orphan children, boys and girls from the old country, frum Ireland mostly. Now watch out fer him. Whur there is so much smoke, there must be some fire."

Bertha thanked her for her concern and asked about all of the Brenners. Then Elvira remembered what she came for and asked, "Mis Gast, can you let me 'ave some brown sugar or some syrup? Even sorghum will do. I'm in a pinch for breakfast, and imagine, no cakes without syrup! There ain't nothin' open at this ungodly hour. Couldn't find no grocery, grog er grub sutler open anywhur neither."

Bertha dipped into her brown sugar bin and filled the tin dipper that Elvira produced from her shawl.

"I'll pay you back when I'm next through Brementown. Go right past your door, you know. How ye enjoyin' all the fuss and 'to-do' a line captain's wife has to do on board the barge?"

Bertha told Mrs. Brenner how they had enjoyed the trip and that it was a good outing for all of them. Elvira sensed that there was another reason for the entire family to come on a cargo trip, which was usually made only by crewmembers. Trying to ferret out more information, Elvira went on tactlessly: "Course, if you were a regular line or cargo boat and used to this every day. . . . However, what with your family, home and all, I do declare that I do marvel. Also, all this cookin' fer all these hands. Goin' to somethin' special up there in Toledo?"

"Mrs. Brenner, we are going to pick up our new boat at the wharf in Toledo. That's why there are so many of us, for we have to man two crews on the way back - one for each barge."

"Law! Now wouldn't yee know. New boat? Whut kind, Miz Gast?"

"It's a special one for our grain company and for the brewery as well. Then it has a passenger packet cabin, for about twenty people - thirty in a pinch if need be," Bertha explained as she walked Elvira to the gangplank.

"That's why we all came. We could save money and time if I cooked for the crew and family." Elvira's jaw dropped down for a moment, but then her good spirits came back with a rush as she giggled with enthusiasm.

"Wal ding-bust my hide. Did you ever? Now that's jist right fine honey. My, my, won't you all be proud? A new packet boat!"

Bertha Gast smiled as she said goodbye to her talkative guest, and hurried back across the gangplank just as the boys were coming to take it back on deck from the towpath berm.

As hurried preparations were made for getting underway, Elvira Brenner turned and peered in the semi-darkness as the grain barge nosed out slowly from the pier. Lines were cast off and the boys jumped back on board. The horses took up the slack on the towline, and their harnesses creaked. The polemen kept the ponderous, slow moving barge out from the banks with their long pikes. Bertha stood for a moment at the steps down into the kitchen cabin and smiled to herself as she heard Elvira complaining to the morning breeze.

"Bricks and stones will break my bones. That's our style, this old barge, and brickbats, and roofing pitch." Then she threw up her hand to wave as she called out, "Have a nice trip now in that new boat, y' hear? See y'all when we git back to Brementown."

Ben and Hermann growled in a low voice that the whole cluster of barges would be awakened by her squalling. The barge was nearly up to full speed now, and the horses fell into an easy gait since the strain of the heavy pull was over.

The barge glided along with little resistance on the glassy surfaced water. Now and then one of the horses gave a short snort as they often do when pulling.

As soon as the barge was clear of the other barges and headed into the open water of the canal, the small village of Junction disappeared in the mist. Bertha Gast set the small table in the kitchen for her husband and brother-in-law. The boys were told they could either take their plates up on deck or wait and eat later. Bertha put them to scrubbing their hands and faces in cold water and then prepared their breakfast plates. She could hear the girls talking and giggling in their curtained-off partition of the small sleeping cabin. In no time, she knew they would be up and ready for breakfast.

August Ben complained to Hermann that they had lost fifteen minutes or more with Mrs. Brenner's visit. It was a wonder that not every other barge in the cluster had gotten underway to clutter up the canal.

Bertha Gast put both men in good spirits with her hot coffee and hearty breakfast. As the morning became lighter, the fog still hung thick to the ground and to the canal's surface. The miles passed slowly but steadily. A sudden blast from an approaching barge caused Ben and Hermann to spring up on deck. In the fog, the boats barely missed bumping, but the drivers handled the lines on the towpath so that no time was lost.

As soon as the men had finished breakfast, the boys brought their plates down from the chilly upper deck. They warmed themselves at the little cook stove. Bertha made them drink some hot chocolate since they were too young for coffee.

Bertha Gast and her sister Bernhardina had married brothers, August Ben and Hermann Gast. Ben and Hermann were much alike and worked well together, sharing each other's troubles, each helping the other at the brewery and grain elevator. It was a different thing with Bertha and her sister Bernhardina, and her other sister, Ernestine, for that matter. Bertha Gast did not put on airs or assume manners; she was satisfied with her station in life and with the economic level that her husband provided for her with the grain business and with his share in the thriving <u>Blue</u> <u>Goose</u> <u>Brewery</u>, in Bremen. However, Bernhardina Gast and her sister, Ernestine Hofermeyer, considered the brewery just a little beneath the dignity of living, even though it provided a good living. Perhaps their wealthy mother, Mrs. Kattmann, had spoiled them with her grand airs, her world travel, and conservative German well-ordered outlook on everything.

Bertha and her husband, August Ben, had laughed to themselves when Hermann was not around. They joked at how dismayed Bernhardina and Ernestine were and how they had shrieked about the rough men, the fights, and the terrible language one heard on the docks. Bernhardina did not see how it could be comfortable or decent to live in such cramped quarters, and with all those men, not only the family, but those rough drivers and crewmen. Unheard of! When Bertha played her trump card, she told her sisters that she would need one of them to go along. They refused outright. Ben and Hermann Gast tried to point out that delivery of the new boat meant more money and more business to all of them concerned. In addition, someone had to go to bring the boat down, especially since *their* mother, Frau Augusta Kattmann, had picked the boat out back somewhere on the Erie Canal. She had financed it for the company in some sort of an arrangement of a long time loan that would allow her to pay for it over time.

Bertha announced that she was taking her older children along for she needed her daughter Josie to help with the cooking and chores aboard. Right away Hermann and Bernhardina's daughter, Louise, or cousin Lou-Lou, as Josie called her, "put up a howl" to go on this wonderful trip to Lake Erie with cousin Josie. Louise's young brother, Ben, joined in the plea. It was out of the question, but Bertha pointed out that it would look better if there were some other women or girls along. August Ben smiled at this, reminding Bertha that he doubted that towns-people would gossip about her going on a barge trip when her husband was along as captain, and her brother-in-law was at the rudder tiller.

It was then that Bertha and Bernhardina's mother, Mrs. Kattmann, stepped into the picture. In her customary way, she listened first to one side, then to the other, putting her hand up for silence while she pondered. Then casting her eyes down, she would motion for the other side to put up their argument. She would ponder some more, then with typical German flair for organization and simplified efficiency, she would announce a decision. No one countered Augusta Kattmann's decision in the family of Kattmann-Gast. Turning to her daughter, Bernhardina, and husband, Hermann Gast, she queried, "Ve need the barge, and someone has to go get it. *Ja?*"

Bernhardina Gast could only nod her head meekly, wondering at her domineering mother's next move. Turning to Bertha and August Ben, Mrs. Kattmann said, "The new boat *vill* make money for both der grain company *und* der brewery. *Ja?* Iss dot not so, *mein* August Benjamin? Und you Bairtha, you need help in der kitchen and some female companionship as well as looks for der respectability. *Ja?*" They both nodded, and Bertha could hardly keep from smiling for she knew her mother was about to explode one of her cannon-like decisions. Mrs. Kattmann had picked up her ever-present black bag that contained nearly everything she would ever need in every situation or any crisis. Poking her fat ample hands deep down inside the bag, Mrs. Kattmann exploded, "Und I spend *mein* good moneys. . . plenty of good, good moneys. . . traveling hundreds of miles. . . find beautiful, *ach so schön* beautiful barge at *gut, ach so gut* bargain for *mein* family to use for business, make moneys, travel, and the like. What do they do? They quibble and simper ovair small ridiculous splitting of der har, *Ja?*" Then glowering like a bull about to charge, her face like a sudden summer storm, she charged into the family in front of her.

"HALTEN! GEHEN SIE, and get der boat! HELIGE. . . Helige. . . Kristkinder! Of course, Louise and Josephine are to go, young Ben too, with Bertha. It wouldn't hurt you, Bernhardina, to go along and keep that *Louveese* in order. She needs to be paddled more to make der lady."

It was settled then. There were neither more words nor protests. Ben and Hermann got out of the room as soon as they could so they could have a good laugh. Sister Ernestine had left in tears of anger.

CHAPTER 3

THERE WAS LITTLE TIME for Bertha Gast to sit at the table with the boys and think back of the words at her mother's town house in New Bremen, and of how the decision was made for her to take this unheard of trip, besides acting as an experienced line boat Captain's wife. She had never ridden on the new passenger packet boat any farther than the neighboring towns of St. Marys or south to Minster and Ft. Loramie. However, now here she was pretending that she knew what she was doing by carrying out her mother's express command. She was thoroughly enjoying it all, and who knew? Perhaps with a little experience she could become a real "canaler" like Elvira Brenner, or that big Russian "Buffalo Woman" whom the rougher men teased from a safe distance from her rocks and clubs.

Without warning, Louise Gast danced out into the kitchen fully dressed with her bouffant skirts swirling around her. She thumped on a tin pan and pretended that she had a tambourine, as Josie followed her through the narrow doorway.

"Aunt Bertha, see what I learned last night from that Spanish gypsy woman on the showboat? I hope they will be there when we come back by. I could soon learn that fandango business." Louise danced by the boys, banging each one on top of the head with her pie pan as she whirled by. She let her rich contralto voice soar into a make-believe Spanish dance, and snapped her fingers to imitate castanets.

"Oh, I'm a Señorita. . . a gay one from Mad-dreed-dah!" Her brother, young Ben, put out his foot as if he were going to trip her. Bertha clapped her hands in dismay as Josie started to follow Louise. Louise stumbled, then turned and slapped Ben across the back. Bertha took up her wooden stirring ladle and gave Louise a light whack across her voluminous skirts, then took Josie by the arm and parted the two dancers.

"Stop it, all of you. Why, *Ach in Himmel*, you'll fall, upset the stove, and get burned."

"Why the *fandango* is the latest rage, Aunt Bert." Louise laughed and said, "Besides, it's *Ach Himmel* or *Gott in Himmel*."

"You'll think fandango, you two. We've got a couple of gallons of green beans to "fandangle" the strings off before noon. All these hands eat enough for a threshing gang."

"You'll see," Bertha scoffed, and then added, "*Himmel* or maybe *zum Teufel*." (Hell)

"What's going on down here?" Ben Gast boomed down the short stair gangway into the kitchen. His voice was full of mock anger. His laughing eyes gave him away. Louise rushed up the stairs to her uncle and hugged him as she called out a good morning greeting.

"The clowning has started already, and what with the sun not up yet. What will it be before we get home?" Bertha replied.

The girls washed their faces and hands and sat down hungrily for breakfast. Louise would not let her aunt wait on them but insisted on preparing breakfast for herself and Josie. Always the buffoon, Louise picked up a piece of ham with her fingers instead of with her fork. She growled like a dog and began gnawing on it with intermittent growls. The boys yelled with laughter, and Bertha Gast knew that once Lou-Lou got started this would be one of *those* days!

Imitating Elvira Brenner, Louise said,

"Satan's bloomers! Ah declare, but ah am shore hankering fer some vittles," and she waded into her breakfast.

As the barge traveled along to the northeast, the fog cleared little by little, and when the sun was well up over the horizon, only a few patches of mist skimmed along the top of the water. Another boat gave a warning blast on its horn as it approached. Then it was past, and the green countryside could be seen on each side. Soon they approached the bank of the Auglaize River and paralleled it. The girls looked down into the cool mist covered water of the wide river as they passed high above when they crossed it on the stone aqueduct.

In a little over an hour and a half the barge had traveled the nine or ten miles to the first stone lock. It was just at the southwest edge of old Fort Defiance. They descended other locks and were soon into the town. Josie saw the numbers cut into the stone abutments: #31 and #32, as they descended the locks right in the middle of town.

The docks, the high mule bridge, and soon the Maumee River were in view. The last lock came into view all at once, and for the first time the girls were frightened. Even Bertha Gast's eyes were wide with misgiving as she looked down from the high lock into the fast current that came after the early summer rains. The last lock, #34, led right down and out into the river.

Since there was traffic ahead of them, Ben stopped the barge long enough to see how the horses were breathing. Satisfied that they were not getting overheated once the barge was underway, and did not pull as hard as they would with a loaded wagon, he gave orders to get underway again. Yes, they were "locking through." They were delighted that they could rest while they waited their turn to descend the last lock into the river.

When the lock gate opened in front of them, the barge glided right out into the current of the river. Bertha was frightened but tried not to show it in front of her children. The drivers got off the horses and led them across the slender, rather frail looking mule bridge that crossed the river. The polemen guided the barge to the other side of the river where the line was again attached and the horses took up the slack, towing as before. Now the towpath was on the river bank. In a short distance, just before the wide dam at Independence, the barge entered a slip and then turned into the canal again. The dam impounded water to raise the canal level so that a series of locks would let the canal down, lock by lock, to the last level at Maumee.

As they traveled northeast along the Maumee River after passing Independence, they met another showboat, or rather a traveling menagerie. The showboat was going south to play the smaller towns for the summer trade. Ben directed his drivers to dismount and lead the horses when they met the circus boats that were pulled by a line of elephants. Of all things, there were elephants on the towpath, and it was only eight or ten feet wide in some places! The horses snorted a few times and stepped sideways upon meeting the elephants, but the drivers held them in check and the meeting passed without incident. Lou-Lou and Josie were excited at seeing two barges, each nearly as long as the length of the locks, being pulled as one by two peaceful lumbering elephants who didn't seem to know they had a couple of circus barges hooked together in tow. Some of the painted women with brass rings in their ears and dressed in gypsy costumes waved and winked at the boys who were standing on the top cabin deck with their mouths open. All of a sudden, a wheezing off-tune steam calliope began its rendition of "O Susannah," and the townspeople began gathering at the canal dock.

"They're putting in here at Independence for a stand," Charley said to Ben and Lou. "Wouldn't we like to go?"

"You all had enough of show last night at the showboat at Junction to do you for a spell, I should think," Bertha told them.

"You should have seen Papa at that side show. He was having his fortune told by that señorita with the high combs and lace in her hair," Lou told his mother, while looking at his father to see if he heard from the tiller.

"Oh? Now this is interesting!" Bertha said with accusation in her voice, while turning a look of askance toward her husband in the stern.

"Everybody get down. Low willow limbs ahead," Ben Gast shouted so that he could change the subject. All those on the top deck ducked down.

He shouted again, "Low bridge just ahead! Watch out for those limbs! Everybody down," he shouted. They all turned to look, but noticed that there were several feet of bridge clearance over them.

As mid-morning came on, the sun came out bright and warm. Bertha Gast washed out some towels and clothing, and put them out to dry in the sun. She used a towline at the bow where the breeze would catch them and dry them faster. Ben and Hermann figured that it was twelve or thirteen miles on to Napoleon, and they wanted to be halfway between there and the small hamlet of Texas by noon.

Bertha brought the green beans up on the cabin deck and put the girls busy helping her string them. When they had the beans done, she kept them busy with other preparations for the noon meal. They made biscuits and peeled potatoes. They couldn't waste any time, or lose any time on the way, if they were to get into Maumee and get unloaded before dark. Maybe they could go aboard their new schooner and some of them could sleep aboard it this coming night. Someone should be aboard it to stand guard, as Elvira Brenner had warned them.

At Independence, they could look across to the river and see the dam that impounded water for miles, and served as a great reservoir to turn water into the canal when needed. The great reservoir at St. Marys was the principal source of water for the northern end of the canal to the Maumee River at Defiance, but dams along the rivers also acted as sources for water that could be turned into the canal if needed. Surplus water sloshed out of the canal through waste-weirs when a certain level was met.

As they passed through the basin at Napoleon they saw the covered weigh locks. There were turn-around basins for barges to be turned for heading back down south. They passed through more locks as they descended lower toward Lake Erie.

At Texas the barge stopped and a change of horses was made. The fresh horses were taken from their stalls on board while the others were brought aboard to rest and be fed. Bertha had the noon lunch ready so that the crew hands could eat when the change was made.

The traffic became heavier and heavier as they approached Grand Rapids where the river started and descended across rocky shoals and a fall of rapids.

After entering the guard lock just before Independence Dam, they left the free water of the river and re-entered the canal again. They would have an uneventful trip without locks for the next 22-mile level that would bring them to the locks at Texas, where three locks would lower them twenty-five feet. The Maumee River was getting gradually wider as it neared its mouth at Maumee Bay on Lake Erie. The barges left the independent canal channel as they neared Grand Rapids, which was a town on the other side of the river to the southeast. To reach Grand Rapids, barges were required to cross the slack water pool of the river, then enter a short canal by means of locks to unload or load produce at the docks or mills in the town. After leaving this side-cut, the barges could proceed in the slack water river pool above the dam for one and a quarter miles where they would enter the canal again through a guard lock, and ride the high grade of the canal to the next lock at Waterville, which would lower them to the next level. This final level would carry them to the locks of the side-cut from the main line of the canal where locks would allow barges to descend into Maumee. The main line would continue on this upper level to the side-cut at Swan Creek in Toledo, and then on for five more miles or so to Manhattanville on the lake. Water impounded by the Providence Dam furnished the canal water for the thirty-four miles to Manhattanville where surplus water sloshed over the sluice down into Lake Erie, which was the end of the main line of the canal.

The men figured their distances by looking at the sun and then their watches. Hermann had a navigator's map in the captain's cabin with every bridge, lock, and hamlet on the canal marked plainly and with mileage marked between. By their nearest calculations, it was nearly sixteen miles to Waterville. That would take them a good three hours or more. It would be the middle of the afternoon when they arrived. With the constant stream of traffic they were meeting, it would probably take them a couple of hours from Waterville, past Fallen Timbers, and on to the locks and dock at Maumee. One thing was certain; no one had passed them, not even a rapid passenger packet. However, they did meet several coming south on their way to Cincinnati, or over into Indiana to Fort Wayne. Others traveled on to Lafayette, or on down to Evansville and the Ohio River.

The peaceful open country opened up from Texas and Florida as the afternoon became almost hot. The breeze from the slow moving barge fanned the occupants on the deck. Bertha Gast found herself dozing in her bench chair.

Just as they were passing Florida at the foot of the river's Flat Rock Ripples, the calm of the warm afternoon was broken by shouts of angry men on the decks of two freight barges. Before anyone could stop them, the men were fighting on the dock, and one knocked the other into the canal. Bertha hurried the girls below into the cabin where they could not hear such vulgar language. The men were fighting over who should go through the lock first, and were arguing over their own rights. The toll-master collected toll from Ben Gast and ordered the two other barges out of the right away. The town constables came running to the docks and the barge captains quickly paid their tolls and headed on south.

Farther up the canal, the girls could hear an old accordion and banjo playing an accompaniment to an old Irish shantyman's caterwauling, drunken song. As they came closer to the man's barge, Bertha herded both the girls and the young boys into the cabin. She knew this rough-mouthed old man. He probably had a name, but everyone on the canal called him the "old Irish codger." He was coming south with a load of merchandise in wooden boxes. Many of the men on the canal would taunt him just to hear him swear and rant at them. They accused him of hauling manure. They said he just put it in store boxes for looks, but that he couldn't get hired for hauling anything else. It was as Elvira said: every lock and hamlet knew him.

The old codger would swear, shake his fist, and then swig from his ever-present bottle. It was hard to understand him in his drunken stupor. Besides that, he had few teeth for enunciation.

"Whuddle-thay, ye golth-blameth old wimmen-th!" He bawled out trying to say, "What do ye say, gol-blamed old wimmen?" His Irish shanty men with him were little better. He always blamed all the ills in the world on meddling old women, and never missed a chance to insult them with ribald oaths or obscene songs. Everyone knew his antics long before Elvira Brenner came to the Ohio Canal.

He became abusive toward a long raft of logs consisting of eight or ten "ricks" lashed together with chains. A huge swarthy foreign woman in a huge felt hat was the captain, and some other long bearded, solemn men were her crew. The old codger became abusive when he could not get past for he wanted to beat her through the locks. If he had to wait for all ten ricks to go through separately, he would be delayed for over half an hour. The Gast grain barge had descended the lock and met the old codger trying to overtake the log raft that was coming south.

When the foreigners, apparently Russians, failed to give him room to pass the slow raft, the "old codger," seeing his favorite quarry, a mere woman, was the cause of all his trouble, as they always were in life, he made the mistake of calling out.

"Stand by there, you old Water Buffalo. Whuddle-thay? Whuddleth? Why, Saints preserve us! It's our old friend from down in the swamp bottoms and mugwumps of Shelby County," he shouted to his Irish brigands, who were rough canalers that had helped dig the canal ten years before. "It's old Hog Eye from the Loramie Creek bottoms."

"Lay over there, you old Wart Hog, you Old Buffalo Female. Let a *real boat* pass."

Ben Gast told his drivers to let the log raft pass since it was longer. "Just unhitch the towline instead of letting it go slack or we'll snag on the logs. Let the poor woman have the right of way on the towpath."

Hermann came back to the tiller. The polemen kept a wary eye on the raft, and on the banks, in order to keep the barge from colliding now that it was coasting free from the towline.

"Ben, there's going to be trouble. That's the Russian woman and her group. No one talks to her that way. Let's get on past," Hermann warned him.

"Do you remember the time she threw a stick of wood or a club, and hit him down home in Brementown in the Cherry Street basin to the south?" Ben asked him.

"Yes I do, and it laid him out for a while. However, there he is at it again, asking for more," Hermann said. Then he continued,

"I always wanted to see that Russian sawmill village hidden away in the woods and swampland south of Loramie. So that's Big Bertha - the Buffalo Woman who runs a barge and hauls rafts of logs to the sawmill.

"Yes, that's the one they call Big Barge Bertha, but that's not her Russian name. The old codger is asking for it," Ben replied. It was so exciting, but Bertha would not let the girls appear on deck near such a vile man on the deck of the other boat they were meeting. It was bad enough just to be able to hear him. There was no use having the drunken derelict of the "auld sod" insult them just because they were wearing dresses. When the huge Russian woman ignored the insulting calls of the old codger, he became furious, and banged on his deck as he called out,

"Hey, Hog Eye! Be ye deaf too? Stand over..." However, that was as far as he got. Big Bertha hurled a rock so fast that it went straight as a bullet, and the old codger caught it in the forehead. He collapsed on deck and toppled into the water. His Irish crew bailed him out but kept silent. The Russian men said not a word, but started up from the log raft. The horses were stopped, and the great bearded dark men pulled curved knives and polished ironwood clubs from their sashes, as they came to the back of the raft. They stopped and stared at the Irish boat. The Irish men were stupefied. Their coasting barge bumped into the log raft and stopped. The Russian men looked at the bow of the boat and then up to the Irish polemen. When the Irish men failed to make a move to fight or to utter a sound, the big Russian poleman, the one they called Big Gregori, grunted, and then spat on the Irish barge. No one moved. The lockmaster blew his horn for traffic to move.

The Russian woman paid her toll, and the Russian men started unhitching the ricks from the raft so that they could be poled through the locks. All was quiet as the Gasts moved on toward Waterville and the last leg of their journey.

The constant flow of traffic kept the warm afternoon from being too dull for there was the constant tenor of the captain's horns somewhere ahead or astern. The crew was so expert at letting the towline go slack so that meeting boats could cross over the line without causing any delay. However, there was a constant stream of traffic going southwest, either for the passage south on the Miami and Erie, or on west through Fort Wayne on the Wabash and Erie. One thing was certain, no other barge overtook Ben and Hermann Gast and caused them to have to lay over, except once when the repair "hurry up boat" passed them on somewhat of an emergency ahead.

If any other captain hurried at the speed of ten or twelve miles an hour, he would be fined ten dollars if caught, but the "hurry up boat" was a different matter. It was a matter of life and death of the canal and its traffic for hours, days, or more, when the repair "hurry up boat" went foaming by with its water washing the banks. An alert path master and the "hurry up boat" might save a whole side of the berm from caving in where a muskrat, mole, or even a crawdad had bored through the levees and caused a small trickle to start washing out into the fields beside it.

The basin at Waterville was passed uneventfully, as was the next lock while they came down lower toward the lake level. Late afternoon passed into early evening, and still the traffic going south did not slacken. In the past two hours at least four passenger packets, each with eighty - one hundred fashionably dressed ladies and gentlemen met them. Providence slipped by. The next small town would be Perrysburg, then Maumee. As late afternoon was growing into evening, Ben Gast became a little concerned. He did not like the congestion that was beginning to gather as he neared the last lock down to the Maumee level after leaving Perrysburg. What if it took hours for all the lined up boats to go through the lock and it grew dark? How would they find their berth at the Maumee docks with all this traffic? If all dock spaces were taken, would they have to turn around and return to a dock in some small village along the way, and wait until the next day? Hermann was not one to worry as much as his brother did. Together with Bertha, he was able to calm Ben's apprehensions.

Some of the crew started muttering darkly when they met a nondescript barge with a surly, furtive captain who neither spoke nor looked anyone in the eye that he met on the canal. No one knew exactly what he hauled or what sort of crew he had. Most of the canal crews were united in disliking the hulking, scar faced man, and especially the way he abused his small boys whom he drove as if they were grown seasoned crewmen. The rumors spread and up and down the canal that he used child labor who were orphan boys from orphanages, and he was able to take children from many of them. No one knew how he did this, but dark shadows followed him. He never stayed at one place along the canals for long, but he did always work out of the large cities on long hauls.

Some whispered this man, Silverman, dealt in contraband materials and was a fence for stolen goods - especially barrels of whiskey. Some said he aided runaway slaves, and then kidnapped and resold them. Others said he pretended to aid them, and then captured runaway slaves and collected the bounty reward. No one knew what the exact truth was. Hermann and Ben Gast were white with anger when they saw him and his crewmen abuse the wretched small boys whom they cuffed about on deck, and made ride the teams for hours on end. There was something very wrong there...and highly profitable...yet very secretive. Hermann and Ben had seen the abuse of these wretched, often sick small boys on previous trips. Talk followed this dark evil man to the remote western Ohio canal all the way from the busy Erie Canal in New York.

At last, Maumee and the final lock were before them. After waiting for what seemed like hours, it was time for Gasts' barge to take its turn in the lock, and be lowered to the last level. Everyone was on the deck above the holds. There was the constant blowing of boat horns in the cargo traffic. Stevedores shouted, and linemen called to each other as they maneuvered the lines to secure boats in the locks, or to lead them through. However, beyond those closed great wooden lock gates lay another world. Josie and Lou-Lou could hardly contain themselves because they wanted to see that other world right away.

Where the great Maumee entered the estuary that led up to Toledo and onto Lake Erie, large lake crafts were moored. The girls could see the masts and stacks of sailing ships as well as smaller steamers. Miles of docks lay ahead where larger ships lay docked in the deep water in front of Toledo at Maumee Bay.

Charley, Lou, and Ben had stopped their teasing because they were too full of amazement at all the sights around them to talk. They only wanted to ask questions from the experienced crewmen who answered them good-naturedly. They were amused by the boyish excitement. Bertha Gast was just as excited as her children were but she tried not to show it.

Now at last they were in the lock. The gate closed behind them. Then the nose of the barge was edged almost against the closed gate ahead. Everything stood still for a few minutes.

The long barge began to sink lower and lower in the canal lock when the sluice wicket panels in the lock gates were opened. The sixty-five foot long barge was not as long, or as trim looking, as the passenger packets, but it had been smooth comfortable riding. Josie Gast stood breathlessly with her cousin, Louise Gast, and her brothers on the deck of the freight barge. Three locks took the boats down to the level of Swan Creek. These three locks along Canal Street in the vicinity between Stanton and Harrison Streets let the barges down into a basin that led directly into a loop of Swan Creek. The barges used the creek itself as a free water basin for a few blocks along Whittleway Street. Beyond that and to the northeast was another loop at Clayton and Short Streets. Coming out of that loop which resembled something of a bayou, the creek proceeded on north. Between Washington and Monroe Streets, it turned at an angle and emptied right into the Maumee River in the middle of Toledo.

There was an additional basin of a sort along the river and just beyond Clayton Street and the large Oliver House. A guard lock gate was situated where the creek joined the Maumee River at Monroe and Washington Streets. It prevented high water from the river, at flood stage, from overflowing and flooding the canal basins.

The extension of the canal from the Harrison Street locks was moved over to Swan Creek on an aqueduct as the canal made its way on to the northeast, between Ontario and Michigan Streets. The remaining five miles took them to the two locks at Manhattanville, on Maumee Bay, near Bay View at the lakefront.

As the barge reached the level of water in the lower basin, the huge wooden lock gate slowly opened. This was the last of the three locks and now the sluice wicket had let the water flow from the lock so that the boat lowered nearly a foot per minute. The lock gates opened and the barge was poled effortlessly into the Swan Creek Basin. The horses took up the slack on the towline as the dock master directed Ben and Hermann to their docking slip. It was down the creek near the grain warehouses that were along Whittleway Street in the freight zone.

Dock stevedores helped pole the grain barges into their assigned slip at the docks to be unloaded.

"I'll bet there are miles and miles of docks like these all the way out to Maumee Bay on Lake Erie," Charley Gast gasped to his father who was seated at the rudder tiller. August Ben Gast was too busy trying to help ease the heavy barge against the hemp fenders that were protecting the barge from the dock pilings to answer his son. Charley, along with Lou and young Benjie Gast, looked all around them and saw blocks, and what seemed to be miles of busy docks. They had never seen such commotion or such commercial bustling like this before, not even at Junction City or Defiance during the busiest days of traffic.

Lou-Lou, Josie, and Bertha Gast sat on the top cabin promenade deck and watched the scenes of the city, the freight docks, and the river traffic beyond. Bertha Gast knew that she could not follow Elvira Brenner's advice and keep the two girls confined in the cabin below so that they would not hear rough talk, or a possible violent exchange of fists between brawling stevedores and unruly barge hands. There was too much to see, and she was almost as excited as the two girls were with the scene before them.

At last the barges were secured to the bollards and snubbing posts of the wooden docks. The great activity of shipping, unloading, berthing, and reloading the barges made the harbor front of Toledo a thriving, humming commercial center. From here, all the produce coming into Toledo from the two canals was trans-shipped on lake vessels to ports on the Great Lakes. However, more importantly, the produce was shipped to Montreal and Quebec on the St. Lawrence River. A great amount of commerce also went from Toledo directly to ports overseas and all over the world. A great amount of shipping also went across Lake Erie and entered the fabulous Erie Canal for shipment to the port of New York.

The barge people from the small interior canal towns of Ohio and Indiana never ceased to wonder and marvel. The same thing was true at the bustling waterfront of Cincinnati, the Queen City, when the riverfront wharfs were lined with river steamboats. The canal basins there were even larger than those of Toledo. There was more gaiety in Cincinnati, more of a carnival spirit at the beer gardens and other attractions such as grand saloons, dance halls, luxurious dining rooms, and restaurants.

The larger lake and ocean going ships were moored at Maumee Bay on the lakefront. However, smaller ships were moored across the deep Maumee River from Toledo at Perrysburg. The docks and wharfs could be seen across the river at times. They resembled a maze of masts, riggings, and sails.

The Wabash and Erie Canal, running the entire length of Indiana, joined the Miami and Erie Canal at Junction City, Ohio. It caused a great increase of shipping and commerce in Toledo. With the passage of the packet, Banner, from Cincinnati to Toledo, in 1845, the entire waterway from the Ohio River to the Great Lakes was opened. In just a few years, the canal business had boomed to close to three-quarters of a million dollars in toll revenues alone.

It was never made certain to the general public, of both the states of Ohio and Indiana, as to who exactly had built this last leg of the canal from Junction City to Toledo. Government federal funds had been given to both states to complete the canal, but since Indiana had been so interested on completing it, the name of Wabash and Erie seemed to stick.

Overnight it seemed that passenger packets appeared, and the commissioners in Cincinnati reported that 40,000 people had traveled the canal as passengers.

It was this emphasis on passenger fares that had brought the Gasts to Toledo. The freight barge they brought to the docks at Maumee was loaded with nearly 2,000 bushels of wheat (nearly 60 tons) in grain sacks. They were there for reshipment on the Great Lakes. The barge would carry back south tons of merchandise for merchants in towns along the way. The freight on the barges included firearms, shoes, wool, bolts of cloth, rum and numerous other articles from lake ports.

Bertha Gast came up on the top deck to join her children in the excitement of seeing the vast bustling port. Ben Gast took the field glasses from his brother, Hermann, and looked up and down the miles of docks as the Maumee River widened into an estuary bay that became the western end of Lake Erie at Manhattan. There was one thing uppermost in all minds of the family on the deck of the barge. They were to pick up their new barge which had been built somewhere in the east, and was brought to the lake on the Erie Canal. It was transferred onto a lake freighter at Buffalo, New York, and was brought to Toledo. The new boat was to be a combination of freight barge, but also had some passenger facilities and the captain's living quarters. Its lines were slimmer than the bull-nosed freight barges and it was to have a slanted cabin space over its freight holds.

"I don't see any light blue barge tied up anywhere yet," Ben Gast told his brother, as he continued to look up and down the endless docks on both sides of the river port. "It must be four or five miles of canal and docks from this side cut basin up to the locks at Manhattan."

"Time enough for that later," Hermann answered him, "but the port master can tell us its berth number when we're ready."

The younger members of the family could not contain their eagerness to see the light blue cargo – "packet" as it was called. It was to belong to the Gast family and their grain elevator and brewery business down south in New Bremen. Louise Gast had told Josie that she had heard her mother tell one of her aunts that Grandma Kattmann had financed it, for she owned the brewery. The grain business belonged to her sons-in-law, the Gasts, but the two businesses worked well together. Grandma Kattmann, or Grandma-Má, as the family always said, while accenting the last "Má," loved to travel, and the canal was ideal. It was dustless, smooth riding, and comfortable as compared to the jolting, dusty coach over wretched backwoods roads of mud, stones or graveled and log corduroy pikes. She could well afford to finance the barge and even though no one knew the actual cost, it was well known that passenger packets cost anywhere from $2,000 to $4,000 each.

CHAPTER 4

THE BARGE WHICH WAS now tied up at its berth seemed very small and inconspicuous, along with the hundreds of others which seemed to extend in lines on both sides of the Maumee Basin for over a half mile. Beyond the basin the canal paralleled the docks of Maumee estuary for what looked like four or five miles. It was almost to the bay on Lake Erie. Huge ships lay moored across on the Perrysburg side. They could see tall masts north at Manhattan's Port.

The crew captain was left in charge of unloading the barge. After the weighing in at the lockmasters, the bills of transaction were handled by Ben and Hermann. Then the load was turned over to the crew and the dock stevedores for unloading.

Huge Negro stevedores and other foreign looking men formed lines as they threw the sacks of grain up out of the holds. The grain was then stacked on horse-drawn wagons that were waiting on the wooden platform between the canal dock on one side and the deep water docks on the other. Produce and merchandise were being unloaded from the holds of ships at the dock onto wooden pallets that were lifted out of the ship's holds by booms and cranes. Steam winches and pulleys screamed overhead as they blended with the calls of the men from ship to dock.

Bertha Gast wondered how on earth any of them could ever sleep that night on their barge now that it was moored in such a noisy place. This was no place for her girls. She began to wonder about the mysterious packet her mother had purchased.

After a while, as early evening came on, Bertha had her family ready for the sightseeing tour up the miles of docks, to see the large ships, and to the passenger depot where they would see the fashionable world in travel costume.

August Ben Gast announced to all of them that they would really treat themselves this one evening, find some respectable, but not too expensive restaurant or inn, and have their supper. The boys shouted their agreement but coaxed a promise from Hermann and Ben not to eat until they had gotten to see the entire length of the dock before darkness set in.

Bertha and the girls were only too glad to agree to eating out for that meant no drudgery over the hot cook stove or washing dishes. Who wanted to dip up this water in all this congestion of hundreds of boats to heat for water or to wash in? They would have to find a pump somewhere and carry their water.

The crew master was given final instructions from Ben and Hermann for they wanted the grain to be unloaded and taken by grain wagon to the waiting ship holds. It could not set out on the docks unprotected from theft at night. There was also the possibility of a night shower, and that would ruin the sacked grain.

As the Gast group made its way up the docks, they inspected both sides: the canal side, and the deep water side on the bay estuary. Ben Gast had gone on ahead to find the number of the berth where the waiting packet passenger-cargo barge waited. He was to meet the rest of them there as they made their way up the miles of wooden platform docks. Each barge and each ship offered some interesting spectacle to the small town group. Tons of merchandise and raw materials of all descriptions formed mountains along the docks. Great warehouses with opened doors displayed tons more of every kind of merchandise, manufactured goods, produce, and raw materials either coming into the port on the lake steamers or on the barges. Most of it would trade from the ships bound for Detroit or Chicago, or on to the St. Lawrence and Montreal and on to other Great Lakes ports.

Charley and Lou Gast marveled at a great pile of iron ore and another pile of some strange orange colored chemical beside it. Great booms overhead catapulted rope nets full of boxes from cargo ship holds down to the dock beside them. Bertha screamed and pushed the children on ahead of her.

Crates of geese put up a noisy clatter when the group passed them. A great hill of stacked cheese boxes blocked their way. Lou-Lou held her nose as she gave the cheese a wide berth, complaining that it smelled like that "vile stuff" from St. Marys down home.

They left the grain area and came into the heavy building material area. Next they passed through loading zones and berths of lumber and wood materials. Great stacks of barrels full of roofing pitch gave off a turpentine aroma. Now they came into a more refined type of merchandise packed in wooden boxes. Josie saw the names of stores in Dayton, Ft. Wayne, and

Cincinnati labeled on the boxes and knew that it was probably clothing, bolts of goods or shoes bound for canal shipment to the south.

There was sugar from New Orleans, and cotton, hemp, rice and indigo from the southern ports. Great hogsheads and casks of whiskey and wine were being trundled into a great brick warehouse. What a beautiful, trim sailing ship was moored across on the deep-water side! Throngs of people, stevedores, travelers, crewmen, and women and children crowded the docks. It kept Bertha Gast and her brother-in-law, Hermann, busy trying to keep all the children together in the face of the crowds they met going both ways.

Bertha Gast wondered if they could find their barge when they came back after dark. She had no idea how far they had walked already. There were fewer warehouses near the passenger packet area. Now the stacks and mounds of merchandise had given way to smaller mounds of trunks, valises, and hatboxes. A few small casks of wine were interspersed with the leather satchels and carpetbags. A well-dressed *crowd* of people took the place of the working classes of the lower cargo docks. Lines of handsome coaches and open horse drawn landaus pulled into the curbs from the side streets near the lock and the aqueduct where the canal extension crossed Swan Creek on its way to Manhattan and the other ticket office.

The depot stood across the canal on the town side. The hitch posts along the curbs were crowded with cabs and coaches of many kinds. Bertha and Hermann herded their group across the high arched bridge, across the canal, and down to the cobbled paving of the flagstone around the passenger depot. Surely, Ben would be waiting for them somewhere near the ticket office.

As they came nearer, runners approached them trying to hire a cab for them, or to sell tickets on one of the packets. As coaches discharged their fares at the curb of the passenger depot, the hired runners of the different packet lines rushed the prospective passengers to solicit their business.

"Come this way, ladies. Consider yourself introduced to the *Maid of the Woods*! It's the most commodious craft on the canal south." The older woman drew back archly.

A rival company would accost them from the other side, even taking them by the arm, and thrusting a card in front of them.

"*Maid of the Woods*? That worm-eaten ark? Take the *Flying Comet*. The cost is four cents a mile. You'll be served three meals a day," he boasted.

"Three meals a day, and with the horses eat hay," a third runner declared. "Let me have your boxes. Take the *Buckeye Belle*."

"You'll be mudlarked on shoal bottoms and hell! If you are canalling south to Cincinnati, take the *Ohio Sandpiper*. You'll have clean sheets, prime food and programs," another one cried.

The ladies shrugged free from their solicitors, and announced that they were shipping on the lake to Buffalo.

"Wal Ladies, yer in the wrong depot. Cross the bridge up the dock to the Old Erie Line station for lake travel." The rival runners pounced on other prospective customers, almost getting into a fight while trading insults. Uniformed police patrolling the area around and through the depot kept an eye on them. When they became too abusive or too insistent, the constables approached them with nightsticks in their hands. The runners ducked and ran for other clients farther away.

The Swan Creek Station was just as busy as the packet depot, but with more elegantly dressed people. Bertha and the girls stood and gaped with wonder at the silk skirts swaying over modest hips. Beautifully trimmed poke bonnets matched lace parasols. Rustling watered silk and moiré skirts over larger, more European looking hooped petticoats rustled by. Elegant gentlemen in beaver top hats and cutaway frock coats escorted the ladies by using beautiful manners. Inside, brass chandeliers and crystal globes blazed with light as twilight grew into darkness. The boisterous calls of the freight yard docks were gone. The conversation was one of sparkling gaiety and polished etiquette. Strange but light perfumes floated from the ladies' fans and lace shoulder stoles. Turkish tobacco scented with sandalwood lent its perfume from men's pipes and small cigars. Gone were the quids of tobacco protruding from the crew's jam, or the amber flash of the squirt of tobacco protruding from the crewmen's jaws, or the amber flash of a squirt of chewing tobacco juice into the canal's sluggish dark water.

Hermann Gast found his brother at one of the ticket windows. Then he came back to tell Bertha and the others that it would be a while before all the papers were cleared on the transaction for the new packet.

"New packet? But where is it?" Bertha exclaimed.

"Yes, Pa," Lou-Lou began, "It will have barnacles and go to the bottom before we ever lay eyes on it."

"Ben will find out all of that, and then he and I will chust go and find it. Have patience, *mein Liebchen Louveese!*"

To pass the time, Bertha and the girls sauntered out on the docks to inspect the handsome packets that were tied up. Passengers in elegant clothes were going aboard for the night trip. One packet boat was festooned with garlands of paper flowers on its bow, and was headed for some sort of a political rally or campaign in Fort Wayne on the Indiana Canal.

As enthralled as they were with the elegance of the world of fashion from the city around them, Bertha and the girls felt rather out of place in their small country town dresses. Bertha whispered to the girls not to stand and stare so, but to try to appear casual, as if they were used to the city and world travel. Lou-Lou giggled at this, but then she loved to act. To Bertha's astonishment, she saw her niece putting on airs as if she were a sophisticated woman of the world.

Josie was glad enough to get outside, but she could not take her eyes off the handsome people in expensive, fashionable clothing inside the depot.

"Let's stand out here on the docks where we can see people getting out of the coaches, and those from the depot going aboard the packets!" Josie complained to her mother. "I feel like Cinderella at the ball in there."

"I'll bet we cut a pretty figure in there with all those society women," Lou-Lou wailed. Then thinking better of it, she straightened up, threw her shoulders back, and strutted on ahead of her Aunt Bertha and her cousin Josie, as she put her hand on her hip.

"Why I'm Mrs. Gold-bags just arriving over from Ottawa and Montreal on one of the lake side-wheelers," she said haughtily, as she pretended to hold make-believe stem glasses out in front of her.

Passing women turned to look at Lou-Lou, and then at Bertha, who bit her lip with embarrassment. Josie started to join in the fun of swaying her skirts unnecessarily, and pursing her lips. The boys took their cue from the girls and began teasing. They had been silent and open-eyed for so long with the amazing sights around them that they welcomed a slight relief from the pent-up tension.

"Come this way, Mrs. Gold-bags! Take the *Bremen-Bloomer-Leg* for a trip you'll never forget nor regret," Charley said as he offered to hand Lou-Lou up to the gangplank of a moored passenger packet. The uniformed barge porter looked somewhat puzzled at the group of young people who were starting to come up his gangplank. They blocked the path of passengers who looked on with some irritation with the delay.

Young Ben took Josie's arm and offered to help her aboard.

"*Theesh vay, Mein Fraulein Pumpernickle-Lemburger!* Der *Bloomer-Leg* nevair lags. Vair iss der lagging luggage?"

Bertha Gast rushed up to the gangplank and pulled her clowning young charges from out of the way of the passengers. They all started babbling in a mixture of German-Dutch-English to make the people around them think they were just newly arrived immigrants from the steerage class. Their action further vexed Bertha.

"*Ach in Himmel!* What on earth ails all of you?" Bertha wailed, while forgetting that she herself was lapsing into her German of earlier years at home. The children set up gales of laughter as other people gathered around laughing with amusement at the show. The stern faced porter at the head of the gangplank of the packet called to Bertha somewhat officiously,

"Madam, are you coming aboard?"

Too embarrassed to speak clearly, she mumbled something to the effect that "she rather hoped not," and hurried the children off to the side as best she could.

"*Vy not, mama? Ja, why not?*" They all cried . . . Bertha shook them by the arms and tried to hush them. She was trying to speak through her teeth with a low determined voice, as she threatened,

"When I get the lot of you back to the barge, won't I blister all of you with that wooden stirring paddle?"

"*Ach, mein Mama, vud you chust look?*" Lou called out and pointed through the crowd. Bertha gave him a blow with her open palm across the back to silence him. The people who were still around, pressed in to watch the "little immigrants".

"*Ach, Good Night*! Why people will think you youngin's have never been any place before! Now stop it. Why, I've never been so mortified in my life. All these people think that you are terrible. Come on and let's do go on down the dock a ways," Bertha commanded. She was anxious to flee from the curious stares of an amused audience. Lou and Charley stopped abruptly, pointed down the lamp lit dock and began to protest to their mother.

"No, really, Mama, look! There goes Papa in a hurry!"

Bertha Gast stared after August Ben with perplex ion.

"That Ben Gast! Now that I need him, he's never here! Where is Hermann? Is he with him?" she asked.

"Uncle Hermann was still at the ticket window when we came out of the depot," Josie told her.

"Then we had better get back there before we all get separated and lost," Bertha announced. "Now one more performance out of you *clowns* and you'll all catch it. I don't care whether you are kids, cousins, nieces and nephews alike. Do you hear me?" She demanded. They all shook their heads like the obedient children they certainly were not, and they dropped their eyes with cow-like servility, and answered in a chorus:

"*Ja mama! Ve hear! Ve be good! Ve be gut kinder.*"

"Now stop that Deutsch gargling, you little impostors!" She commanded as she slapped her hands at them threateningly.

"Now see if you can act like little ladies and gentlemen when we go back inside the depot. If you don't behave, it's right back to the hot barge for all of us. We will do no more sight-seeing. There will be no eating out in the restaurant," she threatened them.

Bertha knew she had scored a victory when she saw their faces go sober.

"You girls can just cook supper on that hot old wood stove while I sit back and supervise. You boys can split kindling, carry water, and clean the horse stalls!"

The group started into the depot single file.

"Single file...duck style...waddle along...string out a mile," the boys sang out in chorus. Bertha snapped her fingers as she hissed at them in a half whisper. Then all of the children repeated,

"*Ve good children, Mama! Ve behave!*"

Knowing that she had been compromised, Bertha Gast shrieked,

"What? What did I just promise you?" She followed them close behind as they ran on ahead of her, laughing as they went up to Hermann Gast. He was in a serious conversation with the depot official behind the barred window.

Lou-Lou and Ben tugged at their father's coat sleeves to get his attention. When he turned to face the group, Bertha could see that he was very serious. There must be more to the boat transaction than she knew about. Hermann did not smile as he admonished his two children.

"Quiet you two. You're not at home now. Chust try to..."

Bertha spoke up quickly, and tried to appear severe.

"Just try indeed, Hermann Gast. Why, I've never been so humiliated and mortified. All of a sudden they began to act up and began to clown... acting like little foreign children from the steerage...talking like little Deutsch immigrants."

"*Lou-veese! Benjie!* What did your mother, Bernhardina, tell you when you left? How did you promise to behave?" The gentle Hermann asked them, but still his mind was far away.

"Behave? It wasn't only those two," Bertha exploded. "My three were just as bad, if not worse. I don't think we can risk taking them to a restaurant to eat. Why, they would probably dig into their plates with their hands, just to embarrass us all."

Lou-Lou answered saucily for all the other children.

"Oh, Papa! We were only playing. I know what Mom said, and what Grandma-Má said, and she imitated her Grandmother.

"Bernhardina!" (pronouncing it very Dutchey as Bairn-hard-deen-nah!) "You chuld paddle dot Lou-veese more. She iss too chubby. She chuld be more lady-like. Vy, dot Benjie, he is sooch good boy!"

"Now *Louvise*," her Father reprimanded her.

"Papa, come on. We are all getting famished. Where did Uncle Ben go in such a hurry? Why are you both stalling so? Are we never to see the new boat?"

Bertha saw that Hermann was silent and did not look at them.

"What is it, Hermann? Where did Ben go?"

"He'll be back soon enough. He went to see the boat. The port director here gave him the berth. He'll be back soon, and take us all to it," Hermann answered evasively. "It's docked in a wide water berth up the canal toward Manhattanville."

"You haven't told all, Hermann. I can tell. What is it?" Hermann assured her that nothing was wrong, only that they were surprised at the terms, and that it was a larger barge than they had expected.

"Did we get a skinning? Is it an old ark?" Bertha demanded.

"No, I'd say that we got too much of a good bargain. There must be a hitch in it somewhere," Hermann answered. "Your mother made the deal up on the Erie earlier this spring, as you know."

"Yes, and she drives a hard bargain, Hermann. She is not one likely to be swindled in a business deal! I'll say that for Mother," Bertha pointed out to him.

"Oh, it's not a swindle. It's just that there is more to it than we know. She knew, all right. You can bet on that, but she didn't tell us everything. We must wait until Ben comes back and takes us to it. I can't believe all of this, nor can I wait to see it."

Bertha and the others were silent with surprise. For once, none of the children started plying their parents with questions. They all walked along in the depot; then they went outside and sauntered along the packet deck. Hermann pointed out a great long passenger packet that was to make the grand tour with the governor about the middle of the month. They all went down alongside the packet to have a look at it. It was long and narrow, with a black hull. The super structure above the waterline was a gleaming white. Brass fixtures such as lamps, railings and handles on the doors gave the barge a look of elegance. Word had been passing down the canal about the event when the governor and nearly a hundred other dignitaries would travel the Miami-and-Erie Canal to Cincinnati and back. They had already done the same honors on the Ohio Canal from Cleveland down to Portsmouth on the Ohio River and back.

After a while, Hermann and Bertha saw August Ben Gast striding down the dock toward the depot. In the dim light of the oil street lamps, along the street that ran along the dock, Bertha thought that she saw her husband. He saw his family just as he was about to enter the depot and came up to them rapidly.

"Hermann! Well, Hermann!" Ben laughed, and then shook his head.

"Ben, is it...?" Hermann asked.

August Ben could only nod his head. Bertha and the girls pounced on him and demanded an explanation.

"Are we to be kept dangling out here in the night while you two talk in riddles? Now I've waited long enough. I want to see this boat, and I want to see it now. I didn't come all this way on a wild goose chase, or cook my fingers to the bone just to be treated to riddles, Ben Gast. Now March!"

Ben could only shrug his shoulders, while half frowning and half laughing, turned an appeal to his brother, Hermann, who could only shake his head back in return. Ben Gast said,

"I only wish your Mother could be here now, Bertha!"

"A lot of good she would do. She has gotten us into some sort of a mess, I can tell. No wonder she played it so sly and sent all of us to Toledo with no explanation. Then she took off on some trip the other direction to Cincinnati on some sort of a medical convention."

They all walked rapidly up the dock. It grew darker as they walked farther away from the brilliantly lighted depot. After a few minutes, they came to some parallel finger berths, which led from the main canal berths at ninety degree angles. They resembled large port piers for ocean ships, which were nosed into the finger berths with widths of docks between.

The canal was much wider here to allow for the turning of the packets and cargo barges that were moored endwise into the finger berths. In the semi-darkness, it was hard to tell how many packets were moored in this fashion, side by side, in the stalls leading off from the main canal basin. There were small pier docks leading back into the berths between the moored barges, each pier being nearly twenty feet wide.

All of the others who were following Ben and Hermann could only marvel at the beauty of the sleek expensive looking passenger packets. All of a sudden, Ben stopped at the entrance to one of the finger piers. With a helpless gesture, he motioned to an unbelievable light blue barge. Hermann stopped speechless.

"This is it, Bertha," August Ben said weakly, expecting an outburst from her. There was only silence. The girls went up to it, and pressed their hands against its sleek smooth gunwales. Its new coat of light blue paint smelled new and felt cool and smooth to the touch.

"Look at the length of her! Ben, it's long and big. Mama Kattmann said it was a medium sized barge, and that it was a combination of cargo and packet."

"Yes, This is true, Hermann. It's all the locks can do to take this one, and the average lock is a hundred feet."

"What could Mother have meant?" Bertha exclaimed, finding words at last.

"You haven't seen nearly all. Wait until you see inside. Take a look up front," Ben Gast said faintly, but he made no effort to lead them up the pier to the bow.

By the street lamp on the pier, Josie and Lou-Lou could see the packet's name, *The Blue Swan*, printed on her stern in an arch of gold letters.

They raced up the finger pier to the bow of the packet-barge, joining the others who had gone on ahead. They were stopped in their tracks with astonishment at what they saw. Ben motioned them all to come up the pier to the cross-over and stand in front of the bow where they could really get a good look from the street lamp, which shone down on the boat. No one could find words.

"What can Mother mean?" Bertha exclaimed. She knew that her mother had told Hermann, and her husband, Ben, that they needed another barge for the brewery deliveries, and a combination of cargo and packet would be profitable. They could haul passengers back north when they delivered barrels of beer and ale south to Dayton and Cincinnati. However, this is a monstrosity! What on earth would they ever do with it? After all, the brewery belonged to her Mother, even though her brother, Ludwig Kattmann, ran it with the help of Hermann and Ben Gast. The grain business, however, belonged to the Gast brothers alone, but Mrs. Kattmann ran it and was always ready to lend a helping hand there too, as long as her advice was sought.

The long light blue barge lay moored to the pier in its finger berth where it rode serenely and majestically, like the *Blue Swan* she was. The bow beam curved back into a majestic wooden neck and head that must have been a good foot in diameter. A brass ring was held in the closed bill of the swan where a navigation lantern could swing when she was once underway. From the curved wide breast of the swan, carved white wings folded back along the gunwale. It then curved up over the sides, and gave the appearance of a swan resting on the surface of a lake. The passenger cabin was nearly hidden by the sweeping white wings, but its two-level height extended back a few yards, and then descended to one level with the brass railing over the entire length of the remaining top deck. A trim brass railed stair companionway led down to the main deck over the cargo holds. At the back, a raised platform deck raised much like an old galleon's poop deck. Back of this, an extended canopy of a carved swan's tail feathers extended over a lower platform deck where the tillsman could stand at the rudder tiller. It was under this carved oaken tail that the arched gold letters, **The Blue Swan**, was written in ornate raised letters.

When once the astonishment was over, the children found words that their elders could not. They whooped and shrieked as they raced up the gangplank and scrambled up on top of the observation deck that was on up a navigator's small cabin deck. From that eerie perch, they could reach over and caress the great head of the swan that looked straight ahead with aristocratic detachment. Almost losing her balance, Josie leaned over to embrace the great swan around the neck, and cried out,

"Oh beautiful swan, I love you!"

Then Lou-Lou took her turn embracing the unbelievable great swan, cooing as she did so.

"It's beautiful, just beautiful! It's the most beautiful swan in the world, and Josie, it's ours!"

"What's the matter with you two? It's only a carved head of wood," Charley reminded them, but he could not help running his hands over the shining brass railing and the doorknobs. While leaning over the sides of the gunwales, he traced his fingers in the fluted carvings that represented wing feathers. He knocked on it with his knuckles, calling to the others as he did so,

"It's real wood all right. It's really hard. It's not some old cheap plaster."

There were more cries of amazement when Ben Gast unlocked the cabin door and lit the lamps inside. It was unbelievable with its carved paneling that looked like walnut in one room, and some lighter wood, probably mahogany, in the other. They went up the few steps into the pilot or navigator observation cabin from where the captain would pilot while underway. It had a long upholstered seat running horizontally across the back of the cabin. It was long enough for the captain to lay down if he so chose. A panel of small panes mullioned in brass instead of wood sashes ran across the front of the cabin. The erect swan's head obstructed only a small portion of the view ahead, but the cabin was nearly hidden from the sides by the upsweeping swan's wings that came to rest up over the back. There was a small seat a few feet wide on the top deck between the tips of the resting wing tips.

Under the captain's observation cabin was the cook's galley. The passenger cabin could be converted into sleeping quarters at night by pulling down shelf-like bunk beds from the wall. It was too exciting to explore all at once, but Josie and Lou-Lou told Bertha that one thing was certain. After they all went out and ate, they must haul all their bed things, clothes and cooking utensils up here, and sleep in the luxury of the new packet that night.

"We'll do no such thing!" Bertha Gast exclaimed.

"Oh Mama," the girls wailed. "You're no fun. Please let us sleep on the new packet just this once."

Chapter 5

After a while, Ben, Hermann and Bertha Gast were able to herd the children down off the *Blue Swan* onto the pier and head for a comfortable "family" restaurant that suited their dress and pocketbooks.

They were directed to a restaurant that was not too far up a side street that led from the city down to the depot on the dock. Once they were inside and seated at a family table with white linen cloth, Bertha was aghast at the thought of unclean hands. She found the washroom and scrubbed her offspring's hands as well as those of Ben and Louise.

They were all interested in the menu; they wanted to order something that they didn't have at home, or wouldn't have on the barge on the way home.

"No more green beans, collard greens, or cornbread," Charley complained.

"How about some sausage floating in grease with some kraut and knuedels, Lou put in. However, Lou-Lou's rapid chatter interrupted him as she scanned the menu.

"Some *karTeufel-kase mit blutwurst* . . . and some of Mrs. Hemel's rank cheese from that rotting pile of junk up there in St. Marys."

"Stop it, all of you. What if our nice waitress can hear you? She'll think we are all rude bumpkins," Bertha warned them. "Now be serious and order something."

It was hard for Hermann and Ben Gast to eat because their minds were not on their meal but the strange problem of the new barge that had suddenly changed their lives. Bertha Gast could not concentrate on her food, even though the roast beef was extremely good. The solicitous woman who waited on their table inquired if the food was to their liking. While the younger members of the family enjoyed their supper with relish, Ben, Hermann and

Bertha became engrossed in a deep conversation of business affairs. Bertha wanted to know what was in the transaction papers and where the boat came from. She also wanted to know how much the agreed price was that Mrs. Kattmann paid

Ben told the others that the check had come through the freight cargo office from a Heinrich Kattmann of *The Blue Goose Brewery* in New Bremen.

"How much was the check, Ben?" Bertha asked. Looking foolishly at his brother Hermann, he answered,

"You know, these packets cost anywhere from $2,000 to $4,000 and more. It's according to all the . . . ."

"August Benjamin! How much was the check for this white elephant we are stuck with?"

"White elephant? Why it's a *Blue Swan!*" He teased.

"Wal, I swan!" Lou-Lou chimed in. "It's a lovely bargain at that."

"Just eat your supper Miss Know-it-all. Don't interrupt!" Hermann told her.

"This is a family of clowns. Honestly! Now Ben, how much did it cost?"

"Now brace yourself, Bertha. It was a bargain. . . only around, say $1,200 when it's all told."

"Now that's impossible, Ben Gast. What is the truth? Hermann, you saw the papers and the check didn't you?" Bertha pressed.

"That is the honest truth. That was what the bill of transaction read. I had no choice. We had to sign it, for they had the check and we would just be out our merchandise. If we didn't sign a receipt of the freight that they were holding for us, we would just be out a packet. and that's all," Ben told her.

"Now can't you just see us riding home in that circus monstrosity?" Bertha said with alarm as the idea struck her.

"Now you have said it. That's just what it was," Hermann said.

"What do you mean, that's what it was? Isn't it a new boat?" Bertha asked.

"It's practically new. You see, according to the papers and from what the office here tells me, it was a circus boat. You remember the one we saw at Junction last night. There is a whole string of them that were used for showboats. "I think they originally came from the canals of Holland, Germany, and France."

"How did Ma get a hold of it?" Bertha questioned him.

"I don't know how she knew about it, but the owners of this show went bankrupt. They needed to raise some ready cash, and didn't want to chance an auction, so they sold outright. Your mother happened along there somewhere on the Erie Canal in the state of New York, and grabbed up the bargain," Ben told her.

"Bargain? Circus boat? What possible use can this outlandish thing ever be to us in our business? Why we will be the laughing stock of the entire length of the canal, to say nothing of Bremen and Minster."

"Oh Bertha, we are lucky. Your mother has some plan, and after all, she financed it for the brewery and for the grain business, as well as for passengers. It can't help but make money. Besides, you should see some of the other boats from that same traveling water circus. They're tied up here somewhere else up the piers. They're all for sale," Ben explained. Then he added, "One has a hippopotamus head. I think it had pink polka dots. Others are: the winged horse; then there's a big lavender elephant; a rooster. . . "Bertha covered her ears in protest and shrieked,

"Are there other showboats?" Josie and Lou-Lou exclaimed, "Where Papa?" The other children began asking questions about the circus packets. They could not wait to finish their suppers so that they could coax their parents into taking them up the piers to see the other showboats. The others would be something to see all right, but none of them could be as beautiful as the gorgeous majestic *Blue Swan*.

"Now about this check and the papers," Bertha began. "I don't understand. Why would it be signed by Papa? You said it was signed by Heinrich August Kattmann. You sure it was not Ma's signature, Augusta Kattmann?"

"We didn't exactly see the check, but the papers were drawn up that way. The port director and the freight agent both verified that the boat had been paid for by a check of that name. I had to produce proof that we, Hermann and I, were the recipients."

"How did you do that? Anyone could say that they were Hermann and Benjamin Gast," Bertha told him.

"Your mother has a wise business head. She had sent a letter to the office here, telling them he was the one and same Heinrich Kattmann, and that upon proof being produced, they were to turn the barge over to Hermann and me. She had sent lading bills from the brewery with our signatures so that the agent here could match signatures and we could get the boat. We are stuck with it, Bertha. The only thing left to do is to get it home," Ben said with finality.

"It would appear so," Bertha sighed.

The affable proprietor of the restaurant came to the table to ask for their orders for dessert. She smiled slyly at the children and told them,

"I know what boys and girls your age like. I have a special treat just for you. You'll see," she promised as she hurried to the kitchen.

Ben, Hermann, and Bertha had ordered fresh strawberry pie, which turned out to be a new kind of a tart or shortcake with whipped cream. The special treat she brought for the children was a bowl of fresh strawberries. The strawberries were especially large and sweet since they were locally grown, and they were in a full bumper crop this early in June. Then she produced something the children had never seen before: frost covered white dishes filled with a sort of frozen custard. They had to pull back the paper foil wrapper from over the top of the dessert dish to get to the "iced cream."

The proprietress enjoyed seeing the children's wide eyes and hearing their squeals of delight as they tasted the iced custard. She showed them how to heap some sweetened strawberries on top of the cream, and urged them to eat it before it melted in the summer heat.

Bertha was flabbergasted. No one had ever heard of such a thing. The proprietress, who was beaming with delight, told her that "it was just the newest thing," and that the recipe had come from Philadelphia and Washington D.C. While the men sampled the iced custard she brought them, she and Bertha fell into a discussion of the recipe.

"Pshaw! It wouldn't be no trouble atoll for you to make, lady," the eager proprietress told Bertha. "You say you have your own ice?" Bertha explained that they sawed ice in the winter from ice ponds and stored it in sawdust in brick warehouses. They used it in their brewery business, especially when they wanted to serve ice cold ale to special customers.

The other lady wrote out the recipe and the instructions for making the "iced cream" and gave it to Bertha. The hard part was the whirling back and forth of a gallon pail submerged in salt ice, and the scraping of the sides as the custard froze until the whole bucket full froze. Then it must be packed and covered with packs of crushed ice for a couple of hours so that it would get solid.

Immediately the children wheedled a promise out of Bertha to try some of it when they got home. "Won't the other boys and girls at home be green with envy?" They exclaimed. "We'll have something new from the big city that we brought home," Josie told the others.

"They'll also be surprised when they see our new packet boat, *The Blue Swan*! No one will believe that it is ours, and they will all be lined up and trying to coax a ride on her," Lou-Lou said.

The kindly lady proprietress, after figuring up the bills for the meals, insisted on showing Bertha the iced cream she had in dishes sitting outside in her ice chest for other customers. She took her down into the cellar under the kitchen; then she showed Bertha the large wooden tub for crushed ice, the gallon water pail for freezing the custard, and the wooden lid she had made to fit over the top of the bucket during the freezing, and for afterward when it was all put down under ice for packing.

The group was in a quieter mood as they sauntered up the dock to the *Blue Swan* again. From time to time passersby stopped to marvel at the unusual barge. Bertha frowned when she heard some ladies remark that it was probably a passing show that was headed for the canal trade for the summer, and then would move on down the Ohio River. Another matronly lady remarked,

"Yes, wouldn't that just be the life though? You know what those show people are like. It looks as if it would be an exciting life from the outside, but you know, those painted women were. . . Well, it's all false and exceedingly low, Blanche. That kind of life is not at all what it looks like."

Ben and Hermann chuckled, then nudged Bertha with their elbows.

"Chust see, Bertha, see what you've been missing? Your mother has it all planned. Now for the bright lights, the big time, the. . . !"

"Oh, do stop it! The idea! The children will hear us. Showboat! Harrumph!"

"Hear what, Mama?" Charley and Lou asked.

"Yes, hear what, Aunt Bert?" Lou-Lou took up the question. Bertha gave the men dark glances and hurried up on the deck. The passing women stopped and looked up at her as the rest of the family followed. Bertha heard their pontification while they turned to shake their heads and take one last look.

"Think of it, Blanche. . . and she looks like a good woman too," the matron said.

"The pity of it - those poor young children. . . having a life like that ahead of them would be terrible," the other one answered. Bertha cast a black look toward the women but held her tongue. She only wished that her mother *were* along! She would know what to say. Anyway, it was all her fault for sending them all up here on this hare-brained scheme. Then the thought struck her. It would be like this everywhere they went. People would stare and make comments.

"Now you see what I mean Ben and Hermann Gast? This will never do. Why this thing is too rich for our blood, too gaudy and impractical for a small town like ours," Bertha protested.

"Think bigger than just Bremen and the small towns. Think of the advertising and the showmanship that the *Blue Swan* will be for our business in Dayton, here in Toledo, and in Cincinnati. It will be better than a large billboard," Hermann pointed out. Ben agreed. "Besides, we'll have to make it work, for we couldn't just throw $1,200 away as if it were chaff."

They walked on up the finger piers to see more of the other packets. Then a squeal from Lou-Lou brought them all to the attention of some barges moored parallel in the berth at right angles to the main canal channel. Bertha came closer and took a good look, first at one barge in its berth, and then she walked on up the main deck looking at the bows of other showboats that were moored with their bows heading into the main dock. She couldn't believe her eyes.

"I don't believe it. Why, that one looks pink. What on earth?" Bertha cried. One barge, painted pink had a huge elephant head at its bow, just as the *Blue Swan* carried a swan's head on its bow stem beam. Another yellow one with spots carried a giraffe's head. Still another blue-gray, or slate colored one, had huge hippopotamus shoulders and a head with its open mouth gaping at them. Bertha cried out,

"Good gracious. *Ach, Mein Helige Gott!* I am in a nightmare! I don't believe my eyes!"

"It's all part of colorful show business, Bertha. Just like the wild animals on the carousel, it attracts paying customers, especially children," Ben explained to her. "Can't you imagine how a whole town and community would flock to the canal berm when they hear the steam calliope leading this troupe of barges into town? A steamboat pulls these on the river too, all tied up in a line."

"I don't think there was much trouping into a town of customers if all this went bankrupt," Bertha scorned. "And we got stuck with the remnants."

Josie and Lou had skipped up closer to the gaping hippopotamus head and squealing with laughter, cried out to Lou-Lou, Ben and Charley,

"Oh look! It looks like Mrs. Peppleman down home."

"It's almost as big," Charley commented. The others laughed wildly.

"Shame on you - and after all the pieces of her pies that she gives you youngsters," August Ben chided them.

Bertha Gast was glad that she did not have to cook for the crew hands when they finally got back to their barge in the cargo area. It was rather hot and congested there. It seemed rough and burley compared to the packet and depot area of the fashionable world.

The children began pleading to take their bedding and other things they needed, and move up into the *Blue Swan* immediately. Bertha hesitated, knowing that it was getting late, and it would be a good bit of trouble to get moved. Hermann and August Ben were as eager as the children were to get onto the new barge. They helped sway Bertha's consent, when they brought a horse drawn dray to the side of the barge for transporting the necessary things.

The huge livery barns were near this end of the docks for the dozens upon dozens of horses owned by the various packet companies, by the line captains, and by captains employed on the state-owned lines of barges. An evening breeze blew from the livery barn toward the lower end of the canal, and across the decks of the Gast grain barge. Lou-Lou began holding her nose and making exaggerated gagging sounds as she staggered across the deck, pleading for air.

"Ach Himmel! We need air, or we'll die here! It must be some more of Mrs. Hemel's brown runny cheese from up St. Marys way!"

Bertha had not counted on the trump that played into the hands of the others who wanted to move. She made a compromise. They would move up there that night, but if she had to cook for the crew hands, all the others would come back with her into this aromatic fog and help her with the noon meal. Ben told her that there was little chance of the crew wanting dinner, for when they got their work done, they would be out on the town until time to start back on the next day. He had told them that they would stay over one day more for sight seeing, and a possible trip out on the lake. Then they would start home the next morning. The boys jumped with delight at the news.

The first night aboard the *Blue Swan* was one of excitement. It was hard for any of them to get to sleep. Bertha tried out the new charcoal burning brazier for a light snack of hot chocolate and cookies. The larger stove used kerosene or whale oil, and was hooded so that the fumes and heat were carried up a flue. Little by little, she was won over to the *Blue Swan* - or at least to where she could see some of its better points.

To her consternation, she found Ben and Hermann tinkering with some sort of contraption, which lifted out of a well hold near the stern. It was a steam calliope, which looked rather rusty, and was more like a pile of brass and rusted iron junk. Hermann and August Ben were delighted with their find. They announced that it would be just the thing for Elihu Sanders to fool with on rainy days, when he wasn't busy back home in Bremen in his tinker shop. Jake Hemel in the blacksmith shop, would be right handy too, they reasoned, for he had a knack of putting things together that were too much for Elihu to handle.

Bertha threw her hands up in the air with an expression of despair. How could she ever get her clowning children to grow up, when their father and uncle set a prime example of the constant adolescent clown? It was too much to cope with, so she prepared herself and the younger ones for bed.

It was a real romp for them all. The boys wanted to sleep up on the open deck for a while - at least since it was a warm night. If it rained, they could always grab up their blankets and duck down into the cabin. Lou-Lou and

Josie took the pilot's cabin up on the second cabin deck behind the arched neck of the beautiful swan. They could see lights of distant ships out on Lake Erie.

"What if Grandma Kattmann had bought that huge elephant or the crowing rooster barge?" Lou-Lou confided to Josie. Then she sat upright as a new thought struck her.

"Maybe she will buy more of them if this one works out. She could buy them, fix them up, sell them for twice what she paid for them, and make money. You know Grandma-Má."

Ben and Hermann talked late into the night as they sat with their pipes at the stern tiller watching the night traffic on the dock which died down as the night wore on. There were some late coaches and carriages going along the streets beside the piers. Night crews worked all through the night down in the heavy freight and cargo area. They could hear the rumble of wagon wheels, the screeching of pulley cables, and the shouts of men on the large ships calling down directions for the booms headed for the deep holds. Sounds from the larger ship ports farther up the bay at the mouth of Lake Erie carried down to them. A few packet and cargo barges left during the night for their journey south. The captains' boat horns pierced the night with their melodious low note, which sounded much like a French horn or a shepherd horn.

It grew cooler during the night. After a while, Ben and Hermann picked up the sleeping boys from the top deck, carried them down into the cabin, and tucked them into the shelf bunk that Bertha had turned down. Sleep came at last as the night with all its strange sounds passed into a peaceful daybreak.

Bertha had hoped that perhaps they could all sleep rather late to get the rest they needed for the coming day, but her hopes were shattered when the boys tumbled out onto the floor, put their clothes on, and went up on the deck overhead to see the busy world of the port around them. There was little sleeping inside the cabin when the boys began dancing around on the deck. It wasn't long before Bertha heard Josie and Lou-Lou prancing around up on the top deck with the boys, and she knew that trying to rest any longer was futile. No telling where these youngsters would go once they got down on the deck.

While keeping an eye on her brood, Bertha prepared breakfast in the new barge's galley. It was compact but so much handier than the old grain barge. Little by little, she was beginning to be won over to *the Blue Swan*, even begrudgingly and reluctantly.

After breakfast Josie, Lou-Lou and the boys had to stroll up and see the other carnival animal barges. They looked so much more unusual if not grotesque in the daylight, but the beautiful *Blue Swan* looked even more majestic to them when they came back to her.

August Ben and Hermann hired an open carriage to take the family for a drive over part of the city. It was all they could do to crowd into it, but the boys sat on the little leather folding seats that folded up from the floor. Ben sat up with the driver who pointed out the best streets for visitors.

That afternoon, after a picnic lunch in the park that overlooked the bay, they all went on an excursion out from Maumee Bay on a lake steamer. They were excited by the chugging and puffing of the steam engines. They could not take their eyes away from the entrancing paddle wheels, which churned the lake and left a foaming wake behind them. Ben and Hermann studied the paddle wheels. They wondered if a barge could have steam paddle wheels for the reservoirs.

The summer excursion crews walked the deck of the large steamer. It was almost as exciting as the depot had been the night before.

"Is this bigger than those side-wheelers on the Ohio and the Mississippi?" Charley wanted to know. Hermann explained that it was not only longer, but its decks were much higher from the water level, which was due to the roughness of the Great Lakes, as compared to the peaceful quiet waters of the rivers.

Before they knew it, it was evening again, and it was time to make ready for the trip home. Their thoughts of leaving were somehow not too sad, for they were anxious to show off the beautiful *Blue Swan* as they traveled down through the canal toward home. They anticipated their arrival home, and hoped that they could reach New Bremen in full daylight. The boys hoped they would meet some of their canal acquaintances along the way. Wouldn't that ornery codger cuss and carry on when he saw the Swan?

"What if other horses shy away and rear up when they meet us?" Bertha asked in dismay. The thought had never occurred to any of them.

"Won't that old Mrs. McKeeters, up above the canal there in St. Marys, where the canal curves behind those high brick flats . . . won't she about fall out of her porch into the canal when she sees us go by under her?" Lou-Lou laughed. "You know, Papa says she never misses a thing. She and that ornery old Irishman have words every time he passes beneath her."

"What about Mrs. Hemel at home? She's always out on her balcony above the blacksmith shop looking down on the towpath. She sees and knows everything that goes on in Brementown. Won't she shout and holler?" Charley said. Young Ben and Lou joined in the fun of imagining what their grand entrance back home in Bremen would be like.

Bertha astounded them all when she said,

"Yes, but what about your mother, Lou-Lou? What is Bernhardina going to say when she sees this thing?"

"Oh, and Aunt Ernestine. . . Won't she lay a goose egg about anything as common and gaudy as this? However, Uncle Ludwig Kattmann will love it!"

"So will Grandpapa Kattmann out at Maria Stein. That is if he ever gets to see it," Lou-Lou told her brother, young Ben. Then Josie said suddenly,

"What about Grandma-Má Kattmann's sister, Great-Aunt Fredericka?" Bertha thought a moment about her own aunt, her mother's sister, who always dramatized the slightest little incident. Then she said simply,

"She will just faint. She will smile and smile at first, then weep, and end up fainting, especially if someone makes light of this barge to her."

They went to eat supper again with the friendly plump lady in her white curtained little restaurant. It was like home, visiting with someone whom they felt they knew. Abigail Vonel knew how to win customers.

It was just growing early evening in the twilight when Ben and Hermann left the *Swan*, went to the freight office, and met with the port director to make final arrangements and to pick up their papers, which were to be ready for them. The grain shipment was settled, the clearance papers for the *Swan* were signed and handed over, and arrangements were made for the payment for rental of horses along the way from the state line companies. It was then that a hurried messenger from the director's office in the depot came to the barge with some other papers for Ben and Hermann at the Port Director's office - or perhaps in the freight office.

Ben and Hermann Gast were completely taken by surprise by the additional paper. It seemed that they had not claimed all the merchandise paid for by the Blue Goose Brewery of Kattmann and Kattmann. The freight agent had a twinkle in his eye when he tried to pretend complete innocence in the matter, thinking that the Gasts had known all along that they had other possessions to claim in the deal with the *Blue Swan*.

A messenger was sent from the office to conduct Ben and Hermann to the livery stable, and to ask for a certain groom and deliver to him an envelope with a paper of transaction inside. It was then that Ben and Hermann learned that there were four magnificent white Percherons with brass buckled harnesses and tassels that were part of the barge deal. The men were speechless, but the paper was certain proof. However, the problem now was how to get all of their possessions home - both the barges and all the horses.

They did not tell Bertha and the girls about the horses. They waited until the next morning when the grooms brought the handsome white geldings to the barge. Bertha could say nothing. She and the girls just sat down on the top deck to watch the crewmen pole the barge out slowly into the canal, and then hitch two of the high stepping horses to the towline.

When Hermann and Ben came back to the barge after their surprise of the ownership of the horses, the Port Director came to the barge and looked it over. Then he told Ben and Hermann of his real mission. A private detective from government sources in Canada was at his office. Upon learning that the Gasts were from down the canal in the environs of New Bremen and Minster, he was particularly anxious to talk with them. It was to be confidential and private. He was as Scotch as his name, Angus MacClintock. Never smiling, he shook hands with the men and thanked them for coming. His eagle eyes pierced them as he began questioning them. He wanted to know if they knew a barge captain by the name of Silvermann, or at least that was the name he went by. The men told MacClintock all they knew, and that his reputation was anything but good. Ben and Herman told how he abused the small children who people knew were orphans. They told him that they had passed him just before coming into Maumee, but that he was often on the lower canal. He seemed to tie up often in the small towns of Minster and Ft. Loramie. He would often stop just out in the country at night, along any stretch of the canal. They told MacClintock that no one seemed to know what Silvermann and his surly crew hauled.

Angus MacClintock thanked them very dryly for their help but disclosed nothing. He asked them if they would mind if he were to call upon them sometime at night when he happened to pass the canal going south. It would be best if nothing were said, but to merely introduce him as a prospective client for shipments of ale from the brewery. With silent amazement, Ben and Hermann agreed. Angus MacClintock did reveal that he probably would be on the excursion packet that was to carry the governor of Ohio and congressional representatives, and other dignitaries along the entire length of the Miami and Erie, and on the way back.

He could not impress upon them enough that his business was not just canal business, nor was it only business concerning the state of Ohio and the United States. His business was that of an international network. Ben and Hermann shook hands in parting and gave their word. It was all very perplexing. They knew it would never do to let a hint of MacClintock's visit drop in front of the family on the barge. There would be no rest night or day until Bertha and the girls ferreted out the secret.

The day had dawned rather cool and cloudy. It was a good day for getting underway. In spite of all the commercial activity on the docks, there was a great bit of activity at the passenger depot. Without giving a hint of recognition, Ben and Hermann recognized the tall, thin man in Scotch plaids even in the summer heat. He was obviously in poor health, and wore his plaid cape, scarf, and plaid billed cap, even in the summer. MacClintock watched the strange but graceful *Blue Swan* pull past the depot. Nearly everyone stopped to look at it, and to marvel at the high prancing geldings pulling it, and their bells and tassels swaying as they walked. Bertha remained inside, but she got her courage back when she noticed that no one laughed or ridiculed the *Blue Swan.* Josie and Lou-Lou twirled their parasols from their seats on the top deck just back of the swan head, and nodded to people. Louise caused Josie to go into a fit of giggles when she commented,

"If we just had a purple silk," she said, "I could sprawl out here and make people think I was Cleopatra coming down the Nile on her royal barge." She went into a short version of an Egyptian serpent slithering with her one hand in front of her, and the other behind. She heard her father call her name from the tiller so she and Josie sat back down on their high seat above the captain's pilot cabin.

So much had happened that it did not seem possible that they were headed home at last. However, it would be good to get home, but they hated to leave all of this. Would they ever get to go to Dayton or to Cincinnati again and see the great river steamers? Could anything equal the large paddlewheelers out on Lake Erie?

The pleasant reverie was spoiled temporarily as they came into the lower cargo dock area and the livery stables. The morning crew of grooms and stable men were hauling great wagonloads of manure from the livery stables, down the dock to the side street that would lead out into the country fields. Lou-Lou gave a gasping groan as the wind caught them high up in their perch between the protective swan's wings. Both girls swung down from their seat and leaped into the passenger cabin.

"Did you ever see so much of that stuff in one great pile?" Lou-Lou complained, when Bertha thought it best to drop the subject, and she started talking about what they would do when they got home.

Their old grain barge was already at the locks. It was ready to rise up the levels into the canal for the passage west to Waterville, Napoleon and Junction. From there they would head south on the Miami and Erie.

The *Blue Swan* rose gracefully in the locks but had just a few feet to spare inside the lock. Everyone along the way marveled at the packet barge. They asked all sorts of questions at the lock. Bertha could hardly suppress smiles at the matter-of-fact way August Ben and Hermann answered the questions asked of them. When asked where they had it built, the men would call back nonchalantly that they had just brought her down from the yards in New York by way of a lake steamer. It had been built in Holland or Germany. This always brought open mouths and exclamations of wonder from the questioners.

Shortly after noon, both barges at Napoleon were ready for the next leg of the journey. The draft horses were changed every ten or fifteen miles to keep them fresh, but the great white Percherons who were splotched with dapples of gray, were berthed on the empty grain barge.

All along the way they met curious people who marveled at the graceful packet, asked questions, marveled some more, and then moved on. People in the towns along the way stopped to look at the barge, which they knew was no showboat because there were no fancy painted people on it.

Night came as they berthed at Junction. They ate supper before dark, and then by renting line horses for the stages along the way, the men thought it best to shove off south toward Delphos so that they could make it on home by dark the next night.

After it grew dark, the lantern was lit and placed at the bow, which was in the bill of the great swan's head. The reflected light on the great beak and curved breast gave the appearance of the Roman Emperor's barge floating along through the night. While Josie and Lou-Lou fell asleep, they were lulled by the pleasant swaying of the barge over the smooth canal's surface.

CHAPTER 6

Soon the lights along the way to small hamlets and farmhouses were extinguished. The *Blue Swan* with her proud arched deck glided along silently in the quiet night. Now and then, the dim lantern of an approaching boat came out of the darkness. With scarcely a loss but of a few minutes the barges passed each other in the canal without touching. Then each went on its way. The melodious tone of a distant boat horn floated through the night at the approach of a lock, but most traffic had stopped for the night.

The barges rose higher in each lock toward the south. Soon they were entering the high mound in the vicinity south of Delphos where the canal was a deep cut lower than the surrounding countryside. Canalers referred to this portion of the canal as the "deep cut at Spencerville." Actually there was a hamlet with shops and houses there called Deep Cut. The canal and towpath were almost fifty feet lower than the top of the summit ridge through which the deep cut was made, and it continued for nearly three quarters of a mile between Kossuth and Spencerville.

Long after midnight, the barges tied up for the night. It would be no hardship to reach home the next day, because they had only a little over twenty-five miles more to go. They had to ascend at least twelve or fourteen more locks up the summit toward New Bremen, and to Lock 1, where they would dock at home. Yes, they would reach home in full daylight. If they started by early daylight, in six hours they should reach Lock 1 by noon. It all depended upon "locking through," and how busy the locks were, but even with traffic delays, they should be home early in the afternoon.

When the curious *Blue Swan* barge with its attendant grain barges curved through St. Marys, ascended the locks there, and paused in the triangular basin, curious townspeople soon gathered on Spring Street and on the quay alongside the basin. The show horses had been hitched to the *Blue Swan* for the next stage of ten miles to rest the draft horses. The stately white and dappled show horses seemed to know when they had an audience. They performed royally. True to Lou-Lou's predictions, the inquisitive Mrs. McKeeters nearly fell off her perch onto her balcony and into the canal. She recognized the Gasts but could not understand their riding in such a magnificent off-canal vessel.

Bertha Gast had put on her better dress clothes of Toledo for the occasion of homecoming. It wasn't long before word of their coming into New Bremen spread over the town. No one in the family was at the docks of the brewery or grain depot to meet them, because no one knew when they were expected. No one was happier to hear of their return than Daisy Baby, Bertha's baby daughter who had been left at home with her Aunt Ernestine and Aunt Bernhardina. The uncertainty of the trip and cramped barge quarters did not make it seem sensible to take a young child on such a trip.

In a short time the barges were docked endwise in their private berths. The grain barge was in the slip at the grain depot. However, the *Blue Swan* went to the special place prepared for her off Washington Street, and between Front and Plum Streets. Her slip was in the basin and in front of the brewery dock. In no time, curious townspeople and admirers pressed alongside the *Blue Swan* and over her decks in order to examine the luxury packet. The *Blue Swan* was also to serve a practical business purpose - that of a cargo transport for the brewery. Some of the gossips began to say that perhaps the Gast and Kattmann family was seriously considering show business. They all put on quite a show most of the time, to say nothing of the clowning antics of the entire family, Mrs. Augusta Kattmann included."

Bertha took the girls and went home. She left August Ben and Hermann to explain the fancy horses and the plush barge to the open-mouthed townspeople. Ludwig Kattmann tried to help Ben and Hermann explain the business angle of the barge but even he was over-awed by the elegance of the *Blue Swan*, the horses, and the rich trapping of the regal harness. "Why when those high stepping horses pranced in that elegance of the *Blue Swan*, the horses had the rich trappings of regal harness," he said... Then he tried again - "Why, when those high stepping horses pranced in that elegance of shining leather, white rings, brass buckles and tinkling brass bells, one would think he were watching a horse parade in front of Windsor Castle or the Esplanade of Vienna's famous Lippizanner Spanish Riding School." It was very amazing to Ludwig Kattmann, but he knew there must be some method to his mother financing such a venture, for no one could ever say that one of his mother's faults was ever wasting money. Every dollar spent or invested must be accounted for in some sort of logical manner.

Bertha sent the girls over to her sister Bernhardina's to get Daisy Baby, for she knew the young child was homesick for them. Even though she had seemed delighted with the idea of visiting her grandmother and her Aunt Bernhardina, she was glad to see her mother and her siblings.

The barge trip home had not been at all tiring. If anything, it had been a leisurely rest, because the *Blue Swan* glided so smoothly along toward home. Even though there were many things that called for attention at home when she got there, Bertha was in no hurry or mood to be encompassed in the humdrum of everyday life. She sat instead on her side perch watching the activity up the canal at the grain depot and brewery docks. Where did all those people come from? She wondered how long it would be before her sisters came to call and to heap ridicule upon the graceful head of the *Blue Swan* that rode at rest in her private slip off the main dock south of Lock 1. Bertha knew not to expect her mother, Mrs. Kattmann. Oh no, Mrs. Kattmann would not show herself until all the novelty had worn off. In her own way and in due time, she would explain all this clandestine purchase and the plans for the new barge. There would be quite a bit of explaining to do, Bertha Gast reckoned, for she knew her sisters, Bernhardina Gast and Ernestine Hofermeyer, would be outraged by all the ridicule heaped on them by derisive townspeople.

They also would nurture polite but cutting jealously thinking that Mrs. Kattmann had showered favors and money on her favored few. Ernestine especially would be sad because she and the mousy hen-pecked Henry Hofermeyer had no financial concern in either the brewery or the grain business. Of course, much of the grain went into the brewery.

The days went by and June became brighter and warmer. The news of the coming excursion of the governor's packet filled the days with anticipation as towns along the canal put up bunting, cleaned up the canal docks, and made general preparations for welcoming receptions.

Bertha's sisters had not made the cutting remarks she expected from them. It seemed strange that she, who had been so critical of the *Blue Swan* at first, was now in position to defend her. She had her speeches prepared for her sister. She had gone out near Maria Stein to visit her father. Heinrich, who knew little about the barge, did not seem to be concerned. That was Augusta's domain and he had his vineyards, his beehives, his hop vines, and some other new enterprises to occupy his contented days at the peaceful country retreat.

Then one day Mrs. Kattmann did come home from her travels. She was careful not to set foot in New Bremen, but she sent a gracious invitation to all the family for a large Sunday dinner at Maria Stein. Bertha knew that this was the time and place of her revelation. It would be like a ceremony.

Now at last they were all to know. If only Bertha could spring a few surprises herself!

Bertha mused to herself as she went about her everyday tasks. Then all at once, the idea struck her. Why not experiment with the iced custard they all had loved in Toledo? It was a great plan, Bertha decided. Elihu Sanders could make her a freezing pail out of a cream can. They still had a full summer's supply of ice in the ice house behind the brewery. Why not try it in her basement cellar? If it worked, she could make a huge batch, pack it in ice, and take it out to her mother's home. She would spring a few surprises herself!

The appointed Sunday came at last. The grandchildren, uncles, aunts, cousins, and even friends of the family swarmed over the grounds of the old cream-colored brick homestead to the east at <u>Willow Haven</u>, or the German <u>Weide Himmel</u> outside of Maria Stein. Mrs. Augusta Kattmann, or Frau Kattmann, as many German people of the community called her, had spared nothing. She had linen covered tables spread under the grape arbors and under spreading willow trees. Her hired women helpers scurried everywhere making preparations for serving the banquet style meal from the brick kitchen.

That morning of the Sunday family dinner, Bertha Gast had kept Ben and the boys busy with freezing the iced cream custard she was preparing. The huge cake of ice from the ice house disappeared as it was broken into smaller chunks. Then the ice was put inside of a gunny sack and beaten by the broadside of an ax until it was crushed into small pieces suitable for freezing. With the use of a great deal of salt for quick freezing and much exertion of whirling the gallon pail back and forth by the bail in the tub of ice, a successful frozen custard was accomplished. After sampling it, Bertha had it packed over the top with layers of crushed ice; then it was put in the back of the spring wagon. Ben and the boys drove on ahead in the buckboard spring wagon. Bertha and the girls, Josie and Daisy Baby, were to come in the carriage with Bernhardina and Hermann and their family. Young Ben rode on with August Ben, Lou and Charley.

Bertha's last instructions to Ben were to make sure to hitch the buckboard in the shade, keep the wet tarpaulins over the ice tub, and to make sure the sacks of wet sawdust were packed securely over the top to keep the ice packs from melting. Above all, the boys were instructed to keep out of the ice, and to tell no one what was in the back of the buckboard. She would pull a few surprises on her sly mother.

The Sunday dinner passed very pleasantly and without any tense moments. Everyone was very agreeable, but Bertha could tell that there was an air of apprehension, of unanswered questions in the actions of her sister. Aunt Fredericka seemed to go around in a blank state of puzzlement; she managed to smile profusely when she remembered herself or someone caught her staring. Apparently, the subject of the *Blue Swan* and the extravagant outlay of money, whether it was a personal whim or an investment, was never brought up until some of the other relatives had left.

Bertha's moment of triumph arrived. She waited until the main deserts of pie, cake, fruit salads, and chilled fruit had been well cleared from the serving tables. When a lull came in the eating of dessert, and after a reasonable time when the appetites might be ready for more dessert, Bertha slipped out to the buckboard with Lou-Lou and Josie to sample the iced custard and to see if it were still solid after being packed in the layers of crushed ice. Much to her delight, she found the frozen cream solid and flinty with crystals of ice. Covering the tub quickly to keep out the warm air, she summoned Ben, Hermann and the boys to cart the tub and its precious contents into the well house just off the brick kitchen.

Much to Mrs. Kattmann's surprise, Bertha announced her surprise and had everyone line up with the dishes the women handed out. Bertha used a huge strong iron spoon to dip up mounds of the iced delicacy to the amazed but delighted relatives. She waited for all of them to be served and waited for their verdict. The cook and housekeeper, Joditha Noffsinger, could only nod in amazed silence to her helpers, Meg Threewits and Mayme Mote, who murmured their delight. When the steel-blue eyes of the Prussian Anna Steinhoge, Mrs. Kattmann's devoted confidant, betrayed her reticent approval, Bertha announced,

"I learned this recipe for frozen custard, or iced cream as they call it, in Toledo. The nicest woman proprietor went to great pains to explain it to me, and took me into her cellar and showed me how it was done."

"Why Bairtha, it's. . . it's wunderbar. . . chust wonderful, "her Aunt Fredericka cooed, nodding to one or the other of her relatives for comment. Then she smiled vacantly into her dish.

"Of course it is always best in June during strawberry season," Bertha added. "Then the proper cake for iced cream is a light banana and hickory nut cake with white icing."

Bertha and the girls brought out their cakes and bowls of strawberries from the cool well house, and from her mother's cellar where they had deposited them upon their arrival. Mrs. Kattmann was pleasantly surprised and somewhat flabbergasted at having her daughter out-do her in her own home, and out-do her other daughters. Mrs. Kattmann knew better than to crowd Bertha, for she knew also that she could not be flattered, cajoled, or dominated the way the other two girls and sister Fredericka could be.

Bertha made it a very pointed statement when she mentioned Toledo, and now when the afternoon wore on and some of the other relatives had left, there was only the immediate family left. In the cool shade of the huge willow tree that overhung the large well house and pump room, Bertha called the family to the table under the huge tree as she dipped more iced dessert from the tub. This huge willow tree, as well as the grove of willows around the house, gave the place its name of <u>Willow Haven</u>. The Kattmann family called it the German <u>Weidenhimmel</u> from an old family home in Bavaria.

The iced dessert would have to be eaten soon for it was beginning to grow soft with melting. The boys did not have to be called twice, nor did Josie, Daisy and Lou-Lou. Huge crock bowls of sweetened strawberries disappeared by the gallon as did the iced cream. The strawberries had been kept cool in their earthen crock containers in the water trough in the pump room. Occasionally more cold water was pumped into the cooling trough where the milk, butter and other foods were kept cool. Where the overflow spouted out on the outside into a grilled tile sink, Daisy Baby gurgled her delight as she waded barefoot in the cool water in the catch basin of the sink. Everyone went silent when Bertha, who handed her mother another bowl of iced cream, and at the same time put the question to her.

"As I said, I learned this in Toledo. You remember that we went up there on your express wish to bring home the new barge. We didn't know at the time what kind of a new barge it would be. You did not choose to let us in on the wild chase we went on, so wouldn't it be a good time now to tell us all just what is to be the purpose of so expensive a piece of equipment?"

Mrs. Augusta Kattmann enjoyed her ice cream and she enjoyed keeping them all waiting. Finally she explained:

"It is chust good business. . . I saw a bargain. . . There vas little time for the deciding. . . ready cash a quick deal. . . und der *Swan* boat vas mine." Ach, I mean ours."

"This investment. . . Mother, how is the new barge to make that much money to repay its investment outlay?" Bertha asked. Ben and Hermann listened.

"Don't you see, mein Bertha. . . that the rather unusual boat is also an eye catcher? In order to catch der eye, der ear, and der pocketbook is what makes the business world turn, Ja?" Augusta Kattmann explained. Heinrich Kattmann who seldom entered into family discussions, looked up from his bowl of iced cream and made a lone comment,

"You will see, Ben, Hermann, Bertha and Bernhardina, that the barge will coin money for you once it is known on the canal as the symbol of the brewery."

"Papa is right," Mrs. Kattmann joined in quickly. "The thing now is to make longer deliveries even if they are only small ones, but travel the length of the canal so that the *Blue Swan* is seen and known as the cleanest, trimmest barge of them all, and that her product she carries, der *Blue Swan Ale*, has her picture on each keg and bottle. I tell you, it *will* double the sales."

"Ja, Papa is right. Der *Blue Swan* has more of der class."

"Why did you purchase such an expensive barge, mama?" Ernestine asked. "Was it needed?"

"Could an old grain and ordinary cargo barge make the long trips?" her mother asked."

"The passenger service will pay for the expense of cargo delivery of the ale," Ben Gast added, coming to Mrs. Kattmann's defense.

"Passenger service, yes," Bertha told him, "as long as it is passengers only and not meals or overnight bedding down. The cost of food and a cook would eat up your profit. Make it daytime travel only with passengers, and let them stay overnight in inns along the way."

Therefore, the incident of the *Blue Swan's* purchase was opened and closed. It remained to be seen whether the *Blue_Swan* would make money. At any rate, Augusta Kattmann planned to have some leisurely trips on her.

"If this one brings in enough to pay for itself, Bertha, we may have mama buy der other showboats and invest in them!" August Ben teased.

Bertha Gast let out a shriek as if she had been stuck with a hat pin.

"Not those monstrosities!" Bertha protested. Lou-Lou and Josie began a lively description of the other showboat barges tied up in the berths in Toledo. They described how the one with the large head of the hippopotamus was the most outstanding one. Mrs. Kattmann listened, but Bertha noticed the fleeting strange expression on her face.

"Oh, Grandma-Má, with its huge head and its mouth wide open, it looked just like Mrs. Peppleman when she is hollering down the street for that no account Charley to come home and split kindling for her!"

"Such disrespect, mein Lou-veese, to your elders."

The day ended and the Gasts all returned home to New Bremen. June in all its promise of glory lay ahead, and the pleasant thought of the governor's visit gave the family to anticipate. Could that fancy passenger packet compare with the glory of the beautiful *Blue Swan*?

All the way back to New Bremen from Maria Stein Bertha thought about the afternoon. Some of the things said and not said did not line up right in Bertha Gast's mind. All during the light supper they had when they got home at dark, Bertha was silent as if she were far away or in deep thought. Ben Gast noticed but pretended not to. After the children had left the table and had gone upstairs, Bertha spoke to him.

"Ben, Ma hasn't told all. There's more to this swan barge deal than we know. Why, we don't know any more about it than we did. I thought sure that today she would reveal everything."

Later on while preparing for bed, as Bertha sat brushing her long light strands of hair, she said to Ben:

"Ben, she's got something up her sleeve. She was too agreeable, too complacent today to be the real Ma. I think today was just to draw us all out to test us. Did you notice that sister Ernestine and Henry didn't say much?"

"Bertha, you're letting your mind work overtime! You are jumping at conclusions," Ben said quietly.

"Ben, that's it! She was just drawing us out. She intends to bide her time to see how the packet passenger service goes, to see if it makes money, and if her first investment was a wise one."

"First investment?" Ben interrupted as she approached the bed still brushing her long tresses furiously.

"Ben! No wonder she was smiling to herself like a *Chessy Cat* instead of admonishing us all and passing out maxims of health, deportment, and morals the way she usually does. Ben! She's got an option on some of those other barges - some of those circus bankruptcy barges - that is if she doesn't already own them!"

"Bertha, you have such an imagination! The *Blue Swan* makes sense with our business. However, how would those others ever fit into our business or make sense?"

"Ben, doesn't it look strange to you why those other barges should be there in the Toledo docks too? Why wouldn't they be scattered and sold here and there? Why were they transported across the lake to Toledo?"

Ben was silent with thought. Then Bertha sat down on the bed looking at the floor as she continued to brush her hair. She stopped suddenly and pointing her upraised brush at Ben, she exclaimed,

"That's it, Ben. A line of packets. . . and you know what I think? She'll put my sister Ernestine, and her husband Henry, in the passenger packet business with maybe an inn or two thrown in along the way."

"It might work." Ben admitted, "Henry hasn't done too well in that clothing business and tailor shop there in Minster. He's too fussy a tailor and doesn't get anything done."

"Nor has he made much at anything he has done. He wouldn't be any good with my brother, Ludwig, in the brewery, nor with you and Hermann in the grain business, and you know he couldn't run a cargo barge."

Lou-Lou and Josie could not help hearing the discussion through the open floor register in their upstairs bedroom. The girls started whispering then fell into giggling.

Lou-Lou whispered, "Pa told Ma that Uncle Henry probably stitched some lace on his own panty-drawers instead of getting his customers' tailoring done on time." Josie laughed in her pillow until she snorted for breath.

Then she added, "I heard Papa tell Mama that they couldn't use him in the grain depot for he was as out of place as a white-robed altar boy cleaning out chimneys."

Both girls shrieked out loud in their laughter. Charley and Lou called out from their room for the girls to be quiet and go to sleep. Bertha heard Josie's last remark and realized too late that the register was left open.

The girls next heard the warning thump of the long broom handle on the ceiling below them. Bertha called up to them to get to sleep and not lie there and giggle all night. Next they heard the register bang shut from below.

In a lower voice Bertha gave her husband her final thoughts concerning her brother-in-law, Henry Hofermeyer.

"I'll bet a pretty penny he'll not like the work it will take, but now wouldn't that jar you if Ma did set them up?"

"Henry will find it will take real work, and a regular schedule, but he will tread water and out distance your mother," Ben answered her.

"Yes, and my sister Ernestine will find it's more than she's been used to doing too. She'll have to learn to get along with people and smile when she meets the public. She can't be correcting their English and manners as she does everyone else's," Bertha went on. "However, we are jumping at conclusions as you say."

"As for the constant smiles, how about getting your Aunt Fredericka for good public appearances? I'll bet she will lie there and smile at her own funeral! Did you notice her today? She seemed sort of blank to me. She was in sort of a daze, but she would look out over the fields at nothing and just smile and smile."

"Ach Helige Gott!" Bertha exclaimed in German, since no English exclamation seemed to express the sense and emotion quite as well.

"But come to think of it, it was rather odd that your father spoke up in defense of the *Blue Swan* today, and usually he never enters into anything concerning the family discussions. Funny he should care, when usually he walks off and sees about his bees or vineyards when the family talks get too involved."

During the night a light rain started falling. After a while, the wind rose and there was a short period of distant thunder and lighting. It was a good night for sleeping but the next morning dawned cool and rainy.

Monday was rather a slow leisurely day. Bertha went about her morning wash day chores in the cellar with the thoughts of the night before still fresh in her mind. Wouldn't it be a real laugh if her mother has invested in those outlandish circus barges to put them into a flamboyant packet service? One thing was for certain: they would attract attention along the way. She had to laugh to herself when she thought of her stiff-necked tight-lipped sister,

Ernestine Hofermeyer, having to help with cooking and bedding on the passenger packets or at the end of the trip. If her mother, Mrs. Kattmann, gave out the order from her fortress at Maria Stein, it would be followed out by the Hofermeyers if they wanted to eat. Prosperity might come later when they could afford it, but first things must come first.

Ben pointed out to Bertha that Henry Hofermeyer was resilient and was quietly tough beneath his quiet gentlemanly appearance. He skated on thin ice where Augusta Kattmann was concerned and survived her domination. He knew where the money was. Yes, if the ice broke momentarily, Henry would tread water until he surfaced again and his fortunes improved with a financial handout from Frau Kattmann.

Bertha laughed at his metaphors, and then commented that Henry knew how to sew a fine seam, survive Ernestine's sarcasm, survive his mother-in-law's domination, and the sleuthing of her detective and bloodhound, Anna Steinhoge.

"Yes, he will come up out of the pond after the dive, as unruffled as a loon, and with his fine manners and soft voice, he will charm us all out of our pocketbooks," Ben told her.

"But imagine a polka-dot-elephant barge!" Bertha exclaimed.

CHAPTER 7

THERE WERE SIGNS OVER town that the mayor and alderman were making preparations for the governor's packet and his party of inspecting senators. As for Ben and Hermann, the rain had called a halt to deliveries from the country grain wagons. It was a good cool day to take it easy up at the depot as well as at the brewery.

It was a good day to tinker with the discarded old calliope on the hold of the *Blue Swan*. Elihu Sanders was as happy as a little boy with a top to have the contraption to experiment with. Ben and Hermann were like schoolboys as they tried to figure out each part and what needed to be done. Jake Hemel, the blacksmith, was a great help for he seemed to have a deft mechanical knack about things of this sort. The few people, who were permitted near the shops at the locks, stepped back of Jake Hemel's blacksmith shop to Elihu Sander's tinker shop to view the calliope and give ideas of how it should look. Mr. MacPherson, the lockmaster, advised that the fine work of brazing the brass fittings should be done by the machine shop men up at St. Marys. He could even fix the church pipe organ in a pinch.

During the ensuing days, a way was found to smuggle the calliope up to the brass welder in St. Marys. Mr. MacPherson and Elihu Sanders danced with glee when they finally heard the wheezing off-key steam organ rasp out its shrill off-key notes. Nevertheless, a way had to be found to keep the player from scalding his fingers for the pistons under the keys needed new packings. There was another delay: then at last, the leaking packings were replaced.

Next the boiler had to be checked and rechecked to make sure the steam gauge was correct. Elihu cackled at his own joke about the uneasiness of the steam organ player being blown into perdition with his heaviest loud playing, and when an inaccurate gauge caused the boiler to go dry.

When the calliope was at last slipped back to New Bremen, the news of its journey and its repair leaked back to Bertha Gast. One afternoon the boys inadvertently let the secret drop in front of Lou-Lou and Josie, and in time it got back to Bertha. She surprised the men at the depot one late afternoon when she suddenly popped into Elihu Sander's tinker shop and found most of the men, including Jake Hemel, polishing up the calliope to make its brass shine like gold.

"Why are all of you acting so secretive?" She called out to the surprised culprits who tried to cover up the calliope. If you're ever going to play it, you know the whole town can hear its squalling!"

Then the question came up of who could play it now that it was repaired. They also wondered where would they play it and for what occasions?

This was an excellent question - one without an answer, Bertha told herself. She was well aware that sisters Ernestine and Bernhardina could play the piano and the melodeon organ as well. Ernestine gave herself great airs on the bench of the church organ, much to the discomfiture of the men who had to pump the bellows levers, especially when she got carried away and pulled all the stops for an impressive passage. Some of the German women were somewhat unkind when they whispered behind their fans that perhaps Ernestine, as well as Bernhardina, imagined themselves to be the reincarnation of Johann Sebastian Bach at the pipe organ in Brandenburg, Germany.

Little by little, a thought kept running through Bertha Gast's head. It was one that grew with amusement the more she thought about it. She found herself smiling to herself as she walked the cobbled and brick streets to the market. People she met smiled back thinking the friendly Bertha was smiling at them, but her thoughts were centered on the men at Elihu Sander's shop. How they had scrambled like little boys in the cookie jar when she found them polishing the calliope! Then her thoughts went deeper with amusement.

She tried to imagine her sisters playing the calliope when the governor's packet came through the town. They would say that it was such commonplace performance! How vulgar and exhibitionistic the sounds would be to them! They, Ernestine and Bernhardina, had studied music laboriously, and mastered the technique and written notes. However, somehow they let the melody and expression elude them. They had both taught music. No, they would go to the executioner's block before submitting to such an earthly comedown.

However, Bertha treated herself to the humor of trying to picture either one of them at the calliope mounted on the docks, or better yet, on the barge as it passed through the town on the canal.

No, if anyone played the calliope, it would have to be Aunt Fredericka for she could lend humor to it. However, then she would probably scald herself or catch her skirts on fire from the embers under the boiler at her feet. Josie and Lou-Lou might be able to learn to play it, but they had not mastered the parlor organ yet. It was all they could do to play the simple songs on the square piano. Organ technique was something else, but the connecting, holding touch was the same for the calliope. No, Bertha reasoned that the only one to play the contraption for the men at the tinker shop was she. Someone had to. She knew that Hermann and Ben would be crestfallen if they did not get to hear that infernal squalling steam organ being played after all their secrecy and work. What was her mother, Mrs. Kattmann, to think once she got wind of the steam organ? It would all be very interesting.

While preparing the evening meal, Bertha sprang her plan on the girls. Lou-Lou always managed to get her work done at home and run back over to Josie's house. Sometimes Josie went over home with her to help her so that her mother would not scold, and besides, two of them could make the work fly faster. They could turn their chores into play as long as it passed the critical inspection of Bernhardina Gast who followed behind them.

Bertha told the girls about the calliope and that someone would have to learn to play it. In time the job would fall to them, she told them. However, for the time being she would have to practice and commit some simple songs to memory. Then she could go out on the barge and practice on the calliope. She didn't want anybody to hear her miserable errors in practicing. Besides, how did she know if she could play the infernal thing anyway? The girls were beside themselves with laughter and excitement at playing the calliope. Why, people would come for miles to hear it. No one ever heard of one, except on the passing showboats, and on the large river paddlewheelers on the Ohio and Mississippi.

Then Bertha hit upon the idea of dressing like the show people they had seen at Junction City the night of the carnival: the dancing señorita, and the colorful costumes. She would have to dress the part if they were to put on a show. The girls squealed with excitement.

"Oh, mama, do you mean it? What will Aunt Bernhardina and Aunt Ernestine say? Will you really dress up?" Josie exclaimed.

"Oh just you wait! Now let's see. . . perhaps a fortuneteller, or a Spanish señorita outfit would do! I'll have to have something simple enough so that I can play and not be all bundled up or confined with furbelows," Bertha said.

"Oh Aunt Bert, you wouldn't dare! Why, Grandma Kattmann will lay an egg!" Lou-Lou wailed.

"Oh, wouldn't I? Can't you just see me? Just you wait. I've been wanting a chance to show the lot of them a thing or two," Ma included. "Did you notice how they all smirked Sunday over the iced custard, and yet they had to admit that it was delicious?"

"Oh, Mama, they will just die - just die, Josie exclaimed.

"It will be worth it. Oh this is rich!" Bertha laughed as her face crinkled with humor. Then she reminded the girls of the horror-stricken faces of those two women on the docks in Toledo when they saw her come aboard the *Blue Swan* and supposed she was a show woman, and how they had remarked in their retreat,

". . . And she was such a nice-looking woman! What a life for those poor children." The girls screamed with laughter as they had peeled the last of the potatoes for the "kartoffel-klase" (potato soup with egg "nudelin").

"However Aunt Bert, you can't get all this ready, and learn to play the calliope all in these few days before the governor's packet arrives," Lou-Lou said.

"No, but we can try. Wouldn't it be rich through to put on a show unbeknownst to Ma and my sisters? Wouldn't the townspeople fall over in a fainting swoon if I were to make a fool of myself up there on the dock when the packet goes into the lock? Mayor Zinndorfer will make his welcome speech, and then I will open up all the steam stops and let loose with some background music!" Bertha found herself laughing as hard as the girls were at the picture she was painting of herself.

It was after supper when Ben and the boys had gone back up to the tinker shop to work on the calliope, to chat with the other men, and perhaps have a game or two of checkers at the depot. Bertha and the other girls carted little Daisy Baby upstairs with them to look through old pattern books and remnants of old cloth that could be used in the costume.

After discarding the señorita with high combs and lace mantilla in favor of the fortuneteller, Bertha remembered the astrologist behind her desk in the little tent booth on the docks during the carnival at Junction City. Of course, that was the costume! That of Fatima, the Turkish clairvoyant with her turban and mask over half her face, and the large full Turkish harem pants gathered at the ankle.

In no time at all, Bertha had devised the headpiece and tried her hand at wrapping a turban in the mirror on the dresser. Next, she found some beaded lace with a filigree of imitation seed pearls twined in an oriental looking pattern. This was just the thing for the face veil. Now for large earrings and all the purple, lavender, and black material she could find. If only she could get into her Mother's trunks of discarded gowns. What velvets, silks, and ribbons she could find there!

In the morning, she went to the little dry goods store where Mrs. MacPherson showed her several bolts of inexpensive cottons, calico and gingham. Bertha reasoned that if Ben and Hermann could be so extravagant as to spend money on the calliope, she could have a fling or two and go hog-wild on her unheard-of naughty Turkish harem costume. Who ever heard of a middle-aged woman, and mother of four children, appearing in public in floppy Turkish bloomer pants instead of modest hoops, and making a spectacle of herself by playing a calliope like a common show woman? It was shocking to say the least, but how they all laughed. They would show those men at the tinker shop a thing or two about secrecy and surprises. New Bremen would never be the same! What would the governor think, and what would newspapers say about all of it?

Bertha shut herself upstairs behind locked doors and went to work in earnest on the Turkish costume. Josie and Lou-Lou did the morning work and kept a sharp weather eye out for Charley, Lou, and young Ben. Daisy Baby was too little to understand any of it and kept busy with her dolls and her "dolly" dishes. No one was to know of their scheme of the costume, especially August Ben and Hermann. The grand debut was to be a complete blasting shock to leave them all agog and their mouths agape. She would teach August Ben and Hermann to sneak around like schoolboys with their first love note from their valentine box. If only there was more time before the governor's packet trip through town.

Bertha stopped at noon and hid their needlework before the boys and men came to dinner, and went down to help Lou-Lou and Josie finish the meal. As soon as they were all gone, she took the girls and rushed up to finish the costume. When it was done, they all marveled at its breath taking beauty when Bertha put it on and strutted around the room admiring herself in the mirror. Nothing would do but what the girls were to have costumes too. They would stand on either side as side attractions to help her with the sheets of music in the wind, tend the fire, and watch the boiler gauge. Of course, Charley, Lou, and young Ben would want in on the fun once they found out. Perhaps they could stoke the fire and carry water for the boiler.

It was no trouble at all to make the señorita costume for Lou-Lou for she had her heart set on it. Josie and Lou-Lou went over to Bernhardina Gast's home and finding her gone as usual, to sister Ernestine's, they ransacked the trunks in the attic. Then they went to Grandmother Kattmann's and found some lovely black lace with black jet embroidered in it. Lou-Lou pounced onto it immediately for her lace, which was to drape from her high comb mantilla.

Josie decided that the weather might be too chilly for the bareback circus girl rider, and settled for the fortuneteller, even though she was a blonde. In no time at all the costumes were made, and little by little all three picked up trinkets, accessories, and jewelry to go with their outfits. The stage was set.

Next all three took turns practicing diligently, first on the piano to learn the music; then they learned to play the same on the parlor organ. Lou-Lou and Josie went over to Lou-Lou's to practice on the instruments there while Bertha pumped away on the parlor melodeon.

She found simple organ arrangements of show tunes, and old German folk waltzes. She had to laugh at herself when she heard her own rendition of "Ach Du Lieber Augustine" on the parlor organ followed by "Du, Du Licht Mir Im Hertzen," "The Skaters," and "Der Snitzelbank." Next she tried the French "Alouette," some old Viennese traditional songs, and some Russian Folk songs. She couldn't leave out "O Susannah," "Clementine," or "Buffalo Gal." They were so dearly beloved by the wagon trains going west in the "forty-nine madness." The girls practiced diligently. Bertha could not remember when they had gone to their practice without being driven by threats, cajoling, and finally the yardstick and flyswatter.

The time came in the next few days when Bertha decided to drop the bomb on Ben. She would tell him that she would consent to play the calliope on the condition that he and Hermann did not breathe a word of it to the other men, or to Mrs. Hemel. If she or Mrs. MacPherson got wind of it, it would be all over town. Mrs. MacPherson might be a bit suspicious already since she seemed a little surprised at the bright colors of the cotton yard goods she had sold her a few mornings back. Ben was not given even the slightest hint about the costumes, but he was overjoyed, as was Hermann, and the other men were at the news that at last they had a player for the calliope.

One afternoon Bertha and the girls slipped aboard the grain barge at the grain depot and Ben and Hermann embarked down the canal on what appeared to be a routine delivery of ale kegs and grain sacks down to Minster and Ft. Loramie. The boys took turns as hoggee drivers. Jake Hemel went along as troubleshooter and to watch the steam gauges, while Ben tended the boiler and the fire under it. Once out of town and out of hearing, Bertha began to experiment. For one thing, it was hot down there in the hold with all that fire, the heat from the boiler, and the closeness. However, she was game, and a little gingerly at first, she tried her fingers on the stiff metal keys. It was almost ludicrous at first, and she warned all of them to keep civil tongues to themselves, for she needed hours of practice to get used to the contraption, if it didn't blow them all into the next county in the meantime.

When they met anyone on the canal, the calliope became silent. However, many farmers in the summer fields turned strange expressions in the directions of the canal, but seeing only a clumsy grain boat, knew the strange off-key music must be coming from somewhere on down the canal. Below Newport the canal turned to the east into deep woods through swamp bottoms. A side-cut canal led back through a dark avenue of trees to the Russian village and the sawmill.

Jake tried to keep the stiff metal lever keys oiled so they would work easier, but the heat from the steam evaporated the oil and he had to repeat it rather often. Lou-Lou and Josie got their turns at practice while Bertha rested up on the deck and cooled off. One thing about it, when they got to the seclusion of the swamp canal near the Russian sawmill, and below Ft. Loramie on Loramie Creek, the men could carry the "infernal contraption from Hades" up on deck. Then Bertha could at least get what summer breeze there was. She began to wonder if she shouldn't change her concealing Turkish costume to a cooler one of a bareback rider or a ballerina. Maybe she should change the outfit to pink tights, like the trapeze and tightrope walker. Wouldn't that give them all something to faint over?

Once they were in the seclusion of the sawmill side-cut canal to the millpond that led off from the canal and Loramie Creek below Newport, Bertha had the calliope brought up on deck. She had mastered the technique well. She didn't mind the curious stares of the Russian mill workers who came out of the sawmill yards, or the lumbermen who came out of the woods on every side of the side-cut sawmill canal when they heard this strange, loud, but entrancing rhapsody of the steam pipes.

The irrepressible Johnny Ivan, the so-called "Mad Russian," even whirled in some Russian folk dances when Bertha swung furiously into a "Kopak" and some wild Cossack folk dances. The Russians all clapped and yelled "Hai" for more when she finished. Ben told them what they were doing there, and after a while they went back to their work. The huge Big Barge Bertha of the rapid "bullet stones" of up Maumee way even appeared on the shaded towpath with her black-eyed boys, and listened with rapt attention to the strange contraption. Ben and Hermann danced a German *Lederhosen* "*shulplatl*" on deck with the traditional shoe-sole and cheek slapping in time with the music of "Augustine." They laughed with glee at their success. Jake Hemel wiped his brow from the heat of the boiler and clapped his hands in approval. Then he helped himself to a half gallon of ale from the bunghole of a barrel.

Bertha smiled to herself at their boyish glee, but smiled more when she whispered to the girls that Ben and Hermann were in for more surprises, if not shocks, later when the women all appeared in their costumed finery.

The boisterous gaiety there in the seclusion of the remote woods was broken and somewhat clouded by Uriah Hornback and his slow oxen team plodding on the towpath. He had a raft of logs in tow to be delivered to the Russian's sawmill. He shook his head at the "Ways of Sin" and "Working of the Devil" when he saw the dancing on board the barge, the Russians dancing on the rough plank dock, and heard the sinful but luring strains of compelling music. He wanted to stand in a trance and listen. However, he remembered lessons from the scripture of the sinful Salome, and of her music and lustful dance, not to mention how it drove sane men mad. He also remembered the scripture lesson of Jezebel, of the music of Baal, of wicked lustful Delilah and her dance and seduction of Samson. All this was called up to Uriah Hornback, who forgot himself for a few moments, and then ducked his head in embarrassed silence. He fought to go on with determination. However, the music was strong, and the flesh was weak. His wife, Sheba, sat crocheting as usual and was nodding her head constantly as if to lend encouragement and assent to the very thoughts going through Uriah's head. Little Orvie and Mahaley stopped playing with their assortments of rocks, mussel shells and fungus brackets long enough to stand transfixed by the music and stare at the brazen world of sin before them. Sheba covered her ears, and with a pleading look she urged Uriah on quickly down the towpath with their cargo of logs for the sawmill. She wanted to get away before their offspring were lured to their doom. She was afraid that in their innocence they would be drawn to this wild siren at the devil's keyboard that was playing those swirling temptations from hell.

Now the stage was set. All the actors knew their parts, and the calliope was a success. They were ready to spring it on an unsuspecting world! Back in New Bremen, as well as other towns along the canal, more preparations were made for the governor's visit with members of the congress. Bunting was strung here and there, rubbish was cleared away, fences were painted, and all in all the towns took on a "spruced up" look. The *Blue Swan* was washed and polished until it gleamed.

The only incident to mar the otherwise perfect preparations was a couple of nights before the arrival of the packet. In fact it was the night after the practicing experiment in the heart of the woods down by the sawmill just off Loramie Creek. A rainstorm came up that night, and after the first severe winds passed with the front, sheets of heavy rain fell in a steady downpour. The path master became uneasy about the banks and berms of the canal, so he took his oil lantern and started his inspection tour after the deluge subsided. Other path masters stationed at Minster and Ft. Loramie, as well as St. Marys, did the same thing. Their duty was to walk their assigned ten miles each day, going down on one side and coming back on the other, to watch for leaks in the built-up banks and berms. A mole's tunnel, a gopher's borough, or a crawfish's hole could start a trickle from the canal through the berm or the towpath bank. In no time, a fine trickle could grow into a gushing breakthrough, and let miles of canal water into the adjoining fields where the canal grade ran higher than the surrounding land.

All at once, the fire bell began to ring and everyone ran into the streets near midnight. The path master had reported to Mr. MacPherson at the locks that there was a leak about halfway down to Minster near the big pond at the edge of the overhanging woods. The emergency call went out for men from house to house and everyone responded for the canal was the lifeline of the community. The repair boat came along and foamed up the water at a fast trot of nearly ten miles an hour. Most people called it the "hurry-up" boat because it was permitted to exceed the speed limit because of its emergency purposes. Men in oilskins and boots piled into the repair boats and hurried to stop the leak in the berm. They got it repaired good enough to hold until daylight when a more complete crew could inspect and make final repairs.

Then in the middle of the night another alarm was sounded. There was a bad leak, because of some accursed muskrats to the north, and beyond Lock 2 at New Paris. It was here that the canal crossed a small tributary of the St. Marys River northeast of New Bremen. Why did those miserable rodents always decide to work at night, and of all times, during a rainy night? It took the Russians from down on Loramie creek and their dogs to hunt down the muskrats and flush them from their swampy boroughs.

August Ben, Hermann and the boys joined the emergency crews and worked well into the morning. After all, they couldn't have the governor's packet delayed by such a disaster. What if it were to happen again just before the packet arrived and caused the canal to run dry, leaving the packet and all its finer people "mudlarked" on the oozy bottom like a mud-puppy wallowing in a swale?

When the tired men came back to town after conquering the rampaging canal, angry farmers were pounding on Gast's doors, hounded Mr. MacPherson for an immediate inspection of their ruined cornfields, and threatening to sue the company if they did not get immediate payment. The townswomen had food and hot coffee ready for the water and mud soaked workers. Bertha and Mrs. Peppleman, along with Mrs. Hemel and other stout-hearted women, took carriages and braved the rain to deliver sandwiches, pie, and hot coffee to the drenched workers who were trying to stem the flow of water. They also were trying to stop the caving banks where the canal grade was built up high to be level with the aqueduct that carried it over the small branch of the St. Marys River.

The night passed and after the repair crews had made the canal safe once more the next day, everyone settled down to a much needed rest. The day after tomorrow was the date for the arrival of the governor's packet and now everything seemed ruined by the storm and by the scare of a dry-bed gully instead of a canal. Another day passed and some repairs were made in town.

The lamps went out early in the town while everyone went to bed early to make ready for the coming event. Downed tree limbs and tree trunks were removed from the streets near the canal and the debris was cleaned up. Some of the bunting was ruined, but the town was quick to gain back some of its gaiety. Soon it appeared like its former self, even if it was tired in body and spirit.

Bertha Gast had little trouble in getting most of her family to bed early. Tomorrow was the big day, and they would all have to be up early in order to be ready for the historic event in the life of the quiet little town asleep on the berm and towpath of the Miami Canal.

CHAPTER 8

AS DAYBREAK WAS ABOUT to show streaks of light in the east, a cool breeze arose and fluttered the curtains in Josephine's window. It was a fine morning for sleeping a little later than usual, but today of all days, that would not be permitted. After the rainstorm had passed and all the excitement of the leak in the banks subsided, the day before had been hot and sultry. The June sun beat down on the little town of German descent in western Ohio along the canal. Josie opened one eye when she heard the far off trumpet sound of the canal boat's approach to the depot and the double locks at Bremen. Then she snuggled down in her warm bed for another snooze before her mother's voice would awaken her. The cuckoo clock peeped its quick six o'clock call. Then before she knew it the little bird popped its head out of the door and called seven o'clock.

"Josie! Josephine? Are you awake? It's time to get up!" After a few minutes more of Josie pretending sleep, Bertha Gast called again. This time she called more sharply and Josie knew that it was time to be up, dressed, and washed for breakfast. This was the *day of days* and reality came spinning back as she became more awake. She heard the sharp rap of the long handle of the broom on the ceiling below her just as her brothers Charley and Lou rushed in and threw a little cold water in her face. They rushed out of the room as she started after them with a pillow. Laughing heartily at their prank, Charley and Lou raced each other outside on the towpath to work up an appetite for breakfast. When Josie came downstairs, little Daisy Baby was giving her dolls breakfast on the bottom stair.

"Jo-Jo," Daisy called to her, "come and have hot oats with Dollie May."

"Later, Daisy Baby," Josie said as she smiled and hurried by to the cistern on the back porch to wash her face and hands in cool, soft water. Her mother set large platters of ham, eggs, and buckwheat cakes on the table as her father and the boys sat down to breakfast. There was a big day ahead with a day's work to be done that morning, because of all the activity at the depot and the canal freight office. The storm and leak in the bank caused several barges to be delayed for loading at the dock. When Josie slipped into her chair after helping her mother finish setting the table, her father patted her cheerfully.

"How is my little Josephine, *mein little fraulein*?"

Lou called out to his mother,

"Mama, Papa is talking Dutch again."

"It's not Dutch, Lou, it's Deutsch," Mrs. Gast corrected.

"And for vy should I not use German Deutsch with *mein* own family, *Ja*? Und could you tell me of not one respectable German family in Bremen and Minster who does not talk to his own family at his own table with at least some Deutsch?"

"And, Charley, take your pigeon away from the table and out of the house," said his mother.

"Oh, Papa," Josie chided him, "how are we going to be able to use English with the other kids our age in school, if we hear German all the time at home?"

Charley spoke up while trying to cover his cakes with syrup.

"Papa, you just use those words with Daisy and Jo-Jo, sorta special like, and Cousin Lou-Lou."

Ben Gast spoke up quickly, as if he had been burnt by his hot coffee.

"*Ach*! Now *Mein Karl*, that iss not true. Chust yesterday in the freight warehouse I spoke to you in Deutsch, *Ja*, now didn't I?"

Charley shook his head and looked surprised.

"When, Papa? I don't remember it!"

Ben Gast, his eyes wrinkling with mirth, laughed and said,

"Vy, yes Charlee, ven you left Mrs. Peppleman's wooden buckets of lard set out on the dock in the sun, ven you should haf put them inside in der cooler shade, *Ja*?"

"Well, what's German about all that?" Lou asked.

"Vell, don't you remember, Charley? I said you wair ein. . . . "

"Oh all right," Charley said loudly, to drown out his father and to save his own embarrassment.

"I DO REMEMBER. I'd better take my pigeon out."

"Remember what, Charley?" Josie teased.

"Yeah, what?" Lou asked his father.

"Vy, I chust said to Mrs. Peppleman ven she complain about soft lard, 'dat Charlee, he iss *mein dumm kopf*!'" Ben Gast said as he tapped his head with his finger, and looked sidewise at Charley who was eating rapidly, and trying not to pay any attention to the joke on him. All the other children laughed and dawdled over their food, expecting more fun making from their father.

"Eat your breakfast, all of you," Bertha Gast spoke up. "I declare, Ben Gast, you spoil them so - and I am the one who has to make them mind."

"Now Berta, it's der light heart that makes the work lighter. A happy breakfast iss a happy day, *Ja*? I want all mein children to be happy. I want them happy at home, and happy out in the world! There are tears enough in dis world."

"There'll be tears for me, Ben, if all of you don't get your breakfast so that I can get my work done, and this house redden up before my sisters and Aunt Fredericka come over this morning. You know how they always inspect everything to see if I keep house as they do. Josie, I'm surprised that your cousin Louise isn't here by now."

"They're coming again this morning, Berta? They wair chust here last night." Ben leaned toward her, squinting his eyes, and pretending to have forgotten.

"Und wot special day iss this, mein Berta? It's work for me at the depot and freight house, chust like any other..."

"Ben Gast! *Gott in Himmel* - sometimes I think you would forget your own birthday."

However, Bertha Gast caught herself lapsing into German when she started to get angry, and Ben roared with laughter, knowing that he had succeeded in getting her *Old Dutch* up. The children squealed with childish glee. Little Daisy clapped her hands and called,

"*Gott-immel, Gott-immel*," as she was trying to imitate her mother, while getting egg yolk on the tablecloth from her baby plate. Bertha Gast had to laugh in spite of herself at her baby's childish gibberish in make-believe German.

"What is going on in here?" a girlish voice called from the porch on the canal side of the house. "Is there a medicine show in town?" Louise Gast came quickly to the morning glory-shaded east window and peeked in. "Or are you getting in practice for taking the *Blue Swan* on tour?"

"Lou-Lou," the boys called out to their favorite cousin, "Come on in. You're next on the program for the 'Ghastly Gast Gas' - that side splitting Dutch minstrel playing daily on the towpath."

"Charley, do be quiet. What will the neighbors think? Do come in, Louise." Bertha picked up the shoo-fly fly swatter and pretended to swat Charley as he was standing up now, waving his arms, and giving his come-on show spiel: "And next, ladees and gentleman, I give you Lou-Lou Gast, that well known Brementown comedian with her own brand of imitations."

However, the swatter caught him across the top of his head, and his mother spoke harshly, even though there were wrinkles of humor around her eyes.

"Now get on with your breakfast, all of you. The neighbors can't help hearing all of this, and they will think we're all *Gerzeit-plopten!* Charley, if that pigeon gets on my curtains!"

"What Mama, *ger*-what?" Ben teased, "Do you mean *gehen geplappern*?"

"You've gone daft, out of your heads, ever since the showboat and Toledo. Oh, never you mind," she answered quickly, and gave her husband a swat across the table. "Now eat your breakfast." Louise came into the kitchen and kissed her Uncle Ben on the cheek, then went around to her Aunt Bertha and hugged her. Bertha Gast went on:

"Ben, I do declare. You're the worst of the lot. *Das geht nicht.* Look at all of our offspring. Comedians, the whole pack of them, and you - you lead them on." Louise pulled up a chair beside Josie, helped herself to a hotcake covered with jam, which she rolled up with some ham, and called it a *Strudel-schnitzel.*

"And Berta, why is this day so special-like? Vot iss dis day?"

Josie interrupted her mother who was about to speak, but she choked with vexation at Ben Gast's question.

"Why, Papa, this is the morning when the first big fancy passenger packet will pass right by here on the canal with the big society folks, on the way down to Cincinnati. . . even the governor. You told us all that up in Toledo when we saw the packet."

"Why yes, Uncle Ben, some elegant ladies from Washington, are coming down the lakes to Toledo, then on down to Cincinnati while inspecting our back country," Louise added.

"And, in addition, some Ohio senators will accompany some of the big people from Washington," Lou added. His eyes grew large with thinking about it. Josie spoke up.

"Mrs. Hemel, across on the other side of the canal and above the forge, said that the barge drivers were saying last week that they had a fancy large boat. A passenger packet will come all the way from the Erie Canal from New York. Then it will come onto our canal on a lake steamer. We saw it at the docks!"

"They will go aboard one of those big river steamboats at Cincinnati, and go on all the way down to New Or-leens," Charley said.

"O Gee-Himmel," Louise sighed. "Just think – that's just down the towpath!"

"Vell, what do you know?" Ben Gast said while shaking his head.

"What do we know? August Ben Gast! You sat right here at this table blowing all about it last week when Mr. Peppleman, Mr. Hemel, and all those other side-kicks of yours from the freight house were here for coffee and crullers. Now don't act so surprised. You saw it at Toledo, didn't you? Get on with your breakfast, and get out of here. I have tracks to make." Berta Gast swatted at him with her flyswatter as he bellowed out a deep laugh, and ducked her arm.

"We'll help, Aunt Bert," Louise assured her. "They'll all be over here on your side porch to watch the show about mid morning. I want to get out of the house. Besides, I would rather work over *here*."

"All? All coming?" Bertha Gast shrieked. "What do you mean by *all?*"

"Why didn't you know that Aunt Ernestine came up from Minster and brought your Aunt Fredericka? Nothing would do them, but they had to send Pa over to Maria Stein to fetch Grandma-Má. Oh, I can tell you. Our house is one bee-hive, one mad house, and I am so sick of tip-toeing around that I could scream," Lou-Lou sighed.

Bertha Gast groaned, and put her hands to her head. "But that ain't all, Aunt Bert. I have had lectures: lectures on deportment, and how a young lady should act in company, and with all this society that is passing through. Why you would think I was being coached for marriage with a foreign prince."

"Lou-Lou Gast, you beat all," her aunt said.

Lou-Lou had an audience now, and she arose from the chair for one of her theatrical imitations, for some of which she had been soundly spanked for disrespect to her proper, but stolid, German elders. She picked up a fork from the table and held it in front of her eyes as if it were stick-glasses, drew herself in, screwed up her lips, and said in a finicky, mincing tone. "Lou-eese, try to valk like theese - slow and deestinct. Lou-eese, a proper young lady doesn't run and skip, but valk, *mein Liebchen*, like a princess of the blood. Lou-eese are you listening to your Aunt Ernestine? Dere! Dots battair." Then Lou-Lou dropped her accent and rose to say out of the side of her mouth, "and darned if she didn't have the gall to pinch me to make me listen."

"Louise. Now I am sure sister Ernestine meant well," Bertha Gast said of her sister, but she did admit to herself that Ernestine did put on airs.

"Und what did your mother say?" Ben Gast asked. He knew his sister-in-law, Bernhardina Gast, had notions toward high society, the same as Ernestine, his wife's other sister. However, she was a little more quiet about it.

"What did Ma say?"

"It's what she does. She just stands to the side, nods her head, walks stiffly back and forth, and nods approval of everything that Aunt Ernestine says. Aunt Fredericka, Ma's Aunt, you know, horns in on everything Ma says and closes her eyes, nods her head, and smiles and smiles."

"Louise, honestly!"

"Oh, Aunt Ernestine is out of another century, Ma is a caution, and Grandma-Má! She is like an old dragon sitting over there on the settee, breathing fire."

"Louise! Is there no stopping you?" You just don't understand your grandmother. She means well!"

"Yes, oh yes man! She sits there, staring at me with those piercing black Bavarian eyes, grumbling in German. "Honestly, I can't understand a thing she is murmuring about. She just keeps saying, 'Ach, Mein Gott.' She is such an impudent kleine fraulein. Bairn-hard-deen Nah! Ach! You should not latt her eat so much. Like a prize heifer she'll be. You should use the paddle-stick more, Bairn-hard-deen-nah. Hair bottom is getting too fat. You should paddle her more, teach hair to mind, and say, "Ja, gnaedige Frau. Ja, mein Mutter." ("Yes respectful lady. Yes my mother.")

"Louise Gast," her Aunt Bertha protested.

Lou-Lou went right on, "And when I stared right back at her, and made a face when Ma and Aunt Ernestine weren't looking, she puffed up like an old owl and started batting her eyes like a toad in a hail storm, sputtering out more German. Then she puts these gold glasses on a stick out in front of her and looks me up and down."

Ben Gast, laughing as if he would burst, said to his wife, "That sounds like Frau Kattmann, your mother."

"Ben Gast, you're no help. You only encourage them, and I have to be the one to put the brakes on. Louise, its no wonder you and your brother Ben get so many paddlings. I should think that barrel stave out in the wood shed would be getting worn thin by now."

"New," Lou-Lou said, dropping her accent and mimicry, "I thrive on it." She rubbed her backside. "The board may be getting thinner, but dragooned if I am." "Aunt Bert, do I look like a young heifer? Do I?"

"Oh Lou-Lou, honestly! Of course you don't. You're no fatter than my Josie. Now tell me truthfully, Ma didn't really say that, did she?"

"Well, I'm no sapling pole, mama," Josie acknowledged, but Lou-Lou took up her aunt's question.

"She sure did, Aunt Bert, as sure as I am standing here. Wish I could imitate a calf bawling like brother Ben can. I'd go around bawling and mooing in front of her."

"Oh, now stop it. Josie, clear up these dishes if the men folk are done, and let's get with it. I can see it all now. We are *really* going to have company. I can see they will all be in fine *fettle*. Scat now - all of you. To arms, to arms, each one to his post," Bertha Gast commanded.

Louise raced on, "Then they'd all get down on their knees in front of the sofa and have prayers and more prayers, and holler and give Satan a going over, and the saloons, and then they always get *way* out on temperance. They always give a spell of a good chunk to temperance and the evils of liquor. Aunt Fredericka fans...and smiles...and takes smelling salts, burnt feather, then smiles, smiles, weeps and smiles, and then hollers and hollers."

"Now Louise," Bertha tried to interrupt her. "You don't understand your grandmother. She has been very generous with all of us. You must not judge by outward appearances only. Some day you will understand her. Have you forgotten the *Blue Swan* already?.

"No, but Aunt Bert, why is she always on me? I get lectured to all the time."

"I think perhaps she rides you because she is fond of you and wants you to grow up to be what she wants you to be. I think she can see herself as a girl in you, for I think she was very outspoken and as full of mischief as you are Lou-Lou," Bertha said. "Her Prussian father used his riding crop on her..."

"Well, you ought to hear them go on when they have prayer services," Lou-Lou protested.

"Now Louise, they don't carry on like that," Bertha scolded.

"Yes they do, don't they Josie? You've been there when they cut loose."

Josie had to admit to her mother that Lou-Lou was telling the truth, and then Lou-Lou went on,

"And when 'the Father' comes and they get started on charity, temperance, and supporting foreign missions for the heathen..."

"Well, we all try to support the foreign missions, and do what we can for temperance causes, Bertha explained.

Lou-Lou turned to her uncle, August Ben.

"Now ain't that a good belly laugh, Uncle Ben? Temperance! Why, Grandma-Má Kattmann's people made their money from distilleries in the old country. Moreover, what do you think about our own Blue Swan Brewery? It belongs to Grandma and Grandpa, and Uncle Ludwig runs it with the help of you, Uncle Ben, and Papa! Why it's one of the finest breweries in the country, better than the Wooden Shoe here in Bremen."

"Louise, honestly, you are too grown up for your years," her aunt replied.

"You mean too big for her britches," Charley said as Lou-Lou slapped at him.

Then Lou-Lou raced right on and said:

"Oh Ma curls up her nose in disgust at the mention of 'beer' as if it was dirt, while I suppose whiskey is refined and high society." At these two last words she put her hand on her hip and pranced sidewise, holding her make believe opera glasses on a stem in front of her.

"Lou-Lou, ach...you will be the death of me," Ben Gast laughed.

"Now August Ben, stop it! You only encourage her and she will get a switching when she gets home if she goes on like this there," Bertha complained.

"And don't the canal make money from our toll from hauling barge load after barge load of beer and ale barrels down the canal to Piqua, Troy, Dayton, and who knows where else? Right on the barrelhead it says <u>Kattmann and Gast, Blue Swan Brewery, New Bremen, Ohio</u>. And won't our new barge really put the final touches on it, since the beautiful *Blue Swan* has come to mean <u>our</u> brewery now that they have taken over the barge-packet?"

"You're just wound up this morning. There's no stopping you and I guess I'll just have to find enough work to keep all of you busy so you won't think so much about questions that have no answer, at least for your young minds. Now get on with breakfast or let's get busy and get this all cleared up. The governor's packet will be here and we will be here chiming about all kinds of nonsense," Bertha announced.

"Lou-Lou! Tell you what," Charley said. Josie and Lou-Lou leaned over toward him. "Why not put an envelope with money in it, say a few bits, for the collection plate and slip it in the Holy Father's mailbox...sign it 'Aunt Fredericka and Grandma,' but be sure to get some of the *Blue Swan Brewery* office letter paper..."

Bertha jumped up and grabbed her large flyswatter, shrieking,

"Lou-Lou! Charley Gast! Why, the idea! No you don't!"

Charley, Lou, Josie and Lou-Lou clapped their hands at the idea, and pounded the table with laughter.

"Yes! Yah, why not?" Lou-Lou asked. "Wouldn't they have a hemorrhage?"

Bertha Gast took the fly swatter and cleared out the kitchen, protesting furiously. Ben Gast took the boys and left for the freight office, laughing all the way up the towpath to the dock landing at the canal basin above the lock. Young Ben Gast, Lou-Lou's brother, and Hermann Gast were waiting for them.

CHAPTER 9

WHEN BEN GAST AND his sons, Lou and Charley, left the towpath, they walked rapidly across the wooden platform of the dock in front of the freight warehouse. His nephew, young Ben Gast, was waiting for them to begin the day's work. He heard them laughing and talking all the way up the towpath toward the freight depot, and called to them,

"Now who has Lou-Lou been imitating?" He called.

"Guess!" Lou answered him.

"I think it would be Grandma-Má Kattmann or our Aunt Fredericka."

The older August Ben Gast soon put the boys busy at the various jobs that needed to be done, but they still exchanged stories about members of the family and the humorous things that had happened.

Ben's brother, Hermann Gast, also worked for the canal company at the freight depot, and took turns as barge captain, along with Ben, when the regular barge captains and drivers were off from work. The boys rode the tow horses as *hoggees* or "haw-gees." Since all the town was excited about the passenger packet that would pass through Bremen at mid-morning, many men of the town had gathered on the platform of the dock to discuss the event.

A wagonload of sacked wheat had to be loaded onto a barge from the warehouse. Another wagonload was on the weighing platform, and its load of wheat would have to be sacked and put on a barge. All slow barges were to get a head start, then tie up in a basin where the canal widened at a dock (at Cherry Street to the South) to let the faster passenger packet pass, and to clear the towpath. The packet would have two teams, four horses, pulling it at a near trot, so the towpath had to be cleared of lines and ropes.

The little town hummed with morning activity. The woolen mill and the large flour mill at the lock seemed busier than usual. The lock gate at Lock 1 held back the flow of water downhill from the south from Minster and the Loramie Reservoir. To prevent flooding and an overflow of the canal banks, the overflow sluice beside the lock permitted the flow to cataract over the sluice, and then to flow back into the canal's lower level. Mills situated here were permitted to use the water from the upper level by turning it into their mill flumes. The water passed over the mill wheels, and down into the lower level of the canal - the same as the sluice overflow. This was true all along the length of the canal. The water rent was cheap and the mills brought business to the canal.

The freight and cargo barges could make about 35 to 50 miles in an eight-hour day by going about 3 or 4 miles an hour. It was all according to how fast walkers the tow horses were, and how often they were replaced along the way with fresh horses. Two horses or mules pulled the small barges for freight. The team that pulled the barge south from Bremen through Minster to Ft. Loramie, a distance of only 6 miles, often would rest a few hours and then pull a return load back north to Bremen. Passenger packets often traveled overnight with fresh horses along the way. Passengers ate and slept on board the packet, if the boat was a through, express packet. However, some of the slower passenger boats tied up overnight at inns or line hotels along the way.

Activity picked up in quiet little Bremen as the morning hours passed. Even the tow horses seemed to know there was something in the air, for their walk seemed more brisk. The barges glided smoothly along while scarcely making rippled waves along the canal banks. Loads of grain went north toward Maumee and Toledo to be shipped on the Great Lakes. Open loads of hay with canvas tied over them went south for the river steamers and the horse barns in Kentucky and Tennessee.

Even the most noted character, and the loudest mouth on the canal, the old codger, had passed that morning with his usual spirited calling out to everyone from his load of sawed lumber. When he had had too much whiskey, his language became rather indecent and abusive, so most of the women and girls on the streets and porches managed to get away from the towpath and out of his sight when he came to the edge of town.

Young boys reveled in the sport of teasing the old codger. They threw mud balls at him from a safe distance just to hear him rave and swear. Some of the older boys, who were more daring, got close enough to the towpath to throw dried horse manure at him. However, they were prepared to run swiftly if they saw one of the rough deck hands jump to the towpath bank with a club.

Hermann Gast stopped from his work long enough in the freight house to nod out the door to the old codger, who was shouting and laughing with some of his rough language as he passed the dock. Turning to his brother, August Ben, he said,

"You would think the company would retire the old codger one of these days. He's getting worse, Ben. Listen to that obscene ditty he's singin'."

"They won't retire him until they have to, Hermann. He always gets his load through in record time, with no mishaps, and can handle lines better than most of the younger barge captains. He makes them money and he knows it."

"Mrs. Hemel says that he would work for nothing just to be on the go all the time, where he can sit there and swill down likker," Charley called down from the grain bin.

"Yes, and holler at all the girls and old women along the way. Why it's a fright, the things he says," young Ben answered.

"Never you boys mind," Hermann called up to them. "Let's get that wheat sacked and ready to load. Lou, watch that grain spout. Your sack is coming loose." However, before Lou could catch it, the sack's wooden hoop holder came loose, and the sack fell over and spilled the wheat on the wooden plank floor. While Lou was sweeping it up, Mr. Hemel came over from the blacksmith forge across the canal bridge, and started telling the older men some funny report that caused the older Ben Gast to start laughing his whooping gasping laugh. The boys upstairs in the grain bin stopped to listen.

While the barge of the Irish O'Hooligan was waiting to go through the lock, to kill time the old codger called out insults to nearly everyone he saw. Then one of the burly Irish polemen took up a mandolin while the old codger started to clog and jig wildly on the deck with his heavy soled shoes and to sing out in a drunken stupor while waving his bottle.

"O what do I bring; the divvel you sing; O don't you wish you knew!
O what's in my barge? O hooch barrels so large. Whist, maybe it's Irish brew!"

Mrs. McKeeters had gotten so angry with the old codger's rough language, his terrible songs, and constantly wagging rough tongue that she had thrown a pail full of her kitchen garbage slops down on his head as he passed below her back porch. Some said that she emptied her night jar on him. The canal curved through the main business part of the little town of St. Marys at the east end of the great reservoir, and the old widow's home was high above the canal's basin just off Spring Street. Jake Hemel had told his wife about it and she thought it was a great idea. More women along the canal path should take up arms. Mrs. Hemel put some water pails on her back porch.

Mrs. Peppleman set out her night jar and even her large earthen bed chamber. Mrs. MacPherson at the lock had a small thunder mug ready.

Mr. Sander's wood shop, or tinker shop as some called it, was an old shack almost on the canal next to the blacksmith shop, and many of the older men liked to sit out front and whittle in the shade of the large cottonwood tree. All kinds of tales were spun there, and from the men who loafed in front of the forge next to it. Old Elihu Sanders could tell the tallest tales of any of them and keep right on working. He would look over his spectacles at his listeners whenever he suspected that they might be doubting his word. He told the same tales over so many times that many of his listeners knew them by heart, but had him tell them anyway. He never told them quite the same way but they were just as hard to believe. They were about three-legged bobcat, the turkey buzzard that whistled, the fur-less ground hog that swam, the whistle-pig, and the duck that was part chicken, or at least he had spurs. All these tall tales never failed to amuse young and old alike. Then he was a dead shot with his tobacco juice. The men out front would place bets on horse flies that would light near old Elihu, and he would take the bets, then take steady aim six feet away and nail the luckless fly with a stream of tobacco amber. The children never tired of his tales while he was repairing their kites or ice skates. Josie, Lou-Lou, and the boys would hold their breath if a hapless sparrow would alight on the opened window's sill, and then shouted with glee when Elihu's deadly amber stream hit the target. Oft times the target would be an old bullfrog who surfaced too near the shop along the canal's towpath.

Shouts of glee would fill the air from the winners of the bets, but old Elihu always took out the cut for the "house" before bets were paid off. Many of the thrifty *Deutsch* housewives would hear the shouting and come by to take their "hoosebands" home and put them to work. Mrs. Peppleman was a huge elephantine woman who always needed split kindling for her cook stove in her pastry shop in her home. Many times she knew where to find Papa Peppleman. When the other men saw her large form coming down the path with the look of a storm cloud over her ample German face, they would warn Charley Peppleman and try to hide him in a large three-barrel hogshead at the rear of the shop, but somehow he never was able to deceive her for long. She would march to the hogshead and rap it smartly with a stick of lumber until poor old Charley's ears rang with the crack of doom. She then put her arms across her chest like a cross Deutsch housewife, or hausfrau, and she would exclaim,

"Iff you are in thair, Charlee, it giffs wan minute to kommen out. You hair me, Char-lee? Ja?"

If he didn't make a move, she would march over to Jake Hemel's forge, take a pail of water from his wooden tubs that he cooled his forged irons in, and then march back and empty the contents into the hogshead. It was so high that she could not peer over the top of it, but it mattered not. She knew he was in there by some secret sense. When Charley started to sputter and protest, she would tap her foot and say with a lowered voice,

"It's been an hour I've been needing kindling for mein stove, and no kindling, no baking, Charlee, and no baking, no money coming in, Charlee."

Then she would explode like a cannon and bang the hogshead with her wooden timber. Water-soaked Charley would scramble out, run toward home - that is, run as fast as his heavy round body could. Mrs. Peppleman sometimes gave him a good whack if she could get close enough to him, then follow him home while mumbling oaths in German. Her face was as cloudy as a summer storm. High tempered Mrs. Hemel, Jake the blacksmith's wife, would watch from her side porch above the forge where she missed nothing up and down the street on one side, and the canal on the other. She heartily approved and she would utter, "Ja, Ja. Thot's wot the fat loafer needs. We ought to clean out that beer tavern up the way where all the loafers hang out."

Bertha Gast's household was one of bustle and hurry. The girls, Josie and Lou-Lou, were hurrying with their assigned chores. The beds made, kitchen dishes done, house gone over again, no details spared, for Bertha Gast knew quite well about the prying eyes of her own mother and sisters and her own Aunt Fredericka. She knew they would descend upon her with great ceremony and expect to be treated like royalty. Bertha had prepared some wafers and she would make some cold lemonade and put it in the cooling basin in the well house. Yes, when the fancy packet came through it would be a holiday - a holiday for everyone except her. How right that impish Lou-Lou was, but she did not dare acknowledge it, and encourage her niece with further complaints about her own immediate family.

After a while they heard a horn blow from a boat going north and old Mr. McPherson, the lockmaster, would have to stop his fiddle sawing above the locks and open the lock for the boat to descend on its way north. Soon after the barge of New Orleans sugar passed, it was followed by two more in close succession that were carrying molasses. Coils of cotton line and cord were piled high on top of the molasses barrels that were bound for some of the sail lofts along Lake Erie. Some of the beeswax, charcoal, and cordwood passed south. The traffic of through line freight barges seemed to increase. How was a passenger packet to make any time on the canal with all this traffic? The men were busy on the docks. Old Mr. McPherson got his Scotch dander up for it took a great deal of push to open and close the heavy lock balance beams that extended out several feet to the side of the lock. His grandson helped him with the other side that was opposite the lock shanty. The old lockmaster would no sooner get settled down to sawing on his old violin, and screeching out some old Scotch ballads in his cackling voice, such as "Flora Mac Donald" or "Flodden Field," when another canal boat horn would blow for the locks to open.

The old codger, who was a red-necked old Irishman from County Cork, was especially disliked by the old lockmaster. Most Scotch, Welsh, and North Irish were loyal Orangemen when they were pitted against the Catholic Irish from the south counties. Therefore, there was a general brawl at the locks when the old codger went through, for he scolded the old Scotsman for being tardy on the lock gates and overcharging on the tolls. Words were exchanged. Jake Hemel shook his fist at the old codger for his foul words and abusive language, and exchanged some words just as bad. Mrs. Hemel heard it from her porch and shouted some admonition of her own, and threatened him with a pail of kitchen slops. Mrs. Peppleman came to the towpath armed with her large hand-made broom. The German born people never understood this "fight at the drop of a hat" among the Irish, Scotch, Welsh and English people. However, neither did the latter understand the German "Dutch" ways. Then It didn't matter. They just lived together in times of stress and plenty. Only the old Irish codger seemed to be facing the world alone.

Mrs. Gertslaecker closed her doors so that her plump daughters could not hear "those terrible words," and slipped on her shawl (even in the early June heat) as she brought the town Marshall to the scene. The old codger made a hasty departure south toward Troy and Piqua, for his crafty eye had not missed Mrs. Hemel's ammunition of slop buckets, and even her night chamber lined up on her back porch railing. He nearly choked on his words and had to bite his tongue to keep still, but he had to pass beneath Frau Hemel's porch, and her sturdy arms could probably hurl a barrel the ten feet to the canal if she was angry enough. He scolded his rider, the *hoggee* boy, to touch up the horses, and he glided rapidly past Mrs. Hemel's glaring eye as she poured out the unending stream of invectives on his head as he passed beneath. She turned and followed his every move from above the lock as he tried to make his getaway to the south, and her ample hands were not far from her jars of ammunition on the railing. He saw Grünwalda Peppleman's large earthenware night chamber with hand painted roses on her steps.

Her last words were, "and don't let me hear of you abusin' those poor horses or that poor orphan *hoggee* boy riding for ye. You old shanty Irish skinflint, d'ye pay him anything?" Then, Mrs. Peppleman, Mrs. Gertslaecker, and Frau Zinndorfer joined Frau Schweitermann sputtering in guttural

German, and were joined by Mrs. Sanders and Mrs. MacPherson who added their Irish and Scotch invectives after the departing evil old Irishman - that ornery old codger. A few corncobs and "road apples" from the boys followed him as he tried to dodge the missiles.

Hermann Gast was dismayed by all the commotion. The boys in the grain bin enjoyed every bit of it, even though the language was not suited to their young ears. Ben Gast and Elihu Sanders laughed until they were weak. Elihu even missed a blue salamander that had crawled up between the platform planks, and his amber streak of tobacco juice scored a miss. They all shrieked at his failing aim.

Therefore, life went on in the little town along the towpath, with laughter, anger, work, gossip, and the little things of everyday life that somehow made the commonplace things seem special and set apart when viewed from a distance of years.

Lou and Charley worked hard to get their work done so that they could be on the loading platform and close to the canal when the high-class passenger packet passed and brought a breath of that great world outside, that imaginative world of high society, big cities, fine clothes and manners from the old world across the ocean. All this was just over the horizon and down the towpath to the north or south. One way led to the Great Lakes, and its cities of Chicago and New York, or up the St. Lawrence to Montreal and Quebec.

"Just think of it," Ben called to Charley, "by putting one foot in that water out there we are connected with New York if we go north. If we go south, we are the same as touching Cincinnati, and the great steamboats down to Louisville and on to New Orleans."

"D'ye suppose we'll ever get to haul or drive on a private boat and see the steamboats at Cincinnati? Or will we ride those sailing ships and lake steamers again on Lake Erie?" Lou asked, while pausing for breath as he heaved another sack of wheat on the pallet to be let down to the first floor to be loaded onto the dock. "It seems like a dream – Toledo and Lake Erie."

"We've got a better chance than most. We're part of the line company; well Pa and Uncle Hermann are, so we are too."

When they had rested a while, and fell to talking and daydreaming, a broom handle rapped on the wooden floor beneath them and Hermann put them back to work.

"Are you boys going to chin up there all morning and miss the canal packet? Let's get our work done first, and talk later." At Hermann Gast's house there was much preparation for the event of the passenger packet, and the carriage trip the few blocks across town to Ben and Bertha Gast's house right on the canal towpath. Hermann's wife, Bernhardina, a sister to Bertha, was entertaining their sister Ernestine from Minister, and her mother, Frau Kattmann from Maria Stein. Grandma-Má Kattmann's sister, Fredericka, as formally High German as Potsdam or Leipzig, was visiting from Pennsylvania, so Bernhardina Gast had quite a house full of relatives. Hermann, his son Ben, and the unpredictable Lou-Lou were happy to be away from the house and the overdose of Teutonic propriety. Hermann said nothing, but young Ben complained,

"Too much is too much whether they are relatives or not." Lou-Lou exploded on learning that the Prussian elite were about to descend on them. Then she burst out,

"Relatives, in-laws and fish all smell after a day or two." Her mother, Bernhardina Gast, stood up archly, closed her eyes, narrowed her lips and boxed her daughter's ears for her brashness. Then Bernhardina lectured to her much as Aunt Ernestine had done so often,

"A proper young lady never says disrespectful things of her elders. A well bred young lady of proper German background and lineage never . . " It went on endlessly, while Lou-Lou was already day dreaming of Elihu Sander's aim on the hapless frogs in the canal, or Mr. MacPherson's Scotch minstrel.

When Lou-Lou was missed, the older women began to complain,

"Now vair is dot Lou-eese? Shay chud be paddled more, Bernhardina. You spoil hair so." Nevertheless, Lou-Lou had skipped out and was having a fine time helping her Aunt Bertha and Jo-Jo with their work. As usual, she never stopped talking and imitating the whole time.

Bertha Gast had not saved her garbage and kitchen scraps as some of the women had, as a possible defense against vile language and obscene songs from the canal men, but sent it out to the chicken lot with little Daisy for the hens. When Josie heard Daisy's frantic screams, she and Lou-Lou ran to the rescue in time to see the mean old Plymouth Rock rooster peck and "flop" her baby sister. Josie took aim.

"Let me at 'im. I'll cold-cock him, so help me." However, her words stopped when the wet cob connected with the rooster's neck and knocked him senseless. He lay fluttering and "flopping" on the ground while Daisy jumped with glee, then fled through the gate, shouted,

"Cold-cock him, cold-cock him."

When the rooster soon regained consciousness, most of his banter and fight was gone, and he ran "flopping" and flew up onto the shed roof, cackling and crying with excitement.

"Let him have it, girls." The old cuss flopped me the other day when I was pulling weeds under the fence," a neighbor woman called.

"Josie, Louise. . . now let that old rooster alone. Do you want to kill him?" Bertha Gast called. Lou-Lou mumbled something about its not being a bad idea, and it would be a good idea to have some pressed chicken sandwiches or a good old rooster stew.

Josie sat the gurgling little Daisy in the rope swing and hurried along into the kitchen for her next chores.

"You girls run to Mrs. Peppleman's and get the pies. Then tell the boys at the warehouse that they are to get her boxes of pies for the inn. She has baked some special ones for the guests on the packet, if they stop long enough. Hurry now."

The girls scurried over the town with their chores, and Mrs. Peppleman cooed over them and patted them, calling them "*mein Liebchen, mein kleine kinder*," and sent her wares along with them, calling out to give her regards to "Frau Gast."

Then Jo-Jo and Lou-Lou went to the freight depot on the landing dock and gave the instructions to Ben, Lou and Charley, who had their wheat sacked and were eager to get out of the hot granary. The girls called cheerfully to Mr. Hemel as they passed the blacksmith shop, and looked in on Elihu Sanders just in time to see him purse his lips. He put his finger to his lips for them to be quiet. Then he put all his force behind one deadly blast of amber toward the canal and caught the old bullfrog dead in the eye. A shout of glee went up from Elihu, as the frog blinked a time or two, then dived under the canal's surface with a "chullunk" from his deep throat like a bull fiddle tuning up.

"Been trying to nail him all mornin," Elihu beamed, wiping his chin on his sleeve, and then cackled with glee. Just then a barge horn sounded from the north for the lockmaster, and Mr. MacPherson cursed as he put down his fiddle. However, when he saw the Gast girls he smiled shyly and apologized, and asked them the time of day as he went about his business with the lock gates. A load of produce from St. Marys glided past, and Lou-Lou said it smelled like some of that strong powerful goat cheese from up that way. She rattled on to Mrs. Hemel that "Only a dumb Dutchman would eat such stuff while most other people would bury it!"

"Young Lay-dee. You chust don't know vat is good," Mrs. Hemel replied. "Sam of that cheese mit sam sauer-kraut, and blutwurst (blood pudding). . . Ach!"

As the girls hurried on down the towpath toward home, Lou-Lou shuddered at the thought of blutwurst (blood pudding) then gasped,

"When on earth does that woman get any of her work done? She sees everything and passes judgment on everyone."

As they neared the Gast house, Lou-Lou stopped short and caught her breath. Then grabbed Josie, or Jo-Jo, as she called her most of the time, and started to go back toward the warehouse.

"Ach! Jo-Jo, they're there, and if they didn't drive the carriage for those few town blocks!" Josie went over on the rise above the towpath to get a better view around the house to the street side, and to be sure she saw the horse and carriage at the hitching post. "Good Heavens! Grandma-Má Kattmann and all the rest!" Lou-Lou suggested running back to the docks.

"We can't turn back now, Lou-Lou. We can't leave Mama with all of them. She needs us."

"Oh you're right," Lou-Lou said. Then squaring her shoulders, she said with much military firmness. "To battle. To arms. . . "

Just then the bells from the twin spired Lutheran church began to toll. After it kept up for a while, people came into the street to look up at the cathedral-like spires. Just then the deep-toned bell in the Catholic Church spire began to toll.

"Mein Gott - Ist thair a fire?" Mrs. Peppleman shouted down the street from her pastry shop at the back of her house. Jake Hemel shouted back with anger in his voice to his wife when she began shrieking questions down to Jake.

"You women. You know that is the signal from the church spire when they sight the passenger packet a couple miles to the north." Mrs. Hemel bullied everyone else, but when big Jake spoke, she quailed, and held her tongue.

Everything was dropped. All work stopped along the canal. Everyone went to his place along the canal to get a good look.

CHAPTER 10

IT WAS ALMOST LIKE a holiday spirit in the little town along the canal. Some of the townspeople who could take the time from their work, had dressed in their "company" clothes. Who could tell? They might get to meet some of the distinguished passenger guests who were passing through. The small shops, groceries, and inns all had hopes that the packet would stop and some of the "people from back east" would come into their shops.

People began to line the docks, the berm of the towpath, the locks, and even the top of the bridge under which the packet would pass. Men and boys working in the fields along the canal heard the signal bell, and had stopped their teams or had driven them near the canal. Many were working the hay fields in this mid-June summer day. Several smaller boys were overjoyed to leave their hoeing in the corn rows to come to the edge of the canal to get a glimpse of the world of fashion and "big city people," or the Governor of Ohio. No one knew just what he expected to see, but it was exciting just to wait for the anticipated surprise. They could hear the great bells of the Catholic Church in St. Marys to the north. The barge was there.

Many of the townswomen had put on dressy ginghams and cotton billowy skirts over their cotton dress. However, when "Frau" Kattmann and her daughters, Bernhardina Gast and Ernestine Hofermeyer, came to descend on Bertha, her daughter who lived along the canal, all eyes turned with surprise to view their silk and satin finery.

There was no time now to get the calliope and costumes ready. It would have to wait. Nevertheless, they could show the *Blue Swan* to the world. The beautiful but astonishing swan barge was turned end for end in her slip beside the brewery so that her head and white wings faced the main line of the canal. She was berthed at the entrance of the slip. No one passing on the canal could miss the huge, unusual packet as she glistened in the June noonday sunshine.

As Lou-Lou and Jo-Jo came closer to the Gast house, approaching from the canal towpath side Lou-Lou grabbed Jo-Jo's arm, and said under her breath,

"Will you take a look at their get-up? You would think they were going to a formal Catholic wedding, a German Lutheran funeral, or a Teutonic Wake of Valkyties."

Josie had noticed this, as had many of the neighbors. Mrs. Peppleman, who had little friendship toward Frau Kattmann, looked them up and down and grunted her disapproval. Mrs. Hemel from her all-seeing porch folded her arms and said aloud,

"Now if that don't beat all. Such a to-do. Such puttin on."

Grandma, "Frau" Kattmann, was decked out in a black satin gown over billowing hoops, her black lace shawl over her plump arms and a dressy Dresden bonnet trimmed with lavender rosebuds, and her black lace parasol. Her daughters, likewise were dressed in black with lavender bonnets and parasols, stepping very archly, nodding formally to this one and that one. Aunt Fredericka was astonishing in her orchid brocade as she carried her purple parasol and mitts. She smiled profusely; yet seemed on the verge of tears.

Bertha Gast welcomed her family and beckoned them to chairs she had set out along the towpath, in case the side porch would not offer as good a view as the chairs that were placed closer. Bertha however, was not overdressed, but looked very pleasant in her lemon colored cotton dress with flounced full skirt. Her lace-trimmed apron was worn over it. She was a little embarrassed when she saw her neighbors looking strangely at the formal dresses of her mother, aunt, and sisters, but she covered it up with cheerful conversation. She spoke first to this one and that one while she welcomed her family to seats of honor along the canal.

It was with a sigh of relief that she called to Josie and Lou-Lou when she saw them edging slowly upon the lawn from the towpath. Hurriedly she directed the girls to get the cold lemonade from the spring house and the tarts from the kitchen. As Josie was giving the glasses of lemonade to her relatives, Lou-Lou followed behind offering little plates with napkins and then the wafer-tarts.

"Und vair haff you been Lou-veese. This whole morning ve haff not see you, eh?" Grandma Kattmann said in a low voice, while she was looking straight ahead. Bernhardina and Ernestine leaned forward waiting for Lou-Lou's answer to their respected aristocratic mother, the "Gnadige Frau."

Bertha Gast sensed the tense feeling and rushed up, pretending to help the girls.

"Maw, I don't know what I would have done without Lou-Lou's helping Josie and me this morning. I have had company all morning. So glad you could spare her this morning, Bernhardina." Mrs. Kattmann looked at her daughters, Ernestine and Bernhardina, and nodded her head as if to say, "It is as I said." Bernhardina Gast merely smiled a forced, formal smile, and answered quietly.

"She can be a great help. I am pleased she was a help, sister Bertha."

With this triumph for her cause, Lou-Lou forced more tarts on her grandmother and aunts, which they minced upon like refined birds. They also sipped some lemonade.

"Maw, we sure have worked up a sweat, Jo-Jo and me. Aunt Ernestine Hofermeyer interrupted her, "Josephine and I. Louise, ladies do not sweat!"

Lou-Lou quick to answer, swung on her heel said somewhat tartly to her aunt,

"Wal neither do dogs, but they can sure get hot just the same and pant," and Lou-Lou put her tongue out and panted like a running dog. Her mother, aunts and grandmother pretended not to notice, but through narrowed eyes they looked the other way at the activity along the canal. Bertha Gast squeezed Lou-Lou's arm and pushed her gently along in front of her with Josie. She thanked the girls for their help and told them they could bring some of the kitchen chairs out on the lawn and rest a while.

"I suspect that I have worked them pretty hard, Bernhardina. They have been doing errands all over town for me and for Mrs. Peppleman."

When Ernestine and her Aunt Fredericka excused themselves to go into the house, Bertha Gast did not tarry long behind. She came into the bedroom quietly but soon enough to catch Ernestine running her mitted hand over the dresser top to inspect for dust, and she suspected her Aunt Fredericka of inspecting the pillow case seams to see if they had been ironed properly before using. Bertha Gast's temper rose, but she managed a smile, knowing she must cover up for Lou-Lou to keep her from getting a paddling for running away from home so early in the morning without permission.

Jo-Jo and Lou-Lou had followed, but they went around on the street side of the house. They were in time to hear the conversation.

"Can you beat those two snoopy old hens?" She whispered to Josie who had put her hand to her mouth to suppress a laugh. Lou-Lou went on and nearly caused Jo-Jo to burst out laughing.

"I'll bet they try to snoop out in the wash house next to see if the week's washing has been done yet, or if the ironing is done. What if they nib around and find our costumes?"

Bertha Gast cleared her throat and asked sweetly.

"Are you ladies comfortable? Could I get you something?" They assured her with much fawning that they were merely adjusting their bonnets and veils, for the morning breeze had made them "a mite untidy" on the ride over. Bertha smiled kindly, and then waited for them to come out. (As if there were a breeze in this hot June heat!) As they came back out onto the porch somewhat guilt-ridden, and as if they were two children caught in the cookie jar. Bertha locked the door behind her, saying very pointedly,

"I believe I had better lock the house with all these people around. Who knows but what a thief might enter while we're so busy out here at the canal. Last summer when the fortuneteller and show barge were here, people had silverware and other things stolen. You can't tell who might be snooping around."

Ernestine and her Aunt Fredericka did not stay long on the porch, but tripped back down to their chairs with as much dignity as they could muster under Bertha Gast's scalding, implied meaning. Frau Kattmann sat with her hands folded in her lap, while batting her eyes and saying nothing, but understanding all.

To the north a horn sounded three short blasts, and everyone seemed to come to attention and look in that direction. It was only the fast repair barge, which was traveling about a mile in front of the packet. It glided through the water making scarcely a ripple along the grassy banks, for it was long, narrow and light. It glided along like a canoe with only two horses almost at a trot.

Canal company rules demanded that a speed of not over four miles per hour be kept because of damage of ripples to the mud banks - which would cause washing. However, on this day Mr. McPherson did not scold, nor did hesitate to open the lock for he knew the repair barge was in a hurry to keep ahead of the packet and to make sure the canal had not sprung any leaks in its berms during the night. At every lock or tollgate, the repair barge captain questioned the path master to find out about any leaks or more muskrat damage. The towpath master or walker walked ten miles or so each day, and then walked back on the other side to inspect for damage. Even the slightest mole hole or muskrat borough could grow into an open breadth in a short time and had to be plugged immediately. It would be an embarrassing incident to have this packet mudlarked on mud bottom, helpless for several hours until the leak could be patched, and water from the reservoirs run back into the canal again.

The repair barge mounted up the locks and glided on as a pilot boat at a good pace south toward Minster and Ft. Loramie. The crowd became one of easy humor and good cheer again. Neighbors visited, and some of the men left their shops and places of business to join the women and children on the canal banks. Children romped and played up and down the berm, racing in the street and over the bridge that went over the canal.

At length, a deep melodious horn gave a long winding blast from the north end of town where it was entering from the first lock at New Paris, called Lock 2, out at the old mill basin. After another long deep toned blast, the gaily-colored packet glided into view in the distance. People at the north end of town sent up a cheer of greeting to the horn. They had never heard one like this one. The steersman at the rear was wearing a tall silk hat, and the man next to him who mounted the platform above the long passenger cabin, wore a gray tall hat. Once again he put the curled brass horn to his lips and blew a long pleasant blast for the lock ahead. The "hoggee" riders on the sleek black double team of horses were not the usual run of the mill "hoggee" in battered hat and rags. These riders were men, not boys. They rode saddles and wore green uniforms with caps to match. The teams brought the long packet quickly into view, and there was hardly a sound from its wash as it glided along. Soon the captain of the packet called: "Low Bridge" and "everybody down." The passengers on the top deck lowered their parasols and sat down on deck chairs as they passed beneath the cross street bridge, even through there was plenty of room to spare. The huge long packet had nearly 100 passengers aboard. The boat was painted black with a white border above the water line near the varnished deck. The cabin that protruded above the main deck was painted white and had brass lamps. It had a brass railing on top that made the foot deck or observation platform. Elegant ladies in colorful, fashionable hooped gowns stood and sat on the top observation deck, and gentlemen in frock and cutaway coats and tall hats stood beside them. Parasols were of every color as were the wide-brimmed bonnets.

The crowd cheered enthusiastically at first, but then quieted as the onlookers became obsessed with the beauty before them.

There was the world of fashion of New York and Montreal before them. Soon these fortunate people would be on the large river steamers, those paddlewheelers and side-wheelers that would take them to the far away dream weekend out into the gulf and across the ocean. Lou-Lou and Josie gasped. It just could not be real. They were too enchanted to waste much of their time with words. They wanted to watch. Charley, Lou, and Ben had joined them but they kept exchanging comments of excitement among themselves, and Ben and pointed to their grandmother. As the society folks glided along toward the lock where the boat would stop before being lifted up its eight feet into the next lock, they passed directly in front of Mrs. Kattmann, her daughters, and the rest of the family. Mrs. Kattmann very archly took her gold stem-glasses in her lace mitted hand and viewed the scene in front of her. Her sister, Fredericka, who was putting on old world courtly manners, almost curtsied but bowed instead. Frau Augusta Kattmann waved regally as if from a throne. People on the top deck platform noticed them and how they stood out from the rest of the crowd in their satin and velvet finery, and nodded back, thinking no doubt that they were some of the dignitaries who would welcome them, but Augusta Kattmann received a bow from the governor.

"Now wouldn't that scald you?" Lou-Lou fumed, and Ben nudged her as she began prancing and holding up her hand with pretended stem glass lorgnette.

"Stop it, Lou-Lou. You'll catch it if they see you."

"I will anyhow. I skipped out this morning," Lou-Lou answered. Then she paddled herself with her hand, and said in a low tone so that the boys laughed loud with an uproar,

"You chud paddle hair, Bairn-hard-deen-nah. She is getting like a heifer, Ja?"

The pranks and joking went unnoticed with all the noise and cheers along the canal path. As the boat docked in the lock just south of the street, the crowd pressed in closer. The captain gave his bill of toll clearance to Mr. MacPherson who received it with a big smile. The town mayor shook hands with the captain and some of the gentlemen on the top deck. Other ladies in various types of bonnets waved out the curtained windows of the passenger cabin. People peered in the windows to see the upholstered seats. The boat was just about all the lock could take with only a few feet to spare. When the gate behind it was closed, the front lock gate wicket was opened and the water began sloshing in with a roaring sound. The boat rose slowly to the upper level of the top of the lock. Mrs. Peppleman, in a large flowered gown and wide-brimmed sunbonnet, delivered a large basket of pies and cookies to the captain. She was beaming like a school girl as she handed over her prize wares and cooed something about,

"Der complementaries of dair town of New Bray-mun. (New Bremen) It giffs velcome, mein captain. You do us great honors iff only mit dair passings through and not dair stayings." She almost blushed, and for once her stormy face was pleasant and almost flushed pink. Perhaps it was the large flowered pink gown, which floated about her huge form like a pink circus tent on a haystack.

The governor and two senators made a brief appearance to inspect Lock Number One's facilities. Ben and Hermann recognized another tall thin man through the cabin window. When the detective, Angus MacClintock, saw the Gast brothers, he nodded slightly and then returned to his book. Augusta Kattmann said not a word but left her astonished family and walked archly to the lock south of them and just across the street. She ignored Mrs. Peppleman and regarded her welcoming outburst as childlike. Augusta walked up the lock incline, went to the governor and shook hands rather familiarly as she made him a formal welcome. They visited informally and it was apparent to the townspeople that they had met before. A brassy voice with a gong-like quality called out above the noisy celebrations to Mrs. Peppleman.

"You tell them, Grünwalda Peppleman. Tell 'em for all of us," Mrs. Hemel called out from her porch high above the canal.

The captain of the boat looked at his watch, then the sun, and shook hands with the town dignitaries. The water had filled the lock and raised the packet up to the last level. Jake Hemel scowled up at his wife. The captain was anxious to get started for there were many miles between New Bremen and Dayton where they planned to tie up for the festivities that evening. With much waving and well wishing, the boat started moving forward when the horses took up the slack on the towline after the last lock gate was opened into the higher water. With a last blast of the beautiful toned shepherd's horn, the packet was moving on up the canal to the south, and it hardly seemed real that it had been there at all. That golden horn - was it a French horn much like the ones used on coaches and carriages in Europe on the turnpikes, or was it a hunter's winding horn? The *Blue Swan* must have one like it, Mrs. Kattmann said to herself with satisfaction.

The breath of elegance from that other world was vanishing almost as unbelievably rapidly as it has come among them. The townspeople looked after it with wonder, and some small disappointment. True, they knew it was making a trial run to test the canal to see if the large passenger packet would be practical for the back country freight canal. Just the same, it seemed that it could have stayed a little longer. Some touched its sleek gunwales.

Grandma-Má Kattmann came back to her daughter's lawn, sat down and closed her eyes while rocking back and forth in her chair, with her hands folded. She then had the last word with her daughters. She coined disgust with Mrs. Peppleman, and brassy Mrs. Hemel.

"I don't belieef it vud be practical to spend that mooch money for so large a packet for dis canal system. From viar and for vat iss der passenger to come and to go? No Fredericka, I say it vud navair pay. Lat them take it back East to the Erie." Let our *Swan* do the local passenger trade."

Others standing near Mrs. Kattmann nodded their heads to each other, agreeing with her, while others who wanted some elegance in their lives were for giving it a try. One could always sell it back east again for what they had in it. After all, the Canal Company could afford it. Many suspected that Mrs. Kattmann was a heavy investor in the bonds, which made the canal a possibility.

Lou-Lou nudged Josie and growled,

"That's right, Grandma-Má, kill it before its hatched. We'll be stuck with stinking cheese, brickbats and hogs. That's our style."

Little by little the crowd scattered, but many lingered to visit in the noonday sun. Some lollied under the shade trees along the canal. Men stood in circles with their arms folded while talking business, and discussing the merits of canal passenger packets on the Miami and Erie. After a while the dinner bells began to sound, and the men drifted off to their noon meal. Soon it would be back to work as usual. Josie and Lou-Lou felt that it would not be quite the same. Something had come into New Bremen and into their lives that caused them to feel unrest. They could not tell what it was, but they knew they just had to explore the world out there. Some way, somehow, they had to have a trip down the canal to the cities along the way, to see the wharves at Dayton and the docks at the riverfront at Cincinnati. Some day the girls wanted to go down the Ohio River, out onto the mighty Mississippi and on to New Orleans. The younger children could talk of nothing else at the noon meal, and their imaginary trip in a packet down the canal.

"Yessir. . . Yesmam. We'll all go. I can see it now," Josie told them all. "Why that would be a wonderful trip. It's just down the towpath. Follow the *Swan*; she'll take us there."

CHAPTER II

As AUGUST BEN GAST left the side porch to descend to the canal towpath beside the lawn, Bertha Gast came up to him from the back kitchen door,

"Ben. . . Ben, now for once be serious. Do you plan on letting the girls go with you to Minster?" She asked.

"Berta. . . I see no harm in it. It would be good for them. Lou-Lou doesn't get away from dose prying hawk eyes very often."

"Well then, what time do you plan on going? I can get the dinner dishes done in no time and get them ready. Ben, now do watch where you go with them and try to keep them away from those rough men and their uncouth tongues along the way. Remember the Toledo trip."

"Ve try Berta, but you know the canal iss not your mother, Mama Kattmann's, closed-off and darkened best parlor."

"What time Ben?" Bertha pressed him.

"I chud say in about an hour ve be ready, give or take a leetle. Doan vorry, Berta. The boys will be along and dey take gude care of Lou-Lou, Josie, and the girls," Ben assured her.

"What on earth are you going to Minster for, Ben?" He told her that they were going to take a company barge down for some repair work, and it would save hiring a line boat captain and driver for the job. Besides, he and Hermann were not too busy today now that they had the heaviest of the old wheat shipped. They needed the barge for the new crop in July and August when the summer grain threshing started, and many farmers did not have storage granaries. They would need every boat for grain shipment.

Bertha hurried the girls through their after dinner chores. They washed the dishes, cleaned the kitchen, and then scoured the wooden handled silverware with brick dust. In their eagerness to go on the barge trip they would have scoured the oak-planked floor with white sand and brickbats, but

Bertha would not hear of it. The floor could wait until Saturday morning. They wasted no time in inviting the other girls.

The girls would have dashed up the towpath bareheaded, but Bertha made them wear wide summer straw hats with chin veils to hold them on. She made them put on mitts and carry parasols like proper young ladies, even if it was only a grain barge instead of a passenger packet for their trip. She knew what sitting in the hot June sun on the top deck for an hour each way would do for their freckles and sunburn. What would her sister, Bernhardina Gast, say if Lou-Lou were to come home sunburned or as brown as a nut?

After a while Charley and Lou came down to see if the girls were ready. The boys were excited with the prospects of being permitted to ride the guide horse, to be the "hoggee" driver. Of course they would take turns riding, but at last they felt grown up with the responsibility of being canal "hoggees." It was just like on the big Erie.

"There couldn't be a better day for a get-a-way from this dead town," Lou-Lou confided to her cousin Lou.

"What do you mean, Lou-Lou?" he asked as they walked along.

"Well Ma, Aunt Ernestine, and Aunt Fredericka are all over to Grandma-Má Kattmann's at Maria Stein. They won't be back until dark and we should be back by then. They'll never know if you boys don't let it out."

"What's the difference? Aunt Bertha said you could go and so did Uncle August Ben," her brother Ben said.

"You know I'll catch it tonight. I sneaked out this morning. Oh, Aunt Bert spoke up for me and tried to cover it up, but you know Ma. Then I'll probably catch it for panting like a dog!" She giggled, and began panting with her tongue out until the others all laughed with her. After a moment as they neared the grain bins at the freight dock, she became serious with thought. She picked up a heavy grain sack of coarse linsey hemp.

"You know, I think I can fool Ma. How about it if I pad my bloomers with several layers of old grain sacks?"

"Oh Lou-Lou, you don't want that coarse stuff under your clothes. You'd break out with a rash with that next to you," Josie warned her.

"Rash? You should see the rash I *will* have from that old butter paddle or cream ladle, whichever they can lay their hands on." Lou-Lou laughed loud at her joke and planned her padding for the bloomer warming she would receive.

"Lou-Lou, you wouldn't get so many 'scutchins' if you would behave now and then," her brother Ben teased her. She gave him a shove, and turned on him saying,

"Listen to him. Behave, is it? Why if I squawked on you just part of the time, you'd be in welts from the razor strap. You think I don't know you boys sneak under the platform back of the loading dock and light up those old pipes you got at the tinker shop? You were smoking coffee and you got sick on a cigar."

"Better be still," Lou warned. "We'll all be caught. Besides, it was only once and we had to 'spearmint,' as Mr. Elihu Sanders said. We told him we wanted to make bubble pipes for blowing bubbles, but the way he smiled told us that he knew what we were going to do."

All at once, Lou-Lou burst out in a fit of high-spirited giggles, and they all turned to see what she was doing.

"Can't you just see them all over at Grandma Kattmann's? Wouldn't they be saying beads for all of us if they only knew?"

"Lou-Lou, honestly," Josie chided her.

"I can see them now - all down on their knees in that holy closed-up parlor, a-hollerin' and goin' on, a-ranting about the evils of beer and drink, wages of sin, the ways of man. Unfortunately, Aunt Fredericka will get all worked up and get to bawling and blowin' her nose into her petticoat, and shoutin' that a man is at the root of all evil things in this world."

They all had a good laugh at Lou-Lou's imitations, for every time she imitated someone's speech, she usually imitated their walk or mannerisms. She ended her mimicry of her great Aunt Fredericka by wrinkling up her face as if she were crying; then she stooped quickly and pretended to blow her nose in one of her many petticoats under her short-hooped full skirt.

Her father, Hermann Gast, saw her and knew what she was doing, for he had seen it many times.

"Lou-eese, do try to behave yourself in public – for shame!"

The boys started skipping rocks from the path on the surface of the canal. Just then, they saw old Elihu take aim at a sparrow that had perched on his open window sill.

"Ja get 'em, Lihu?" They called while racing to his tinker shop door. "Did ja nail 'em?"

Hermann and Ben had the boys help bring the team to the towpath and hitch them in line to the towline. The boys drew pebbles from the fist to see who would ride first and in what turn. Another team was led across the portable gangplank and onto the barge. They were then put in the stalls at the back. Since the barge would be exchanged for one already repaired in the boatyard at Minster, a fresh team would be needed to rest the horses along the way back. Lou had the first turn as the "hoggee" rider - calling first "*haw*" and then "*gee*."

Hermann would take the tiller to control the rudder, and Ben would be captain on the trip to Minster. The girls skipped around on the open deck, then peered down into the hold where loose grain was usually stored.

Ben Gast had put a springed wagon bench seat on the deck for the girls. Usually he and Hermann sat on nail kegs with a sheepskin cushion. Lou-Lou could not contain her high spirits any longer, and she tapped her brother, Ben, and cousin, Charley on the shoulder as she hopped up on the ledge of the lock and walked gingerly, with one foot in front of the other on the narrow stone ledge.

"I'm on my way to Minster. I'm on my way to Minster," she sang out gaily in nursery rhyme style. Her father gave her flouncing skirts a resounding whack in the back as she jumped over the water's edge back down into the boat, and commanded,

"Stop prancing on the parapet like a goat, or you'll be left high and dry in Bremen. Now let's get ready to shove off."

They mounted the lock and left Bremen at a near trot for the empty barge skimmed along, riding high in the water.

The high spirits and good humor of all five girls was infectious, but Lou-Lou was the center from which all the gaiety and song radiated.

Ludmilla Vogelsang had gotten herself ready for the canal barge voyage in a hurry when Josie so breathlessly invited her. Ludmilla had tied her light summer straw hat on at her mother's insistence, and then ran back to gather up her small harp-like zither which she often carried with her all over town.

As the countryside opened up to them at the south end of town, the brilliant June day beckoned them from every side. The boys who were permitted to ride "hoggee" on the tow horses, were in high spirits and called back and forth to each other.

The girls at last settled down on the wooden bench on the top of the barge cabin. Along with their small girl-talk, they began to harmonize some of the songs they knew. Ludmilla led out with her harp-like zither; then the other girls joined in with their voices.

Gerta Langhorst started complaining about the "goody-goody" song that the group of girls would have to sing in the coming Church Children's Day program. Lou-Lou took up the tirade and started pantomiming the program where the group of her young girl friends would have to carry bunches of flowers, and twirl parasols as they sang the song called "One Summer" in harmony. Ludmilla started it out, admonishing them all that today would be a good time for all of them to get a good practice, and sing in the way they wanted to without Mrs. Zinndorfer and those other "old harpies" correcting them. It would be worth something to be able to practice out of hearing from "Old Lady Kattmann," and that "Sergeant Steinhoge."

They started out but got only part of the way through when they forgot the words. Dort Waterman and Ludmilla went through the song together, not singing it, but merely saying the words of the lyric. They all repeated it until they had it letter perfect.

> "One summer's day, we locked through on our way.
> The open towpath calls us to see the green world,
> and the wild flowers along its way.
> We crossed each stream; then lost in childhood's dream,
> we drifted with ease, beneath arched trees,
> and thought deep June would always stay."

The irrepressible Lou-Lou jumped up and started to pantomime.

> "The bluebells traded their sprightly heads, and
> ground squirrels scurried across our way.
> The kingfisher dipped so low to bathe,
> that he frightened all the frogs away."

> "As we locked on down, through fabled Lockington town,
> we slipped through six locks, all downhill in a row.
> As we crossed Loramie Creek, free of that flume,
> we took a peek at the white blossomed pond where sweet
> lilies grow."

The girls all got up from the bench and stood with arms entwined as the beauty of the song seemed to touch them.

> "If we just could, how I only wish we could
> hold those days forever still, and never let those sweet hours
> get away.
> Sweet memories stay of a sweet June Day,
> on the towpath that brightened one summer's day."

Ben and Hermann Gast listened attentively and then applauded. The girls curtsied to them and then went on to some other songs. The boys on the horses started baying and howlin' like dogs at the music, but the girls ignored them.

"Now no church songs," Lou-Lou admonished Ludmilla. "We're not going to no mournful funeral today. Today is ours."

They started singing some lively tunes. Ludmilla even tried to pick up the tune of the ditty the old Irish codger, Hooligan, sang. However, she changed to something else when Ben and Hermann frowned on it.

As they left the limits of the town, the open country began to stretch out before them. The girls felt a sense of freedom, and the breeze was pleasant on the gently rocking barge – even in the bright June sun. Hermann and August Ben sat at the tiller at the back of the empty barge, swishing the huge rudder now and then to keep the boat in the main channel of the canal. Young Charley and his cousin called out to Lou, who was taking his turn as first driver hoggee. It was rather hard to keep the slack out of the towline since the barge was empty and glided along with little resistance. They sang up on deck in harmony while Louise plucked the zither. Hermann and his brother, August Ben, talked of the wheat crop as they viewed fields along the way of newly shocked wheat fields. Some fields were dead ripe and needed to be cut and shocked before a summer storm flattened them.

Some late fields of hay smelled sweet as their red clover bloom scent drifted across the canal. Lou-Lou had stopped her play-acting and clowning, and was pleasantly occupied with the *peacefulness* of the green countryside.

The canal went almost in a straight line south toward Minster. By now the top of the brewery's brick smokestacks, and the gold weathervane on the top of the brewery's brick smokestacks, the gold weathervane atop the church spire, and other buildings of Bremen had begun to look small in the distance as the barge glided on to the south. Hermann and Ben exchanged greetings with other barge captains when they met or when they overtook a slow one. Many coming from the south told of tying up in wider basins when warned by the pilot boat of the Governor's appearance.

They all talked about its sleek lines, its speed, and its well-dressed occupants. Many wondered if there would be packets like it on the Miami and Erie between Toledo and Cincinnati. The Ohio and Erie Canal from Cleveland to Portsmouth bragged of many fine packets.

As the canal entered a stretch of wooded land, and the trees on each side shaded the canal, Josie removed the white brimmed straw hat and veil so that she could enjoy the cool air from the woods. The boys amused themselves with their reed blowguns and enjoyed the cool air from the woods. A flipper scolded them from the cattails and reeds along the bank when the barge disturbed them. Some redwings also scolded them from the cattails and reeds. Purple martins and swallows darted low over the water catching winged insects. Now and then one of the boys slapped at a mosquito. Charley took aim with his sling at a sparrow hawk that hung motionless in the air above them. It fluttered its wings while it scanned the woodland below for some unsuspecting small bird.

Ahead of them several barges in line came into sight, and Hermann called to Lou to let the towline slack. The boat went slower and slower; then finally, Ben and Hermann put it gently to the bank on the other side from the towpath. Lou caught the loop when Charley threw it to him from the ring in the bow post. He then drew his horses to the side of the towpath to let the oncoming span pass. Young Ben had jumped to the towpath because it was his turn next to ride, and as an experienced driver, he helped Lou get the wet towline out of the way of the other barges so there would be no tangled lines.

A line of four barges was laden with stacked bricks from the kilns somewhere below Ft. Loramie. They were headed north for some new buildings in St. Marys. Some dressed stone from below Dayton followed in other barges that rode low in the water.

The barge captain thanked Ben for giving him the right of way, spoke of having met the Governor's packet, and was on his way with his mule spans towing the barges. The boys tossed the towline back to Charley in the bow, Ben mounted the third horse, and when the boat came near enough to the tow side, Lou jumped onto the gangplank his father put over for him, and the barge slid on toward Minster. The twin spires of the church came into sight through the trees, and then suddenly they were out of the shaded area. Josie put on her straw hat and tied the veil beneath her chin.

Before long, the three mile trip was over and the barge was tied up in the boatyard basin at the north end of Minster. While Hermann and Ben busied themselves with the business of repairing the rammed gunwale, they gave the girls permission to visit the town up and down the streets, and told the boys not to wander too far. The quaint little town was much like Brenner's; yet it was different. The girls stood on the bridge on the main street and looked north toward the boatyard. They were amazed to see the weighted bridge north of them start to rise slowly at one end. The bridge tender seemed to be turning a ratchet that wound cables that pulled the bridge up while weights and levers on the other end helped. A larger barge with high box-like sides came under the raised bridge and tied up at a brick warehouse halfway down the block where the girls were.

Next to their barge, a company-owned line boat was tied up for some repairs, so Jo-Jo and Lou-Lou had a chance to satisfy their curiosity. Whole families often lived on the line boat as it traveled up and down the canal with its cargoes. Hermann and August Ben visited with Joel Brenner (the captain) who invited them aboard his barge. It was going to be put up in drydock for seam caulking. The bottom of the barge would also be painted below the waterline.

Line boats were often owned by freight companies. A freight shipping company might also own many barges that traveled up and down the canals in Ohio, Pennsylvania, New York and Indiana. The lifeboats paid a little different toll rate than privately owned barges did because they hauled more freight and used the canal more. Thus they were making more toll income for the canal.

Joel Brenner was a friendly, good-natured man from Indiana who hauled on Indiana's Wabash and Erie Canal. That long canal system joined the Miami and Erie at Junction City, near Defiance, Ohio, with its southern terminus at Evansville, Indiana, at the other end of the state on the Ohio River. Joel pulled kegs to sit on up on the top deck and the men started to exchange canal talk and barge business.

Elvira Brenner was a homespun Indiana woman from the southern part of the state, thin and wiry, with hair pulled back in a tight knot, a cheery parrot-like voice, and hearty Hoosier welcome for all who came aboard her water-borne home. She welcomed the girls when she saw them holding back on the dock after their fathers went aboard over the gangplank.

"Wal howdy," she called to them, "c'mon up. O'm a-ironin', and I'll declare I'd adore to have some wimmen folk to talk to." Jo-Jo and Lou-Lou did not need further invitation and bounded aboard. They wanted to see what a floating barge home was like.

These line boats were often the only homes many captains and their families knew. Jo-Jo and Lou-Lou were so interested in looking at everything that Elvira Brenner stopped her work to show them her small home. They marveled at the tiny but handy kitchen with its built-in cupboards, and a small cook stove under a copper hood. They were so surprised to see how she could do so much in so little space. After she did her washing, she took it up on the top deck to dry on low lines she stretched between removable posts. Her own children, Melissa and Bub, stood around their mother with little to say, and just looked at the Sunday dresses and veiled straw hats the girls were wearing.

At the back of the boat by the tiller were covered stalls for the horses when they were rotated and brought on board. When they were not pulling the barge or grazing along the towpath, they were brought aboard and put in their stalls for oats and hay. In a way, these horses became part of the family, along with the dog and cat, to say nothing of Elvira's parrot who rattled out his jargon to all who passed his cage. The garden plot was a window box crammed with every kind of flower that could be crammed into it; however, the problem was to keep the cat from digging in the flower box instead of her sandbox.

The tapping of feet and scraping of chairs, kegs and boxes on the deck above did not hamper Elvira's talking, for she raced on above the noise. Her bird-like form was going back and forth to her hot stove with flat irons as she exchanged them. After she finished ironing the few dampened pieces she had left to do, she showed the girls the small berths they'd used for beds. They were much like the folding shelves that she folded up out of the way in the daytime so that there would be "settin'" room in the little parlor.

"It ain't much. Taint nothin' so fine as your swan boat! However, it's home, and we're plenty content," she said.

After a while, Joel Brenner called down to her as he came down the recessed stairs to her kitchen cabin,

"Elviry, could you scare up some hot coffee? We can invite the folks to some coffee, can't we?"

"Why, shure thing. I wuz just thinkin' of fixin' sumthin' for the kids and these young ladies here." Then she stepped out and called up to Ben and Hermann on the top deck,

"Right smart looking young ladies ye got here, Ben Gast. You too, Hermann. Ain't seen' em around the docks for a while, and it beats all how they shoot up."

When they were up on the cooler top deck having coffee and slices of bread with strawberry jam, a large heavy barge appeared. It was down the canal coming north toward Bremen. It had a high piled cargo of lumber on its top deck. As it came closer two little boys in large brimmed hats could be seen as the riders. Later when the boat could be seen from a side view, a huge stern faced woman stood at the tiller. Elvira's children started giggling and saying to one another that it was Big Barge Bertha.

"Now you youngin's mind your tongues. Don't stare and don't stand around whispering. Why she'd come aboard here and clean us all up good and proper if we wuz to make the slightest light of her," Elvira Brenner warned.

One of the colorful persons on the canal, about whom little or nothing was known, was Big Barge Bertha, who from all appearances was a widow with three dark beady-eyed children scampering around her decks. She belonged to the Rooshian sawmill village on south of Ft. Loramie. Her older two boys rode the tow horses, never smiling nor speaking much - even to one another. Big Bertha smiled seldom and talked even less, and then only to a few trusted people she knew along the way. Elviry Brenner was one she always visited with and told the news from along the way.

Big Barge Bertha got her name from the huge barge she towed. It was usually stacked with heavy lumber, but sometimes she hauled coal or barrels of roofing pitch. She kept some goats aboard and a ferocious mastiff dog. Some said she kept a cow in the horse stall. She was a solid giant of a woman who was built like an ox, and was solid and heavy in the shoulder. Her broad Slavic face told of European origin, but little was known of her. Men along the way who joked about her, but seldom to her, said she was a Pollock or Ukrainian honkey who came to Cincinnati from Pittsburgh. She could do the work of three men, and with a stern jaw, and a cigar clamped between her teeth, she was her own stevedore. She slammed the lumber she unloaded from her shoulders onto the docks. Her children scampered around the decks, slipping under tarpaulins or behind barrels when strangers came near, but those black beady eyes of theirs missed very little. A few short words from their mother in that strange foreign tongue was all that was needed for them to either get to work or fall below in the cabin out of sight. Dressed in men's work trousers of denim, and wearing a hat, she usually sat at the tiller and looked neither to the right nor to the left as she passed through the towns or went through the locks. She paid her toll, and attended strictly to business, unless she was to exchange words with Elvira Brenner or Grünwalda Peppleman in Bremen.

Some of the rougher men would make sport of her from a safe distance by calling out the nickname she hated, "Big Barge Bertha," and others that enraged her such as "Hog Eye" and "Water Buffalo." Men and boys who called such names were usually hidden at a safe distance on some mill's second floor or in an upstairs window, and were ready to run at a moment's notice of pursuit. She had been known to go into a saloon along the canal in Cincinnati, grab two men at the bar who had insulted her, slam their heads together, then dash them to the floor with crushed ribs.

Bertha also chased some men in St. Marys and brought them down with rocks. She knocked a stevedore overboard from a lake steamer in Toledo when he winked at her and called out "Hog Eye." Of course they all remembered her rock slinging up near Maumee.

As the huge gray Percheon horses came nearer with their barge in tow, Elvira spoke up and said,

"It's a cryin' shame about the brutal life that wommin has had. All she has ever known was brute slave labor in the old country. Don't know why them ornery men along the way have to torment her. Heard she carries scars from slave labor in the czar's labor gangs."

"They wouldn't do it if she didn't get so fighting mad. They just do it for the excitement of having her chase them. If she would ever hit one of the men with them rocks she throws, she would kill them for sure. Why, she can throw like a cannon ball," Hermann said.

When she came closer, Elvira went to the side of the deck, waved to her, and gave her a big smile. The placid mask on the face of the Slavic woman changed, and her broad face broke into a smile of recognition. She said one command in foreign tongue to her two boys on the huge grey Percheon, and they let the boat glide to a stop along the berm. Elvira said softly to the others that since there were strangers aboard, Bertha would never come aboard their barge. Therefore, Elvira said that she would go and speak with her instead.

Elvira took a tin cup of black coffee with her to the other barge and gave it to Bertha, who welcomed her aboard with a broad smile - a thing few people along the canal saw from her. From the way she started talking to Elvira with much gesturing of her heavy thick hands, the men knew that something along the way had happened to arouse her anger. They tried to overhear the conversation, but they could not make out many of her words. Elvira shook her head from time to time, put her hands to her face, and exclaimed,

"Mercy on us! A cryin' shame!"

Chapter 12

Josie and Lou-Lou sensed that something exciting was about to unfold when they saw the stricken face of Elvira Brenner after she left Big Bertha's barge deck and came back up the towpath to her own barge. The silent boys mounted their Percherons, which were grazing in some green grass along the towpath berm. At a command from the Russian Bertha, they took up the slack on the towline and the heavy barge inched slowly out from the berm into the deeper canal. When Elvira waved good-bye, Bertha scowled darkly at the men on the top deck, but threw up her hand to Elvira and nodded her head emphatically, as if to say, "It's all true, and we will talk about it later."

When Elvira came back aboard, she sat down and didn't say much. Then her husband, Joel Brenner taunted her.

"Wal now speak up, Elviry. What did the Water Buffalo tell you that has got you so?"

"Now shame! Don't you be callin' her that. Poor widow woman has to make her way in a man's world, doin' a man's work. It's a cryin' shame. There's more good in her behind her quiet Rooshian ways than a body would think fer," Elvira spoke up smartly.

"What's wrong, Elviry. Might as well get it out," Joel said. Ben and Hermann waited silently while finishing their coffee.

"Wal ye know that barge captain, Silvermann, at least he says that's his name. We pass him from time to time. Wal we all thought that the old Irish codger was about the orneriest talking old reprobate on the canal, but this Silvermann is the meanest, plumb cruel, and vilest man on this stretch of earth," she exploded.

No one along the entire length of the canal liked the dark, beetle-browed Gustav Silvermann. He was known as a liar, and he tried to cheat every lock-tender and toll master on every canal he traveled. The men talked about him and all agreed that these charges were true. His darkest crime was taking orphan boys from orphanages, or lost orphans from the streets, with the guise of giving them a home. Then he would put them to work the hardest slave labor on his barge - loading and unloading heavy cargo. The lot of the little boys he forced to ride "hoggee" in all kinds of weather was the worst of all, and everyone who saw it along the canal was incensed by it, but no one knew what to do. There were no laws to protect children from slave labor, and who was to stand up for an unknown orphan and plead his case in court, an orphan without people, family, or funds to fight his case?

Many Irish, as well as German children, were orphaned when their parents died at sea in the steerage of ships on the voyage over to the United States. There oft times were no relatives to take care of them. Ship captains simply put them off on the docks to shift for themselves. There were no funds for a return voyage back to their origins, and oft times there were no homes or relatives to return to in Ireland or anywhere else in Europe.

Elvira then got to the point and told that Bertha had seen him beating those little boys with a thick stick or club, and their cries tore her heart. She said one of them was bruised very badly. He looked very sick as well. She thought that he might fall off his horse into the canal. Bertha had waited behind him while he was stalled, for one of the boys was too sick to ride on and Silvermann got into a rage, beat him. Bertha almost took a crowbar over his head, for she hated him, but she managed to get her towlines cleared and get around him. He swore at her, and was not going to let her past him, but when she got out on the berm with her iron bar, he changed his mind. However, he threatened her with a pistol if she came on the deck of his boat. Ben and Hermann's smiles faded. This was serious business.

Bertha had told Elvira all this in her anger. She also told her that his real name was either Gottlieb or Lehman and she knew that he was in hiding for some crooked dealing, maybe a crime back east in New York or Pennsylvania. She had heard it in a riverfront tavern when she was having her pint of beer. Now those dark beady eyes of hers were peering into the past, and she had put together something from the clues. They did not call her "Hog Eye" for nothing. She remembered seeing a drawn sketch of him wanted for some unspeakable charges back east. It was all coming back to her now, little by little.

Bertha was going to tie up for the night up in Bremen and she would tell Grünwalda Peppleman about it as they sat together soaking their feet in huge wooden tubs of suds, and having their beer. Even the advice of Gerta Hemel would come in handy for she always gave it whether it was sought or not.

No, there was no use to consult the men because they were never any help. It seemed to be the women folk who made the decisions in the German households of the United States, and that the men spent their time in joking, checkers, and laughing. Life was one big happy time. As long as there was a roof over their heads and food to eat, why worry? This seemed strange because in the old country, German men lorded it over their wives, but when they became transplanted in Pennsylvania and Ohio, it seemed that the tables were turned.

Therefore, with her goats and her shy wild children scampering over the laden decks, Big Barge Bertha made her way up the canal to Bremen where she would prepare the evening meal and put her barge in the basin beside the freight depot.

After the excitement of Big Bertha's news, Elvira became so lost in thought that she had little to say. The men got busy helping the repair men pry and clamp new shiplap planking in the barge's stoved-in gunwale, and secured it there with wooden pegs and screws. Then they caulked it with tar and hemp.

The girls went sightseeing all over the town, and stopped at the various shops and stores on the main street and along the canal. There were many kinds of businesses that had sprung up along the canal for the barge business. There were tinker shops, groceries, inns, restaurants, chandlers and hardware shops. Lou-Lou and Josie bought some lemon drops and peppermint sticks at a little store that displayed all sorts of candies in glass jars. There were also tempting pastries. They recognized some of Mrs. Peppleman's pies from her shop, which she had sent down on the local freight express run.

Lou, Ben, and Charley loitered around the blacksmith shops, and then helped their fathers with the barge repair. When they grew tired of playing horseshoe in the lot by the boatyard, they got their lines and some bait from Mrs. Brenner before they went to try their luck fishing for catfish in the canal. One day they would talk their fathers into taking them fishing out in a boat on Loramie reservoir for some of those big bass and trout Charley Peppleman was always bragging about, but never showed to anyone.

Evening grew out of the late afternoon, and traffic seemed to be heavier on the canal. All the barges, which had docked to let the passenger packet pass, were now coming north. Many passed going south and it kept the hoggee drivers busy managing towlines accurately to allow for enough slack. There were tales of dilatory hoggees and linemen who did not handle their lines properly, or without enough slack to let the line rest on the bottom of the canal. Heavy oncoming barges had intercepted the line and dragged teams and drivers into the canal. There was one tale on the Erie of horses and riders who were drowned when pulled into the canal by a passing barge. The crew was unable to cut the line free. Therefore, the horses were dragged beneath the coasting barge, ground into the oozy mud beneath, and drowned. Ben and Hermann Gast usually cast their lines off the bow when the boys were riding hoggee. Big Bertha did likewise for her boys were still children, but older experienced men riders usually tried to save time by merely letting the lines go slack to let the oncoming barge next to the towpath have the right of way.

After the barge was repaired, Ben Gast blew his boat horn for the children to come back to the boatyard and get aboard. Brenner's barge could not get into the drydock until the next afternoon, so Joel figured that he might as well go on up to Bremen and come back the next day. However, there was another reason, for Elvira had a "hankerin" to get up there to get in on the commotion when Grünwalda Peppleman found out the tale Big Bertha would tell her. Then as the evening shadows began to lengthen, there was an increasing reason.

After the Gast barge had pulled out from its berth, a slow lumbering barge of cordwood and kindling passed through Minster. Elvira Brenner and Joel recognized the severe face of the so-called Gustav Silvermann. Elvira pretended to go out on the towpath to get some mop water out of the canal so that she could get a closer look. Her heart failed her when she saw the tear stained face of the sick little boy trying to stay on his horse ahead of the barge.

She knew that if she said anything or even looked angry, the black-eyed devil at the tiller would only take it out on those poor orphan boys. The other boy sat in the bow splitting kindling out of larger cordwood and stacking it in small piles that he bound with hemp cord to be sold along the way to housewives. Nevertheless, the boy in the bow kept a sharp eye on the sick boy that was weaving back and forth on the horse. He was afraid that the boy would fall. Elvira did not see the third boy anywhere, and Silvermann usually had three or four boys. She did notice that the boy in the bow had darkened eyes and bruises about his face. There was no telling what his frail little body could show. With all the kindness she dared to muster, Elvira Brenner spoke to each of the boys and told them she was glad to see them. A feeble smile of recognition came over their faces, but faded when they stole a glance at the iron face of Silvermann at the tiller. Joel Brenner waved to him and Elvira called out greetings to him. He relaxed his stern grimace and to Brenners' surprise, he waved back. Just ahead of the boatyard he called a halt; then after a while he came back along the towpath and asked Joel if he would keep an eye on his barge and boys while he stopped into the shop up the way for some things he needed.

When he had gone, Elvira sent one of her boys to see where he went but not to let on, nor to notice too much, but just to act like he was playing along the street. She took the opportunity to slip some homemade bread and jam to each of the famished boys that was followed by glasses of milk. Watching the towpath carefully she slipped them more food, and asked them when they had last eaten. She helped the sick boy off the horse, but he was terrified to get down lest Silvermann would some back and catch him. She washed his face and gave him some hot soup she had made for supper. Joel Brenner kept watch for her as she tried to minister to the crying needs of the miserable boys. When Elvira asked where the other boys were, the two boys clammed up. They were stricken with terror. They would not dare talk and Elvira knew that something had terrified them. Elvira sensed that she was in the midst of some terrible tragedy.

The boys confided that they would run away, and had tried it once, but that he had about killed them. There was no place they could go, because the law would return them to Silvermann or take them to the orphanage. Silverman could then take them out again. Elvira turned down the ragged shirt collar of one of the boys and showed welts and scabs to her husband without saying a word. He nodded and then looked the other way so that the boy would not know that he saw it.

One of the Brenner children came scampering back along the towpath and told them that Silvermann was leaving the waterfront where he had eaten in a tavern and was heading toward the barge. Immediately the boy tried to scamper back on the big black horse but was so weak he could not. Joel Brenner helped him up, and patted his back affectionately. The boy cried out and jumped with pain. Joel realized that his back must have been one great welt of sores from beatings. His heart sank but anger came rushing back. He knew that he must not show it in talking with Silvermann, or he would say more than he should. Then the boys would pay with more suffering and abuse.

The two terrified boys thanked them for their kindness, but asked them to leave them alone, because Silvermann had warned them not to talk with anyone, or they would get the blacksnake whip.

Silvermann came back, said a few words to Joel Brenner, and went aboard. Joel tried to make pleasant conversation, and said a few words about canal traffic and the weather; then Silvermann and his piteous group were off up toward Bremen.

Elvira Brenner's skinny girls, Ellen and Malissy, got busy and cleared up their supper dishes, but wondered at their mother's longer than usual grace that she said before the meal. It was almost a heart to heart talk with God, and all her family wondered what was to happen next in their lives. Elvira tried to do her work, but after a while she left the hot boat for the cool towpath and took a little walk while fanning herself with her sunbonnet. As she disappeared in the twilight, Joel thought to call after her, but the girls stopped him and told him,

"Not now, Pa. Ma is having herself a good cry." Joel Brenner kicked a keg out of his way, then curried down his horses. The boys each took a horse along the green grass of the towpath to graze while they sat talking. The boys let the horses wander on their long tethers.

"I'll betcha we don't stay here for the night," Bub said, and the other brother answered,

"New. Sumthin' is awful wrong. I'll bet we go on up to Bremen tonight or at least early in the morning, drydock or not."

It wasn't long before Elvira came hurrying back to the barge and began clearing things away right and left. She was apparently in a hurry but said nothing. She blew her nose and wiped her eyes, and the girls knew not to ask questions, and to stay out of her way. She and Joel were exchanging heated words on the top deck and the girls strained to listen. They motioned to the boys in the twilight, and pointed to the top deck and nodded their heads.

"Wal if nuthin' else will do, that's what we'll do, Elviry," Joel exclaimed. "There'll be no peace on this boat unless we do."

"There is something dreadful going on. I'll bet he's done something with those other boys, and none of us are the wiser. They're <u>dead</u> back there in the thickets below Loramie in them swamp bottoms!"

"D'ye suppose them two other boys could be lying down in the bottom of that boat too sick to move and here I didn't know it? I coulda took them sumthin to eat, but law! How's a-body to know? Parbly dead though."

"Now Elviry, don't go getting all worked up and jumpin' at conclusions. We don't know that. Them scared boys would have surely told us."

"New they wudn't. They didn't dare. Couldn't ye tell they was almost afraid even to breathe?" Elvira went on and then another thought struck her. "Layin' down there sick? Joel, they might nigh be dead and he's transportin' them somewhere to get rid of them." Joel's mouth stood open, and the children gathered around their mother. Elvira exploded,

"Joel Brenner, if you air a Christian man, git them horses hitched up and let's git to making tracks to New Bremen."

"But, Elviry, we just got them out to pasture a little while ago. Let them have a few more mouthfuls of green grass."

"Fiddlesticks, Joel Brenner. They have been grazing this blessed day while we've been tied up here in this hot boatyard. They're so full o' green grass now that they'll have the squitters all the way to Bremen. Now come on. All you youngin's get your things collected and get ready to get underway in tow," she commanded.

Joel counseled that it would be better to go very slow so as not to get too close behind Silvermann. Be better if he didn't know they were behind him for he knew they were tied up for drydock. Elvira cautioned that she needed to tell Big Bertha what she had discovered and to tell Mrs. Peppleman and the others

"But what can we do?" Joel asked, while trying to figure out how paying an expensive toll just to go to Bremen to satisfy curiosity made any sense.

"Pshaw and fiddlesticks," Elvira retorted. "If we have one shred of decency about us, it's the least Christian thing we can do."

"But we can't settle all the problems of the world, and undo all the sin and meanness in the world alone, Elviry. We have all the mouths of our own that we can feed, and we can't take on all the mistreated orphans in the world."

"No, but we can try. We can do that little bit that the good Lord has given us to do. We can try, and we will know that we cared, and maybe got to others who can do more than we can, Joel." Elvira's hands flew at her work as she shrieked after Joel, who left to get the horses hitched in tow, and to make arrangements with the dry dock master about a later day to dry dock.

"We will know that we didn't leave the sick and dying at our gates for the dogs to lick his sores like it tells about in the Bible. We didn't cast stones on the poor fallen. . . "

"Oh Maw, stop yelling. People will hear us and think we were shanty Irish a-fightin'," one of Elvira's daughters cautioned her.

"Now Missy, don't you tell yer mother what to do." Then she caught herself, wiped her eyes, and began to smile when she thought of what her daughter had said. She was right. No use to yell, but rather act, and act fast. Deeds, not words, them wuz what counted. "Yes Malissy, we're not Uriah Hornback yet."

The evening breeze was soothing on the top deck as Brenner's barge, the *Wabash Loon*, skimmed along the canal, while riding high in the water without its usual load of cargo. It was all Elvira could do not to get out and run, for Joel was holding the horses back for fear of overtaking Silvermann. An oil lantern swung from the short bow mast and another one from the stern above the rudder.

The more Elvira thought about the injustice of Silvermann, the more her blood boiled. Her own boys had told her that Silvermann had gone into that little restaurant on the canal berm and had himself some supper and a stein of beer. In addition, to think of it, those poor hoggee boys were already sick and miserable with abuse, had not had food since morning, and had not had supper yet. No tellin' what that black devil would feed them - probably bread scraps and the cheapest thing he could, if indeed he fed them at all.

Darkness fell all about them as they glided along in the early night. There were no lanterns of oncomin' boats ahead of them, nor could they see any barges following them. They felt alone out in the middle of nowhere in the velvety silence of the night. Occasionally they passed a lighted farmhouse but there would be no locks until they got to New Bremen. Joel and Elvira talked. He told of having heard many cases of crooked barge captains who mistreated their young boy hoggees. Worst of all, orphan boys had no place else to go - not even an orphanage. Many captains mistreated and cheated their hoggee drivers on purpose so that they would run away toward the end of the season and the captains would not have to pay them their small wages. Seasoned men drivers got twelve dollars a month, while young boys got only nine and ten dollars. Young boys were easier to bully and cheat out of their wages. In frustrated desperation, they often ran away and left the barge stranded. However, with orphan boys it was different. They got no wages, only their keep, such as it was. They had to take care of the horses, put them out to graze, work two shifts a day, and if there was any time left, curl up in their clothes in the hay on board or in a freight yard stable for a few hours of troubled sleep. Then there was the cold weather and rains of early spring, fall, and early winter. They rode in all sorts of weather to make their wage and to keep the barge moving. However, there were various church societies, and mission societies, who tried to help the miserable lot of the boy hoggees. The conditions were much worse on the larger canals on the Erie and the Pennsylvania canals back east. It was because they were closer to large cities and the crime that went with them. On the Miami and Erie, and on the Wabash and Erie, these conditions of cruelty, thievery, and abuse were not so common because the unsophisticated backwoods people of the rustic small town were "home folks." Such things just did not go on, or at least not in broad daylight. Therefore, folks knew nothing about them.

The plight of many orphan boys who were "let out" to farmers was a life of plodding slavery and misery. Then there were instances where the boys received good homes. They were often adopted. Elvira remembered of hearing a big city barge captain from back east telling of mean river and canal captains throwing out sick *hoggees* in forlorn swamps and bayous, and no one was ever the wiser for their identity was unknown. They were dead when they were found, and could not tell of their captain's crime.

Elvira and Joel were both uneasy, and knew that they would not sleep that night when they did tie up in Bremen. The boys riding out in front were keeping up a steady stream of talk as they rode along in the ever-gathering darkness. The horses snorted from time to time as they often do when walking or pulling.

A few more houses passed in the darkness. There was no traffic on the canal now for it was dark and most of the captains had tied up for the night. Elvira thought to herself that only a fool would be out "moonin" around in the night, but still she reasoned that they must try to do what they could to help.

One thing puzzled Elvira. What happened to the young girl orphans or lost waifs on the streets and docks? No one talked about them. What was their fate? They couldn't all live by begging. Were they enslaved into drudgery work in taverns, inns, or farm homes? Then the truth began to dawn on Elvira. Of course, they too were exploited into the unspeakable life of prostitution. No one ever spoke of this or acknowledged that it existed.

CHAPTER 13

BRENNER'S *WABASH LOON* WAS the lone solitary traveler on the canal the entire trip from Minster up to New Bremen. An overcast sky hid the late rising moon so that the three-mile night journey was completed in near darkness, save for the wan lights of the pale lanterns. It was excitement to the Brenner children, for although they did not comprehend all that was hidden beneath their parent's strange behavior; they shared in the suspense of what might unfold in New Bremen.

At the edge of town, Joel Brenner slowed the tow horses to a very slow walk; then when within a few hundred yards of the street lamps at the lock, he nosed the *Loon* into the bank. He stood guard on the towpath for oncoming barges while he sent one of the boys ahead to inspect the basin to see if Silvermann or Big Bertha were tied up there. No use stumbling into a bear's den unprepared and foil all of Elvira's plans.

When the boy soon returned with the alarming news that Silvermann's barge was high and dry up on the weighing cradle scale in the weigh lock by the grain depot, Elvira was at first thwarted; then she decided that perhaps it was a good thing. Joel was to keep the barge there where the canal was widest in case of traffic, and keep the children together so that no one would know they were in town. Elvira secured her bonnet tightly by the bow strings, and crossed the canal by the stone bridge. She crept up into town by the side streets until she was even with Big Bertha's lumber barge in the basin. She tried vainly to think of a way to slip onto the barge without being seen. After waiting in the shadows for what seemed a long time, she decided that all was quiet on Silvermann's barge and that he was probably at one of the taverns along the berm. The skinny frail form of Mrs. Brenner scurried over the cobblestones onto the berm along the basin to the lumber barge and scampered aboard the barge, banking low as she landed on the deck. She could be less visible from the street. Immediately Big Bertha's sleeping hulk under her blanket on deck came to life, and she was standing over Elvira Brenner with her protective club in her hand. No one would steal from her boat or harm her wards for she slept like an escaped convict - trusting no one.

"It's me, Berthy. Elviry Brenner," Elvira gasped out in a hushed voice, and just in the nick of time. Then she removed her bonnet in the semi-darkness and explained to Bertha why she must see her. Big Bertha sensed something in Elvira's face before Elvira could pour out all of her story. Bertha motioned her below into the tiny cabin of her spotless kitchen where they sat in the shadows of a low-burning whale oil lamp. The two women sat close together, and the silhouette of their shadows against the plank wall looked like David and Goliath. Bertha could say little but kept saying "Yah, Yah," and urged Elvira on. She always called Elvira "Little Missus." With her immense large brimmed hat removed, and her coal black hair stringing over her shoulders, Big Bertha in her night clothes created a strange picture that Elvira had never seen. Strange indeed, but a friend in need, ears that listened to every syllable, and eyes that searched her face.

Elvira raced on in a half whispered voice to tell why they had come, and why they had docked back there in the dark. She told Bertha about Silvermann's boys, of the terrible things she saw, the bruises and welts, the heart-break of those miserable abused boys. The huge broad face of the Slavic woman darkened with anger. Her coal black eyes smoldered with unspoken rage, but Big Bertha could not put her feelings or the pent-up anger of years that were inside her into English words. She worried about the sick boy on the horse, as well as the other little boys. They were all going without food, and they were being beaten. Who could tell what else they suffered? All this was unleashing a pent-up flood of anger that could become dangerous once Big Bertha went into action. Bertha's own children peered from the shadows of the adjoining bunker sleeping room, but never a word escaped their lips.

Without a word, Bertha began to put on her work clothes and grabbed her hat. She addressed her oldest boy in that foreign tongue, telling him where she was going and that he was to stand guard with the fierce dog against thieves. Elvira shook with fright. The dog! She had completely forgotten about that huge dog. Why she could have been torn to pieces, but he had never even growled. Why, he must have known her by her scent!

Bertha then turned to Elvira and said curtly,

"Come, Little Missus, we go up dark side of the street to Pie Woman. She know. . . .but the two other boys. . . dead, I tank."

Elvira looked at her without understanding, "Pie Woman?" Bertha nodded slowly "Yah. Beeg Missus. Shure, **you** know, Zat Pepples." Then

Elvira knew she meant Grünwalda Peppleman of the famous pies. Bertha caught up her heavy ironwood club from the deck and grumbled in a low tone to Elvira,

"I tank. I tank I be-geen to remembers. Not zure - but maybees zat Zilvermann ees somebodies else. Eef I for zure, little Missus, I tank I keel heem, Yah!"

"Why, land o Goshen, Berthy! What on earth d'ye mean?" As they walked stealthily up the darkened street toward Mrs. Peppleman's pastry shop on the canal, Bertha continued after a long silence.

"Not sure. Doan you worry, Little Missus, but sumthing vair bad in past. Eef he be who I tanks, he black evil man not deserves to live. He has keel people, Little Missus, Yah, keel!" Elvira's blood ran cold. Maybe her worse fears for the missing boys were not her imagination. She stopped in her tracks and clutched Bertha, who stopped and looked down at her quickly, while she panted out to her what she feared might be down in the hold of that Silvermann barge up there on the weighing cradle. As they walked on, Bertha whispered to Elvira that there had been trouble. Silvermann, as usual, tried to lie and cheat his way through the locks, but Ian MacPherson was in a no play mood and refused to open the locks. Elihu Sanders and Jake Hemel backed him up, and when Silvermann tried to undo the lock gates, Jake Hemel knocked him down with his sledge handle and called the constable. The Gast brothers and the constable immediately ordered his barge into the weigh lock for weighing and there was where it remained - up there in the weighing cradle. Elvira fanned herself at all this news and longed to run back to tell Joel, but braced herself for the ordeal ahead. This was just a start. The barge should be searched.

Big Bertha also told her that she had just come from "Mrs. Pepples'" a short while before, and where she had some ale and a good hot soak." The two women stayed on the street side in the shadows and went to the back door of Mrs. Peppleman's. High voices of laughter rang out in the night from her open door, and first they heard the low voice of huge Grünwalda Peppleman, then the grating harsh voice of Gerta Hemel's, then the high shrieking voice of Mrs. Gertslaeker. First they would sing a ditty in German, then the clink of mugs and steins, then an avalanche of hysterical, yet abdominal, hearty laughter. Each one had to take turns making up verses of "Ach Du Lieber Augustine," and some of the funny but naughty things he did. "Ich liebe dich so." "Hafe mir nich lafe. Alle ist tauschen." (All is deception or delusive.)

Bertha gave a short rap at the door, and then she led Elvira in behind her onto the dark porch. Grünwalda finally heard them and called out, "Ja? Vell, gecommen in out dair."

Before any of the women could call out their names in welcome, Bertha put her hand up to her mouth and gave a loud "sh-h and hiss;" then she shook her head for them not to speak. Quickly she motioned for Elvira to come on into the room. Without any introduction, Bertha, her face full of pent-up expression that she could not express, exploded in a half-spoken whisper.

"Dair beeg troubles. Bad troubles. Little Missus, you tell." Grünwalda and Elvira knew each other, and Elvira knew Gerta Hemel from passing beneath her little porch over the forge, but she did not know the other woman. Grünwalda nodded that it was all right for Elvira to speak, so she told all that she knew.

Upon entering the kitchen, Elvira almost retched when she saw all three of the huge women with their feet soaking in wooden tubs of steaming suds, with steins of ale in their hands and a mixture of food on a table in front of them. The smell of ale and kraut, and some vile cheese floated over the scent of soap suds and hot tubs. Elvira tried to tell her tale, but stopped in amazement when she saw Mrs. Hemel heap some of that evil smelling, brown runny cheese ("Schmere-kase")on top of a plate of cottage cheese. Then she almost gagged when she saw that Grünwalda was stowing away huge forkfuls of apple pie with sauerkraut heaped on top of it, and wash it down with copious draughts of ale slopped out of a huge mug.

"Satan's drawers! Where on airth did they ever dream up sech heathen vittles? Why heathens in Borneo wouldn't eat sech stuff," she swore to herself, but was stopped short by her own retching when she saw Mrs. Gertslaecker breaking apart pickled pig-knuckles and sucking marrow out of the bones. The crackling racket almost drowned out the story Elvira was trying to tell. Bertha saw that Elvira looked sick, and put her hand up for the other women to listen, then cautioned.

"Listen. Zis turrible bad. Ve got beeg trouble - maybe killings." At this, all eyes turned first from Big Bertha to little Elvira Brenner. Bertha could not sit down, but paced the room like a huge jungle animal stalking prey or hunting for an escape from a trap, first looking out of the door into the night, then out of the window. She looked as menacing as a cape buffalo. As Elvira went on, her story getting worse by each passing minute, Bertha punctuated her story with an occasional "Yah," or "You zee?"

First one, then another of the women stopped their eating, spell bound by the piteous outpourings of Elvira Brenner, and one by one they put their plates and steins down on the table. Mrs. Hemel said some terrible words and her narrow turtle eyes became beady with anger. As Grünwalda Peppleman's former jolly face now became clouded with anger and dark as a thundercloud. She said not a word, but started drying her feet, and then announced to the others.

"Dair time has come for action. Ve go?"

Then Bertha gathered them all together at the table where they sat in council and told them that she suspected that Silvermann was a terrible evil man who had done great mortal wrongs in the old country. Many years had passed. He looked different but little by little, she was beginning to remember him through his disguise. Mrs. Gertslacker was now almost in tears, and she moaned over and over: "Poor motherless boys. Dair poor *kleine* souls."

Grünwalda Peppleman came to a reasonable solution at last. It was time for some of the responsible people in the community to wake up and take a hand in things. Her wrath turned toward the men who were always having "dair jolly times" at the poker tables, or checkers, up in that grain depot or freight warehouse.

Mrs. Hemel said it was time for the law, the big law to step in, not that ornery shiftless town constable and his lazy ways. Bertha, who was always cautious out of years of ingrained habit, told them they must act in secret and have proof, or the law would look the other way. It would take swearing an oath and perhaps money, if they went to court. Could any of them raise money? All became silent until Grünwalda took a deep breath and swelled up her huge full size, and burst out while slamming her hand down on the table.

"Dat Kattmann. Dat Frau Kattmann is always hollerin' about reforms, foreign missions, and temperance. She is always sendin' money to convert the heathen, and money to help Abolitionists in Boston."

Mrs. Hemel looked strangely at Mrs. Peppleman, wondering why she was bringing her arch enemy, Mrs. Augusta Kattmann, into it.

"And what has Gusta Kattmann to do with it, Grünwalda?" she asked.

Mrs. Hemel continued pursing her lips and narrowing her eyes with conviction.

"She can practice her Christianity right here at home. Now and here is dair place. She got plenty of moneys. Know all beeg people aivrywhere. Decorated by dair Kaiser for bravery and service in der wars when she doctor and nurse both in big wars. She know right people, Senators and Governor, know how get beeg law here, and she have money to do right Christian thing if she the true Christian she preach."

Mrs. Hemel exploded an unspeakable one-syllable word that women just weren't supposed to know about, let alone ever say. Then she said,

"Grünwalda, you are running a temperature. You know that tight-fisted old Pharisee wouldn't look down on us peasants and lend a helping hand. You're wasting your breath."

"She will dis time, or we'll lock horns. If she such know-it-all, big doctor, mid-wife, nurse and money-bags, now is time to help or else shut up all that hollerin' and preachin'. We got her up against the wall, and she can't squirm out. I'll put it to her in front of all dair town people and she can't sneak out and save face. I'll put some of der burrs under her fat tail."

Grünwalda then girded for action. She warned them all that the night was wearing on, and those poor boys were suffering by the hour while they sat chattering. Yes, it was time for action.

Elvira put on her bonnet, tied it beneath her chin, and followed Bertha out into the night. Grünwalda and her troop would go break up the "shiftless" men at their checkers, get the law, search that barge, and rescue those boys. Then they would descend on Frau Kattmann and shake her down out of her tree house of dreams, and her unheard of *Blue Swan* canal packet.

Elvira had to trot to keep up with Big Bertha. When they came to her lumber barge, Bertha told Elvira to go have her husband bring the *Wabash Loon* up to the basin and tie up right beside her. There was no use to fear Silvermann, because he could not get his barge free until he paid Mr. MacPherson the toll, and after the barge was weighed again in the morning.

Elvira fairly flew down the darkened towpath to the *Loon*, where she told everything that had happened, and all the news about Silvermann and his brush with the toll master at the locks. In a short while Joel Brenner and the boys had tied up their barge beside Big Bertha, and in no time Bertha and Elvira were ready to join Grünwalda and her women in their crusade.

Lou-Lou and Josie were having a good time taking turns playing the pump-organ melodeon and trying to sing the popular songs. Bertha Gast stopped them when they tried to pick out by ear and sing one of the ditties that they heard the old Irish codger sing beneath their windows as he caterwauled his way through town down the canal thoroughfare. Their merriment was interrupted by a curt knock at the door, and the stern faced Mrs. Peppleman and Mrs. Hemel trudged into the kitchen, promptly told Bertha Gast they needed to see August Ben Gast, Hermann, and all the rest of the "Canal Company freight peoples." Bertha Gast knew something more had come out of the incident at the weigh locks when she called Ben up from the cool cellar, where he and Jake Hemel were listening to Elihu Sanders' tall tales. Ben came quickly for he too sensed that something was very wrong. Jake Hemel followed and stood in the stairway listening.

The little house on the canal towpath became silent, empty, and forlorn. Lou-Lou and Josie, along with the boys, stood quietly at the side looking on and listening to their elders. Just then, Hermann Gast drove up on the street side in Frau Kattmann's sleek brass trimmed carriage. He had come for Lou-Lou to take her home. Bernhardina Gast, her sister, and her mother had all returned from Maria Stein to Bremen, and it was time that Lou-Lou and young Ben were home in bed. Bertha Gast was surprised to hear that her mother had decided to stay in her "town house" for a day or two to take care of some business at the church. Some foreign mission society people were coming down the canal from Fort Wayne. Therefore, Frau Kattmann preferred to entertain them in her town house since it would be so much more convenient. Besides, Heinrich August Kattmann preferred the quiet solitude of the country house at Maria Stein with his hired man, the housekeeper, and his own world that was <u>Willow Haven</u>. He seldom came over to supervise the brewery in his later years. He and Frau Kattmann saw less of each other each passing year as their interests became so widely different.

He preferred his curved meerschraum pipe, his hounds, beehives, vineyards, and hop vines to all the bustle in the world, and all that "hollerin' and reform." Therefore, Frau Kattmann left her husband, Heinrich August, who was much older than she, to his <u>senile</u> interests in the country. Then she went abroad into the world to set some of its wrongs to right. Little did she suspect the mantrap she was to stumble into at the hands of the disgusting, common plebeian, Grünwalda Peppleman.

CHAPTER 14

JOSIE AND HER BROTHERS tried to go to sleep after they were ordered to bed when the hour grew late. At last, quietness fell over the town as the carriage wheels became faint in the distance when Hermann took Lou-Lou home. Ben and Bertha Gast accompanied him, for Grünwalda Peppleman reasoned at Mrs. Hemel's urging that it would be best for Ben Gast to talk with Mrs. Kattmann. She always seemed to listen to him or Hermann, while she always disagreed with her daughters out of force of habit. Bertha Gast seldom gave her mother the chance to advise, reprimand, or disagree with her.

Grünwalda Peppleman, Mrs. Hemel, Mrs. Gertslacker, along with Elvira and Big Bertha, called upon Mrs. Sanders behind the tinker shop. She in turn ran and got Mrs. MacPherson. In a short time most of the town knew what terrible abuse the lonesome, homeless orphan boys of Silvermann's barge were enduring, and of the black suspicion Elvira and Bertha held concerning the "missing" boys. Some of the husbands were home where they should have been, and they soon learned of the black heart of Silvermann. However, Grünwalda missed several of the others, especially Charley Peppleman.

Going out on the towpath, Grünwalda turned her head first one direction and then in the other to listen. Surely enough, after a while she heard loud guffawing of men's voices.

Creeping nearer the grain depot and close to the freight house, her women followers were coming in single file behind her along the towpath. Grünwalda pinpointed the source of the laughter and knew where the "loafers'" lair was. Enraged, her women accomplices urged her on to victory. They all looked like a file of Druid priests about to attend a ritual of human sacrifice on the stone altar.

Silently they entered the ground floor of the depot, where Grünwalda grasped a huge granary broom weighing at least ten pounds, and ascended the rough plank stairs to the grain bins above. There in the passage ways between the bins of stored wheat was the lair. A barrel with table boards across the top served as the checker table, and under some oil lanterns, at least a dozen men sat around in a circle laughing, and lifting their mugs while those at the board played their game furiously. Grünwalda charged in furious disgust when she saw that the game was not checkers but poker, and she saw money stacked on the board. No wonder they were shouting and going on so it sounded like old lady Kattmann's revival meeting. There was a keg of ale with a wooden spout across a wooden rack, and to her anger, she saw Charley acting as bartender, and he was keeping the mugs filled as they were passed to him. Raising her huge broom high, roaring in that deep bass voice of hers, Grünwalda raced in, brought the broom down on the table, and sent boards, chips and money flying in all directions. Before Charley could run for cover into one of the many corridors between grain bins, Grünwalda caught him in the seat of the britches with the huge broom and nearly lifted him off his feet with the impact. He howled with pain. She swung right and left. The other women put up a screech like the end of the world. The men, not knowing what had happened, leaped and dodged the flying heavy push broom. Some jumped into the bins of wheat, some to the rafters and others jumped out the windows or down the stairs. Grünwalda bellowed condemnation on their lazy shiftless ways and warned them all to get home for they were needed, and that terrible things had descended upon the town. Not one dared to defy her, for they would just as soon have stood up to a charging elephant or an enraged rhinoceros in the African bush country. Charley howled as he held his backsides and tried to run for home. It did Big Bertha a world of good to see the dispersion of the evil clan. She recognized some of the "brave" runners of the retreat as some of those same ones who so bravely called from a distance to her on the canal, "Hog Eye," or "Water Buffalo," and who so bravely ducked out of sight when she took to the street with her ironwood club and handful of good-sized rocks.

After the excitement was over the women went to their homes. Jake Hemel came for Gerta and after a few terse commands, he told her to mind her own business and set her own household in order before gadding around town in the middle of the night in a "petticoat posse." Gerta had no harsh sharp words for the powerful blacksmith who was her husband and master. She ducked her head as she slipped out from Peppleman's kitchen gasping,

"Wal, fer pity sakes. Mercy!"

Wasting no time, she skipped along home and mounted the steps up to her flat above the forge, keeping her scolding, raucous mouth to herself, put out her light, and promptly jumped into bed. She knew better than to open her mouth when Jake Hemel was as angry as he was this night, and if he did not come in until daylight, she knew not to open her lips or to utter one word of complaint. She found fault with everyone else, and gave the whole world tactless advice from her eerie perch above the forge. She was much like a ruffled cross hen perched on a rail fence. However, when Jake barked at last, she leaped from her perch and ran for cover as though an old hawk were overhead.

In the stuffy velvet and brocaded parlor of Augusta Kattmann's town house, the beaded, glass prism of the hanging lamps reflected different colors of light. The room smelled of polish and hospital-like cleanliness, but also of being shut up against dust, and of disuse. It was the Sunday-best parlor full of overdone furniture which filled every valuable space, but it was inviting to the grandchildren who were permitted to look in through the door now and then, and only if they were obedient.

As Ben and Hermann unfolded the evidence that had been brought to them, Bernhardina Gast and Aunt Fredericka sat silent, their eyes wide with apprehensive fear. They looked slowly from the men to Frau Kattmann, who sat silently, and for once did not bat her eyelids or look down in bored contempt. Instead, her eyes were large and intent. She was listening, and in that Teutonic mind of clockwork, organized perfection was already organizing work battalions for different levels of personnel. She sat in a large padded chair of red velvet plush, much like a tribal chieftain or jungle queen that was listening to the war counsel. When they were all finished, a babble of voices took over, but she put her hand up for her emotional daughters to be quiet. Bertha Gast alone said but a few words, but her sister, Ernestine Hofermeyer, was for having a public whipping post or the rack. Bernhardina wondered why the old-fashioned stock and pillory, and hot pitch tar would not be a fine idea. In impatience with their childish lack of insight, Frau Kattmann clapped her hands and lowered her eyes, waiting for them to subside and give her the floor. When she upbraided them for their immature emotionalism, their faces sank and Aunt Fredericka gave way to tears. Immediately the daughters put up a protest. Bertha Gast wanted to tell her mother that her own domination had made the girls immature and subservient to her. However, she held her tongue. Her mother very archly rapped on the marble-top table for silence.

"Bernhardina, Ernestine, Sister Fredericka," she called out. They turned to her and answered out of habit, as if responding to a roll call. When Mrs. Kattmann saw that she was in command, she said simply,

"Shut-up! Halten!" After waiting a minute with her head lowered and her eyes shut, she turned to Ben and Hermann. Ludwig, her only son, stood silently, for he left such matters to the sons-in-law. The brewery was his long suit. Augusta Kattmann outlined the plan of action. She was flattered by the attention paid to her, but she was a different woman now. This was a crisis and some of her former self came to the surface in the emergency; her fidelity as a competent nurse, midwife, and almost doctor, took command.

"Mein sons, Hermann and August Benjamin, we go into action in dair morning, but the sheriff must be sent for at the county seat tonight. It's too much for skinny, shiftless Misters Bushman. We send word to packet for company detective Angus MacClintock if need be, but we see. We investigate, get truth from those canal womens, have sheriff examine poor children's bodies, file charges, have wards taken from Silvermann. We go to work on that orphanage system which permits such things. I think dat county judge who make unfortunate childs wards of court and hand over to *Schwartz Teufel*, dot infamous black devil, also chust as guilty. Ve make investigate, put pressure on, press charges."

It was all perfectly clear to Augusta Kattmann just the exact plan of action that must be taken. There were many more plans that took place in her head upon hearing the evidence. She fell in with the plan to prosecute the evil wrong doing, and money did not seem to be any obstacle. Augusta Kattmann knew the problem would be further complicated because the origins of a great percentage of the lost children could not be traced. Many had no connections with either orphanages, workhouses in the cities, foster homes, or relatives. A great bulk of these children, both boys and girls, were orphans whose parents had died on board the immigrant ships and had left them nothing to live on. They were without relatives, and without money for the return trip to Ireland or to other ports in Europe. They were simply left stranded by ship captains on the docks when they landed. There they were seized by ruthless factory owners, barge captains and kidnappers. There were a whole lot of men with evil purposes who were just like Silvermann. She asked Hermann and August Ben to bring that Brenner woman and that Bertha woman to her that night, but her eyes flashed when she admonished them.

"Do not bring that Pepples woman, and certainly not that Hemel's fishwife – not to my house!"

Bertha Gast reasoned to herself as she and Ben were walking home through the night, that it had been a stroke of pure luck that Hermann and Ben had been the ones to tell her mother, and not those other women, especially Mrs. Peppleman.

Some of the younger men who had sneaked back to the grain bins after Grünwalda's house cleaning were waiting for Ben and Hermann. Mr. MacPherson and Elihu Sanders, along with Jake Hemel, were sitting in the wane lamp light while offering their ideas of how the whole affair should be handled. Two young men of the group readily agreed to ride to the county seat in Wapokoneta with the constable's request for help, and the written account of the resistance to arrest after attempting to cheat the lockmaster and toll collector - a state offense. Jake Hemel would see to it that Silvermann's barge would not get down out of the weigh lock cradle and sneak out of town before daylight.

As the old clock in the church tower struck midnight, peace began to settle over the little town on the canal. Off in the distance some cattle could be heard lowing and a cowbell tinkled faintly. The nightriders to the Auglaize county seat rode out to the north toward Lock 2. Then they took the county road by-passes, which by their angling, made the trip shorter than the pike from St. Marys.

Quiet came at last, but many wondered what the morning would bring. Elvira Brenner could not sleep, but Big Bertha slept soundly with her ironwood cudgel by her side. There would be time enough on the morrow to settle all the things that pressed in, and a good rest would help her remember.

A rather cool overcast June morning started the new day, which promised to be as cheerless as it was cool. Josie and her brothers, Charley and Lou, tried not to ask too many questions. The boys would get to go to the freight house and locks with their father, but Josie was wondering how she and Lou-Lou could get out of the house. Perhaps when, and if, Lou-Lou came over, they could think of a way. Ben Gast had given Bertha instructions that it would be best if the girls were to stay clear of the weigh lock, for there would be some bad business, and perhaps rough words would be spoken there when the sheriff came.

Before breakfast was over at the Gast kitchen, Bertha saw her mother's glossy black closed carriage go by. Mrs. Kattmann had her son, Ludwig, drive her over town to get the lay of the land before the morning offensive began. She drove up one street and down another, past the freight office and the weigh lock. Her face was severe, and she was dressed simply in plain black, with almost the look of a nun's unaffected simplicity. Her expensive dress bonnet was replaced by a white kerchief, which was bound closely around her head like a turban. It gave her the appearance of a nurse or caretaker. Most of the townspeople saw that carriage and saw Augusta Kattmann's look of severe determination, and simple attire, as if she was ready for the ordeal.

Big Bertha's kitchen was a place of activity early in the morning as she prepared breakfast for her sons, and then took care of her tow horses in their stalls. She dallied at getting started on her day's work; then Elvira Brenner convinced her that she should "just tarry a spell" to see what the day would bring. The promise of activity at the weigh lock was soon fulfilled. It was as if a keystone was pulled from an arch, and the rest of the masonry soon fell down in noisy disarray.

Silvermann knew that he was cornered, so early in the morning he readily handed over the toll that he had refused to pay the night before, and he even agreed that the weigh bill was correct.

Mr. MacPherson still would not budge the lock, nor would he let the boat cradle down in the weigh lock so that the Silvermann barge could be waterborne again. Constable Bushman scratched his head, while wavering in his duty, for he was not sure that he could hold Silvermann now that he agreed to pay his toll.

Elihu Sanders tried to make Bushman see that he had to hold him now that he had sent to the county seat for the sheriff. He had attempted to cheat the state tolls; he had resisted arrest. When Silvermann heard about the sheriff, he panicked. He dodged every way he could to find a way out of that wretched town. He would do anything to get those dilatory hoggee boys on the move. He became rampant, yelling and threatening.

He swore at Big Bertha and shouted "Sow, Hog Eye," which was his undoing. She threatened to make him eat his words with her club. Then Silvermann drew his pistol. Bushman then stepped in to arrest him for disturbing the peace. Silvermann attempted to throw the lock gate to flood the weigh lock when Bertha caught him with a rock that knocked him to the deck. At that instant, his black low-crowned hat fell off, and Big Bertha saw a long, bald scar across the top of his head. Recognition came flooding back. She stepped closer with club upraised and saw that his hair near the scar was red, but the rest of his hair had been colored black. The heavy black beard was the camouflage, and she remembered the scars across her back from a long black whip. It was when she and members of her family were driven out of their village in Ukraine like swine to the slaughter. They were driven across the ice, down ice-covered rivers into Siberia, to the salt mines, but she had lived to come back. This was the black hearted demon. Now she knew him. This was not Gustav Silvermann; this was Gottlieb Lehman, the German mercenary of the Czar. She had inscribed his black name in her memory in order to remember with vengeance until her dying day, and she had inscribed the same name in the souls of her sons.

Big Bertha was livid with an insane rage. Without knowing what she was doing, Bertha rushed back to her barge for her iron crowbar. She then advanced on Silvermann for the kill. She called out to him by his real name; then shouted out his crimes to the bystanders. By this time, a throng of bystanders who had witnessed the commotion of the night before had gathered on the dock and the canal towpath. Mrs. Hemel had missed nothing and had gone for Grünwalda Peppleman. Elvira tried to tug at Big Bertha in order to hold her back, but a group of men succeeded where Elvira failed. Elvira's words sank home when she pleaded to Bertha to think of her own boys, and that if she wuz hanged for murder, her own boys would be orphans and fall into the same fate as those poor orphan hoggees of Silvermann's.

Jake Hemel moved in, along with Grünwalda, and reasoned with Bertha to let the law take over and do its duty. There would be time enough if that failed to "put on the dark robes and ride at night." Silvermann picked himself up, but turned on his hoggee boys who stood by transfixed with fright. Silvermann, in his frustration, took his wrath out on the boy nearest to him. He positioned his whip around the boy's back, and shouted for him to get the horses ready. They were pulling out. The very roof of the sky seemed to fall in with this. The tortured cries of the boy electrified Big Bertha who could not be contained. She broke free of the men and grappled Silvermann. He then pulled a knife. She gave him a severe clubbing, and hurled him into the canal as a cat would a mouse, and then jumped in after him. The bloody Silvermann, who was not as heavy as she, managed to swim away from her. He struggled out on the berm and ran down the towpath yelling like a banshee. A posse of men cornered him. Constable Bushman stood on the dock with his mouth open while watching the unexpected action.

A heavy ten pound grain broom caught the wavering Bushman in the seat of the pants, and as he was catapulted into the canal. Grünwalda Peppleman's deep bass voice boomed out,

"Acts. Do your duties! Ve pay your salaries for chust looking?"

Constable Bushman scrambled out of the canal with Grünwalda breathing fire down his neck. Then he slipped wrist irons on Silvermann. The posse helped Bushman drag the cringing Silvermann to the local log and brick jail where he was to await the sheriff.

Jake Hemel and Mr. MacPherson had Silvermann's barge let down out of the weigh lock cradle to free the weigh lock for the day's business. Mr. Bushman tied up the tow horses in the city livery barn. When it was secured at the dock in the basin and out of the way of traffic, Jake ran a huge chain through the bow ring and locked the barge to a piling on the dock. If worst had come to worst, he was ready back there at the weigh lock to heave in one of the planks below the waterline with one mighty blow of his ten-pound sledge from the forge. Silvermann's barge, even if tying up traffic, would be mudlarked on the bottom of the basin with its cargo ruined. The barge was searched but no other boys were found.

Augusta Kattmann sat back in her carriage from the noise of the throng at the dock that surrounded Silvermann's barge, but her owl-like eyes missed nothing. She had left her daughters and sister Fredericka at home, but with her instead was one of her trusted fellow nurses, Mrs. Steinhoge. Her square Hessian face would top the hard rock of the upper Rhine, but whose blue eyes were colder than the ice caves in the grottoes of the Bavarian Alps. Nodding to Mrs. Steinhoge, Frau Kattmann said with finality,

"Effective, Anna, *Ja*! However, those women were <u>diss-guss-ting</u>! <u>Ach</u>!" Mrs. Steinhoge nodded in agreement, and then waited for further orders.

Josie and Lou-Lou managed to sneak up the canal berm in time to see the end of all the fracas. They were more astonished when they saw their grandmother sitting there in her fine carriage watching the complete performance as if she had been in a royal box at the Dresden opera. When Elvira and Big Bertha attempted to give the little hoggee boys of Silvermann some breakfast, Frau Kattmann and her aide, Frau Steinhoge, marched in and took over. To the astonished, but somewhat shaken-up Constable Bushman, the two Prussian Drillmasters announced that they were taking the boys. They were to have a thorough physical inspection at the doctor's office; then all the findings would be recorded. First, she and Mrs. Steinhoge would see that the boys had a nourishing breakfast, and were thoroughly cleaned for the inspection. Afterwards, they would have proper rest and nursing to begin to halt the ravages of tuberculosis. It was feared that the boys might already be in an advanced stage through malnutrition. Constable Bushman stood speechless again at this outburst of the medicinal knowledge, and readily gave way to the two determined women.

Lou-Lou and Josie looked at one another in amazement. This must be a dream. That's it. They had gotten up too early and this was just not real. This couldn't be Grandma Kattmann. Why it didn't even look like her in that black and white garment. No, she must have been a mother superior from the wards of some convent convalescent home, but not Grandma Augusta Kattmann.

They did have to admit that it was a real carriage that the two bewildered and relieved boys were put into. They were frisked away before anyone really knew what happened.

Gerta Hemel jabbed Grünwalda Peppleman in the well padded ribs with her elbow, and grunted with amusement as they watched the carriage.

"Grünwalda Peppleman! It worked! She's right inside the carriage with the boys!" Mrs. Peppleman admitted that she was right, and her thundercloud face lighted into a smile of satisfaction as she patted Mrs. Hemel's back.

"She fell for it like der ton of bricks. Ve say dis for de old walrus, rub her de right vay, and I suppose she got heart." They both laughed at their good luck and joined Mrs. Gertslaecker as they walked down the towpath toward Mrs. Peppleman's pie shop.

Lou-Lou turned to Josie, and swatting herself on her backsides as she watched her grandmother's disappearing carriage, said weakly,

"Bern-hair-deen-ah! You chud paddle her more. Wal dog my cats. Come, we got to tell your mother, Josie."

CHAPTER 15

AFTER THE EXCITEMENT OF the morning had subsided a little, Lou-Lou and Josie wondered what they would do with the day. Lou, Charley and young Ben wanted to go back down to Minster if the Gast Grain company boat went again anytime soon. They had their heads set on a journey farther south. They wanted to go to Ft. Loramie. It would make a perfect day if they could get a rowboat out on the lake at Ft. Loramie, or the reservoir, as most people called it. They could swim, fish, and just have a general good time, that is if Bertha Gast would let them take a basket dinner with them. Josie and Lou-Lou heard of their half-formed plans and set up an immediate plan to go with them. The boys were not going to have their day spoiled with "girls" tagging along, but then Lou-Lou knew enough secret goods on her brother Ben, and her cousins, Charley and Lou, to blackmail them when the time came. She had no doubts but that she and Jo-Jo would be along on the lake trip.

Business at the basin and on the docks picked up as the early morning passed into mid-morning. Barge traffic became heavier as the day wore on. There was much activity on the loading docks as freight for Bremen was unloaded there. Some produce and other freight was stacked there from a local area barge to be reloaded on another barge that was making the long haul to Cincinnati and the river trade on south.

Big Bertha, after chatting with Elvira Brenner for a while in the private seclusion of her barge cabin kitchen, was ready for work again. She was a heroine of sort to the townspeople, as the story of her fearlessness spread from house to house and over back fences. Not once during the morning did the insulting, angering call of Hog Eye, taunt her from the distance as she busied herself with her heavy work. Elvira Brenner and Joel left for Minster to put the *Loon* in drydock in the boat yard. Big Bertha and her

143

boys stacked the cordwood at one place on the shipping docks, and the heavy lumber from the sawmill at another place. Horse drawn drays were soon busy transporting the lumber to the lumberman and to building contractors. The coal was brought up out of the hold and stored in wooden bins on the dock for another merchant. When the barge was unloaded, the horses were brought back to the towpath from their grazing along the berm to the south of the lock. It was early noon, so Bertha gave her boys an early lunch for they had all worked hard. As her barge left the basin and ascended the lock, many hands were raised to recognize her and say good-bye. She was no longer the "foreign Rooshins woman." Somewhat embarrassed by the unaccustomed attention, Big Bertha raised her gloved hand to return the salute, and even though she could not smile, she nodded her head. As the barge left the lock and headed for the straight open canal south to Minster, Bertha sat down on a keg, took the tiller, lighted a long-awaited cigar, and was alone at last with her many thoughts. The muffled hoof beats of her gray Percheron horses and occasional words of her boys broke the silence of the cool gray day.

In an hour, they had traveled the three-mile tow to Minister. After exchanging a few last words with Elvira Brenner, Big Bertha and her boys were on their way south to the sawmill powered by the water wheel on Loramie Creek, and those strange silent dark men who ran the mill and spoke that strange Slavic tongue.

In a half hour or more, they would be at their destination near Ft. Loramie. They would spend the afternoon loading another stack of lumber from the sawmill on the creek to the southwest.

Before long, they went under the bridge where the pike crossed the canal. It was about a mile above Ft. Loramie. In another quarter of a mile, they would pass over the stone aqueduct that carried the canal over Loramie Creek. Just a few rods from the aqueduct, the feeder canal from Loramie Reservoir emptied into the canal. This feeder supplied the water to keep the level of water high enough for barge keels for the trip south on to Tipp City and Dayton. Dams on the Miami River supplied the necessary intake of water for the southern end of the canal that traveled on through Hamilton and Cincinnati to the great basin at the wharfs on the Ohio River.

Big Bertha's horses slowed down for the stop out of habit, for here was the loading point near the junction of the feeder and the canal. The overflow from the reservoir, when not needed for the canal, could be diverted over the dam spillway at the southwest end of the reservoir. It would empty into Loramie creek in case the lake became flooded from an unusual wet winter and spring. The reservoir had been created by building a huge levee and dam across Loramie creek about a mile north of Ft. Loramie. Here was the high ground that divided the northern watershed to the St. Marys River, and

Lake Erie from the southern watershed into the valley of the Great Miami River called Loramie Summit. A line from the east ran through Ft. Loramie and on to Ft. Recovery at the Indiana line, where it dipped southwest to the Ohio River to form the "gore" in Indiana and the first land opened to white settlers in former Indian territory. This was the Greenville Treaty line of 1795. General Anthony Wayne had forced the Indians to cede land to the white settlers after the battle of Fallen Timbers. Statehood came soon for Ohio in 1805, but the "gore" in what was to become Indiana, was opened to white settlers from the south and east almost twenty years before the enabling act permitted the settlers to form the new Hoosier state of Indiana.

When the Gasts had explained all this to Elvira and Joel Brenner about the point at Ft. Recovery where the gore line for Indiana started, and how the string of forts all along the western side of Ohio made the winning of Indiana territory possible, Elvira could only push her bonnet to the back of her head and exclaim,

"Land-O-Goshen! And so this is whar it all happened!" Elvira wondered why all the dutchy Germanish people who built the canals and reservoirs stayed in the towns in Ohio, for she didn't know of many in her Hoosier state. Most folks she knew had roots from "Kaintucky, Tennessee, and Virginny." They spoke like them too. There were no unpronounceable German names that she knew much about in Indianny, and "no heathen vittles sech as blood puddin', kraut what's rotted, or noodles cooked in beer."

After securing her barge to wooden posts on the berm opposite the towpath, Big Bertha and her boys began hauling the lumber onto the barge and stacking it. When the remainder of the stack was loaded aboard the barge, Bertha hitched one of the fresh tow horses from her stall aboard the barge to a flat sled on wide runners. They called it a "mud boat." Then Bertha started back the trail into the woods along the feeder canal and to the sawmill on Loramie Creek. Then they would load cordwood for customers in towns along the way. For heavier beams and timbers for barn sills, Bertha would pry them up, slip a chain around them and by means of a sort of windlass winch, and lift them up to the axles of huge logging wheels, which her Percheron horses could pull with ease to the barge. Passing farmers marveled at the Big Buffalo Woman, and how she could use those crank winches to haul the heavy twenty foot beams onto the deck of her barge as if they were split rails. Moreover, how could those huge Slav woodsmen fell huge oak and tulip poplars with flashing wide axes?

Elvira Brenner and her girls sat up in their barge in the drydock with the chores of everyday living. It was all Elvira could do to keep her mind on her work after the "to-do" of the day and night before. The green beans seemed to snip faster as she kept up a light chatter about the "goings on" up in

Bremen, wondering if the sheriff had come yet, and if she and Berthy would be questioned. After several spoonfuls of green beans had been snipped and strung, the girls set up a "ruckus" by wishing that there was some early sweet corn to go with the green beans, but Elvira did not hear them. She was thinking of the faces of those two abused orphan drivers ("hoggee boys"). Their faces seemed to light up when they knew that they were away from Silvermann. Nevertheless, they were fearful of the future, for they knew the bitter disappointment of being returned to the orphanage, or worse, to the workhouse. The boys knew that they could be bound out again, perhaps to the same heartless master. Even at their young age, they knew better than to trust luck and have hope when there was no cause for hope. Their childhood had been robbed from them and the years had made them cynical with bitterness. They hoped for a better life, but expected nothing but hard knocks.

Frau Augusta Kattmann did not know exactly what she did plan on doing with the mistreated boys, but she had made her stand and, disciplined soldier that she was, she would see it through with complete organization of every detail.

Bertha Gast, the only daughter of Mrs. Kattmann who could talk bluntly to her with a few terse words, went directly to her mother's town house upon learning that she had taken the boys from Constable Bushman. She was grateful that the poor frightened little tikes would not be frightened more by being taken to the jail for custody until the sheriff came. Bertha Gast knew her mother's direct, tactless manner, even when she meant well, and Mrs. Steinhoge was just as direct and militaristic.

Bertha said directly to her mother without hesitation,

"Mother, Mein Mama, these boys are only young children. You must be very gentle and understanding with them. It has been a long while since you reared all of us. These children fear everyone." Mrs. Kattmann, busy with her preparations for cleanliness and inspection, looked up for a moment to her daughter.

"Ja! Dot is so. But why to tell me this, Bair-thah?"

Bertha explained that she needed to gain the boys' confidence first before frightening them with strict, intense questioning about their missing hoggee companions. Perhaps the best way was by fixing them a warm home cooked food. Bertha stayed to help Ernestine and Bernhardina prepare food for them. She cautioned the others that too much fussiness and bother would make the boys uncomfortable. They needed common nourishing foods, with everyday plates and a common kitchen table. They should not use white linen and fine china now. Let them sit at the wooden table. Since Bertha was a devoted mother, and knew the way of children, the boys trusted her more. They would answer her before they would talk to the strange women with the "dutchy" words and "funny accents." Frau Kattmann was amazed at Bertha's success and, for once, there were no disagreements or loud arguments in front of the boys.

When they had been fed a good breakfasts of ham, eggs, and cooked cereals with plenty of milk, the two boys ventured to smile in a half-afraid piteous way. Bertha knew how to place her hands on their arms or pat them gently while the other women felt awkward at their attempts.

When Bertha knelt beside them while helping her mother wash their grimy feet and legs, then their neck and ears, she told them that they could jump into the huge wooden tubs and bathe themselves. She gave them towels for drying that they were afraid to use, for they were so white and soft. Bertha went to her home and got outgrown clothes from her own boys for the two small hoggees. Frau Kattmann announced to Ernestine and Bernhardina that they would need to get the townswomen in and do some sewing. The Needle Guild at the church - that was it! It would do them good. It would give them a chance to do some "missionary work" right here at home, and where on earth was it more sorely needed? Bertha had to bite her lip to keep from smiling because this, coming from her mother, was amusing, especially when many people had said this very thing to Frau Kattmann but with little avail. Now it had hit home. Grünwalda Peppleman was correct in her planning to bait Frau Kattmann; she had a wise head on that huge body.

After the boys were bathed and while dressing them, Frau Kattmann, Mrs. Steinhoge, and Bertha made detailed notice of the scars, welts, and bruises on their frail bodies. Mrs. Kattmann said but little, but her determined jaw with lips turned down let the others know that she was boiling with determined rage inside at the cruel injustice she was uncovering. She and Mrs. Anna Steinhoge doctored the wounds, and bandaged where they could with torn bed sheeting to keep the clean clothing out of the wounds. Mrs. Kattmann made detailed written notes of all that they had observed. Then Mrs. Anna Steinhoge went to bring the village doctor. He had to explain to waiting patients, but Mrs. Steinhoge was firm and unyielding. He had to come on the run. There had to be a doctor's signature to the abuses, along with the nurse's, so that it would stand up in a court hearing. Frau Kattmann was determined not to go far away to get blood. It was time to convert the heathen right here at home: in the state legislature, the county courts, and to do something about hospitals, orphanages, old people's homes, welfare caseworkers for the trustee, and mental cases.

The boys were frightened with the doctor's appearance for they had been examined before at the orphanages. Those doctors told the boys that they were lazy when they complained of being sick or mistreated.

After all the examination was over, Bertha took the boys along with her for a drive while Mrs. Kattmann and Mrs. Steinhoge were busy in consultation with the doctor. Surely the sheriff would come in the afternoon. Once alone with them and out of hearing of others, Bertha assured them that their days with Silvermann were over, and that he could not get his hands on them again, and that they could trust her. They would be making their homes here in Bremen for the time being, and when the boys looked up at her with fearful expectation of the future, she raced on to assure them that all the good people of the community would help find them good homes with good people who would be like a father and mother to them.

After a while, Bertha felt she had their confidence, so she questioned them about the other missing hoggees. Her blood went cold with fear when they blurted out what little they knew about them, but told her that Silvermann had taken them away with another man in a buggy, for they were "terrible sick." When Bertha tried to find out how sick, they told her that the boys were beyond knowing with fever, and that they were unconscious. They could only tell Bertha that it was along the towpath some time at night when the boys were taken off, and to their counting, it had been the night before last. However, they did not know where the boys were taken. They only heard it said that the sick boys would be taken to a place to be taken care of. Bertha tried not to show her consternation in front of the boys. She knew that the sheriff must be told this, and soon. These boys could have been thrown out in some woods to die, as Elvira Brenner warned.

When the two little boys began nodding with sleep, Bertha took them back to her mother's town house and put them to bed for a nap even though it was not yet noon. They had gone without sleep for so many nights, and then when they did manage to get a few hours to curl up in the hay for sleep, it was always broken by some interruption. Constant fear robbed them of whatever peaceful sleep they might have gotten otherwise, but now they floated off to sleep in the great feather bed in the darkened room.

Wasting no time after telling her mother and Mrs. Steinhoge, along with the doctor, what the little boys had told her about the other missing hoggee boys, Bertha Gast went immediately to her husband at the grain depot on the dock and told him what she had learned.

Sheriff's deputies arrived in New Bremen by mid-morning to start the investigation into the charges. The sheriff himself would come in the afternoon. Ben and Hermann Gast sent an official company letter down the canal on the through mail on the freight barge to alert canal company officials to the trouble in New Bremen. They wanted the company officials to put out search parties in their vicinities to see if there was information of possible stray hoggee boys, news of any very ill ones, or news of recent deaths.

When the doctor and the two women nurses presented the sheriff with their evidence that afternoon, he immediately put the sullen Silvermann to severe questioning with threats of dire consequences. In spite of his bruised condition from Big Bertha's clubbing, he still was arrogant in his manner, and refused to talk.

The sheriff authorized his deputies to form a posse in New Bremen and Minster for the purpose of searching the countryside, especially in the wooded areas along the canal right of way and on down below Newport to Lockington. The news soon spread from town to town along the canal as barges spread the word up and down the canal on their hourly runs. Barge captains hated the sight of his driving those poor frail boys night and day and his mistreatment of them. There was little that these travelers on the canal did not know about their fellow travelers and barge people. The hoggees had a grapevine of news and scandal that they passed along upon meeting others, or during idle minutes when they grouped at the locks between loads. The suspicion surrounding the missing hoggee boys of Silvermann's came as no surprise to these other captains who liked to think of themselves as respectable, and who did an honest days work without child abuse to make their honest dollar.

However, the story that made canal folks up and down the canal sit back and take notice was the tale of Big Bertha beating up Silvermann, throwing him in the canal, and jumping in to throttle him when he whipped one of the boys. Of course the tale became somewhat exaggerated as it was repeated that morning on the waterway, but all captains now had respect for the "Water Buffalo," who had done to Silvermann what someone should have done many years before. Yes, they would raise their caps in salute to Big Bertha, the big "Rooshin" or "Bulgar," whichever she was.

Lou-Lou confided to Josie that things were much quieter at her house since Grandma-Má Kattmann had seemed to retire Bernhardina and Ernestine from her immediate household, and had taken Mrs. Steinhoge and the doctor into her confidence. Then in this time of stress, she had relied upon Bertha Gast rather than her other two emotional daughters. Bertha knew what to do in times of stress and trouble, and crying out in hysteria was not on her list of actions.

Charley, Lou, and young Ben had their Saturday work nearly done at the freight house and the depot, so they had some time to play horseshoe and throw some ball in the grassy lot along the canal berm. They started making plans for the outing to Lake Loramie on Sunday, but wondered if they had much chance for success because of the commotion at the dock. They knew their fathers would never let them go out on the reservoir unless some of the elders were along, and it did not look as if either August Ben or Hermann would be free now that she sheriff's posse was being formed. They knew that they were too young to be included but it would be exciting to go along.

Big Bertha led her gray horse that was hitched to mud sleds, down the trail through the woods, and along the feeder canal where it left the main canal. There was a gentle curve through the trees as the trail led away from the feeder to the sawmill and between the feeder and Loramie creek. An earthen levee formed a millpond for impounding water for the waterwheel that powered the vertical saws of the mill. The dam across the creek diverted water into a millrace, which carried the water into the millpond. From there it raced down a flume over the water wheel to set the machinery in motion for the sawmill. Log huts were set apart from the mill in the clearing.

Bertha was leading one gray Percheon while her son was leading the second one. All of a sudden, the horse shied from something at the side of the woods trail that frightened it. The horse stopped, then arched its neck and gave several short snorts. Bertha knew something was wrong. She stroked the horse gently to soothe it; then called her sons behind her to come and hold her horse. She moved cautiously to the side of the trail, parted the bushes and branches, and raised her ironwood club high to be ready for whatever "varmint" might be in the bushes.

Big Bertha gave a short guttural grunt and an oath, in her Slavic tongue, which brought her son to her side with a bound. They both looked at the ground and the matted grass and wood plants. Lying face down at the edge of the trail was a small boy in rags. From the looks of the undergrowth, he had crawled there sometime during the morning hours or perhaps during the night. Once she was over her first alarm, Bertha knelt to examine the body that she feared was dead. To her surprise, his small body was still warm and there was a slight pulse. Immediately she marked the spot with a stick forced into the soft black ground; then Bertha took up the small half dead body and hurried back the trail with him to her barge. She sent her second son back to help with the horses and to return them to the barge. Then Bertha told her older son to go on to the sawmill and tell the men there.

The men at the sawmill knew something of the fracas of the morning, because some of the lumbermen who were felling the trees for the sawmill had been at the tavern in New Bremen. Some were on their way to work in the woods when they heard about it in Minster from Ivan, the so-called "Mad Russian" (Johnny Ivan). By noon, word of the sheriff's posse had passed up and down the canal by passing barge captains, and from line boats whose women folk exchanged news and gossip when they overtook or passed each other on the canal.

Big Bertha put the dying boy on a cot in her kitchen cabin, and kept him out of the cool drafts. She then covered him with warm coverlets to get his body temperature back to normal. She bathed his arms and face with hot water to try to get his circulation back. After a while she thought that his heartbeat was stronger.

When the men came from the sawmill, Bertha told them that she suspected that this was one of the missing hoggee driver boys, for her own son thought that the dying boy looked very much like one of Silvermann's hoggee drivers. The men cursed Slavic oaths as Big Bertha told them about the sheriff's posse, which was being formed before she left New Bremen near noon. She told them in rapid Slav uttering that there were two missing boys, and that they should follow the trail from the stake she had driven down and fan out to search for him. She felt that they should try to follow the trail the boy had made as he crawled from somewhere in the woods to the lumber trail where she found him. They could use the dogs to "scent out" the trail he left. However, she knew her duty was to get the boy to a doctor at Ft. Loramie in Minster and to report to the authorities, and she hurried up the canal to Minster.

CHAPTER 16

WORK AT THE SAWMILL stopped, but it was Saturday afternoon anyway, and work usually ended early in the afternoon at the end of the week. Farmers in the vicinity took up the search along with the sawmill hands. Uriah Hornback, with his slow plodding oxen team hitched to his barge of split rails, clapboards, and split roof shakes, usually held up traffic along the canal. It was difficult to pass him for he did not handle his towlines very well. The slow oxen were difficult to move out of the way of the horses. Even barefoot Uriah tied up his barge-raft, and left his wife, Sheba, to watch the rails and barge, and help the kids, Orville and Mahaley, tie up the oxen.

The repair barge from New Bremen came foaming along at top speed, spread the news along the canal, and picked up posse members. The posse was to pick up accomplices of Silvermann. The word now spread that the other members of the heartless group were a gang of interstate kidnappers. They sold children that they managed to get from orphanages or lost children off immigrant ships. Others were from other sources of welfare where the children were neither wanted nor missed. Big Bertha met the repair barge just at the edge of Minster and flagged them down. She told the sheriff deputy that she had found a half-dead boy who might well be one of the missing hoggee drivers. The deputy urged Bertha on to a doctor in Minster after coming aboard to see the boy on the cot in her kitchen cabin.

Bertha urged one of the men to come along with her to take the tiller of her barge into town so that she could be free to look after the boy. She told the deputy that the sawmill men and some of the local farmers were searching the area where the boy was found, and that they could show him the stake she had put in the ground to mark the spot where she found the boy by the trail.

When Elvira and Joel Brenner saw Big Bertha's barge coming into Minster from the south with only a half load, and a strange man at the tiller, they knew something was wrong. When Elvira did not see Bertha on the top deck at the tiller, she began to wonder if there had been an accident and that Bertha was hurt.

"It would be no wonder if she were hurt. Why that woman was tugging them heavy logs and barn sills around like she was a circus elephant."

When Bertha's barge passed the drydock in the boatyards and came abreast of the *Wabash Loon* which was up in the dock, Bertha came on deck and halted her horses so that she could call up to Elvira. Motioning for her to come on board, Bertha put the barge into the berm and put across her gangplank for Elvira. Elvira scrambled up out of the little rocker she had on deck where she had plopped down to set a spell. She tied her bonnet strings beneath her chin, skittered like a squirrel, got off the *Loon* via the ladder of the drydock, and skipped onto the deck of the lumber barge. Bertha met her at the gunwale, and took her by the arm, looked down into her face, and blurted out,

"Little Missus! Turrible thing. Can you help?"

"Berthy! You look pale. Course I can help. What on airth?"

Bertha took her below and into the cabin and pointed to the delirious boy, but would not let Elvira go closer. She warned Elvira that he might have a raging fever, or a bad case of something, and there was no use for her to carry it back to her family. Bertha reasoned that she had never been sick and that nothing would ever touch her, for she had survived death several times by escaping from the salt mines of Siberia and seemed to thrive on it. Elvira could only open her mouth in amazement. This was all too much, but Big Bertha needed Elvira to be her mouthpiece to help find the doctor and ask him what they should do. If only - if only they were in Bremen - and had Mrs. Pepples, the pie woman - and above all, if only they had the advice and expert nurse care of that Kattmann nurse-doctor. They would know what to do, but that was another hour away, and the boy might not live that long.

From his breathing, Elvira bet her life that the poor boy had "new-moan-ey" from being exposed out in the chilly night air. He could already be sick from the cold weather, or perhaps he was faint from being overworked and underfed. Pneumonia? The very word spread a chill over Bertha, who usually allowed nothing to dismay her. But that word? Didn't it usually mean death? What if it were smallpox, or one of the other fatal plagues? What had she done? She thought of her own boys, and of Elvira's family. However, Bertha straightened her shoulders for strength and told Elvira that something had to be done, someone had to do it, and there was not much time.

"Ve do in this wor-reld, vot we must. Ve doan hav choice," Bertha said with determination. Elvira nodded rapidly.

"Law, yes. Now Berthy, you watch over him. I'll tell Joel. Land a sakes, the youngin's and all of us can surely find a doctor."

Just as Elvira was about to run up on deck to go back to her own barge, the delirious boy started to moan. Bertha moistened his parched feverish lips with warm water, and replaced the blanket he was fighting in his feverish deliria. Elvira listened carefully and motioned for Bertha to listen also. The boy's whispered complaint finally made sense to them. They tried to soothe him and ask him over again what he was saying. They finally made out that he was trying to get help by motioning with his hand to the side and moaning: "my brother. . . Robbie. . . dying, help him. . . back in swamp." They tried to ask him where but he kept repeating the same thing, and motioning with his hand. Bertha knew in a flash that he meant that his brother was back there from where he had crawled, and he was trying to get aid for him when he collapsed. Big Bertha, in spite of her great size and weight, fairly sprang up the stairs to the deputy aid at her rudder tiller, and told him. Elvira followed her up on the deck in time to hear Bertha tell the man that her "oldest boy" could take the horses and go back to find the deputy and the posse and tell them. Maybe they could find the boy before it was too late. Elvira was puzzled, and she said in disbelief,

"Satan's drawers! There *is* another youngin'. Then it's all true." Bertha had left the deck and was preparing to send her oldest boy on the errand of mercy into the swamp trail. Elvira came to her senses, ran after her, and tugged at her arm.

"Now Berthy, we ain't sendin your youngins by themselves on such a mission as this. Them horses is tired, and this ain't nuthin' for a boy to be doin'. Our horses are Morgan stock from southern Indianny and they kin run. They're rested too. Let that young man, that deputy feller there, take our horse and gallop back there to ketch up with that repair boat and the posse." Bertha nodded and said that this made better sense. Then Elvira said,

"What with meanin' no disrespect ner bad apples about yer own horses Berthy, but them smaller black Morgans and Tennessee walkers kin outrun them big hoofed Percherons any day, and every minute counts."

In a few minutes, Elvira Brenner had told Joel about all the excitement on Bertha's barge. The deputy first galloped by the constable's office to tell him what Bertha had discovered. Joel Brenner and the deputy galloped down the towpath toward the feeder canal and the woods trail. The constable and his aide soon hitched up to a light two-wheeled cart, and left a dust trail behind them as they raced down the pike toward Ft. Loramie. They were going to the bridge over the canal that was near where the woods trail started on its way back to the Russians' sawmill.

The canal was the "main street" through Ft. Loramie, with houses, shops, and even mills lining the wide canal on both sides. There were brick streets on either side of the canal. The towpath went through the small town to the wide water basin and turn-around south of the village. Then it descended south to Newport. By this time, the men were on the brick walk outside of the constable's home in Minster. They were running to find the village doctor. When he arrived and examined the boy, he concurred with Elvira and Bertha that he thought he was dying from pneumonia, over exposure, and the effects of being beaten.

There would have to be a place found to take care of him that was near the doctor. Elvira wailed aloud that if only they were in New Bremen where that Kattmann woman nurse was. The doctor inquired if she knew Frau Kattmann, and Elvira and Bertha both nodded that they did, and that Mrs. Kattmann had taken the other two boys from the dock to feed and nurse them. The doctor pursed his lips in deep thought. Then he added that there was no one in Minster who could compare to Frau Kattmann when it came to sickness. All he had was his office in his home, and that his wife was too old and sickly to take on a full nursing responsibility. The doctor ordered all the young boys and girls away from the barge for this could well be a case of the dreaded smallpox, along with the pneumonia. He wanted Elvira and Bertha to keep to their barges and not go out in the streets. He was mulling something over in his mind. He too voiced his lament that if only Frau Kattmann and Mrs. Steinhoge were here. He remarked that he had seen them nurse cases back to health when doctors had given up. Mrs. Kattmann was a doctor in her own rights, and used home remedies, German medical knowledge, and even Indian herbs in her doctoring. She would have none of that foolish "bleeding" that some doctors had used in the first part of the century in order to let out bad blood. She reasoned that the body needed all its blood. Elvira said outright,

"But Mrs. Kattmann is up there. We air down here, Doctor."

Bertha added uneasily as she eyed the suffering boy.

"We need do something here and now, Mr. Doctor. You say - we do!"

Then the doctor made the wild proposal. He would stay with the boy, and bring his medical bag and supplies with him. He would be just as well off there as in his own office - perhaps better. If they could maneuver the barge up to New Bremen, he would go along and stay right with the boy. The barge would ride so much more easily than a carriage on the bumpy pike. The patient could not stand the jolting and the dust of the pike. Bertha shook her head in agreement, and Elvira told her children that they should stay put on the *Loon* until she got back. Indeed, she was going on to New Bremen and her kids knew how to take care of themselves.

Just as they were about to get under way, the *Blue Swan* barge of Gast's brewery tied up ahead of them to deliver some kegs of <u>The Blue Swan Ale and Beer</u> on the dock for the local taverns. Elvira's thoughts raced ahead of her, but in a moment she told Ludwig Kattmann and Hermann Gast what had happened, and that they needed to take the boy back for Mrs. Kattmann's expert care. Compared to Big Bertha's lumber and coal barge, the brewery's *Blue Swan* barge was a luxury yacht with a paneled cabin interior. Also, its cabin was much larger. Even though Bertha was willing to make the trip, Elvira persuaded her to let the *Blue Swan* make the trip and save her horses because the Gasts had fresh horses on board for the return trip. Ben Gast was with the posse down stream. They were now fanning the woods and underbrush to find the boy before dark. In no time, Hermann Gast and his brother-in-law, Ludwig Kattmann, had stacked the barrels on the dock. Charley and Lou brought the fresh horses from their stall and hitched them to the tow span while young Ben led the tired horses back on board, across the gangplank to their stalls and to hay and oats. Charley dipped into the canal with wooden buckets and brought water up to the horses. They nickered their content and made "slobbering" snorts as they nuzzled into the water buckets. The horses sprayed Charley as they did so.

The old doctor called to some men on the dock to help Hermann and Ludwig manage the well-covered cot. The sick boy from Bertha's barge was carried into the *Blue Swan's* clean cabin below the deck. Big Bertha jumped to the task before the men could help, for lifting heavy loads was no new thing to her.

Gasts kept their light *Blue Swan* moving rapidly up the placid green flecked canal, even though there was a fine for speeding much beyond five miles an hour. Backwash and ripples from speeding barges caused erosion and washing to the banks of the canal, so even passenger packets were warned of the speed limit. Many captains, in order to make time, raced on anyway and paid their fines when caught. The captains thought they had the better end of the bargain. The light *Blue Swan* rode high in the water with its load of ale kegs now stacked on the deck. The fresh white horses trotted along as they clipped off close to ten miles an hour. In no time the barge was in Bremen, but it seemed like hours to Elvira Brenner, who had to be content with assisting Big Bertha and the Doctor from a distance. No one was permitted near the feverish boy since his affliction was feared to be some dreaded fatal disease. The terrible cholera plague of ten years before, in the 1840's and 1850's, was not forgotten along the canal. Hundreds of Irish workers, as well as civilians along the way died of the dreaded plague, which came down the Great Lakes and on down the Ohio River. Then the plague found its way down the canals that opened into them.

The Gast men hurried to Mrs. Kattmann's town house as soon as the *Swan* was docked, and gave the electrifying news to Augusta Kattmann and Mrs. Steinhoge. When the carriage came to the dock, Mrs. Kattmann descended rapidly and went aboard the barge to the doctor and the sick boy.

By his breathing and the sound of his chest, Augusta Kattmann satisfied herself that the affliction was truly pneumonia and that the time was short. There could be no risk of over-exposure in transferring him to the carriage with his feverish state. While the doctor and Mrs. Kattmann made the patient ready for transfer, Big Bertha, who was not used to delays in times of emergencies, wrapped the blanket around the boy, took him in her strong arms, and carried him horizontally as one would a baby. Then she cried,

"Mr. Doctor! Ve Go! Words later!"

Elvira scrambled along in front of her to help at the steps up to the dock, but Bertha bounded up with the lithe grace of a panther in spite of her great size. Bertha held the boy in the carriage without a word, and Mrs. Kattmann marveled at the strong, strange woman's ability to keep silent while Elvira's tongue rattled on incessantly as she called out to everyone along the way.

Once in the confines of Mrs. Kattmann's house, the shades were drawn, shutters closed, and the curious onlookers were kept beyond the closed paling gate. Many people gathered in the street when the news was first spread that Gast's barge had brought the dead boy to town. Then word spread that no one was permitted near the house for fear of a reoccurrence of the dread cholera plague of ten years earlier. Next, word spread that the boy was already dead. Dark rumors grew in the huddles of men in the tavern, or in a corner of the alley under the umbrella of an overhanging plum tree. The late afternoon shade was more concealing there. Word reached Constable Bushman by way of Jake Hemel that black talk was spreading about taking that criminal Silvermann, or Lehmann, out of the town's small feeble jail at the end of a rope. The sheriff put the question to Bushman and to the Gast brothers: "What proof did anyone have that this last boy they brought in was a hoggee driver, or that he was Silvermann's, and that Silvermann had caused his death?"

These questions reached Augusta Kattmann's ever-sensitive ears, which missed but little and she pondered the questions in her mind. There would be no problem. It was very orderly and clear-cut to her. She would merely have the two hoggee boys identify this new boy in her care. Certainly, that was it! They should be awakened anyhow, and rushed over to Bertha Gast's in case there was some disease. In their low state of health, they would be susceptible to any illness that came along.

Mrs. Kattmann had it all planned. Sister Fredericka and Ernestine could help Bertha for the time being, but in the long run Augusta Kattmann reasoned that the boys would recover better away from the curious stares of well-meaning townspeople. Yes, <u>Willow Haven</u>, her country estate with its vast orchards, vineyards, and farmlands near Maria Stein would be the ideal place for a couple of boys to grow back to health.

Anna Steinhoge and the doctor advised against having the sickly hoggee boys in the same room with the new arrival for a very long time, and Mrs. Kattmann readily agreed. However, she knew that much depended upon having an accurate identification of the dying boy as soon as possible. Only these two boys could identify him because Silvermann would dangle from a noose before he would ever confess knowing or having even seen the frail boy discarded in the swamp.

When the two little boys were brought into the room, and held up over the bed to see the other unconscious boy, they both cried. They were afraid to talk until Bertha Gast knelt with them in her arms and assured them that their wicked barge captain had been arrested, and that he could never touch them again. It was then that they told her that the sick boy was Will - little Willie Fleener, and that he had a brother, Robbie, who had been taken away from the barge when they both got sick.

Augusta Kattmann walked the floor in unspoken raging anger. She exchanged words in German to Anna Steinhoge, whose piercing ice-blue eyes betrayed her inner rage and hatred toward Silvermann, and men like him, as well as toward a lax society that permitted such things.

CHAPTER 17

WHEN THE *BLUE SWAN* brewery barge delivered Big Bertha and Elvira Brenner
to the boatyards in Minster, the afternoon was growing into evening. The
reluctant sun shone but little between periods of cloudiness and the days remained cool and damp, unusually so for late in June. Upon inquiry from the
Brenner children, and from Bertha's two boys who stood watch on the lumber barge, the women learned that there was no news concerning the other
missing boy. The different parties of searchers had found nothing and still
they traced back and forth through the dense woods along Loramie Creek
and the feeder canal surrounding the clearing at the Russian sawmill. The
deputized posse had reported nothing from the swampy bottoms along Mile
Creek to the west.

Big Bertha was strangely dejected. She hardly answered Elvira when
they parted. Bertha and her boys turned their lumber barge around in the
boatyard basin and headed back down to the feeder canal to the trail to the
sawmill, pausing to let the horses rest in Ft. Loramie. She could tie up in the
feeder canal so that she would be out of the traffic on the main canal after she
left Newport.

Bertha talked to the Slavic men at the sawmill who had reported back
to the grizzled black bearded Gregori, foreman of the Russian sawmill; then
she went back to the trail to the stake she had driven down in the black
earth and stood there pondering. There must be a clue here. There must be
something they were all overlooking. Her own boys stood silently beside her
and watched her every move. Some of the Russian men from the sawmill
clearing and the log huts where they lived, joined Bertha after a while, and
they all exchanged short, terse Slavic comments. Every one of them knew the
silent presence of death. They had lived in its chill presence, and they knew
the meaning of a solitary trail of escape through dense forest. They also knew

how one false move could have betrayed them. They would be put back under the granite-tipped knot of the whip master at the Siberian out post. For the exiles, it was a slow death in the gripping and merciless cold.

Elvira could not stand the suspense of not knowing. She put her oldest daughter, Mirandy, in charge of the younger children and prepared an early supper for them. Then taking one of the horses, she tucked up her wide gingham skirts and rode sidesaddle down the towpath to the sawmill trail. Surely somebody somewhere would know something. Joel Brenner could not dissuade her.

When she spotted the lumber barge tied up along the trail in the feeder canal, Elvira knew that Bertha must be nearby. Elvira tied her horse to a sapling along the berm near the lumber barge. Then she picked up a stick at her feet and started down the lumber trail in search of Big Bertha. The strange hump-backed hound on Bertha's barge beat his tail a couple of times in recognition. Then he lay back down on the top deck while holding his head high with ears pricked. Elvira, thinking that she heard voices in the dense woods along the trail ahead, called out,

"Berthy! Berthy, air you up there?"

A deep voice called back to Elvira, who then knew that it was Bertha up there with some men, because Bertha called back "Little Missus." As she came nearer, Elvira rounded a clump of underbrush that protruded over the path. She saw Bertha and called out to her again,

"Berthy! I can't stand sittin' back there doin' nuthin' when maybe there's something come up that I can do."

The dark bearded huge Russian men looked strangely at Bertha when Elvira called her that, then back to Elvira. Elvira noticed that when they spoke to her they called her something in that foreign tongue like "Katyna" or "Ekaterin-ya." When Elvira called her "Berthy" again, one of the smaller men had a trace of a smile around his mouth. No one had ever dared call her Bertha to her face for "Big Barge Bertha" had been a nickname along the canal - the same as "Buffalo Woman" or "Hog Eye." However, Elvira did not know any different for "Berthy" was all she had ever heard. Big Bertha gave the men a nod of her head and uttered something in her own language to them for them to keep silent, and Elvira went right on calling her "Berthy."

Almost as if there were no others present, Bertha walked up and down the trail in deep thought as if she were walking in some sort of a compelling trance. Where would be the logical place to look that the dozens of men had not searched this past afternoon? Elvira fell into pace with Bertha and the two women began to think aloud. Soon, another younger and more handsome Russian man came up the trail and was greeted by the others. Elvira remembered having seen him dance those wild dances of the Russian

Steppes, those wild Cossack songs, as he whirled and leaped with that strange looking square stringed instrument. Yes, she recognized him as "Johnny Russ," as the men called him on the docks. Bertha called him "Ivan," and Elvira tried to imitate her, but ended up not with the "ee-von" but more like "ev-vun." It would continue to be for her, Johnny for the Russian Ivan, yes, Johnny Evan, the "Mad Rooshian" who danced like a wild mad dervish. He leaped, yelled, and drowned his Tartar melancholy in streams of vodka, and yelled "Hai."

Having known suffering herself, Bertha was sensitive to it in others. She felt so guilty and so helpless. Elvira tried to think with her. Bertha said aloud that the lost boy perhaps, if not dead, might lie dying from neglect and abuse. He might be waiting for someone to find him, and hoping that his brother had made it to safety. Bertha said that here they were within a stone's throw if they only knew where to look. Bertha satisfied herself that not one of the searchers had followed the crawling boy's trail to the lumber trail, and that they had lost it somewhere down in the woods. Her black eyes studied the matted undergrowth in the fading light, and she started slowly to follow the faint trail that the crawling boy had left.

Seeing her crouching along as if she were picking up a scent caused Elvira to exclaim,

"Berthy, that's it! A hound could foller this trail!" Bertha straightened up, came back to the lumber trail and said something in quick excitement to the Russian men. Then Bertha's face fell when she said aloud that a piece of clothing with the scent would have to be used first to condition the hound before he could pick up the trace. Then Elvira remembered some of the rags they had taken off the boy when they washed him on the barge. Immediately both women went back to the barge, and they were followed by the Russian men. One of the men put that strange hump-backed hound on a leash. Another Russian went to the log huts and brought another large hound that might have been a bloodhound. However, Elvira wasn't sure for she had never seen such strange dogs before. For that matter, she had never seen such strange people before either.

Bertha went in front a few yards, her eyes finding every disturbed twig, every broken stick and bent woodland growth. To her satisfaction, she saw that the dogs were following exactly the trail in the soft earth that she found. She stepped aside when she was sure the hounds had the trail scent. Once she thought that they had missed it, and she had them brought back to re-run the trail a second time. The dogs followed the same trail again, so the party went on following them. There were no words now; the hounds did not leap on the leash but walked very precisely, stopping to sniff now and then, and when sure, walked on a few paces further. There were no deep bellowing bays from either hound but only detached concentration.

Elvira decided against further penetration of the woods. The growing shadows made her shudder and she decided to go back to Bertha's barge with the two black-eyed boys. They did not speak with her but kept up short, low-voiced conversation between themselves. After a while, they fell to playing a strange sort of game to amuse themselves. They tossed a knife into the air a certain way and observed how it fell. They made great sport of each other as they knelt down and inspected the angle of the knife's penetration of the black ground. When one of the boys made an apparent error or lost, the other said some special words and gave the other one a few blows with the back of his hand across the other's forehead. It was great sport to them by their facial expressions, but they never laughed aloud.

As the evening shadows deepened, the cloudy day seemed to grow chillier. However, the western sky was almost clear and the setting sun made an orange-red halo as it settled in the northwest on this day near the summer solstice - the longest day of the year.

Elvira built a little fire in the cook range in Bertha's cabin kitchen, and then when it grew dark, she called the boys in. She knew her horse was safe while it was tied there beside the barge. She lit the bow and stern lanterns just in case a boat might come down the feeder from the canal and crash into them in the dark. She settled down with a light blanket shawl around her shoulders on the bench on the deck where she could hear and see anything that went on in the night when darkness came. She tried to make conversation with the boys but their answers were short with usually a "yes" or "no." Elvira entertained herself with thinking of what all she had stumbled onto in these past two days. "Law, no one in Indianny would believe she had been on sech neighborly terms with so many furriners, et sech vittles, and heard sech strange, funny talkin'!"

She could hear hoof beats of teams and single horses on the pike out beside the main canal. It seemed that she heard a barge horn every twenty minutes; traffic passed every so often. It seemed that the canal was alive with traffic, which was unusual at night. She could begin to see the flecks of lantern lights from time to time through the trees in the distance, and she knew the searching parties had not given up.

Elvira was startled when one of the Russian men came back on board and spoke to the boys. He asked for an oil lantern, and one of the boys gave him one. After lighting it, he disappeared in the gathering darkness of the woods, and Elvira started humming some old church hymns to herself to keep up her hope and courage. Insects of the night began their night mournful moaning.

Elvira tied her bonnet strings tighter and drew the shawl around her shoulders with determination.

Yet, she reasoned that there was little use in letting herself get all upset and skittery. One had to have hope, and she reasoned that there was more hope and trust in these new Russian friends than she had seen anywhere else. Who else knew these deep woods better than the Russian woodsmen? Didn't they spend their time surveying the woods back and forth and marking select trees for the owners to have cut and sold? In addition, with Bertha out there as well, Elvira felt that someway, somehow, that if anybody could find that poor boy before it was too late, then Bertha and her fellow countrymen could.

After a while, Elvira thought that she saw a lantern back down the lumber trail near where the stake was, but the underbrush cut the view. She thought she heard muffled voices, but then the lantern seemed to veer off down the trail toward the sawmill clearing instead of coming to the barge. It surely was not Big Bertha and the Russian men; yet Elvira thought she heard men's voices talking to the dogs.

Her hair crawled on her scalp. She wondered to herself if they had indeed found some terrible thing. It could be the dead boy, and maybe they had taken him to the log huts on the other side of the sawmill clearing by the millpond. She would not give up! They would tell her if they had found anything, and in due time. It was all she could do to sit still up on deck in the night air. No, it wouldn't do to sit still up on deck in the night air. No, it wouldn't do to send one of Bertha's boys to ask, not out by himself in the dark night. No, she wouldn't send a youngin' on such an errand. In her heart, Elvira knew something had been discovered.

Groups of restless citizens gathered in small groups in the shadows in the little towns along the canal, but especially in New Bremen, Minster and Ft. Loramie. The people here were more closely concerned since the events of the past two days had happened in these towns and the townspeople, as well as the people in the surrounding county, felt involved in it and that they were sharing the responsibility of the outcome.

The word reached the sheriff through his deputies from Newport. They had heard the ugly rumors from other men in the posse, that Silvermann might leave the small town jail on the end of a rope. It could be worse if the boy at Mrs. Kattmann's died, or if another dead boy was found abandoned in the swampland along Loramie Creek, or Mile Creek. Fearing ambush from country roads on the way to the county seat of Auglaize at "Wapuck," the sheriff organized another armed posse to help him escort the prisoner to the county jail at Wapokoneta. Believing a barge to St. Marys would be a safer way, the sheriff and his deputies led the handcuffed and leg-chained Silvermann to the barge where he immediately got underway for St. Marys to the north. Once there, he put the prisoner in the jail temporarily, planning to bring a closed cab from the county seat on the next day, and transport the prisoner on to the county jail. It was all done so quickly, that few people in New Bremen knew it had been done until it was over.

Augusta Kattmann stood in exacting attendance on her patient. The old doctor had been in consultation with the local doctor. Finally, after he discharged his patient to the younger man, he was taken to the carriage for his ride home to Minster.

Mrs. Kattmann and Anna Steinhoge sat by the bedside every minute with a pale lamp burning at the side of the room. They knew how to conduct a sick room, and no one dared to breach their strict discipline. After a while, Mrs. Steinhoge took the first three-hour shift so that Mrs. Kattmann could rest; then they were to exchange shifts. The younger doctor was urged to remain during the night; his makeshift bed was prepared on the sofa with a light coverlet over him. No callers were permitted in the house. Bernhardina Gast was to see to that, but Fredericka and Ernestine had been banished to Bertha Gast's home. They were just not the type Frau Kattmann wanted to have on a case in the sick room. Talk, emotions, and tears were certainly not needed there, but only efficiency, discipline, and composed deportment devoted to one single purpose - duty.

Even with her own house filled with her own family and the new additions, plus her relatives who had been sent to assist, Bertha Gast found time to talk with her two new boys and to make them feel at home. Visitors came and left, but Bertha saw to it that the two shy sickly boys were not on display. They were not to be stared at and pitied by a curious array of sympathetic townspeople. She knew she could rely on Charley, young Ben, and Lou to help out, along with Josie and Lou-Lou. When it grew dark, she sent the children upstairs in the large hall room at the top of the stairs where they could romp and play. She urged Charley and Lou to try to draw the little boys out, and to get them to take part in some of the games. It would be good for them to forget themselves for a while. Lou-Lou came to the rescue, for if anybody could draw out a laugh, it was Lou-Lou. Little Daisy laughed and clapped her hands in amusement. Weak as the two new boys were, they began to laugh and join in the fun little by little, even though they were a little shy. After a while, Aunt Ernestine brought some fresh doughnuts and cookies with cool milk from the cellar. Knowing that Bertha Gast had extra people to cook for, Mrs. Peppleman came to call bringing a couple of large warm pies from her own kitchen shop. Bertha Gast knew that the men would sit out in the cool night along the canal bank smoking their pipes to keep the mosquitoes away as they talked until late into the night. At least she wouldn't have all that pipe and cigar smoke coming up from her cellar until all hours of the night.

Everyone kept coming to ask about the other boy at Mrs. Kattmann's home. Finally, the truth that he was alive spread over town and killed the first rumor that the boy had died soon upon his arrival.

No one dared to bother Augusta Kattmann's door, or to try her locked picket gate. Ludwig Kattmann had been posted at the gate to give out any news his mother might pass on to him, but his chief duty was to turn people away and to keep it quiet along the street in front of Mrs. Kattmann's home. After a while, Bertha Gast turned some of the lamps down in her home and extinguished others. Many of her guests took the hint and started leaving. She explained that the boys were weak and that they must be put to bed early. Then tomorrow was Sunday and it was time to attend church. After church, Bertha had Sunday dinner to prepare for an untold number of people. There was no telling what all tomorrow would bring - or even tonight once the search parties and posse returned to town.

Before going to bed, Bertha and Ben stole over to Mrs. Kattmann's to see if help was needed, and to learn if there was any change in the delirious boy for whom they feared morning would never come.

Nearly all of the young people met Josie, Lou-Lou and the boys at the lower end of the side lawn near the towpath. They managed to keep their excited voices down as they talked, all the while watching the towpath for a barge lantern from the south above the lock which might bring news from the posse scouring the swamp lowland.

Charley, Ben, and Lou, along with Jakey Backhaus, Fritzie Witt, and the Schroeder boys were disgruntled because they were not permitted to help search the swamp bottoms with the older men and the other older boys.

Ian McPherson, the lockmaster, along with his brother Angus, the path master, and with the Gast brothers, Hermann and Ben, had formed another search party with some other lumbermen south of Loramie who knew that woods terrain well. Ian had permitted the older boys, his lock gate helpers, to go along. Hank Speckman, Schani Schlesselmann, and Frederick Langhorst were able to ride horseback with their fathers' saddles, but Alby Wiemeyer and Alby Lemkuhl had to be content with riding work mules with only a folded grain sack for a saddle blanket.

It was all exciting for the young boys about to become men. It was equally exciting for Josie, Lou-Lou and their intimate girl friends. Milly Vogelsang ran back and forth on the towpath to the lock across the cross street and to the south to see if she could see anything or hear any news from below Newport and Loramie.

Charley, Ben, and Lou could hardly be restrained, but they knew that their fathers meant serious business when they had said "No" to their pleas. Jakey and Fritzie were no help, but Fritzie had a few well chosen black words to use to express himself. He had picked them up at the blacksmith shop and the livery barns.

CHAPTER 18

SUNDAY MORNING DAWNED BRIGHT and sunny with a cool briskness about it. Bertha Gast was up shortly after dawn to begin her preparations for Sunday dinner. There had not been time for all the Saturday night scrubbings with so much company, but boilers of water were put on the little wood range in the summer kitchen for the wooden bathtubs. There was always some last minute ironing to do but Ernestine was quick and handy with that. While looking down the canal from her kitchen window, Bertha could see wisps of misty fog rising from the still quiet water. The frogs had kept her awake for a while the past night. When the traffic on the canal died down for the night, the frogs became bolder; then it seemed that all of them joined in the chorus. They were safe at night from Elihu Sander's deadly aim, so all of them came to the surface, opened their throats to a full swelling, and sang until daylight.

When Ernestine got up, Bertha left her to watch the kitchen stove and keep the fire going while she drew her shawl over her shoulders and went to her mother's house to see how the night had gone. To her amazed relief, she found that the boy was alive and he seemed to be much better. Of course Mrs. Kattmann, who was always on the cautious side, warned that a feverish patient is always better of the morning and more restless at night. Nevertheless, the fact remained that his breathing was better. Bertha told her mother that as soon as the crisis was over, that she and some of the town women could come in and take shifts. She told her mother that she and Mrs. Steinhoge should take a much deserved rest. No one knew what might lie ahead!

Instead of being exhausted after their intermittent shifts of nurse duty, Anna Steinhoge and Mrs. Kattmann seemed to have new energy. Even though she was very sparse with words and cautious with her predictions, inwardly Augusta Kattmann felt that the boy's condition looked favorable.

She felt that unless some new development set in, he stood a good chance for recovery.

Both nurses were pleased with his faint progress, but they knew that his weak frail body needed nourishment after the ravages of deprivation he had suffered. As his breathing grew easier and the rattling in his lungs quieted somewhat, he seemed to go into an untroubled sleep with real rest.

After an hour or so when the bright morning light found its way through the drawn shutter, he opened his eyes. When he saw the two strange women, he closed his eyes again and had a trace of a frown on his young face. Augusta Kattmann waited for him to open his eyes again while Mrs. Steinhoge withdrew from the bed. When he opened his eyes again, he turned his head slightly to look at Mrs. Kattmann. She spoke to him very softly. Without asking who she was and with great effort he formed words with his lips. After a while, he managed to ask in a half whisper,

"Robbie? Robbie - here?"

The women knew his troubled state of mind made him keep trying to help his brother back there somewhere in the woods. They tried to pacify him and put his mind at ease. They told him in simple words that dozens of people had been searching the woods for miles around ever since he had been found. This seemed to put his mind at rest for a while and then he dozed. When he rallied again, Anna Steinhoge had a bowl of chicken broth with small bits of bread ready for him. It was held over a candle in a chafing dish to keep it warm. At first, he fought the nourishment: then after taking small sips at long intervals, he seemed to begin to like it. He was to be fed at short intervals, but only a little at a time, until his stomach and body were ready for it. He relished the few sips of cold water Mrs. Kattmann gave him through a goose quill straw.

Word spread from the house to the street that the boy was slightly better and that he had rallied for a little while. He had also taken his first nourishment. Sympathetic people who had been saddened by this unspeakable cruelty now found encouragement. The older people shook their heads and had to acknowledge that here was another case where Mrs. Kattmann had nourished a patient back to life when doctors had given up. Mrs. Hemel was not so kind when she commented to Mrs. Peppleman after hearing that the boy had rallied. Of course the patient would live. With Frau Kattmann's bulldog tenacity and German discipline the patient would not dare die.

The first bells for church began to ring, and then they were silent. Next the large bell in the Lutheran steeple began to toll as if for a funeral. Bertha Gast listened and then turned a fixed gaze of wonder and dread upon her husband. As they hurried to church, the bell continued to toll - just one light chime on one side, but not the familiar and regularly paced double "ding-dong." With apprehension, the early churchgoers gathered in front of the church while wondering and waiting for some sort of an announcement.

Without putting it into words, the townspeople looked at each other; then whispered what they feared

"That poor little boy has died - ."

The church doors were opened, and the white haired minister in his dark frock robe beckoned the people up to the steps. In sorrowing words, he announced something else that stunned, surprised, and saddened his listeners.

"My good people," his steady voice went on, "the bell is not tolling for the little soul in Augusta Kattmann's house. He lives, and thanks to almighty God, he is better this Sabbath morning. It is a far sadder thing I have to tell you." After a few moments of hesitation, he went on as others joined the throng at the curb in front of the church steps. "Another little boy - the second little unfortunate soul has been found." Murmurs of relief and thanksgiving went up from his small throng. Then the pastor put up his hand, and lowering his gray head, and shaking it slowly, he added, "has been found dead in an old well. The well is in the swamp bottoms in the woods south of Minster, below Ft. Loramie and along Mile Creek."

With this sad announcement, the old pastor beckoned his throng inside the church to begin the worship of the Sabbath. Instead of following the usual Lutheran litany and dogma, the organ rolled into a hymn of salvation that sounded very much like a requiem. The pastor began services by kneeling at the chancel instead of going to his pulpit, and led the congregation in a heartfelt prayer. The organ accented his words in the background.

The word spread all over the town in a short time as it had spread up the canal from Minster. Bertha Gast and her family were just coming to church when they joined the throng on the curb in time to hear the saddening announcement.

After church, Ben and Hermann Gast went to Mrs. Kattmann's home to bring Anna Steinhoge over for Sunday dinner so that she could go back and stand watch while Augusta Kattmann came and ate. Bernhardina Gast did not like it too well when it seemed that her sister, Bertha, got all the attention, and that her mother seemed to rely more on Bertha in an emergency instead of her when her own house was only a stone's throw from her mother's.

It was then that Josie and Lou-Lou, who were in the back seat of the carriage, learned how the news got to New Bremen. Ben Gast was explaining it to Mrs. Kattmann. She wanted facts for she had heard so many false rumors during the past day and night that she reasoned this too could be a false report or rumor.

It was Uriah Hornback, who was considered by many to be a slow nuisance with his plodding oxen team on the towpath, who had brought the news. His log rafts often tied up the canal and as Elvira Brenner had complained, "he was so deef that he couldn't hear thunder." At the locks he was roundly cursed, for he had the right of way the same as anyone else, and when he untied his rafts and put through the "ricks" of a dozen or more logs chained together, traffic was delayed for over an hour.

Old Uriah had been plodding along with his rafts of lumber while heading up to St. Marys. His wife Sheba sat on a stool on the raft and embroidered while little Orvie and Mahalie played on the logs. The Russians especially did not like Uriah too much, for he was a competitor in the lumber hauling business which they'd taken pretty much for granted as theirs in that neck of the canal along Loramie and Mile Creek.

Uriah's small cabin and clearing was in the deep woods on the other side of the sawmill. He was first suspicious of something when his dog put up such a "fuss" at the well sweep, and he heard him barking back there. At sundown Uriah went back to dip water for his livestock that were in the woods running wild. His brown brindle dog started circling the well and the hackles rose on his back. The dog would stand and bark toward the rock well curb. Uriah was afraid of a panther or wildcat, although he had never seen one. However, he knew something was wrong.

He finally got the courage to call one of the Russian men to come with his lantern. Bertha and her group had traced with their hound repeatedly. They were within a few rods of the old well when the dog lost the scent. It had been very perplexing.

With the lantern's wan light, and the presence of the Russians with their knives and large clubs, Uriah became more bold, even though he could not hear nor understand what they were saying. When the men were certain that there was no wild animal in the well, they began to wind up the windlass to bring the huge wooden bucket to the top. It was then that Uriah's dog began to run in circles again. All they found in the wooden bucket was a boy's jacket or shirt. "Why would that crazy dog carry on so," Bertha asked the men in Russian?

Acting upon a hunch, one of the men took the jacket that was not entirely wet because it was across the top of the bail of the suspended bucket. The Russian gentleman gave it to the massive bloodhound. He held it for the dog to sniff for a few minutes, and the dog circled the well a few times. Then Uriah's dog seemed to go into fits and his barking reached a new pitch. What did it all mean?

The frightened Uriah beat a hasty retreat, but not until Bertha motioned for him to take his dog with him. Its hysteria could not aid them in any way.

Uriah did not understand any of it. He was horrified that part of that poor boy's clothes had been found in his well. Uriah was certain that the boy was at the bottom of the well. Bertha had great fears of it, and after Uriah left, she had the agile Johnny Russ, the "Mad Russian" so to speak, shinny down the rope with a lantern while the others stood guard at the top. There was no body floating in the shallow well. The Russians took a rail from a nearby fence to probe the bottom of the well and rile up the water. However, no corpse came to the surface, nor did their rail detect anything in the well's bottom. Only the Mad Russian would risk diving in icy water in a dangerous old well. It was in the middle of the woods and in the dark of night, but they did so. They were much like sea otters. Unfortunately, they came up with nothing.

From a distance, the short staccato bellow of big Gregori arrested the attention of those at the well. After drying themselves the best they could, they followed Big Bertha who was bounding down through the forest.

The large Russian hound had led them to the body! Still, no deep bays came from the large mournful looking dog that pawed at a brush pile. Gregori and Big Bertha hurled the brush aside and there in a shallow hollow in the ground lay a little boy who from all appearances was dead. Bertha took off her jacket and covered the little body. She found it cold but not stiff as in death. Then she hurried up through the woods with the little boy. She went toward the log cabins in the sawmill clearing. It was this commotion of lanterns, and terse excited foreign voices, that Elvira had thought she heard in the middle of the night while she kept watch up on the lumber barge deck.

Uriah Hornback had not stayed to see the outcome because he was so frightened and shocked. He almost ran barefoot into Ft. Loramie and on up to Minster on the towpath. He forgot his oxen, old Sheba and the rest. Like a clarion of doom, he spread the word of "the dead boy found drowned in his well," but no one could make him hear if they asked for details. He was too excited to make sense, and when the posse tried to find the well, he couldn't tell them how to find it. When they finally did reach the well, they found nothing. No one was there. When they questioned the waiting Elvira long after midnight, she could tell them nothing about where the Russians were. They had never come back with the hounds, and for all she knew, they "wair still out there beatin' the bresh."

Sometime later in the night, Bertha sent two of the Russian men from the sawmill to the barge to retrieve Elvira and her own boys. The men hitched to the barge and pulled it on down the feeder canal to the branch that led to the millpond for the sawmill, and tied it up in the millpond. Elvira was amazed to find a hidden Russian village in the other clearing on the other side of the sawmill. She couldn't see too much by the lantern light, but saw an orderly row of log houses with some sawed scroll work on the gables and eaves. The village gave an appearance of a Siberian outpost of cabins with their red stain. They certainly didn't look like American pioneer cabins. Here in this secret retreat was Bertha's home. Elvira would have never known for few, if any outsiders had been invited inside of this compound hidden in the forest that surrounded by a strange interwoven fence of posts, rails, and saplings driven into the ground.

The Russian men rattled a little brass bell at the door, and Elvira knew that she was at the house of Big Bertha. When she was admitted, Bertha drew her over quickly to a candlelit pallet where she had been administering aid to the stricken body, and had applied a heat compress of heated clothes under the blankets. There was no pulse, and the heartbeat, if there was any, was too faint to be detected. However, to Bertha's expert eyes and ears, there was a light and hesitant breathing. Where there was life there was hope, and every minute counted.

The women were too occupied in trying to revive life into the frail, over-exposed body to think of sending word to the posse or the sheriff. The Russian men were so aloof and silent that they would not think of it unless Bertha (their "Katyna") told them to do it.

Uriah Hornback had spread the news during the night. His wailing wife, Sheba, sat nodding her head up and down, as she always did, as if to say, "It is so! Yes. . . Yes. . . it is as we feared. O, there is murder among us!" When the searchers and the posse heard the story and could find no one who had seen the body, they began to suspect the Russian clearing. However, no one ventured in there uninvited and alone. People did not go into the Russian compound in the dark and long after midnight.

Finally, a group of brave deputies came to the clearing, and bravely called out to the Russians from the outside. The growling wolfhounds slinked inside of the wooden palisade, and their eyes shown green in the lantern light. It was then that Bertha and Elvira, along with Johnny Ivan, realized that the authorities had not been notified. Elvira acted as spokesman and related the story to the deputies. All agreed that Bertha had done the sane thing in the emergency, and that it was important to get the boy to shelter and nursing attention. The deputies went to bring a middle-aged doctor from Ft. Loramie for they thought that the old doctor from Minster was still up in New Bremen.

Bertha kept Elvira by her side while all the strangers were in her house; she needed a mouthpiece and someone she trusted. The doctor could see how difficult it would be to keep the boy there in the Russian village, so far away from town, and out there in the wilderness in an almost unknown and inaccessible place. With Elvira's help and Big Bertha in attendance, they prepared the pallet as if it were a litter. They covered the boy with blankets to keep the chilly early morning dampness from his congested lungs. The young boy was transferred to the barge. He was then carried in the barge to the doctor's home in Ft. Loramie. After having breakfast with Bertha in her quaint but spacious log home, Elvira was ready to get her horse and get back to her family in Minster at the drydock. As she was having thick black coffee, Elvira couldn't help but marvel at the great brass "coffee pot" which bubbled on a heavy wooden table, and the idea of these "furrin Rooshins" making soup in their coffee pot. Law, there's no tellin what they would have to drink out of! She eyed the earthen jars with suspicious apprehension. The mug handles protruded from beneath the shelf-like beds extending from the log walls.

In addition, as the samovar bubbled on its song of peace and contentment, Elvira wondered "who on airth" that hollow faced big-eyed woman was that was engraved on that brass or copper pitcher. With that candle burning in front of it over there in the corner, Elvira, knew that it wouldn't be polite to ask personal questions. She contented herself with supposing that the picture on the brass pitcher must have been a relative who recently passed on, God rest her soul. Why, of course these "Rooshins" had people, feelins', family connections, and "relations" back in the old country! They didn't just hatch out on a stump!" Before she knew it, Elvira saw that it was time to go to her own family. The whole thing just wasn't real. She had fallen in a well and had come up in a foreign country, an unreal Never-Never Land. This past night was just a nightmare, but now she must mount the night horse and ride back to reality.

As soon as the excitement died down on the *Wabash Loon*, Elvira made her preparations for the Sunday dinner in Minster. She knew she could never make it to church this Sunday, but her kids were not to miss out very often if she could help it, even though they had to go in clothing with patches. One thing, they might be in plain homespun and gingham calico, but they would be clean, if she had to scrub them with sand. (That is if they got too poor to buy soap.) Nevertheless, with dinner no sooner finished that Elvira was seized with a new restlessness. She wondered how the other boy was up at Mrs. Kattmann's home. She wished that there were some way to get this other boy that they just found, into the expert nursing care of Mrs. Kattmann. Then a thought struck her that caused her to get up and pace the deck of the barge. Joel Brenner, who was trying to nap after his all-night foray in the woods with the search parties, commanded her to be quiet and quit "clacking" the deck with her leather heels. Elvira turned her new idea over and over in her mind. Without a doubt, Mrs. Kattmann didn't know a thing about the second boy being found. Elvira felt that if the two expert nurses and the doctor up there in New Bremen knew about the second boy, they would know how to doctor him.

It made sense to her that this boy's case would be the same as the others. He was suffering from the same malady, and up there was the place he should be. As long as he was carried in his bed and sheltered inside of the barge cabin, he wouldn't suffer any more exposure, and he could be taken there. How could she get the word to Mrs. Kattmann to see if she didn't think the same way? Elvira went down off the barge on to the drydock and paced back and forth. She went for a short walk on the towpath where her children were playing among themselves. She didn't want to ride back out to Big Bertha's and impose on her, but she knew Bertha would be very willing to do what she could. She didn't know how she would get up to Bremen but she <u>would</u> get there.

She came back on board and fixed herself up to look respectable for Sunday. Putting on a smaller poke bonnet to replace her everyday sun bonnet, and a tidy lace shawl stole over her gingham dress with a freshly ironed frilly apron, Elvira told her children she was off to New Bremen, and set out on the towpath on her adventure. Surely, there would be some way. There was bound to be someone on the canal today that she knew, even if it were that ornery old Irish codger, or old Uriah. Now that she was all prettied up, Elvira didn't want to ride horseback. She would just walk. Someone would overtake her and she could always get a ride back. The important thing was to get there and deliver her "ideas about carin' fer the sick." She also wanted to satisfy her own curiosity. Elvira would share her wild night's adventure while she basked in the glory of the rescue. She would also get all the latest gossip from Mrs. Peppleman or Gerta Hemel. They surely wouldn't be eating any of the "vile stuff" on Sunday.

As she walked along the canal on the quiet sunny afternoon, Elvira thought aloud to herself,

"Law, if I have to skeet up and down this canal and trek through swampy bottoms, I might as well have web feet!" As luck would have it, the light repair barge with the deputies overtook her. She hailed it down and climbed aboard while telling the chief deputy of her errand and message.

It was with great astonishment that Bertha Gast received the news Elvira brought with her, for Elvira had stopped at there since their house was close to the canal. It was then that Elvira learned of the report given in church that morning saying that the boy had been found dead. Elvira wasted no words, explained how it really was and why it probably had looked that way. Then she told Bertha Gast why she had come. Immediately Bertha and Ben Gast rushed over to Mrs. Kattmann's with the news that Elvira had brought, and of her plea to have the boy brought up to Augusta Kattmann and the young doctor's care with the other boy.

Mrs. Kattmann was puzzled with the new turn of events. As usual, all the rumors and reports were false or misrepresented. Of course the boy must be brought up to her, but how would they get him there without further risking his life? There was only one way. She could safely leave Anna Steinhoge and the doctor with little Will for a few hours, and go into the field of battle like a true Valkyrie to bring back the fallen herb to Vahalla. Ben and Hermann were to get the *Blue Swan* ready immediately. No the repair barge wouldn't do. It was not sheltered and it did not have good cabin facilities. It didn't even have an oil stove for heating water. Taking her medical supplies, blankets and sheets, Augusta Kattmann marched aboard the *Blue Swan* with Elvira and Bertha Gast by her side, and her son-in-law as captain. Then she gave the orders to shove off.

"*Gehen Sie! Ein steigen! Beeilen Sie dich!*"

"*Go! Get going! Hurry up!*"

Charley and Lou got to ride as driver hoggees and young Ben was a reserve. Bernhardina was commanded to keep the home fires burning, and Augusta Kattmann cast a baleful eye on the mischievous Lou-Lou and Josie as they tried to sneak aboard. However, with a clap of her ample hands, Frau Kattmann shooed them off the gangplank as one would a stray cat.

"*Out! Heraus! Ausgang! Gehen sie hinaus,*" she commanded sharply, and the girls ran down the towpath away from the *Blue Swan* as it got underway. They complained to their aunt Ernestine that they never got to go anywhere as the boys did. Lou-Lou stood on the berm with her arms akimbo; then imitated her grandmother, and began clapping her hands and repeating, "*Out! Out! Heraus! Aus, mit du*"!

It was a quiet Sunday afternoon for the girls, but the other townspeople were beginning to pass the new word they had just heard. Many were at the dock to see Frau Augusta Kattmann off on her latest errand of mercy. Lou-Lou, in disappointment at not getting to go to Ft. Loramie, told Josie that they should go to the grain elevator and get some corn silk, and go down under the dock pilings like Charley, Lou, and Ben and smoke up a storm. Her aunt Ernestine heard the girls mumbling and promptly got them busy doing the Sunday dinner dishes and entertaining little Daisy.

Chapter 19

As the night grew late and the barge did not return, the townspeople as well as the immediate Kattmann and Gast families did not despair. However, they were fearful that a bad turn of events had reached a crisis. Whatever happened, they felt secure in knowing that Augusta Kattmann was there with the boy and the doctor, and if anything could be done, it certainly would be. If they were too late, it was certainly a great pity. However, they had tried. At any rate, the new day would bring some sort of news whether it was bad or good. Evening church services were quiet, but it seemed that there were larger congregations in attendance in all the churches.

Monday dawned clear and bright. The everyday routine of a workweek began, and in no time, many wash lines along the canal were multicolored with the Monday washings billowing in the morning breeze. Work went along smoothly at the brewery. The mill hands kept the grain elevator and depot work going steadily even with the absence of Ben and Hermann Gast - to say nothing of the boisterous Gast boys.

Growing somewhat uneasy near the noon hour when the barge had not appeared, Bernhardina Gast came over to see if Ernestine had heard anything, and to see how she was getting along with Lou-Lou and Jo-Jo. Ludwig Kattmann, who was never one to grow impatient nor anxious, calmed all of them down when he told them that it might be a day or two before they came back. After all, they were all prepared aboard the barge to live for a while if they needed to, and to be assured that Mrs. Kattmann would make whatever decisions were for the best.

The dull afternoon wore on and Ernestine saw that Josie and Lou-Lou were kept busy ironing the newly dried washing as it was brought from the lines. Even everyday sheets for the beds were to be ironed with the same care as the white shirts.

Aunt Ernestine, who was more tactful than her sister Bernhardina was, promised the girls that they would take a drive in the late afternoon if they got their ironing done. They might even take the two hoggee boys with them out in the fresh air and hot sun. A drive out to Maria Stein to Grandpa Kattmann's would be fine in a few days, but it would be too long a trip for the short afternoon. They expected the *Blue Swan* at any time. Surely it would appear to the south this evening before dark. Elihu Sanders and Mr. MacPherson kept a weather eye out for the barge, as did Mrs. MacPherson from her high booth above the lock, and Mrs. Hemel from her high perch above the blacksmith shop. All kept watching the canal to the south. From all inquiries below, both of them could only answer that there was no sight of them yet. Mrs. Gertslaecker called up cheerfully to the dismayed Mrs. Hemel:

"Don't look too glum, Mein Gerta. No news is sometimes good news."

When Mrs. Peppleman saw that Mrs. Gertslaecker had taken some fresh strawberry preserves to the Gast residence, she was not to be outdone. Immediately she took some fresh fruit pies from her oven and slipping them into her huge basket while they were still steaming hot, she took them down the towpath to the Gast family.

Gerta Hemel was also feeling somewhat outdone. Therefore, she got busy and made some of her special noodles that she stewed in chicken broth added some stewed chicken and dumplings and put them in a large covered vessel. She delivered them herself to Mrs. Steinhoge at Augusta Kattmann's town house. The sick boy and his nurse as well as Bernhardina Gast needed good food and help too. Other townspeople brought food to the door, but no one was permitted to loiter very long or allowed to enter the house.

The scene at Ft. Loramie was anything but encouraging. Life hung in the balance, and each hour counted. Augusta Kattmann could see in a moment that the doctor's office was no place for the sick boy. However, it was dangerous to move him about in drafts. She could see that it was hard for the doctor to take care of him there for a very long period, and when she suggested that she take over his nursing care, neither the doctor nor his wife raised much protest. After all, who was to pay the bill for the medicines and services?

All through that Sunday night, Mrs. Kattmann sat up with the barely alive boy. Ben Gast slept just outside the inner office on the doctor's couch. The doctor himself had a cot in the next room so that Mrs. Kattmann could call him when needed. Somehow, Bertha Gast managed to take short catnaps on the *Blue Swan* while the boys snored peacefully in their bunks. Hermann and the crewmen slept either in the pilot cabin or in the holds.

The long silent watches of the night passed without much change. Bertha fully expected her husband, Ben, to come aboard at daylight with the news that the unfortunate little boy was dead. Still he lived on, and by morning his breathing was stronger and his pulse much stronger and more rapid. With this encouragement, Bertha persuaded her mother to take her rest on the couch in the darkened room to the side of the office. It was impossible to get her to come to the barge for a complete rest. She assured all of them that she could do that when the crisis was over.

By afternoon, it was apparent that some sort of a decision would have to be made. They could not stay indefinitely at the doctor's home. There was not another suitable place to use as a hospital except aboard the *Blue Swan*. Augusta Kattmann made her decision. The passenger cabin of the packet barge was made into the hospital room as was planned on the trip down. All preparations were made for provisions for the trip home and for the transfer. The litter was prepared and the delirious boy was placed on it. Mrs. Kattmann and Bertha used yardsticks for supports to hold a bed sheet over the boy like a tent in order to keep drafts away from his head.

He was placed on the cot that was prepared for him on the barge without incident. In the closed cabin, with all the hospital-like prearrangements that had been made, Mrs. Kattmann and Bertha could administer to him all the medications that he had in the doctor's office. The doctor accompanied them on the return trip. Since it was growing toward evening, Bertha had prepared a light supper on the barge for all of them. It took a little over two hours for the packet to approach the dock basin at New Bremen.

Gerta Hemel had first spotted the unmistakable *Blue Swan* in the distance, much to the discomfiture of Mr. MacPherson, who had watched the canal to the south with dogged attention day and night. Mrs. Hemel's clarion voice alerted Grünwalda Peppleman to the south of her just beyond the locks. Mrs. Peppleman's booming brass voice alerted the townspeople of the approach of the packet-barge. The barge docked at her berth that led in from the canal to the grain depot; then it continued into a slip and to the brewery because it was nearer to Mrs. Kattmann's town house. Augusta Kattmann scowled at the gathering groups of curious townspeople.

Little news of encouragement was given out, except to say that the boy was barely alive and that his pulse was somewhat stronger than it was the day before. There was only a bare glimmer of hope that life could continue in the frail and emaciated body. However, as long as life continued there was always hope.

Bertha and Hermann hurried on to Augusta Kattmann's dwelling to help Mrs. Steinhoge make ready for bringing the new patient into the makeshift hospital. Preparations had been made before departure for this eventuality and now it was a reality.

Mrs. Kattmann and the doctor waited until the barge was docked, the crewmembers had the necessary lines secured, and the horses led off to the livery stables before making any concrete plans for moving their patient. The townspeople left the side of the barge when it was apparent that Mrs. Kattmann would stay on the barge with the doctor.

When the way was clear, Augusta Kattmann and Bertha assisted the doctor and Ben, along with Hermann and some other men, to take the covered litter to her home where the invalid was placed on the cot that was prepared for him. The hospital vigil began anew with hushed voices, dim lights and assigned tasks for the various watches of the oncoming night.

Another night passed without much improvement, but neither was there a worsening of the boy's condition. The first little boy, Will, passed his crisis and began a slow, painful, almost snail-like progress. Another day passed.

Another doctor from St. Marys, upon hearing about the heroic dedication of Mrs. Kattmann, and of the support of the town toward the four pathetic orphan boys, came to New Bremen on a morning packet and offered his services if needed. The older doctor went back to Minster where he was needed, and the other one went back to Ft. Loramie. Word soon spread of strangers in the town and community - detectives or federal marshals who were questioning various people about many things.

Several more days passed, and it seemed as if the young doctor and Mrs. Kattmann performed miracles, if only for a borrowed amount of time. They had snatched the two frail bodies from what looked like certain death. At least life held on, and in the case of the second boy, Robbie, perhaps if no insidious complications set in, he might have a chance. He was far from free of danger for who knew what strange sudden turns pneumonia could take. Tuberculosis lurked just one step behind - ready to spread its ravages on the defenseless child's body. A medical board of inquiry from the state capitol visited Mrs. Kattmann's hospital.

Life went on in the small villages along the canal. The grain business flourished with the summer crops. Uriah Hornback came through town now and then and tied up traffic at the docks with his interminable log rafters. The Russian lumbermen and their rafts waited behind. Neither could communicate with the other, but looks darker than their voluminous black beards scowled down on the witless Uriah, while his wife, Sheba, intoned psalms and nodded her head. The boiling hot sun did not wilt her evangelistic ardor. The *Blue Swan* became a familiar sight up and down the canal with its cargo and packet business, and Ludwig Kattmann complained that he needed more boys' hands for packing and loading. He could use some boys for "hop and malt" work too.

It was difficult to find time to spare for anything else with the pressing needs of everyday living, the countless tasks of the household, the pressing needs at the depot brewery, and caring for the sick. There was no time to think of the future of the four little boys once their health and lives were saved. There were hardly enough hours at the present to think of the trial of the infamous brute, Silvermann, once the investigations were concluded. There was time enough for that later, but that time arrived one day too.

On the trip down to Ft. Loramie on the *Blue Swan*, Elvira Brenner had accompanied the Gasts and Mrs. Kattmann as far as the dry docks at Minster. Then she left them to go to her own barge and family. She had been only too willing to try to help, but upon being assured that all of them could surely do what was needed, she left reluctantly. Big Bertha was so far from being able to concentrate on her work at the clearing, and on the heavy loading of the big timber that she needed to get moving from the sawmill to the building contractors along the canal. Bertha Gast and her mother were too preoccupied to notice, as they carried the sheet-canopy over the unconscious boy, that Big Bertha and Elvira were standing silently along the towpath ready to lend their help if called upon. Elvira had learned from Hermann and Ben that there was progress being made, and relayed the news on to Big Bertha who asked often about the boys.

Elvira found herself a welcome visitor back in the sheltered Russian village deep in the cloistered silent woods where few outsiders had ever ventured. The huge Russian woman's face wore an expression of stoic but grave and fatalistic sadness. She was used to the tragic turn of events and never dared to look for the optimistic turn. As Elvira related to her what she had learned from the doctor's office in Ft. Loramie, Bertha could only close her huge dark eyes momentarily. Then with an awe-stricken face, she turned to that strange picture in brass that looked down from behind the burning candle. Big Bertha crossed herself and intoned something about "Mother Russia and the strength that came from the soil - each leaf, each blade of grass - " and ended with something about "St. Catherine hear us and have mercy on us all. . ."

Not wanting to appear heathen in the presence of such sincere devotion, Elvira, without knowing what she was doing, followed Big Bertha and nodded her head then fumbled at her brooch as if crossing herself. When she looked up, Elvira caught the sly Johnny Ivan (the irrepressible Mad Rooshin') looking at her through those narrow-slit Cossack eyes. He had a sly trace of a smile on his face until a flash of black eyes from Big Bertha (Katyna) arrested him, and his eyes fell to the floor.

Joel Brenner got his *Wabash Loon* out of drydock at Minster after a few days. It seemed like he was kept busy hauling day and night from the brick kilns up to St. Marys. It gave Elvira a chance to inquire about the boys from the Gasts, as she passed through, and relayed the news to Big Bertha when she met her from time to time on the canal. The new mills, livery stables, and other buildings included in the building boom in St. Marys required a constant supply of bricks, stone, and heavy lumber. It kept Big Bertha and her Russians busy supplying the timbers and rough siding. Brenners had the contract for the brick. Uriah Hornback switched from log rafts, when a slack time permitted, to towing a flat box-like ark loaded with mortar, sand, gravel, and burnt lime for the masons from up north and south of Troy. Trouble arose when the old Irish codger tried to edge in on the local hauling instead of continuing his long hauls of merchandise in wooden boxes from Maumee to Dayton. He took over hauling in Silvermann's place. The contractors knew he would be worthless for short hauls of much needed raw materials. He would be too intoxicated to get the loading and unloading done. He would tie up the docks and cause constant trouble among all the other haulers, to say nothing of the stevedores and day laborers on the docks. No, they would not give him an order in St. Marys now - or in the future. He swore at them vehemently. Then he was put off the dock and onto his barge. The experience only brought more profanity from him as he departed reluctantly down the canal on his makeshift barge. He could still sing his obscene ditties when he was drunk and angry.

He made the mistake of continuing thick-tongued Gaelic abuse under old Mrs. McKeeter's balcony over the canal for she was as Irish as he was. She tried not to pay him any mind at first as she busied herself with her potted geraniums. However, he spotted her up there puttering with her re-potting operations, and made her the special target of his vituperative abuse. Before he could dodge her aim, he received the full impact of her bucketful of rich rotted rabbit and sheep manure she was using to enrich the mulch of her potted balcony garden. As he swore and tried to shake the malodorant black mulch from his hair, beard and hat brim, a great part of it sifted down inside of his shirt collar and down his back. Before his crew could clear the barge from Mrs. McKeeter's range, the old codger received another barrage directly in the face as he raised his face toward the flowered balcony landing. He leaned back while shaking his fists and bellowing out unspeakable obscenities to the skinny birdlike woman. The contents of her garbage swill (peelings, coffee grounds, and slop water mixed with the black mulch) covered the old codger and his deck, and made the result a great slick black mess. The Irish crewmembers stepped up the horses to get down range from the evil-smelling missiles, but still the old codger stomped the deck, threw down his battered top hat and swore unspeakable vile language at the old woman. Mrs. McKeeters, in her wild anger, skittered about her balcony shrieking shrilly much like a cornered wet monkey trying vainly to find something else to hurl at her tormentor. She ducked into her flat, and emerged almost instantly from the door with her earthen "night jar" (or chamber) but the old codger was out of range of her deadly aim. The amber contents only splashed on the deck near the tiller, and the Irishman at the till leaped to the side while bawling madly when some of it splashed up on him.

"Faith - and the old she-devil's got me! Begorra - and let's get out of here!"

Men on the canal basin and on Spring Street roared with laughter.

The Irish barge was now being towed with horses at a near trot, but not a minute too soon, for Mrs. McKeeters scrambled down her wooden stairs and scampered down into town for the town marshal. She pounded on the desk at the town hall and demanded to know why that old vagabond with the vile mouth couldn't be locked up in the callaboose the same as any other drunks who violated the law. Why couldn't a "god-fearing, law-abidin', poor widder" be protected by the law, even in her home?

The Irish barge was well outside the town limits of St. Marys before the town constable could get moving and apprehend him. They would wait for him the next time, if only someone would tip them off when he made his next appearance. Mrs. McKeeters grumbled to herself as she went to the edge of town for another basketful of mulch.

Elvira Brenner and Joel were unloading bricks at the St. Marys quay when they heard all the commotion. Needless to say, Elvira wasted no time in repeating the entire fracas to everyone up and down the canal - especially to Big Bertha and Grünwalda Peppleman. It was the nearest that anyone had come to seeing the huge Russian woman laugh; she became rather crinkled around the eyes and pursed her lips to suppress an abdominal laugh, but Grünwalda bellowed with glee while slapping her amble thighs and stomping on her wooden porch until it shook.

One day Elvira happened to remember the cup of brown sugar she had borrowed from Bertha Gast, and since it gave her a perfect opening for a visit, she dropped in "for a spell" to repay the sugar and to inquire about the young boys. Then she wanted to know more about the mysterious strangers who popped up out of nowhere and questioned everyone. It seemed to her that there was more in the offing than met the eye, and this Silvermann, not to mention the orphan boys he had almost killed. There was a rumor about the old Irish codger passing by in one of his more sober moments as he went through the locks. Elvira raced on to make it clear that she did not waste time listening to the likes of his vile mouth. However, now and then he did drop some things that did make sense - or at least some good gossip.

"Now I don't mean to even hint that we are friendly with the likes of that - that fugitive codger from County Cork," and she twittered at her own alliterative play on words, "but then Joel and me have to get along with people on the canal, for our livin' depends on it. There's only Joel, me, the kids and our hired men we have from time to time. We caint' afford to get into a scrap with that old codger, and all that. . . rough Irish crew of his'n that are drunk and mean half the time."

"What did you hear from the old codger that has made you suspicious, Elvira?" Bertha asked in trying to get her informer to come to the point.

"Wal, now I wasn't egzackly told. I only overheared him tellin my man, Joel, but it seems this Silvermann, or I guess his name is something German, like Lehman, er somethin', but he's really in deep. It beats all how that old codger can hear things, but later on you find that ther is some truth in it."

"What did Joel overhear, Elvira?" Bertha asked patiently.

"Wal, you know all these strangers askin' questions around, all up and down the canal, have been tracin' things clean acrost the country frum San Franciskey and Canady, Toledo plumb down to Cincinnaty, from New York clean acrost the Erie to Buffalo and the lakes, and - and now they air here, Miz Gast. They air here!"

"Yes, Elvira, they are here, and I am glad they are. We want the law to get to the bottom of this, and have it all handled in due process (the law) in court."

"The law? In court? Pshaw, Miz Gast. He'll just beat them all slick and clean, git out, and do it all over again in some other part of the country. There's money of some sort back of that slick, low skunk, and money talks, Miz Gast!" Elvira assured her.

"Elvira, did you know that after that first little hoggee orphan was brought up here to my mother's that the men here were up in arms, and that there was talk of taking that Silvermann out of jail at the end of a rope?" Bertha told her.

"Do tell! New, I hadn't heared any sech thing as that!" Elvira's eyes grew large.

"Yes, and the sheriff and his deputies moved him out at night up to Wapokoneta to the county jail. They moved him at night with an armed guard so that he could have a fair trial and equal protection under the law, Elvira."

"Wal, I'll swan! Now thet does take the rag right off'n the bush! Oh, but I am afeerd that wair a mistake, Miz Gast. Oughter' let the men finish the job, if you knowed how slick and mean a man this'n is. He'll slip right through their hands, and murder all of us who helped do him in. He'll slit our throats while we sleep."

"What did you hear from the old codger that makes you think Silvermann is more of a criminal than we think he is? Bertha asked her. "You said he was in deep, Elvira."

"So that murderin' copperhead snake is in the callaboose in Wapuck? They better take him to Washington, Diss-trick of Columby and put him in irons behind strong bars in the United States jail. There must be one there somewhurs." Then Elvira moved her kitchen chair up a little closer to Bertha Gast, and looked to make sure Lou-Lou or Josie were not listening from the door, she began her tale.

"Oh, this usin' orphan boys for slave labor, then murderin' them to git rid of them when they get sick, or the law gets too hot fer him, is small stuff fer that Silvermann, or Lehman, and others like him have done in New York on the Erie. Big Berthy has tole me some of it, but law! Miz Gast, don't breathe a word of this, or mention her name, fer she is scairt plumb silly of the law and doan want no part of any detectives investigatin' around. She'll just clam up plumb tight if they try to question her, even as bad as she hates Silvermann. She knows him from way back - something in the old country. She can't afford to have it all brought out in the open, for she lies awake nights now that this has happened. Berthy is afeared she will be sent back to the old country and be exiled in Sibeerey agin, and be whupped like beasts. . . and. . . and. . . ."

"I will not mention her name, Elvira. What do you think Silvermann has done?"

"Wal, he is some part of every mean thing there is in the world where there is big money. He has double-crossed someone along the line, probably back there in Rooshey on that Sibeerey deal. He's made off with a bunch of jewels and money that he stole from Polish and Rooshin nobles. He was paid to drive them off into the frozen wastes of Sibeerey to die; only he made off with the fortunes he was supposed to turn back to the government. The government had confistercated their properties after the nobles were sent to Sibeerey."

"That Russian woman, Bertha, told you this? Bertha Gast asked her.

"Law no! She won't talk much about it, but some of the Rooshin men at the sawmill, when they get likkered up on that vodkey stuff, you know, that distilled lye water they make out of rotten taters in a barrel. Wal, they talk when they get likkered up. They sing, then cry, then dance like possessed wild demons. Then they slink down on the floor and moan, cry and then open up and talk. Joel says it's turrible, the things they tell of whut has happened to them: They talk of heir sufferin, their scars that they show from lead and stone tipped whips, and the scars from actual brandin' irons."

"Oh, Elvira," Bertha pressed her, "what else has he done?"

"And oh, the untold names of the ones they tole about who wuz shot in the snow, strangled, even drowned by the dozens. They were poked alive through holes cut in the thick ice in that back country, Sibeerian wilderness," Elvira wailed.   Bertha knew that her informer was the just now getting warmed up so she pressed further. Lou-Lou and Josie had not missed a word from the upstairs register in the ceiling. They were still as mice and took turns at keeping little Daisy Baby occupied in the next room with her dolls so that she would not give them away.

"I think these federal men (detectives) are after something big, Mis Gast. Mebbe it's like hundreds of thousands of dollars worth of jewels and Rooshin rubles. Then there is the hint of the story that this Silvermann and his gang run out on the Rooshin authorities, and took off with all the fortunes of the dead nobles that they had drove into Sibeerey. They got here from Chiny by way of Hong Kong. You see, Berthy and them other Rooshins came here from Chiny where they'd escaped to, and got into San Franciskey somehow or other. Probably had to work it off like slaves, for they couldn't have any money when coming from Sibeerey."

"Elvira! *Ach in Himmel!* How can you know and remember all of this?" Bertha asked.

"Shucks Miz Gast, I ain't tole half yet. Law, you won't believe, and Joel Brenner would skin me if he knowed I wuz tellin' what he heard from them drunken broodin' Rooshins. It's a fright on Sattidy night when they git likkered up on the vodkey stuff - especially with them red pepper pods in it. Those pepper pods fire yer insides all the way clean through - I mean clean through. - Why you would have to - to fan yer behind in the outhouse. . . it's so hot."

"Elvira! What is the rest of it you haven't told the half of? Are you sure you remember correctly all of this?" Bertha baited her to get her to continue. She poured her more black coffee, which Elvira gulped, and soon was ready for more. Then she lowered her voice as she nudged up closer to Bertha, so that Lou-Lou and Josie could hardly hear.

"This barge business is just a front. The Rooshins know this and are just waitin'. If Berthy hadn't lost her head and clubbed him good there at the weigh lock, the Rooshin men planned to get him some night along the dark canal. Then none of us would have ever heard of him nor his barge agin. Ya see, he dint recognize Big Berthy for who she really is, dint remember having done her dirty, and havin dealin's with the likes of them in the old country at the prison camps."

"Elvira! I can't believe all of this happening right here in this small town!"

"Wal, try this fer size and see how it grabs you, Miz Gast. This barge haulin' is just a cover up. He gets rid of these boys, these orphan slaves he gets fer nothin, once they git too wise to his thievin' inhuman ways or git sick. Why, he gets rid of them. He gets rid of crewmembers. He took grown men who crossed him, or were no longer any use to him. Miz Gast, I'm tellin' ya'. He kills them, and gets rid of their bodies in the swamps - in the quagmires. He don't dare leave them in the canal for they will come to the top and float, all swell-up like!"

"Elvira! How horrible," Bertha gasped. Elvira swilled down more coffee.

"And now see how this sets with you. You know it must be the truth, for them tight-lipped, gloomy, broodin' Rooshins wouldn't lie in their sleep or when they're drunk. They cry like babies, and fall all over each other, men kissin' each other, rollin' on the floor and tellin all this terrible stuff that has happened to them, and crying out the name of that vile devil Silvermann - only they call him Lehman. Now you know it's the truth, for they repeat the same thing exactly each time they're drunk. They don't know they have told all of it when they come to. The Rooshins are ready for work at the sawmill, or they are out swingin' them mammoth axes and cuttin' heavy timber in the forest. Then it is ready for the mill on Monday. I'll tell you, Miz Gast, it's enough to make Satan's drawers flop in the wind on Halley-een night!"

"Good gracious! *Ach Helige Gott!* Elvira, how long have you known this?"

"Oh, fer a good long spell, but more of it in this past year since we've been workin' this Miami-Erie canal here in Ohi-yee. Also, bein' in and out of the Rooshin sawmill, fer Joel has had more dealin's with them. Then he does get into the saloons and taverns with them now and then. You know how it is, men bein' what they air!"

"Is this all of it, Elvira? He's a murderer many times over, as well as a kidnapper, brutal prison-warder, and thief?"

"Law no! Human slavery! First let me tell ye. I'm gittin' ahead of myself. He delivered boatload after boatload of helpless Chineese men and wimmen who were bound at hand and foot. They were hog tied like a shoat fer market into San Franciskey to be sold. Yes, they were sold fer coolie slave labor out in them minin' camps. . . fer diggin', cookin', washin'. . . and," Elvira put her hand up to her mouth and whispered something about the fate of hundreds of women who were kept in opium dens and underground caves. . . the "brothel cribs."

Bertha put her hands up to the side of her face in shocked horror.

"And now this, Miz Gast. It's got too hot fer him in the old country: in Sibeerey, in Chiny and in San Franciskey. Now what's he doin' here on this dinkey little old canal, this small time haulin' stuff, bringin' big time crime and corruption to decent country people?" Elvira asked her hostess, who could only shake her head in disbelief.

"Why I'll tell you. He has decided to put on a air of decency, and make folks believe he is helping them unfortunate poor run-a-way slaves from the south, who sneak acrost the river into Cincinnati, and try to git away up north in to Canady. Some of them come up acrost Indianny through Richmond, Winchester, Ft. Wayne and on into Canady by the 'underground railroad,' or so it is called. You know, they travel at night and sleep during the day, while being hidden by folks along the way. Wal, this agent of Satan, this Silvermann, is transportin' them in holds of his barge in them large boxes that looks like boxes to store merchandise in. You know: dry goods, pianners, and other stuff in big boxes. They pay him good money, and God only knows how they kin raise any money. Berthy, that is Big Berthy, has helped a few but she doan take no money. She would help more but she is afeered of the law snoopin' and she kaint take no chances."

"But the money he could make from those poor unfortunate blacks is small compared to the big money he has made from big crime, Elvira. Why would they bother with this?" Bertha demanded.

"Mebbe he has lost out, and the people he has double-crossed, along with divine providence, is breathin' down his back," Elvira said suspiciously. While waiting for Bertha's agreement, she rushed in with her next point - words for the eye-opener.

"And then mebbe, just may-bee, he gets these poor helpless black niggers almost to their destination in Toledo that are ready to be shipped across the lake to Canady or up the coast to Detroit. Then he turns them over to waiting bounty hunters who have been tipped off, and then shares part of the reward money offered by their masters. You see, they is protected by the federal law, for he is only returning property to the rightful owners. Pretty slick ain't it? It is happening right under our noses."

"The fugitive slave law is coming home right here in this small community - to us!" Bertha gasped. She bit her lip to keep from saying what would alert Elvira. After talking about the outcome of it all, and the possible future of the boys, Elvira put Bertha to thinking with one of her blunt questions.

"What will be the outcome fer them young orphan boys? There are four extra mouths and growin' up, that is if they all live and survive all this. It would be cruel to send them back even if Silvermann hangs, as he deserves to. Can't adopt all of them? They're too young to work and make their own way."

Bertha shook her head, but assured Elvira that her mother would come up with the right answer when the time came. Next, Bertha began to ponder a question of her own. What would Augusta Kattmann do when she learned of the betrayed black people?

Elvira's other news from other canalers to the south, from Hamilton and Cincinnati areas, was that the governor's packet would be coming back north before too long. It would be when the senators and others returned from a trip on the Ohio and Mississippi Rivers on the steamboats. The governor had gone on to Columbus. He went up the Ohio with the senators on the steamboat to Portsmouth, where he took a packet barge up the Ohio and Erie Canal via Circleville and on to the capitol.

After Elvira had gone to get Joel Brenner at the blacksmith shop and start their return trip, Bertha went quietly up the stairs. She pointed to the open register in the floor of the bedroom. Then she took her toe and closed it. Taking both girls by the arm, she took them downstairs and sat them at the kitchen table. Without raising her voice, she did not give them a chance to deny that they heard the electrifying conversation she had with Elvira Brenner. Instead, she impressed upon them how serious it was. She told them that they must not even breathe a word of it - not even to the boys - or to any of their playmates. Too many lives were at stake. This was serious business for the federal marshals and it must not be fumbled. In fact, Bertha did not quite know what course she should take, but one thing was certain: nothing must be said that would put the Russian men or Big Bertha in jeopardy. Now she knew why detectives and federal men were investigating along the towpath.

That night, when the right moment presented itself, Bertha, upon pretense of visiting with her mother, waited until Mrs. Steinhoge was out of hearing, and until her sisters, Bernhardina and Ernestine were out of the room. Then she whispered to her mother that she had something of a frightful nature, and great importance to tell her, but that under no circumstances could she chance telling her when anyone else was around. Mrs. Kattmann knew her daughter Bertha, and knew that it was not an emotional outburst of gossip that she had to tell her.

Later in the evening her mother announced to her that in the morning, if no time came before then, she would come after her in the carriage and they would drive out toward Maria Stein to Weidenhimmel (her country home).

While having a mug of thick Turkish coffee with her mother, Bertha had the distinct feeling that her mother was expecting her to bring some news, but it seemed to Bertha that she was not overly anxious or surprised. It was as if she already knew, or at least Mrs. Kattmann took a great deal of time to prepare the special coffee treat. The *Schlagergober* treat was a delicacy from south Germany, but more exactly so from Austria. It was a thick Turkish coffee, strong and rich that was served in hot mugs with meringue and whipped cream on top, and sometimes it had a nut meat or red cherry on top. Usually small *tortes*, cupcakes, or slices of rich chocolate cake were served with the mugs of thick *Schlagergober*. Bertha mused to herself how amusing it would be to serve this to Elvira Brenner some day when she popped in, just to see and hear her reaction! Everyone of the German community had been amused by her tale of the brass Russian coffee pot at "Big Barge Bertha's," which bubbled over its own fire, and from which "them people drunk soup, broth, and about everything."

As they sat and talked, the hour grew late by the time Bertha brought up the subject of the young boys. Health and hospital care was a subject dear and sacred to the heart of Augusta Kattmann. She had a doctor's dedication to her cause.

The two boys, who had been brought first to Mrs. Kattmann's after being taken from Silvermann's barge at the locks, had made great progress. In the few weeks time that they had been under proper care with rest, food, and mental relief from their former anguish, they showed an improvement. Their bodies had taken on a few pounds, their eyes were brighter and their skin was more ruddy looking. The biggest change was in their facial expressions. They smiled when they talked, and fastened their blue eyes on everyone they spoke with as if they were measuring them to see if there was trust and sincerity in them.

The little boy, Will, whom Big Bertha had found by the trail along the towpath in the sawmill woods, was now developing an appetite. He was also making noticeable, but slow progress. Mrs. Kattmann told Bertha that it would be several months before his stunted condition made a marked change, and perhaps not until he came into early adolescence, for he was only ten years old. As for the fourth orphaned boy, Robbie, (the brother of Will) who was found near the old well by the Russians, was a different matter. The crisis was over at last. After nearly a week of being in a coma, he regained consciousness. He was eating now but he was too weak to be out of bed much. However, Mrs. Kattmann was a firm believer in getting the patient up as soon as possible, if only for a few minutes at a time. His unused muscles and out of shape limbs, as well as cramped body organs needed to get back in proper alignment so that they could function normally again. The first few times that she and Mrs. Steinhoge lifted the boy to a sitting position to feed him, he responded favorably, but when they held him between them to stand him on his feet and take his first steps, he fainted. Frau Kattmann was not one to be dismayed by setbacks. She continued the walking exercise now and then. After he became strong enough to stop fainting, she allowed him to take a few steps by himself.

The whole town breathed a sigh of relief now that it was apparent that the boy would live, but Augusta Kattmann assured them all that the fight was far from over.

Now her mind started to grasp at the enormity of the crime along the peaceful canal - this terrible thing about the traffic in returning fugitive slaves.

A Stevedore

Abigail Wigtver

Alby Lehmkuhl

Angus MacClintock

Angus MacClintock

Angus MadPherson

Anna Steinhoge

Arrival at Swan Creek Canal Depot

August Ben Gast

August Ludwig Kattman

Augusta Kattman

Augusta Kattman

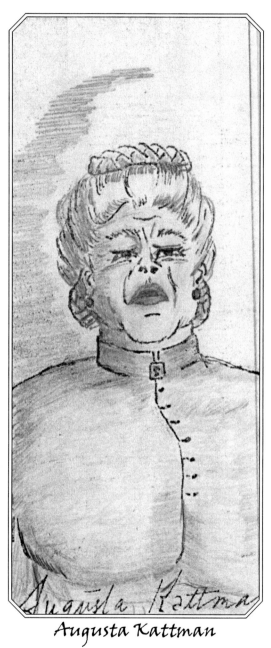

Augusta Kattman

Augusta Kattman

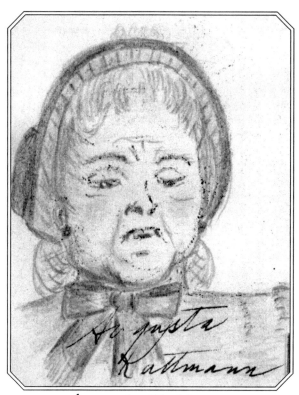

Augusta Kattman

Augusta Kattman

Barge crewman and poleman

Benjie Gast & haw-gee boys

Bernhardina
Gast
[Lou-Lou's mother]
"I wonder it Mother
is in complete charge
of her faculties.
Such schemes!"

Bernhardina Gast

Bertha Kattmann Gast

Big Gregori

Bilge-keel O'Reilly

The Blue Swan

Charley Gast

Charley Peppleman and Redy Schlossel

Daisy Gast

Elihu Sanders

Elvira Brenner

Emilie Vogelsang

Emilie Vogelsang

Ernestine Hofermeyer

Frederica Keller

Frederick Landhorst, Hank Speckman, and
Albert Alby Wiemeyer

Fritzie Witte   Jakey Backhaus

Fritzie Witte and Jakey Backhaus

Fritzy Wittr

Gertrude Gerta Langhorst and
Johann Schani Schlesselman

Gottlieb Sielbermann

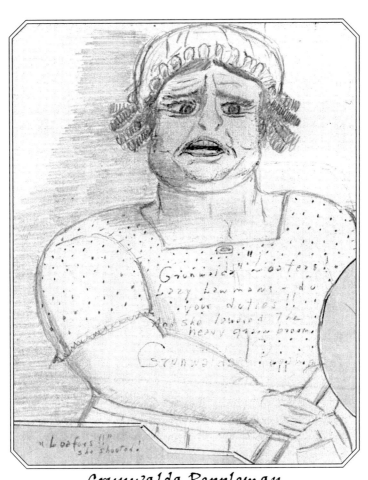

Grunwalda Peppleman

Gusta Kattmann

Henry (Heinrich) Hofermeyer

Henry (Heinrich) Hofermeyer

Henry Bachman

Henry Backhaus

Hermann Gast

Hoggee boys Patrick, Tommy, Willie, and Robbie

Irish Canal Foreman

Irish crewman

Jakey Backhaus

Johnny Ivan

Johnny Ivan

Josephine and Louise

Josie dozed off

Karl Zinnderfer

Katyna Vladmirevna Big Bertha

Leo Wiemeyer

Leo Wiemeyer, Patrick O'Flaherty, and Hoggee Chris Schroeder

Louise (Lou-Lou) Gast

Louise, Lou, Charley, Josie, and Ben Gast

Lou-Lou and Josie

Ludmilla Milly Vogelsang

Ludmilla Milly Vogelsang

Ludmilla Vogelsang, Gertrude Langhorst, and
Dorothea Watermann

Ludwig Kattmann

Ludwig Watermann

As Martha Schwieterman
delivered her homemade lye soap
she called out with her high laugh
to Henry Backhaus at the flour mill.
"Got any Kron berries? <u>Wo Wachsen</u>
Sie?"

Martha Schwieterman

Mary Hogan

Mrs McKeeters

O'Halloran

O'Halloran

Old Vladmir

Squaw of Copper Wares

The Dockmaster

The Fatima

The Port Director

Toledo Banker

Uriah Hornback

Vassily

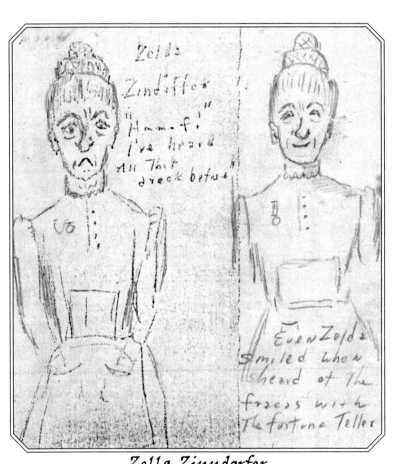

Zella Zinndorfer

CHAPTER 20

IT BECAME MORE EVIDENT with each passing week that the canal was growing up and coming into its own. Traffic in both directions picked up with the summer. Businesses along the canal flourished. Farm produce, manufactured goods, building materials and nearly everything that had been land-locked to the people in central Ohio now had access to market up and down the canal. It was true that towns and villages, to say nothing of the farmers who lived great distances from the canal, still were at a disadvantage. It was a great hardship to drive or haul livestock, or bring wagonloads of produce forty and fifty miles from either the east or west side of the canal to the docks for shipping. People living along the Ohio River or along Lake Erie could ship their surplus goods on those waterways to market. However, the people living in the central section had no way to market their produce. They would have to take long unprofitable drives on foot. They drove cattle, hogs, turkeys, and geese on eighty and one hundred mile trips to the market in Cincinnati.

The Miami and Erie, and its connecting link with the long Indiana canal, the Wabash and Erie, served the needs of the western side of the state. The branching central canal system of the Ohio and Erie, which ran from Cleveland down to Portsmouth on the Ohio River, was a commercial boon to that part of the state. Its branches connected Columbus, the state capitol, with Athens, Marietta and other river ports.

The lower southern end of the Miami and Erie was enjoying a prosperity boom, especially in the passenger packet business from Dayton, down through Middletown and Hamilton and on into Cincinnati. It was reported from the passenger depots that upwards of two thousand persons a week were traveling the canal between Dayton and Cincinnati. A person could travel from Cleveland to Portsmouth on the Ohio and Erie Canal for a little over $6.00. The entire trip with layovers and delays for locks and heavy traffic were taking only 70 to 80 hours. The same was true for the western canal, the Miami and Erie, but for less money and shorter hours in route.

Augusta Kattmann talked about many things on the carriage ride out to Weidenhimmel, or Willow Haven, her rambling country home near Maria Stein. She picked up her daughter, Bertha Gast, but was adamant in her refusal to permit Lou-Lou or Josie to go along. The children were all to eat their noon meal over at their Aunt Bernhardina's, who was preparing the noon meal for the men from the grain depot. Bertha was astonished to find that her mother had planned the day as if it were on some sort of prearranged schedule. She wondered why they were taking this trip all the way down to Minster, and then west the five miles or so to Maria Stein. Why, this trip would be an all day affair! Bertha reasoned to herself that it would only have taken a short trip around town for her to have time to share with her mother the ghastly information she had received from Elvira Brenner the day before. Her mother, like the Almighty, worked in strange and mysterious ways her wonders to perform, and strangely enough, she usually accomplished what she set her head to do.

Augusta Kattmann related to Bertha the information she had about the booming freight and passenger business on the southern end of the canal. The same was true of the northern end, especially from Junction City on north to Maumee and Toledo. The middle section from St. Marys on south through New Bremen, Minster, and Ft. Loramie to Lockington was the slow section. Colonel John Johnston of Piqua was instrumental in getting the northern extension of the canal built from Dayton on north to its completion all the way to Toledo in 1845. Still, the middle section lacked the business that the other sections enjoyed. Even from Piqua and Sidney on south through Tipp City and Troy there was a greater freight business - to say nothing of the passenger packet service.

Seeing her daughter receptive to her train of thought, Mrs. Kattmann suggested that it was time that the *Blue Swan* earned her salt. She had been put through the "shake down" cruise, as it were, and all experimentation on her proved her to be canal worthy and efficient to operate. It was time that she claimed some of the passenger fares that other packets, which were less commodious, were carrying on the lower stretches of the canal.

"What range should we set for the limit of our passenger service?" Bertha asked.

"Ve could decide after a few trial runs. Perhaps the *Blue Swan* could go from Dayton north to St. Marys, or say, from Dayton up north through Tipp City, Troy, and Piqua, over to Sidney and then back, and on up to St. Marys. We could try the short shuttle service at first, mein Bairtha."

"Mother! Who from Dayton is going to want to stop in St. Marys? Passengers from the large cities will want through service, or at least connecting service, all the way through from Toledo, south through Dayton and on to Cincinnati," Bertha protested.

"And I suppose die business mens, buyers, sellers, and retailers from smaller towns don't need to travel back and forth?"

"Well, that's true, but I haven't seen the two thousand a week passenger trade going through Minster and Bremen, unless they are traveling at night!"

"Bairtha! Dere is a lively passenger trade going on in our section now. Each week it picks up. Dots vy we need advertising and suitable packets in operation. With better time schedules there will be more travel," Mrs. Kattmann persisted.

"We need more suitable packets?" Bertha asked, knowing what the answer must be. She had known it since that Sunday dinner at Maria Stein.

"Vell, the *Blue Swan* can't handle it all once the business starts der increase, now can it? Ve see! Maybe ve add more packets to our business and start a company line if der *Swan* proves a profit."

"I knew it. Mother, I can tell it by your facial expression that you attempt to keep so well guarded. We're in for more packets. You want to add those carousel comic monstrosities at Toledo. You have your eye on them, don't you? I knew it!" Bertha let her voice trail.

"Time will tell, mein Bairtha. Ve see. However, ve don't want the *Blue Swan* to get too far from Brementown. Ve vant it as a special show piece, der advertisement for der brewery, Ja? Ve vill need other barges for our everyday money-makers," Mrs. Kattmann said.

"Oh, I see it all now. I just knew it. Mind you, don't get ideas that I am going to run an inn along the way, or go along as cabin maid and linen woman on any packet barge. This is all your business venture. Ben and I are brewery and grain business."

"Vy Bairtha. How do you run on! I haf naiver asked mein own family to vork for charity. Of course ve hire people, and if mein family vork on the line, packet or overnight inn, dey are paid."

"I can see Ernestine and Heinrich Hoffermeyer in it somewhere," Bertha said meekly while waiting for her mother's next words.

When Mrs. Kattmann let the horses slow down to a slow walk, Bertha took the reins to rest her mother. Augusta Kattmann allowed a slow smile to play on her face as she turned to Bertha and said,

"Vould that be such a bad idea? Dot Heinrich! Nothing has worked for him. They are thinking of moving their clothing and tailor shop from Minster up to St. Marys, but I don't think it vill prosper there either. Heinrich has a

vay with meeting der peoples dat Ernestine does not! He vould be good as a
passenger boat captain or as a proprietor of one of the inns along the way. Vot
you think?" Mrs. Kattmann asked.

Bertha knew that her mother's mind was made up and that all decisions
were made. It would be best to just wait and see. She shuddered to think
of seeing Heinrich Hofermeyer in a resplendent top hat and cut-away coat
on the deck of that elephant or hippopotamus barge. He would be smiling,
along with Ernestine or Aunt Fredericka, at prospective customers on the
docks in front of the depots. Wouldn't they make a fine picture here in this
back country with small towns putting on large city airs? It might work. She
remembered how dead set she had been against the *Blue Swan* and how she
had been won over to it. She also remembered the steam calliope and how
she had been won over to it as well. Unfortunately, the right time had not
presented itself for the grand debut. The tragic episode of the orphan boys had
dampened all spirits, and there had not been time for such indulgence of the
ridiculous because of the emergency operations going on. Cooking, washing,
housekeeping and hospital care had just about taken up all the time.

However, now the tension had let up at last. There was time to relax and
ponder new questions that arose with everyday living.

"These four boys, mother. Some day a decision will have to be made
concerning their lives and their futures," Bertha said simply.

"Yes! Yes, mein Bairtha. Yes indeed. I haf given much thought to that,
but there is time enough in the coming months to work something out. I haf
many plans in mein head . . ."

"I have never once doubted that, Mother," Bertha added quickly.

"Vell, dis might chust work," her mother said. For one thing, as we
expand our brewery business and the passenger business, ve will need to train
more help. As you say, ve can't keep it all in the family. Der children grow up
and go avay on chobs and lives of their own. It might chust be that ve could
manage to vork these boys into chobs along the canal. . . Oh, don't look so
horrified, mein Bairtha! I would not treat them like dot evil Silvermann! Not
free child slave labor, but more to train them and then put them on salary or
wages, teach them to save and to be der own managers. Den there is school
to be considered. Dey must be schooled."

It all had seemed so complicated to Bertha when she tried to think of
how the future of these orphan boys would turn out. It was enough of a
problem to try to think of how her own brood would turn out. Now that
her mother had put it in words, somehow the whole business seemed simpler.
"A place and time for everything, and everything in its place at the right
time" had always been her mother's motto with typical Prussian method and

efficiency. Bertha knew that somehow that it would be taken care of, and that all the pieces would fall into place.

Since her mother had mentioned Silvermann, Bertha seized upon the opportunity to take her mother into her confidence. She warned her mother that she was under oath not to betray a confidence. She felt that she should tell her mother and help her decide what the best course to follow was. Mrs. Kattmann agreed after Bertha told her of the precarious position such a betrayal might put the Russian woman in, Big Barge Bertha, as well as the other Russian men at the sawmill camp.

"Ach, I <u>do</u> vish we had another name for her! Dot name is so offensive to her and yet ve know no other name. Ve could not pronounce it if ve did," Augusta Kattmann complained. "Onglisch is hard enough!"

"I know. Elvira Brenner says the other Russians call her something that sounds like 'Katyna' or 'Kateenya.' It's those last names of several syllables that will throw us. They are much worse than those long German names and much harder to pronounce," Bertha said.

Not to be sidetracked, Bertha launched directly, but slowly, into the ghastly tale that Elvira had told her. Mrs. Kattmann stopped her from time to time to make sure she understood and then repeated the phrases that Bertha used. When she had finished, Mrs. Kattmann questioned her, and then had her to repeat it all very slowly to her again while she registered it all in her mind.

"You see, Mother, I don't think it is a figment of Elvira's imagination. Goodness knows she does ramble on, but she could not dream this up."

"No, it is not a wild tale, Bairtha. The fact that those Russian men report the same thing when they are sad or are drunk on dot vodka stuff proves that it is something real dot has happened, or not all of dem would tell the same thing in the same vay each time they tell it. No, it begins to fit together. You have done vell, mein Bairtha, to tell me," Augusta reassured her.

"I agree, Mother, but some authorities should know this. How do we go about it without incriminating that poor Russian woman and those men? They are good hard working people and they have suffered inhuman burdens."

"The authorities do know, mein Bairtha. They have known much about all of this for some time, and have been investigating and getting actual proof. I have talked late at night many times with these detectives and investigators at my darkened living room. I am determined to get some state legislation to correct dese deplorable conditions with the poor, dese insane, those Negroes, dese elderly, and especially wayward girls and orphans. I vant to see hospitals and schools for dese peoples dat need them so."

"Mother! You can't cure all the world's ails by yourself."

"No, but I can try. It is easy to sit back and say dot, but every drop of vater in der ocean helps to bring up die level, Ja?"

"You say the authorities do already know. How much do they know, mother?"

"Quite a good bit, but dis Silvermann, or actually Lehman, is only von fish in der pond. Ve are fishing for bigger game."

"What do you mean, 'We?' Are you in on this too, Mother?"

"Vell, aren't ve all? Do ve vant justice and criminal clean up all der vay from top down, or chust be satisfied with a lot of radical emotional men stringing up one criminal on a rope?"

"I don't understand, Mother!" Bertha said quickly. "You're evasive."

"Vell you vill as soon as we get to <u>Weidenhimmel</u> (Willow Heaven or Haven). Don't you see, ve are using dis Silvermann as bait. Others will come out in the open ven he starts to talk ven ve put der squeezings on him. Some of the others vill probably try to keep him from talking. Therefore, he must be guarded most carefully. He is our prize bait, and ve intend to use him fully and for a long time. You see. Vait until ve get home."

"Mother you never cease to amaze me," Bertha admitted.

"Ach! Mein Gott! I never cease to amaze meinself Bairtha," her mother confessed. Then she laughed a throaty deep chuckle.

"How much of your sleuthing detective work does Sister Ernestine or Bernhardina know?" Bertha demanded.

"Absolutely noss-sing, not one hint," Mrs. Kattmann answered.

"And Aunt Fredericka?"

"Not the first thing! Fredericka! Ach, she would weep her eyes out with fear, and not sleep dot first wink if she wair to know of any of this. These orphan boys, and all the care for them to keep life in dair bodies has nearly worried Sister Fredericka to her death," Mrs. Kattmann sighed.

Bertha went on rapidly to assure her mother that she had told no one a word of this, but she was worried that Elvira would probably tell Mrs. Peppleman or Gerta Hemel some of it. It was too choice to keep and Elvira loved the dramatic, especially if she had such an expressive and talkative audience. Mrs. Kattmann admitted the truth of what Bertha had said, but also pointed out that perhaps she could be warned to keep very quiet if she were made to realize the danger she put Big Bertha and the other Russians in. They could be murdered by Silvermann's accomplices when the heat was put on. The heat would be applied soon once the whole trial proceedings got under way in Columbus. Then Bertha and the Russian village stood a chance of being arrested or deported for illegal entry into the country. However, perhaps if respectable people of property in the county vouched for them and stood as guardians for them, and if they turned state's witness in the prosecution against the Silvermann murderers, maybe a way could be found for making them citizens of this country. Surely Elvira could be frightened into silence if she realized how much was at stake. Bertha shuddered when she remembered that Lou-Lou and Josie had heard Elvira's words. Her mother would have a stroke of apoplexy if she knew this.

The pleasant countryside to the west of the canal soon passed. Recent rains kept the country from being dusty, which was also a blessing, for sometimes in mid-summer the carriage and buggy wheels picked up the inch-deep dust and caused a cloud of it to choke the luckless passengers back of the horses.

After leaving Maria Stein and the tall spires of the cathedral, the two women drove into the driveway through the *Willowdale* of <u>Willow Haven</u> with its pleasant cream-colored brick buildings and willow trees. Truly it was <u>Weide Himmel</u>, and it looked as much German middle class as if it were in the south German countryside.

After greeting her father, who was happily tending his garden and walking in the pleasant shade of his arbored vineyards, Bertha went back into the house. Her mother had her housekeeper prepare some cool refreshment out of the well house for them.

Then, as if to prepare her for a surprise, Augusta Kattmann took Bertha by the arm and led her into the little office off the library. Some gentlemen were in a deep discussion as they looked over some notebooks and written files. To her astonishment, Bertha recognized the gaunt stern face of Angus MacClintock, the Scotch detective from Montreal whom they had met in Toledo, and whom they had seen pass on the governor's passenger packet that day in route to Cincinnati. Bertha was astonished. Why hadn't her mother mentioned this? She felt a cold chill go over her. No wonder her father had seemed rather strange when she had talked with him in the vineyard.

"Bairtha, this is Angus MacClintock. He is international police, and it is very important that you sit here with us and repeat with me exactly and word for word, what you have learned. Dese other gentlemen are working hard on the case," Augusta Kattmann said. Very slowly and solemnly, the others were introduced to her.

The afternoon wore on as Bertha and her mother related their findings to the men. They took careful notes about the happenings. Once when Mrs. Kattmann added her opinion on why such and such a thing had been done, Angus MacClintock interrupted her.

"The facts, Mrs. Kattmann – give us the facts only if you please." His voice had a tomb-like hollow sound and yet it was dry and stern. Even in the warmth of summer, he still had a scarf around his throat. He sat stiff and straight while looking Bertha and her mother straight in the eye. He was almost like an eagle about to swoop for its prey. Bertha felt very uncomfortable, but Augusta Kattmann was up to the occasion and neither flinched nor batted an eye. After all, she was their hostess and they were being sheltered secretly under her roof.

Bertha recognized some of the men that were present in the little office as men she supposed were businessmen passing through town. She definitely recognized two men who came to the house later in the afternoon as men who had posed as brewery supply salesmen. She began to wonder just who some of the travelers were who passed through on the canal. Were they actual travelers, or were they investigators in disguise?

On the way back home that late afternoon, Augusta Kattmann dropped a few more informative bombshells on Bertha. When all the drawstrings were drawn tight, and the case opened at a federal court in the state capitol, Mrs. Kattmann explained that Mr. MacClintock had made it clear that he wanted a good number of witnesses to back him up. It was Mrs. Kattmann's job to prepare the way for this, to ease the fear for many of the small town people, and especially the foreign Russians back on Sawmill Creek.

While reeling from that blow, Bertha then heard confirmation of the fact that her mother intended on financing a line of packets and small inns. She intended to use the trade name of *The Blue Swan Line* on all the inns as well. All of the inns were to be painted alike, have the same curtains and fixtures, and a huge wooden *Blue Swan* sign would hang over the door. *The Blue Swan* barge would be the flagship of the fleet, and of course, the *Blue Swan Ale* would be pushed as the leading beer and ale all up and down the canal. Bertha was flabbergasted. Then the next blow rained down on her. Yes, those other barges up in Toledo would soon belong to the company. Mrs. Kattmann had made down payments on them, and they were to be held until she could talk earnestly with August Ben, Ludwig and Hermann. Of course Heinrich Hofermeyer must be taken into account once the deal was made, but not until.

"Where are the inns to be, Mother?" Bertha asked feebly.

"Why, of course ve need one at the home port there in Brementown. That will be der home office for bookkeeping, accounts and servicing. It will be a good place to break in dot Heinrich and haf him close so as to keep a vatch on him, and help him over the rough spots until he gets experience - mit no loafing."

"What about the food and restaurant part of the deal?" Bertha asked. Mrs. Kattmann looked down into her lap rather sourly with a wry mouth and said,

"Dot Pepples woman! I vas thinking dot perhaps you could be vairy influential in persuading her to expand her shop and take on der food part of it. It would be good money and you know she needs the money. The fact is that she has to make it - if any is made. Und dot loud-mouthed brassy Hemels woman - a good job is what she needs to keep her out of gossip while sitting up there on dot perch above the blacksmith. It will keep her from squawking like a parrot all day."

"Mother! Do you actually think all of this will work?"

"Of course it vill work! Once the money starts coming in, everything vill click. You vill see," her confident mother assured her.

"But they are all such cronies. Will they get anything done?"

"Money talks!" Mrs. Kattmann ejaculated as she patted her ever-present black handbag while nodding to her daughter knowingly.

"And Mrs. Gertslaeker? She'll be there all the time!"

"Den ve work her in too! She needs the money vot with her daughters growing up and all. The little money she makes from odd jobs such as sewing, having overnight renters in der rooms, and cleaning houses vill help!"

"Mother! When will you learn that you can't just sit down, and plan everyone else's life and work for them? You <u>must</u> at least consult them first," Bertha complained.

"I have already talked with that Jake Hemels. He is all in favor of it, not only for the money, but also as der ideal vay to keep dot fishwife scold of Gerta Hemel busy and out of other people's business."

"Well, I'll have to give you credit for planning and trying."

"Ve see. You chust vait! It vill all work out, I am sure," her mother said with determination.

"I am sure you are sure, Mother!" Bertha admitted. "And now what other choice bits of information have you for me? Do you ever let your mind rest?"

"A busy life is a happy one, mein Bairtha! If people are busy with correct planning and direction, is good for everyone. Too many peoples fill dair lives with useless frivolity, utterly useless time-killers and pastimes. Our main direction in our lives in this world should be purpose and duty."

"Spare me the lecture on ethics, Mother. What other plans do you have for the world around you?"

"Vell, you know nursing and medicine is mein main purpose in life. Mein father was a doctor in Germany as you vill remember. My life ambition vas always to follow his footsteps, to attend classes in Leipzig, and finally to sit in his chair at Dresden and in the University of Vienna, but ach," she sighed.

"Mother! You know that is unheard of! Who ever heard of a woman attending the world's leading medical college? Why, only the top cream of the crop male doctors ever make that grade - Leipzig, Prague, Dresden and Vienna, indeed!"

"Ach Himmel. Ja, dot is true. . . at least for now, but I intend to protest, and protest hard against such injustice. Vy do you think that men haf a special edge on the brains in this vorld? Iss dair a physical difference in the tissue, or gray matter, between women and men's brains? Ach! Teufel im Hoelle. No! Nein! Nein! You know, and I know it is not so," Mrs. Kattmann fumed.

"We're off the subject. You started to tell me of another one of your pet projects," Bertha reminded her.

"Ach, yess-ss, so I vas. Mein Bairtha, I can talk to you like I cannot talk to your sisters or your Aunt Fredericka. Even I cannot talk with Papa for he cares only for his vineyards, his garden and eternal peace."

"Yes, Mother. Now go on with your project. I shall keep silent."

"Bairtha, vile you were away up north in Toledo ven you go to fetch back the *Blue Swan*, I vas also gone, as you remember."

"Yes, I remember, and you did not come home until after we did. In fact you did not come home for several days after we did."

"I was on special commission from around here to represent several counties at a meeting in Columbus with the governor."

"The governor? What on earth did you see him about? Was it temperance, crime, medical health. . . or let me see. . . orphanages, or perhaps hospitals?"

"I intend to take all dose things up in duc time, and more," Augusta Kattmann said jutting her chin out defiantly, "but for the time at hand, let us chust say that ve discussed hospitals. I vant to get one in this area. Ve need one. Papa and I have discussed it, and ve feel that we could leave no better memorial to our family and name than to give land for a home type hospital or sanatorium of some sort. You chuld see the ones at the health resorts and springs such as 'Baden Baden' in south Germany. There are also wonderful springs at Ischl in the resort area of Austria, in the Salzgammergut."

"Oh, mother. Now you are dreaming. Be practical. Do you think that people would come to a health resort out here in the backwoods?" Bertha asked her mother in disbelief.

"People are sick here just as much, iff not vorse than in the city. Ve need doctors, nurses, and places to nurse the sick. In fact, I am thinking of leaving Willow Haven out at Maria Stein for chust such purpose after Papa and I are through with it. None of you evair vant to live there."

"What came of your meeting with the governor and his committee?"

"I have reason to be encouraged. It looks like a promising thing for we have nothing here in the central western part of the state."

"I don't think I can stand much more, Mother. This has been rather much for one day. Ach Himmel!"

"And as for those unfortunate boys, they may be a fortunate blessing in disguise. If I pull logs for Angus MacClintock, he pulls them for me. When the papers in the capitol play up the news item, and Mr. MacClintock will see that they do, about how I've nursed those boys back to health from the jaws of death. He will tell how my little cottage town house served as a hospital. You can see that none of it will harm the cause that I am sponsoring for a hospital of some sort."

"Mother, this is downright amazing. And you actually have faith in all these dreams as if they could happen?" Bertha asked.

"Of course it *can* happen, and it *vill* happen," her mother said with dogged determination. "And I have one other little item to share with you, Bairtha. I chust decided today that I am going to keep those four boys. I don't know just how I will fight this corruption and disgrace with orphanage practices and with wards of der courts, but I intend to do something. I shall start mit keeping those boys. I shall educate them chust as I shall help you and August Ben, and Bernhardina and Hermann educate your children."

"And how is all this to be done? Where are these boys to live? You can't disturb Papa's peace of mind in his last years out there at <u>Willow Haven</u>. Four boys, regardless of how good they are, would ruin the rustic peace and simplicity of his life."

"You are probably right, but dose boys do need country air, sun, and work, along with the good food. They also need rich cream and milk und cheeses."

"But surely you won't put them out there?"

"I haven't decided all of this yet but one thing I do know is that for the time being, I am going to fit out that old carriage house back of my town house with bunk beds and the like. Sister Fredericka can act as a house mother. It will be good for her to have something to do besides der smiling. I shall hire tutors for their schooling and ve vill share some of the tutors for yours and Bernhardina's children. <u>Dat Louveese</u>! She needs a good tutor with a paddle."

"Mother, why don't you quit picking on Louise? She is the image of you and has your personality, get-up and nerve. You will never be able to break or curb her. She is too much like you."

"Vy Bairtha! I nevair thought of it like dot. I believe you are right. Maybe I can make good doctor, or at least nurse of our Louveese, but she will have to be disciplined. <u>Ach, dot girl</u>!"

When Bertha got home, the girls had supper ready, and Bertha persuaded her mother to stay for supper. Lou-Lou and Josie were unusually silent because they wondered just what had taken place on the long trip. They also wondered just what steps their tenacious grandmother would take concerning the information that she must have received.

Charley and Lou kept up a lively banter and little Daisy Baby was more playful than usual. If Ben suspected that anything had been discussed, he did not show it. Bertha passed the trip off as a much belated trip out to see her father.

Mrs. Kattmann did not stay long but was anxious to get over to her cottage to see how Mrs. Steinhoge was getting along with her nursing chores. When she got there, she was relieved to see that Bernhardina Gast and Aunt Fredericka had taken care of the evening meal and that young Ben had come over to play with the other boys.

Bertha went out with her mother to look at the spacious carriage house. The horses were stabled at the brewery livery barn. There was no need to keep those unused old stable stalls any longer. The carriage was usually kept in Hermann Gast's carriage house anyway since they used it the most. Yes, this would be an ideal place to start remodeling for the combination of a nursery, hospital, school and home. This was the beginning of a very big dream dear to the heart of Augusta Kattmann.

Bertha could not drive from her mind the statement her mother made concerning how fate or divine providence of God sometimes came about in disguise. The tragic despair of these unfortunate orphan boys were the instruments of the beginning of hope in the lives of many other distressed unfortunate beings.

The willow trees swaying in the breezes at <u>Willow Haven</u> must have known many secrets but they kept their tales to themselves.

CHAPTER 21

THE DAY SEEMED TO dawn full of promise. Ben and Herman Gast were in a high mood when Bertha and the girls came to the grain depot at mid morning. They announced that word had come that the special passenger packet would be coming back through with all the dignitaries bound for Toledo. However, the Governor had already gone back to Columbus.

Along in the afternoon, Charley, Lou, and young Ben came dashing down the towpath and called up to the upstairs window to Lou-Lou and Josie. They heard on their grain delivery trip in Minster that the circus and showboats were going to play there a few nights. After that, they would be up for an extended stay in Old Brementown.

Immediately the girls raced downstairs and cornered Bertha.

"The time has come at last Aunt Bert," Lou-Lou sang.

Bertha looked amazed as she sat dressing a fat chicken for frying. Josie went on to explain to her mother.

"Now will be the time. We can really make that old calliope sing out. Didn't you hear Charley and Lou? The governor's passenger packet will be coming through in a few days, but the showboats and circus from Minster will be up here soon. It's a big show too, and it's coming all the way from Cincinnati. It will be up here soon. Oh, won't we show them? We'll really spook Grandma Kattmann and all the rest of them good!"

Bertha smiled to herself. Yes, after all the serious things that had taken place, a little relief would be a good tonic. Right away both girls started practicing on the parlor organ.

The next morning the old Irish codger passed through while going north again. Ben Gast scratched his head; then he turned to his brother Hermann. They both came out on the dock in front of the grain depot and stood on the scales as they watched him pass. The minute the old Irishman saw them watching him, he began to put on his irascible and obscene act. He began cursing old Mr. MacPherson for being tardy with the lock gate. Elihu Sanders was not one to allow his friend the lockmaster take abuse. He appeared at the door of his tinker shop and let fly a stream of amber that barely missed the old Irishman's head. The old man ducked and lost his top hat as the amber missile whisked in front of his nose. He redoubled his insults while shaking his fists and then gave himself renewed energy from his always-present jug. Jake Hemel appeared at the door of the smithy with a heavy sledge hammer as the Irish barge raced on down through the lock gates, and on north toward St. Marys at a fast clip.

Gerta Hemel was dismayed for she had wanted to pay her respects to his foul mouth for quite some time. When she heard the disturbance below her, she came out on her porch above her husband's blacksmith shop armed with a huge white earthen night jar. Grünwalda Peppleman heard the commotion and appeared on her shop porch armed with the huge push broom she used to clean the streets and sidewalks in front of her little shop.

Ben watched all the commotion much as if he were watching a familiar play that he had seen many times. Each member of the cast reacted much as they had in past years.

"Hermann, there is a strange pattern to all this with the old Irish codger. You know, it is strange, but what does he carry on that infernal old barge? I don't remember ever seeing him unload a thing here in town. He doesn't pick up anything either. How does he make it?"

"I don't either. I have talked to others up and down the canal, and no one actually has seen him make a delivery in any of the small towns along our neck of the canal. It's very odd."

"Hermann, does it seem to you that he always has different crewmen? If all of them are Irishmen from those Irish camps over around Akron and Cleveland, each end up here at St. Patrick's Day. How does he get all of them? I don't recollect ever seeing any of these who were with him before."

"Yes, Ben, it is strange. Come to think of it, all those flannel-mouthed Irishmen are doing as Shanty Irish, or maybe a step up to Lace Curtain Irish, but I don't think they are at all."

"Suppose they are hustling some sort of contraband up to Toledo to go on into Canada? It wouldn't hurt to tip off old Angus MacClintock," Ben remarked.

"*Ach! Helige katzen*! It beats all how all at once the outside world suddenly descends on our little German village," Hermann said.

"That's the price we pay, Hermann, now that we are living along a main artery of traffic between large cities, the Great Lakes and the Ohio River. We are no longer isolated backwoods, Hermann, but the world is coming to our doorstep."

There was a lull in the morning work at the grain depot. Ludwig Kattmann had the boys over at the brewery helping him unload some sacks of malt and hops. They had already trundled several cartloads of grain for making mash for the great copper cookers. Since the men had a little while to wait for the dinner bell, and there was no traffic in sight on the canal to keep the lockmaster busy, Mr. MacPherson came down from his lookout booth above the weigh lock. He produced the checkerboard and called to Jake Hemel who was sitting out front on a keg. He also called to Elihu Sanders to come from his tinker shop. Then Mr. MacPherson spread the board on a barrel top in the open driveway of the grain depot. A game soon developed and the usual players appeared from the towpath. Ben and Hermann joined in, but when the lanky path master came in from his morning inspection stroll, they all complained that checkers was too slow and that only two people could play at a time. Elihu scratched his head and thought a moment; then by taking a careful aim, he splattered a thoughtless sparrow that had landed on the plank floor to scratch at some spilled grain. Laughing at his success, Elihu announced,

"It 'pears to me boys, that the board is too small. *Yessir, it's too small.*" He went to his tinker shop and brought back a large walnut folding board, which was inlaid with cherry and curly maple squares.

"Now Elihu, how in tarnation are we all going to play chess? You're no help," Mr. MacPherson complained. With an air of high handedness, Elihu chewed furiously on his tobacco quid; then he let fly another stream of amber toward the canal. Then he said,

"You boys ain't got no imagination in a time of crisis." Then he unfolded the board and turned it over to make a large four foot square on the barrel top. "If'n ye kaint climb the mountain, then fetch the mountain top down to yew," he cackled at his own wit.

The other men booed and joshed him but pulled boxes and kegs up around the improvised table. They marveled at his handiwork for he had "tinkered" in his spare time, and he had made a magnificent and intricate inlaid game board. It was laid off in sections with light maple dividers for faro banks, loo, whilst, or for roulette. While all of them marveled at his handiwork and admired the inlaid aces, the hearts, clubs, and the rest of the suites, Elihu hurried back to his shop. He brought a carved and turned roulette cup wheel made of walnut. Jake Hemel had helped him make the turning bearing on the base for the wheel to turn on. All of the men marveled at the new addition. Just as the game of roulette was getting underway, Charley Peppleman appeared in the opened breezeway at the double doors.

"Vell chentlemens, vair iss dair refreshments?" He asked upon not seeing the usual wooden pail of ale or, the huge earthen steins with lead caps.

"It's only noon Charley! Respectable people don't take spirits and beverage until after dinner in the evening," Ian MacPherson called out in high spirits, while he arched his little finger, and put on high society airs like Ernestine Hofermeyer always did.

"Ach, go along, Ian MacPherson! Deal me in. "Charley laughed but stepped back out on the dock to look up the canal to Grünwalda's pastry shop. He wanted to make sure she had not seen him slip into the depot from the lower level tunnel under the dock planks.

"I think we have all worked hard this morning, and I believe that a ladle of ale is in keeping for all of us. We have earned it," Ben Gast announced while attempting to rationalize his reasoning. Without further delay he and Hermann slipped out the wide doors on the street side, and stole up along the finger slip beside the moored *Blue Swan*. They went to the brewery icehouse and produced a keg of cold ale from the damp sawdust down next to the huge blocks of ice. They put it inside an open topped malt box to hide it, and brought it back to the depot. Charley Peppleman rubbed his hands in glee, and then massaged his ample bulging stomach in anticipation. In no time, a wooden spigot was attached to the opened end bunghole, and the golden ale flowed freely into the ladles. With the flow of ale, the spirits rose, and with it, good-natured banter, jokes, and tall stories. Jake Hemel said it was about time to make some "summer cider" from the early ripening summer russets. Elihu complained that it would get "hard" too soon in the summer heat, but Ian MacPherson assured them that there was nothing better than summer cider allowed to get hard. Then stop it by adding mustard and caraway seed to it that would be tied up in muslin balls.

The tension of the past few weeks was lifting. The old time neighborliness, good-natured banter over the back fence, or shouting down the canal towpath was coming back to the little town.

Just as the game and fun was getting into high swing Charley Peppleman stepped cautiously out on the street side of the depot to look for signs of trouble, and upon seeing none, stole out on the dock on the canal berm side and looked up and down the basin. He heard gay laughter and high chatter with German accents interspersed. He slapped his thighs in disgust and groaned a warning to the men inside the open driveway. Coming up the lock stairs on the berm footpath were Gerta Hemel and Mrs. Gertslaecker in their shawls and church bonnets. They usually took either the towpath or the berm footpath rather than the street for it took them directly to their back doors. Charley passed the warning and the men stood their ground as they formed a formidable phalanx with crossed arms ready for trouble.

The women stopped their high-spirited chatter and laughing. Then Mrs. Gertslaecker called out to the group of men who eyed them suspiciously.

"Vell, vot have we here? Ach, look Gerta! De boys are haffing a party. Ve go to church meeting of der Ladies Society and vot do ve find on de vay back? It's poker, cards, and ale!"

"Wouldn't you know it, Griselda Gertslaecker," as Gerta Hemel started her brassy-voiced tirade.

"Old woman," Jake Hemel growled, "hold it right there. We are just having a rest before dinner. You have been gadding this whole morning and I suppose there is nothing cooked for dinner, is there?"

"Mercy," Gerta gasped, and stepped over behind her ample sized companion. We were just on our way home from the meeting." Jake fondled a hickory axe handle in the palm of his hand, and Griselda Gertslaecker rushed on to say,

"We had quite a meeting this morning. Sit down boys. No harm in a little game, is there Gerta? Now wait until you hear!"

Gerta Hemel stepped to the dock and saw Grünwalda Peppleman on her porch with her arms akimbo, and knew that she was wondering what the women were doing in the grain elevator with all the men. Gerta waved to Grünwalda. Then Jake saw her motion to Grünwalda, and called out to her sharply.

"Old woman, you are just itching for trouble. Can't you keep out of nibbing into other people's business?"

"Wal Mercy! For pity sakes," Gerta gasped. She edged farther away from Jake because she expected to receive a whack across her broad backsides any minute. "But Grünwalda orter be here and hear this, Jake. We really got a hatful to tell you."

"Yeah! Sit down Gerta. Jake, shut up and lissen. We got more dirt to dish out. We're like two old elephants! Have we got a trunk load of dirt to unload on you!" Mrs. Gertslaecker said as she shrieked with laughter. Jake simmered down a little, and the rest of the men sat down at their card table.

"Oh, ice cold ale, is it? Griselda hinted. "Wal, pass it around. We are hot from walking and I'm bustin' with thirst!"

Soon the good-natured spirit of the party scene was in swing again, and they all had cold ale to quench their thirst. Everyone began talking at once, and the high shrill laughter of the women could be heard above the loud guffaws of the men. Grünwalda Peppleman could stand the suspense no longer, and she knew that something must really be afoot or Gerta would not have motioned for her to come. Then she wiped her face and rearranged her apron. She started down the towpath toward the grain depot. Charley Peppleman spotted her as she crossed the high foot bridge to come across from the towpath side to the berm side and the depot docks. Mrs. MacPherson and Mrs. Sanders heard all the laughing and high shrieks and came out on the berm. Grünwalda motioned them to come along, and all three women came up onto the planks of the dock. Charley started to hop around, while calling and wailing,

"Mein Gott! Mein Gott!"

"Now you men just stand your ground. Put the cards and chips away but keep the ale. Gerta and me, ve take care of Grünwalda!" Jake said.

Just then, Grünwalda Peppleman and the other two women came to the open wide doors and looked in at the scene of noisy gaiety.

"Vell, vot on airth iss going on here, Gerta?" Grünwalda demanded. Then she looked over at Charley who was standing apart from the others. He was near the street side door, and was ready to retreat.

"Chust on my way home, love," Charley answered angelically.

"Ladees! Ladees! Come in, *do come in*," Ben Gast called. He was putting on the act of the perfect host while pulling up wood chairs, kegs, and store boxes for seats.

"Elihu Sanders," his wife called sharply. "No wonder you can't hear me callin for dinner. Now you git home and git washed up."

"And the same goes for you, Ian MacPherson. The idee! You men carry on like a pack of boys with marbles. It's dinner time," Mrs. MacPherson said sharply. Mrs. Gertslaecker saved the situation by raising her mug of ale and waving to the other women.

"Stow all that, girls. Now stop cackling like a bunch of old hens, and sit down and lissen. Gerta and me here, have quite a bit to tell you."

Charley pulled up a low grain tub made out of a hollowed out sycamore log and offered it to his huge wife and said,

"Here love! Rest yourself," and he turned his head and mumbled mischievously, "I think dis orter hold you!" He ducked his head as she slapped at him and missed. Good humored jokes and gay banter soon had the newcomers laughing and joining in on the noonday fun.

Bertha Gast rang her dinner bell for the first early call, but only the boys came from the brewery. There was no sign of Hermann and August Ben. Lou-Lou and Josie took a stroll up the towpath to look across the canal and into the open grain depot, and to motion to the men to come home to dinner. Still they did not come.

After a while Grünwalda could stand the sight of the inviting ale keg no longer, and she motioned for the only too willing Charley Peppleman to give her a mug of the delicious yellow liquid. Mrs. MacPherson and Mrs. Sanders, not being of German blood, disdained the horrid bitter stuff. They did sip a little now and then at Grünwalda's urging, and admitted that it was less "horrid" than most of it. However, at its best it was only good for a "physic" or to wash your feet in. The way was clear and everyone was in a gay receptive mood. The jokes flew rapidly, and a few German songs floated out on the townspeople's ears. Grünwalda made the heavy plank floor boards groan when she did a short German ladler dance while the rest of them sang the ditty about "Iss diss den ein Snitzelbank."

Elihu brought out a jug of wine from the oats bin and urged it onto his wife, Clara Nell, and to Marybelle MacPherson. The deceptively sweet wine slowly won over the two women as they became jovial with the others as they shrieked with laughter. Lou-Lou and Josie watched from the other side of the canal in transfixed fascination. Lou-Lou laughed as she said to Josie,

"Why this is better than the show at Junction City. It's better than a side show too! What do you suppose is going on?"

"There ain't no telling. They had a big meeting up at church this morning and I heard Aunt Ernestine tell Mama when she came by on her way home, that Grandma really floored them all. I don't know what all she told them, but plenty, I'll bet!"

"Charley and his brother Ben said they were awfully loud and that Grandma-Má really got to hollering and pounded her fists together. She scairt Aunt Fredericka so much that she started crying, and almost fell off the organ stool when she was playin' for all their choral singing. Papa and Uncle Ben will have to install that steam calliope so the music can be heard above all their hollerin' and whoopin'." Both girls laughed at their observations but kept an eye on the group across the canal that was having such a good time.

Charley Gast called up to the girls from the side porch,

"Ma says for you girls to come on and eat. If Pa and Uncle Hermann don't know enough to quit work and eat while they kin eat high on the hog, then they will have to take leftovers and scraps." The girls nodded their heads and waved to Charley as he rang the dinner bell again.

Griselda Gertslaecker, always the life of any party with her pleasant broad face and hearty shrill laugh, was in fine shape. When Grünwalda finished her act, Griselda and Gerta took turns at telling jokes that the others had to fill in or guess the answers. While turning to Ben Gast, she addressed a riddle to him,

"Mein Ben, Do you know what the fork said to the spoon?" Ben remembered the old worn out minstrel joke, but could not think of the answer. He knew it was a pun on words of some sort.

"New, Griselda! What did the fork say to the spoon?"

"Who was that ladle I saw you out with last night?" she asked. Ben scratched his head while trying to remember. He shook his head as she shouted in high laughter,

"That was no ladle! That was my knife!"

Charley Peppleman shouted with laughter that was louder than any of them, but he quieted down when he saw Grünwalda's laugh fade into a scowl as she looked at him squarely. He patted her cheek and stepped around her gingerly as he teased,

"Papa love mamma! Mamma love Papa!"

Even Jake Hemel joined in the fun and forgot his seriousness. Gerta noticed his humor and joined the other ladies in loud fun. Upon Hermann Gast's urging about the morning session of the Ladies Society, Temperance Society, or Society of Foreign Missions, whatever this one was, Griselda Gertslaecker launched into her recital.

"Now you just ask Gerta here if I ain't tellin it right. You won't believe your ears. As you know, Frau Augusta Kattmann called the meetin' and what a meetin' it was. Why I never been so . . ."

"You better get on with it, Griselda, before old lady Kattmann comes in here and catches us drinking up all the profit from *The Blue Swan Brewery*," Gerta said with her brassy shrill voice.

"Woman! Watch your tongue," Jake warned her while looking at Ben and Hermann to see if they took offense with the reference to their mother-in-law. Some of the others started digging into their pockets for small coin tips to pay for the ale, when Ben put up his hand in protest, and said smiling,

"It's all on the house. Besides, it pays to advertise!"

Mrs. Gertslaecker launched into her story a second time,

"You never heard such a spirited meetin'. Frau Kattmann really was in fine voice. You could hear her hollerin' over the noise of the grist mill at the edge of town, if you wuz listenin'!"

"What was it all about?" Hermann asked, anxious to hear about his illustrious mother-in-law, even if only second-handed.

"After all our business (dull stuff) was over, dues paid, tithes promised, aid boxes collected and the like, she really let us have it. Know what? She is going to remodel that large carriage house of hers out back of her cottage over there and make it into a sort of a second school and dormitory for them orphan boys."

"That ain't all. She is going to hire tutors and teachers and her own grandkids are going to attend school too! Yessir-ee! And you know what? The rest of us can send our kids too, that is if we all help out with tuition to help pay for the tutors. Now smoke that!"

"That sounds like a good thing. It's cheaper than for the rest of the parents to have to hire teachers just for their own kids," Jake Hemel said while the MacPhersons nodded their heads in agreement.

"Now let me see. What else did she say, Gerta? Oh, yes, she is going to put the finances of this town on its feet. She is going to make jobs for more of us. There is going to be a line of passenger packets called *The Blue Swan Line* that will have inns for overnight guests as well as food places all up and down the canal." Ben slapped Hermann on the back and said,

"I told you, Hermann. Bertha was right. She hit it."

"She wants us all to chip in and help with sewing for them boys: curtains, bed clothes and the like. It's sorta going to be a community project with all of us helpin' out, with the school, that is."

"Well now, don't that beat all? That woman! There is no limit to what she can do once her mind is put to it. She'll be running for public office next," Mrs. Sanders exclaimed. Just then Mr. Bushman, town constable, who herd all the loud voices, sauntered into their midst. Grünwalda scoffed upon seeing him,

"She could do a better job than some of our public officers."

Griselda did not want the audience she had to lose its receptiveness, nor for the feelings of the constable to be hurt, so she handed him a mug of ale and then went on hurriedly,

"And you know what? She has been to Columbus to a special committee meeting with the governor. She was summoned there by him. No wonder there was all that bowing and scraping, and dressin' up in wedding finery when the governor's packet went through here. Did you see him bow to Gusta Kattmann and her sister Fredericka? He was bowing and curtsyin' back like they wuz royalty or something. It was that day when yer whole clan, Ben, was congregated there on your lawn along the towpath." Griselda sputtered as she gasped for breath.

"What was the special committee, Zelda?" Mrs. Sanders asked.

"Why it's something or other about starting a sanatorium or hospital of some sort in this area. God knows this section of the country needs something, and Augusta Kattmann and Mrs. Steinhoge would be the very ones to run it. They know more than most of our quack doctors around here - those old saw-bones!" Gerta spoke up while Griselda got her breath and Grünwalda grunted.

"Now I'll admit there is much to be done. Mrs. Kattmann says there is a cryin' need for reform laws, something to curb the evil practices like what happened to them four orphan boys, some other bad things, and to keep sech things frum happenin' again. God only knows how many times this sort of criminal abuse goes on that we don't know about."

"That's right, old woman. Get *your* teeth into it," Jake exclaimed.

"I intend to do just that, Jake Hemel!" She retorted defiantly.

After a few more exchanges of comments the surprised listeners had more ale. They had much to think about. Then the conversation fell to discussing the fate of the boys, the Russian sawmill people and all the strange suspicious law people who were questioning people in a quiet but firm sort of way. The sheriff in the county seat was pretty upset about it, for none of them talked to him or took him into their confidence. Mr. Bushman wanted to appear to know more than he did. Then Grünwalda told him to be quiet, that he did not know anything all, and never did.

"It would have done all yer hearts good though," Gerta asserted, "to have seen old lady Kattmann holding them all spellbound like puppets on a string. She got to waving her arms and carryin' on like the old cat in the shavings and raisin box . . ."

Jake cleared his throat and growled at her when Griselda Gertslaecker said,

"And that final doxology. . . Why, Fredericka nearly fell off the organ stool while trying to watch Augusta, and play for the singin' at the same time!"

". . . And, that final speech just before the prayer for letting out. She really let us all have it - told us what our Christian duty wuz, and to dig deep in our purses to help the causes. But you know, I think old lady Kattmann had had a nip or two. She was so happy. . . and <u>Loud</u>! The way she got to hollerin' on that last dismissal prayer! Whew! I never heard her holler so loud, and Fredericka forgot herself, tied up her bonnet strings and started playin' before Augusta was through! The good Lord surely heard that one!"

They all laughed at the story Griselda and Gerta told; then the conversation turned to more mundane things: the coming showboats, carnival, and circus. Grünwalda arose to start home saying,

"This is a week-day/work-day. I have pies to fix for the packet to pick up this afternoon for delivery on south. Ben, Hermann, much thanks for the ale." She looked out the wide street side doors and up at the brick smokestack of the brewery, pointed to the huge <u>Blue Swan Ale</u> advertising sign high up on the stack, and she called out to it in a booming voice,

"Old Swan, this golden stuff you lay ain't eggs but you neffer let us down. Your squirtin's don't get rotten - they just mellow with age." All the rest of them clapped their hands as they shouted and laughed in agreement. Then Grünwalda turned to Ben,

"And Mein Ben! Hermann! You better get rid of dese loafers here if you vant work done. They will drink you out of house, home, brewery and depot. You better smash dis playing board here for only evil will come of it," she declared, as she tapped the board.

Charley's Grünwalda did not get far.

"Hands off that board woman," Jake Hemel said while stepping up. The rest of the men formed a defensive cordon around Elihu's precious piece of handiwork. Grünwalda stepped back. She was surprised at the spunk of the men. Griselda and Gerta led her off to the side when Jake Hemel flexed his blacksmith muscles, and slapped the axe handle in the palm of his hand. Elihu, Ben, and the others stood with him.

"This is a work of art, Grünwalda Peppleman," Jake said, "and one small act to deface or desecrate it, and <u>whist</u>! It's into the canal with you."

"Wal mercy! Pity sakes, Jake Hemel!" Gerta almost whimpered, but Jake laughed showing white teeth through his walrus like moustache.

"Wal I never! Did you ever?" Grünwalda gasped in disbelief.

"No and neither will you, if you don't get home love," Charley said to her affectionately. "Come, love, let us go to dinner."

As the two huge people left the dock and started up the berm path arm in arm, the rest of the party laughed at their departure. Lou-Lou and Josie watched and then went home to report to Bertha what they had seen and heard.

Charley and Grünwalda Peppleman did not get far along the towpath's berm after leaving the grain depot's canal basin where there was a mere widening of the canal into wide water, upon which the loading docks of the grain warehouse fronted. There they met Marta Schweitermann, Charley's sister and the mayor's wife, Zelda Zinndorfer who had heard the boisterous laughter and the singing coming from the grain depot. The women hurried their steps in order to get in on the fun - whatever it was. They were coming from the south from the vicinity of the large Cherry Street canal basin and were walking on Canal Street, when they looked over and saw Grünwalda and Charley on the berm of the canal. The women called to them.

When they overtook Charley and Grünwalda, Martha asked at once what had been going on at the depot. When she learned that she had missed the singing, ale, and good stories, she was crestfallen but not for long. Her indomitable good spirits and sense of outrageous humor came rushing back. Zelda Zinndorfer was sober faced as usual, and her pursed mouth was drawn into a thin line when Augusta Kattmann's name or that of the ramrod-stiff Anna Steinhoge was mentioned. The two women told Grünwalda that they had been delivering some ironing and some homemade laundry soap to Mrs. Lanfersieck, who lived there by the ice house, when Mrs. Schulenberg and Birte Brüggemann came in to "sit a spell," and before they knew it, it was noon.

Grünwalda mentioned to Marta about the coming carnival and fair and that some of the women mentioned setting up a church bazaar or food booth to make money for the church. It seemed that Mrs. Kattmann had mentioned it in her "loud hollerin'" that morning at the church meeting. Zelda Zinndorfer sniffed at this revelation.

"Hm-n-f! If there is money to be concerned, you can be sure that old lady Kattmann will have her hand in the till first." Marta, who was unable to repress her humorous mimicry, drew her large form very erect, and held her ample knees tightly together as she attempted to hobble along with menacing steps to imitate Anna Steinhoge.

"Hess, yes-s-s, Ja, Gnädig Frau Kattmann, you are precisely correct. That is what we shall do. *Das ist korreckt. Rechtig.*"

"Dot is almost exactly what she *did* say when Gusta Kattmann mentioned the bazaar, or anything else she mentioned," Grünwalda told Marta. "Und den she socks dat useless glass monicker in her eye and stares at us like a dead fish."

Even the usually stoic expression of Zelda Zinndorfer melted into a sheepish grin that she couldn't hide. The other women and Charley could not help laughing at the mimicry. Then Marta became serious as she told Grünwalda,

"Valta, why not vouldn't the bazaar be a good idea to make monies for the church?" Marta always pronounced Grünwalda's name with the umlaut "u" sound, so that it sounded more like the correct German, and pronounced "Gryn-valta" and not "Groon-waldy" as some of the second and third German-American generations said it.

"Hump-f!" Zelda said grudgingly, "It would make more money and be so much easier than all that quilting we do to sell our homemade quilts. All that spinning and weaving for them coverlets and the like takes a lot more time than food preparation."

"Valta, she iss so right. Don't you see, ve get most of the food donated by soliciting our church people and townspeople alike. Most of the food will be prepared at home. Come on back and let's go tell them while ve got them all cornered," Marta exclaimed.

They turned their steps back to the grain depot, but as they neared the depot dock, Henry Backhaus called to Marta from the flour mill door at the lock. His musical high baritone voice was rippling with hidden laughter as he asked,

"Oh Marta, were there any new stories this morning from down at the basin? Are there any more 'kronsbeere?'"

"And good day to you, Henry. *Kronsbeere? Vass ist? Wo wachsen sie?*"

"*Wo wachsen sie?* Where do they grow?" Henry asked her. Lou-Lou and Josie had been watching from across the canal on the wide towpath side of the main canal right of way. Lou-Lou exclaimed,

"There is that dumb old joke they think is so funny. They never will tell it aloud whenever any of us kids are around. I can't find out from Papa or Aunt Bert."

"Well, it must be something not intended for our tender young ears. It's something about some dumb old cranberries that grow down in the swamp bottoms and river marshes," Josie told her.

"And did you see old Marta imitating that stiff Steinhoge? Now if I do that around home, I get my ears boxed," Lou-Lou complained.

"That cranberry thing is a joke on Grandma Kattmann. It's some dumb thing she said somewhere over in the old country (Germany). Maybe it is a play on words, for she is always getting her English slang mixed up with her garbled mixture of German and English," Josie said. The girls listened as the charade continued when Ludwig Watermann at the woolen mill next to Henry's flour mill called from his landing,

"Ja, Marta, vere do they grow, Wo wachsen sie?"

Griselda and Gerta heard the loud shrieks of laughter, and the yelping short laughs of Ludwig Watermann above Henry Backhaus' high tenor.

"You know where," Marta fairly screamed in laughter as she patted her ample backsides and said, "in th' marsh!"

Lou-Lou and Josie were astonished at the high shrieking laugh that came from Griselda at the grain depot's doorway.

"Now that is really hilarious. What is funny about a marsh?" Lou-Lou said sarcastically. Charley and Lou had come up the towpath to get the girls to come to dinner, and to call their fathers for the second time for their noonday meal. Young Ben came running behind, but all of them heard the exchange of jokes between Martha and Henry. Charley told Lou-Lou when he heard her complaint,

"If you knew what it meant, and knew the German dialect, you would see the funny side of it." (In the marsh is almost vulgar German. "Im arsch - in the a--.")

"Well, do you boys know?" Josie pressed her brother, Charley.

"Well, yes, we know the general gist of it, but it's too ornery to tell you girls. You'll tell on us and then we'll ketch it."

"Charley Gast," Lou-Lou exploded, "Have we ever told on you guys?" Charley, Lou and Ben admitted that they never had.

"No, and we won't, not unless you go and spill your insides on Josie and me," Louise Gast said threateningly. "Not that we don't have a trunk full of stuff on you. Come on and tell us Charley."

"I can't, Lou-Lou, I mean I don't know the German dialect and the play on English and German words that make it funny. Tell you what, if you won't get us in trouble, I'll get Jakey Backhaus to tell it. He can imitate his old man, Henry, to a perfect 't.' However, it's sorta bad."

"We promise," Louise and Josie told the boys as they urged them on.

"Not here, but maybe tonight when we can all get together away from all-prying ears, and away from the stern looks from home."

"What do you mean? Do you have a 'trunk full' on us?" Lou Gast asked.

"Lou Gast, and you too Charley, and Ben; do you think we girls don't know when you have been smoking that coffee, or that corn silk in them corn-cob pipes you have hidden up in the rafters above the granary?

"When was this? How can you tell?" The boys asked almost in chorus.

"How can we tell? Anybody can tell if they get close to you. You boys need to wash your hands and face good in hot water and some of Marta's lye soap fer that stuff smells. Someday Mama and Papa will catch you."

"Albert Wiemeyer got caught and was paddled fer it," Ben told the others, "but he said it was because he forgot to chew peppermint and chop some green onion tops fer his breath."

"Did it stop him?" Josie asked her brothers, as she smiled slyly.

"Why, heck no," Lou said bravely. "He smokes like a chimney."

"We're about ready to try some dried tobacco leaves. The Langhorst boys are drying some that they filched from their old man's patch out along the canal toward Lock 2. I don't know if I'm game yet or not," Ben said.

"Well, I don't know what you get out of that choking, strangling stuff; it's enough to kill you. I don't see how the real tobacco leaf could be any worse," Lou-Lou admonished them.

"How do ye know it's so strangling?" Ben asked his sister suspiciously.

"Yeah, yeah, come on and do tell!" Charley and Ben teased them. "You have tried it too, hain't ye?"

The girls knew they were trapped and would have to confess honestly if they expected the boys to share their confidences with them.

"Well, jest once. Jest a little mind you, but it was jest awful," Louise admitted. Josie nodded her head while pretending to fan her mouth.

"Kin you top this?" The boys asked each other laughing loud at the huge joke. "When did you do it? Where did ja get it?"

"Well, it was only once, but it was real tobacco. It was Uncle Henry Hofermeyer's pipe. Dear God it was awful, but he left that curled stemmed long pipe on his smoke stand one day when we were there. The room reeked worse than a Turkish smoking den, so we were safe, and the thing still was burning when he left it to tend to some customers."

"And you girls took a long drag on that thing?" Lou asked.

"And Josie, did you too?" Her brother, Lou, asked in disbelief.

"As I live and breathe, but never again. Why we couldn't get our breath without wheezing for several minutes," Josie laughed.

"*Gee-zooks! Ach himmel!*" Charley laughed as he wheeled on his heels and clapped his hands. "Can't you imagine Aunt Ernestine and all her fine manners fer fine young ladies? Can't you imagine her face if she had caught you?"

"Oh, she would have laid a goose egg right there! Land, would we have ever have caught it! Why Grandma Kattmann would have sent us to a girls' boarding school over in the old country somewhere," Lou-Lou laughed in glee.

"How did ja know we smoked and where we hid our pipes and stuff?"

"That was no big secret. We followed you and watched you. We found yer pipes and some corn silk wrapped in thin corn shucks up there in them rafters that are high above the granary where Papa and Uncle Hermann would never find them. However, you fellows better watch, for you might carry some sparks or embers and set the depot on fire," Josie told them emphatically.

"Yes, and we know you got real bold and smoked down under the dock planks right here on the canal wide water basin. We could smell the smoke, and see it comin' up through them planks one day when Papa and Uncle Ben were gone to Minster with some grain," Lou-Lou told them. The boys were quite surprised.

"Yes, and one day when you guys wouldn't take us along, and Papa let you take the horse and rig to go fishing up on the St. Marys River north of town," Josie added. "Why we girls, Lou-Lou, me, the Langhorst girls, and Dorothea Waterman followed you."

"You followed and spied on us?" Lou accused his sister.

"Oh, we made it look all up and up. You see, we were all going on a picnic outing for the girls our age. We took Waterman's carriage because our baskets were heavy. Oh, it was fun," Lou-Lou said.

"But we knew some secrets you boys didn't know we found out. Gertrude Langhorst, or Gertie, as we girls call her, found out some way that her brothers had some homemade wine, and their smoking, hidden away in the tile works. You know, all them sprawling acres of buildings up there at William Langhorst's Tile Works on the canal toward Lock 2.

"You didn't!" Charley and the other boys gasped in surprise. "If you ever let out a hint of that we will really catch it. It wasn't wine. Jakey Backhaus, Wiemeyer, Chris Schroeder and Johnny Schlesselman all learned how to make some home brew beer from Schlesselmann's brewery, or maybe they got some of the lager out of the vats and made the real thing. It sure tasted good even if it was bitter," Lou told them.

"What do you mean <u>was</u> bitter? It still is, and it's still there," Lou-Lou told them through her giggles. "Oh, that is vile - real bad!"

"You found that too?" Charley cried out in alarmed surprise.

"There's nothing hard about that. Gertie and her younger sister, and Bert Waterman sampled it one hot day and they all got sick. They had to make up some story about too many green apples in Waterman's orchard."

"Well, if that don't beat all," Ben and Charley said in unison.

"Now you gonna tell us about them dumb cranberries and where they grow?" Lou-Lou pressed them. She knew the boys were in a corner.

"Tonight, if we can get Jakey to come over. We gotta think of a place where we can meet and the folks won't suspect anything," Lou said.

"That is an agreement. Now the worst thing about follering you that day was that we had to be careful. We saw where you jaybirds tied up along the river bank, and had to tie our carriage rig up a long ways back in the woods so you wouldn't see us," Josie explained.

"After we had our picnic, we sneaked up through all that underbrush along the St. Marys so you wouldn't see us. It was little fishin' you were doing. It looked more like Indians around a campfire the way you were all trying to fire up from that small fire of sticks you had there on the bank," Lou-Lou told them. The boys sat down on a plank bench just off the towpath as if their legs were failing them.

Just then they heard Bertha Gast beating a wooden spoon on the bottom of a large kettle to get their attention. She had rung the dinner bell again, but no one had noticed it. She wondered why Charley and Lou had not brought the others down the towpath and home to dinner. She waved at them and beckoned to them to come on home.

The merry high-jinks quieted down on the other side of the canal as Marta and the others went back into the wide center hall of a driveway of the depot to join the group they had just left.

Bertha Gast rang her dinner bell again in vexation; then she beat on the large brass kettle. Josie and Charley waved back to her as she beckoned to them from the home on the canal which was just beyond First Street, and a little over a couple of town blocks to the north.

Leo Wiemeyer called from his flax seed mill to Thomas Speckman at the woolen mill next to him,

"What on earth did that Marta Schweitermann tell Henry and Ludwig? There'll be no work done today, either at Gasts' grain depot or at those flour mills this day, by the way they are going. What is going on up at the depot anyhow? It seems like everybody is going up there."

Without delays or formal prelude, both Grünwalda and Marta launched directly into their subject with concerted purpose. They sprang the idea of a church bazaar to sell not only their handiwork (needlework) at the fair, but also to sell food.

Then it seemed as if everyone started talking at once. They all seemed to feel the enthusiasm of Marta and Grünwalda's idea. Zelda Zinndorfer did not stay long. She was the lone Catholic in the group, and she began to get ideas of her own. She would go immediately to the Father and then her husband, the mayor, and see if it would not be a good idea for the Catholic Church down there on Walnut Street to have their own bazaar and food booth. Why let the German Lutheran Church up there on Herman Street hog the whole show? Pretty soon all the other smaller churches would get the idea, and there would be too many for them to make a profit.

The group in the grain depot decided that a larger group meeting was necessary to get the plan in action. They would call a larger meeting for that night right there in the grain depot. There was no use going up to Herman Street to the church. They would not have to dress up very much but could go as they were to the grain warehouse depot.

Grünwalda and Marta seized upon the idea of sending the Gast children, along with some of their friends, to the homes of most of the church members to tell them to come to the depot for a meeting to make plans for the coming fair and carnival.

Ben and Hermann Gast called their boys and girls to come from across the canal to the depot.

"Ach, since you are so busy eavesdropping, mein liebchens," Griselda told them, "it giffs you something bigger to fasten your teeth in."

"Ja, and der laigs too. Ve need all of you to help." Grünwalda added. Ben and Hermann Gast explained to the young boys and girls what their chore was as soon as they had eaten their dinners.

"Lou-Lou, Josie and the boys watched the others leave, especially Charley and Grünwalda Peppleman as they walked arm in arm down the towpath. They almost took up the whole width! They reported to Bertha what they had seen when they got home. In desperation, Bertha set all of them down to their meal; then she took her kettle and wooden spoon and started up the towpath. She crossed over the bridge to Canal Street, and went straight to the depot.

The party was still boisterous, even though it was about to break up by the time Bertha came over the foot bridge and onto the depot's dock. No one paid any attention to her for they were all looking out the other doors and down the street. Gerta Hemel had spied Augusta Kattmann's open carriage in the distance. It looked as if she, Fredericka, and Mrs. Steinhoge were taking the four little boys for an open-air ride in the sun, and they were coming down the side street, which would bring them past the brewery and on to the dead end where the street branched into a "t" at the grain depot.

"*Mein Helige Gott*! Let's all get out of here. She iss headed this way!" Mrs. Hemel and Mrs. Gertslaecker made a dash for the canal side of the depot when Bertha shocked all of them into silence by pounding on the huge brass dishpan with the heavy wooden spoon, and calling shrilly to her husband,

"Ben Gast! I have rung that bell until I have rope calluses! No wonder none of you heard it. Now it's past dinner time!"

"Ah, Berta, Mein Liebchen," Ben lapsed into affectionate German, "Ve vair chust having a town committee meeting to plan for the coming showboat and circus. Ve business men here must plan . . . ."

"Ja! Dots right, mein Berta," Griselda Gertslaecker cooed while pinching Bertha's cheek as she passed. We had a 'Business meeting!'"

"Monkey business! It smells like a brewery here. I suppose that board on the barrel is for the 'Board Meeting' you just had! Really, Ben!"

Mrs. MacPherson and Mrs. Sanders made a quiet get-away, and smiled sheepishly at Bertha, who by this time has lost her anger and was tempted to smile at the child-like scene of gaiety before her.

"Here comes Mother and Mrs. Steinhoge. All the neighbors are looking this way," Bertha warned Ben and Hermann.

"Quick, get that ale keg, Ben," Elihu moaned. Jake Hemel picked up the nearly empty keg and hurled it back into an oats bin where the path master quickly covered it with grain sacks. The women dashed back into the depot and made a quick sweep of the beer and ale mugs that were still sitting on the floor, ground, and on the playing board. They gathered them up not a minute too soon and put them inside the malt box. Ian MacPherson threw some grain sacks over the mugs, covered the top of the open box with the folded playing board and sat down on it. Elihu had already gathered up the chips and roulette wheel and had made his getaway up the canal side of the depot to his tinker shop.

When Augusta Kattmann and Mrs. Steinhoge passed the depot, only Bertha, Ben and Hermann were in the driveway, and Jake and Ian MacPherson stood talking. Bertha waved gaily at her mother, as did Ben and Hermann, while calling out greetings. Mrs. Kattmann, without stopping the horses, looked them all up and down with her stem glasses. Then she smiled and called that they were taking the boys for a ride in the open air and sun. The little boys smiled brightly. They were glad for a chance to be out in the open at last. However, the little boy that was last found half dead, was propped up and wrapped in a light coverlet blanket. Everyone along the way waved to them and called out cheerfully to them.

After the carriage passed, Bertha said severely,

"And now you two culprits, march home to dinner! You can get hot water and soap and wash those mugs yourselves."

Chapter 22

Bertha and Ben Gast went with Hermann to talk with his wife, Bernhardina, about the planned meeting. They all thought it best to talk it over with Augusta Kattmann because all things connected with the German Lutheran Church deeply concerned her. The same was true of the German Catholic Church. Many said that Augusta contributed heavily to it since Anna Steinhoge was one of the arch pillars of that church.

Augusta Kattmann turned her head to listen to one and then to another. After they had spoken, she closed her eyes, batted them a few times as she did when in deep thought. Then she answered simply and directly.

"Ja, mein Bairtha, Bernhardina, Ben, and Hermann, the idea is gut, very *sehr gut*. In fact, I have long been thinking of chust this. Ve need to make moneys for the church, and how bettair than this? Ja, go ahead, haf der meeting up at the depot and we won't haf to sweep out der church, dust and the like."

Bertha smiled at Ben and Hermann; then nodded to Bernhardina as if to say, "Give them sugar and they will take the bit." Then Augusta went on and her words struggled to keep up with her mind,

"And mein Ben and Hermann, vy not get Ludwig to stir up the brewery, and make some extra barrels of *The Blue Swan Ale*? We strike vile the iron is hot, *sehr heiss*, kill many of der goose with one swan. Ve need to haf a large sign. Elihu can make us a sign mit a picture of der Swan, and you boys make der stand and sell der ale. Now we can't sell ale in the church bazaar. Of course der Catholics might, eh Anna? However, ve, ve cannot. It is the way to make moneys. People will be dry, und you know these Deutsch people. They take cold beer and ale any day to water." She dismissed them with a wave of her thick arm.

"Ja, it has my blessing. Get to it. Ve haven't so much of der time."

When they had left her parlor, Augusta Kattmann told Anna Steinhoge, "Now, mein Anna, I don't think ve should go to der meeting. I haf given my blessing, and that is enough. I think our presence there might dampen the spirits - 'put brakes on the project!'" Anna Steinhoge stiffened a little, compressed her lips, and did not quite know how to take the statement. However, she agreed.

Bertha and Ben did not tarry long at Hermann and Bernhardina's gate, but knew that they should get home and set their project in order. They hurried on home in a few minutes in order to get Josie and the boys started on their errands, as well as getting Lou-Lou and her brother, Benjie, to help them. It would be a good thing to keep all of those other neighborhood town kids busy helping by going all over town to summon the parishioners to the meeting. As for those living in the countryside, they would just have to go ahead without them and hope there would be no hard feelings because they were not consulted on this project of the church.

While spreading the word about the meeting in the depot for the coming fair, carnival, or showboat and circus, whichever first came to mind, Lou-Lou, Josie, and the boys also spread their own word about their own secret party. They would all walk innocently down the towpath to the northeast in a group, as many of the young people oft times did. Then after dark, when the coast seemed clear, they would gather inside the Langhorst Tile warehouse and have their own party. Nearly all of their parents would be at the depot meeting. It promised to be a great lark, and Jakey Backhaus agreed to tell them the German dialect jokes - with no holds barred. However, the girls all had to agree to listen and not to go home and tell it all.

Hermann and Ben took the large reflector bow lamp from the beak of the swan on the *Blue Swan* barge and brought it to the grain depot. They hung it high up on the wall to one side of the depot's center hall driveway. Benches were made by putting planks over small kegs for makeshift seats. Many kegs were spread around for other people to use as seats. Other lanterns were lit, and the smell from the flames filled the interior of the depot with their slight odor. There was an air of carnival spirit and excitement that seemed to fill the arriving crowd with anticipation.

Hermann and Ben opened the informal meeting with a cheerful greeting and then turned the meeting over to Griselda, Grünwalda and Marta. However, they could not ignore Gerta Hemel because she called out her ideas from time to time. Bertha and Bernhardina also made comments. They wondered what their sister (Ernestine Hofermeyer) down at Minster would think of it. They also wondered what Aunt Fredericka would think of having the church traffic in a carnival huckster booth to make money. Would they faint when they learned that Mrs. Kattmann had suggested, even ordered, that they have a separate stand for *Blue Swan Ale*?

Marybelle MacPherson, along with Clara Nell Sanders, told them all that the best way to get a great deal of solicited food was to make out lists of what was needed. Then they could have different ones sign up for what they would bring. If they waited for the ladies to bring donations at random, the bazaar would flounder. They would do much better if they told the ladies what was expected of them. After all, the slate of the church roof <u>did</u> need repair, and the rains did not wait, nor were they respecters of persons. Everyone was in an agreeable mood. All of them agreed on the committees and the proposed ideas. The men fell to discussing the best plans, shapes, and sizes for the needlework booth and on the larger one for the food. They would have a large square booth with counters around the outside. There would be bench seats at the counters. The overflow crowd would be served in an adjoining space that would look much like an outdoor cafe with tables and chairs. There would be girls and women to serve them.

As the evening wore on, Marta, Griselda, Henry Backhaus and some of the other men from the adjoining mills, grew louder and louder with their laughter. Gerta Hemel and Grünwalda had to pound on a heavy oak work table with a wooden mallet to demand order. Everyone knew that there was an exchange of stories making the rounds on the side and in the granary where they were sittin'. The voice of Ludwig Waterman could be heard with his distinctive yelping "ho-ho-ho," along with Leo Wiemeyer's outbursts. Charley Peppleman's rapid grunting belly laughs were interspersed with Jake Hemel's deep guttural guffaws. Marta could keep up with the best of them and never ran out of stories.

Marta avoided the "cranberry story" for fear of offending the Gasts and their wives, who were daughters of Mrs. Augusta Kattmann. The story made Augusta the butt of the joke, but everyone in town loved it.

The business meeting, which had been a huge success, was about over when Ludwig Kattmann, with the help of some of the brewery men, namely Johann Vogelsang and the Fechlenberg men, came to the depot floor with kegs of cold ale from the brewery icehouse down the slip. The festive mood fell into full swing, and so did Marta, Grünwalda and Griselda. In a smaller group at the side of the granary and away from the main floor, this group became so loud with their laughter that everyone else was fascinated by them. They wondered what Marta was telling.

Her stories were always even more interesting because they were anecdotes about living people. They were stories that actually had happened. In addition, her acting out the characters, her mimicry and her dialect made the stories priceless to her listeners. She was a born storyteller. No one thought anything about the fact that she was a widow, and that her listeners were not only some of her women friends, but also included a good many of the married men who were businessmen downtown and on the towpath. The same was true of Griselda's stories. She was also a widow who had to make her own living in the town. No one thought anything about it. Marta was Marta, Griselda was Griselda, and that was that. No one or no thing would change them. The town loved to hear their shrill laughter in early morning as it rang over the downtown and up and down the canal. It was like a morning clarion calling the whole town to life. The same was true of the high tenor laugh of Henry Backhaus and the distinctive yelping laugh of Ludwig Waterman.

Marta was in fine form as she launched into another story that she had just heard that morning down on the Cherry Street Basin while she was visiting some of her lady soap customers and delivering some ironing.

"It seemed there was a family of five bachelor brothers named Schwede who lived out in the country. Maybe they lived up north near Fledderjohn's sawmill at the lock."

(Marta told them that the Schwedes were related to the Brinkmeyers.) Gerta Hemel and Grünwalda urged her on, as did Henry, Jake and the others.

"Now these brothers had a younger brother dat dey made do all dere drudgery chobs such as clean der house, cook der food and clean up after them. The older brothers worked de fields and did der general farm work. They had one bad habit - that of slapping der poor younger brother around when de food didn't suit them. Dey kept all the farm money and gave him only a small bit. Now dis went on for years - dis abuse of der poor younger brother. Now it seems that one day when dey wair older, dese brothers got religion."

Gerta sighed with this and Grünwalda murmured,

"Ach, iss gut."

"Yes, dey got the religion bad, and began to repent of the way they had mistreated the poor younger brother all those years. They knew they had to make der amends in order to be forgiven."

Her listeners went along with her acting, nodded their heads and anticipated the punch line to the story, or the surprise ending. Their faces were as full of expectancy as those of children were at Christmas time.

"So dese older brothers took the younger brother into their confidence, dese Schwede boys, but they were older men by now. Dey asked his forgiveness, told him that they were going to gif him his share of the money dey had saved as well as his share of de land. The little brother was somewhat skeptical, or how you say, not believing. He asked de brothers,

"You no beat me any more?"

"Ach nein, no we never beat you anymore," the brothers answered.

"Good, *iss gut*. Then I no pee in der coffee pot anymore."

Shouts went up from the listeners in the granary, and Grünwalda Peppleman's deep throaty guffaws almost drowned out those of Charley, her husband. Henry Backhaus rolled on the smooth granary floor, convulsed with laughter. Many of the others, who were almost out of control, doubled over and laughed harder. Griselda Gertslaecker was shrieking in her high soprano voice and tears were streaming down her face. Bertha, and Bernhardina, along with Marybelle MacPherson, could not control their faces even though they had not heard the story.

Augusta Kattmann and Anna Steinhoge took a short evening walk, out of curiosity, and that took them nearer the grain depot whose wide doors were left open. They heard all the babble of voices and then the almost hysterical explosion of laughter from Marta's story.

"And that," Anna said slowly with a hint of disapproval, "is a church bazaar committee meeting?"

"Yess-s, Ja, it would seem so Anna," Augusta said simply, "but if you keep them happy and well fed, dey work harder to make der money."

"Keep them well fed? You mean, keep them well soused with ale," Anna Steinhoge said rather dryly. "How many kegs do you suppose that mob in the depot will swill down?"

"Ja, tis true, but mein Anna, ve chust chalk it off to business as a necessary loss or expense. It takes moneys to make moneys," Augusta reasoned. "Dot is good advertising. Dey come back for more and spread de word. Und besides, ve chust stir up another vat of der brew and make more barrels of it, absorb the price of making more as a business cost, and in the long run, ve haf a good, ach so gut profit. Der *Blue Swan* stroke of good luck iss chust starting, Anna."

"Let us hope so," Anna said with some skepticism. "Let us hope."

Augusta and Anna by-passed the boisterous grain depot. They walked past it on the Canal Street slide, then back to Washington and Front Streets, on down to the bridge across the canal, and then on down beyond First Street to Bertha's house. They thought it odd that they found only a neighbor with Daisy baby, and that apparently Bertha had let the other children go visiting for a while.

"Odd I don't hear that Louveese and dat Josephine," Augusta said.

"Precisely, it's very odd," Anna commented. "It isn't likely that they are with their parents at that so-called Bazaar meeting."

"Not likely, Anna," Augusta said, "but then it must have been arranged with Bernhardina and Bertha, for you see they have arranged for der nursemaid neighbor woman to care for der baby Daisy."

After a short inspection of the premises, Anna and Augusta walked on back toward home. They did not wish to leave the young orphan boys by themselves too long at a time, even though they were old for their young years - far too old.

Before they got very far back up Washington Street to the south, Augusta and Anna heard the laughing voices change into musical choruses. Where did that small orchestra and zither come from? Had this been planned all along? They could hear the fine singing even when they were over on Walnut Street to the east.

Out at Langhorst's tile kilns and warehouses, Josie and Lou-Lou, along with their brothers and the other neighborhood kids of the town, were holding their silent tryst in the cavernous shadows of the warehouse between great stacks of tile and brick. It was all very exciting, and was all the more so because it was so secret and forbidden. What would happen if they were caught? It was hard to suppress giggles of laughter and excited exchanges of words, but they knew they had to be quiet to escape detection. Why the town would be shocked if they even so much as thought that young boys and girls, children and adolescents, were meeting together in a darkened ware shed at night with only a dim lantern to make the forbidden cavern all the more eerie. . . and they met without chaperones.

Charley Gast and Jakey Backhaus passed the corncob pipe around with their first attempt at smoking some of their own dried tobacco leaves. It was exciting. Gertie led the girls in taking the first puff on the pipe, but one puff was enough. They had all been to Babylon and had sinned. It was exciting and gratifying, but once was enough. Next they sampled the wine, and then the home brew. Ludmilla Vogelsang clowned and pretended to walk crazily as the old Irish codger did when he went through town on his canal barge.

It was time for Jakey Backhaus to regale them with Marta's story and educate them to the forbidden word used in the cranberry story. He explained that it wouldn't be funny unless they heard Marta or his father tell it with dialect, facial expression, and an imitation of Augusta Kattmann walking in the market place with the stiff Anna Steinhoge.

Jakey hemmed and hawed with hesitation at first, but the others urged him on, for they had been in the dark long enough. They were tired of hearing the older generation going into hysterics at the mere mention of the ubiquitous, omnipresent cranberry, "der kronsbeere."

He told the story but explained that the humor in it was the play on words. The mistaken English word that was taken for a word in German

was not spoken in polite or respectable circles. It was like the innocent
English words for sleigh ride, or sleigh trip, that come out in German as
"Schlittenfahrt," and which in turn sounds so much like an English crudity
that is spoken only in crude circles. The girls giggled but knew the wan light
would hide their blushes in case any of them weakened. Louise took another
swig of the detested brew and then made a face.

"I need some ammunition to fortify me," she cautioned the others.

"Cluck-cluck-cluck, chick-chick!" Charley teased. "You are not going
to turn chicken hearted on us, are you Lou-Lou? Remember you almost
blackmailed us into telling you!"

"I remember and I'm game. I never back out on my agreements," Louise
said bravely. Then she went on to clown as she stood with her eyes closed. I
am ready to walk the plank or go to the block, whichever." They all sat in a
circle in the wan light as Jakey tried to tell them the story, and to explain what
it all meant. He fumbled through the pantomime of Mrs. Kattmann walking
in a market place in Europe and getting her English, poor as it was, mixed up
with her German, which was even poorer. He imitated Anna Steinhoge's walk,
and her fumbling with her counterfeit monocle, and Augusta Kattmann's
out of place opera stem glasses as she inspected the fruit and berries in this
market place, or *naschtmarkt*. He got it mixed up but came out with the play
on words when the market salesman told her that the cranberries grew "in a
marsh." He said it so rapidly that Augusta had trouble understanding him
and asked him again. When he answered somewhat pointedly with irritation,
"in the marsh," she thought that he had been rude and said "*IM arsch*" in
German, which the listeners on the floor knew meant an unspeakable phrase
"In the a--."

They all laughed at the joke. They laughed harder when Jakey told them
that she still did not understand, and was going to get the law on the rude,
brash, offender.

"So that is what it is all about," Lou-Lou exploded." Wait until I have the
chance to spring this when I hear Marta, Ludwig, Henry and Griselda going
into hysterics over their little joke. Won't I get them?"

"You won't dare say that right out!" Josie and Gerta told her.

"You think I won't? You can bet I will say it, and right out loud in the
street. Of course I won't say it in front of Ma, Grandma or Papa."

After they had put their hidden contraband brew and tobacco away
with their other secret cache, somewhere back in the secret passages of the
watershed, and stacked tile and brick around it, the boys were ready to put
out the lantern and join the girls out on the towpath and head back into
town. Ben, Lou and Charley passed spearmint leaves and some green onion

tops around for all of them to chew on to cover their telltale breath. They all giggled with their secret as they moved along the towpath.

"Now we need to do some group singing, and walk slowly like we always do when we take these evening walks. We have to make it look natural," Josie told them. Lou-Lou balked at the idea.

"Why should we, when all our folks and all them good church people are lying around up there above the lock in that grain depot, a-swillin' ale and tellin' worse tales than the dumb cranberry story?"

"Easy for you to say, Lou-Lou," her brother Ben said, "that is if you are itching for that hard ash paddle. I'm not. Oh, it is in the marsh!"

The rest of them laughed. Soon one of them started an easy old song and the rest of them followed, but it was hard to keep down their laughter as they thought of what they had all just done, and no one else knew it. They started singing the old, well-known folk tune called The Carousel. They made up different words for different verses as they went along and improvised where they had forgotten. They thought about the carousels that they had ridden in Toledo, and in summers before, right there on the side street when the carnival and circus showboats had come to Brementown. The horse-propelled carousel had its own mechanical organ that had to be turned by hand to play it. Some carousels had their organs turned by a belt attached to the center spindle upon which the entire carousel rotated. They sang the words:

"Ride the carousel, and fall into its spell as we turn.
Keep on turning, while we're yearning, for one more ride with you..."
As we leap up high, how we yearn to fly, then we swoop low, and at last know where whales blow and dolphins flow."

Their imaginations brought many variations of the old waltz melody with words that betrayed their secret yearning for far away places.

The spirit of camaraderie and general good feeling had claimed nearly all of the participants in the grain depot songfest. When Griselda lined up her members of the foursome who dominated the church choir, the others knew they would hear some fine singing - and not church hymns. Grünwalda, Griselda, Gerta and Marta took the floor and sang an old Teutonic song of thanksgiving. At least it appeared so on the surface, but later it seemed to be a song praising wine and ale.

"Come one... come all... to that grain bin's smooth floor.
Up the towpath, across the footbridge; right now is the hour."

Much to the delight of the listeners and fellow revelers, the women who said they were "ladies of the chorus" began to improvise and substitute words and names as it suited their purpose. Different ones in the audience laughed aloud or called out to them when they heard their names used in the parodies.

"Call Grünwalda and Griselda - Gertie - limber up them legs!
"Get Elihu, call to Jake too, and seat the ladies on kegs."

As they soared into their high soprano refrain, the women substituted words shamelessly. They inserted words to suit the occasion of the moment, that of the song festival of such good heartedness stimulated by the free-flowing ale. It was hard to recognize the group of women now as the pious women of the choir, or the artistic musicians of the high-sounding "Kanal Damen Musik Verein" (the Ladies of the Canal Music Circle). They threw their heads back and sang without restraint.

Mit der Swan ale, from der ice house, der cold beer and der wine.
There's no time, girls, to be sad girls, but trod again that plank floor.
Toss another mug down, then tanz and waltz till you're sore."

There were shouts of approval from the audience and wild clapping of applause. There were other songs and parodies, but Marta led in the clowning with her pantomimed skits while others sang; then she became braver with more ale and launched into some of the funny but naughty parodies of old German folk songs handed down by tradition. The authors were lost in the anonymity of time.

There were variations and parodies upon the legendary mischievous Augustine, who was not German, but Austrian, and made his appearance in the Volksprater of Vienna's beloved playground park. Each prank of Augustine got bolder as different ones of the women added a new parodied version. Henry, Jake and Charley would "egg them on" by asking from the side, "Then what did he do? What did he say?" Even Zelda Zinndorfer, who had come to the meeting out of curiosity, and because she belonged to the Kanal Damen Musik Verein, could not keep from joining into the high jinks of the hour. Her usually dour expression softened into a relaxed hint of a smile at times, and then actually broke into a soft laugh.

Grünwalda's stern dark face lost some of its austerity as she joined in the fun. Her deep alto voice could be heard above the others when she indulged in a throaty deep "guffaw." Then she led them all with bravado in some off-color versions of the old, "Du, Du lich mir im Hertzen," but her broken

German highly Anglicized ending sounded more like "Vice nich veer goot ich deer bin."

The different Germanic families disagreed upon words, translations and pronunciations, because the different German families there in German township and New Bremen, did not come from the same origins in Germany. For example, the Gasts, who descended from Uncle Gregor and Papa Hermann, came from Strasbourg in Alsance and Lorraine, the Saar Valley. They had French blood also and their dark hair, facial contours and quick Gallic wit belied their French blood. However, Bertha Gast's side, the Kattmann's, Kellers, and Kitsners had the blonde Teutonic features (blue and gray eyes) of central and northern Germany. Some of the other families who were first and second generation German Americans had originated in southern Bavaria in the high alpine country and spoke high or "hoch" German. Others came from the Palatinate of central Germany and some came from northern Pomerania. Many were good old Württembergers, Hanoverians, and some from the original Bremen. They liked to call it "Old Brementown." There were also some families of Swiss origin.

The younger generation did not study it in grammar books nor could they write it, but knew it only by ear like Jakey Backhaus. Many like Lou-Lou did not care at all and thought it all very "dumb."

Lou-Lou, Josie, Gertie Langhorst, Charley, Jakey Backhaus and the others walked slowly along the towpath engrossed in their group unison singing. Josie knew that her brothers, along with Jakey and August Schlesselman, were lagging behind listening to Fritzy Witte and Albrecht Lehmkuhl telling off-color stories of what the older boys and men at the brickyards told about the Fatima Fortuneteller, and some of their showboats that had been run out of town. Even Marshal Bechman had been involved in some shady practices. There were whispers from the group of boys, and some loud spontaneous laughs. Then there were more whispers from the group of boys, and more loud spontaneous laughs. The girls scolded them and made them join in with the singing. By this time, they were nearing the bridge over the canal at Second Street. They decided to follow along the towpath that was on the west side of the canal.

Marta and Griselda beckoned to some of the other women who had not been taking part in the singing to join them. These women were the ones that been laughing the hardest. After all of them had taken part in the group round singing of "Snitzelbank," Marta inserted some objects not usually included in the round of nouns to be described and sung about. The men would shout the answers (in not very musical tones) to the objects pointed out in the old round. Then the way was left open for Marta to land back into some of the funny but vulgar doings of "du Lieber Augustine." Everyone joined after drinking more ale, for no one wanted to be accused of being too "nicety-nice" to get into the spirit. They would allow Marta or Grünwalda to sing the choice old parts, telling of some outrageous thing that the mythical Augustine had done or said. The other women would end the verse with repeating the last line in the chorus.

Henry Backhaus made the mistake of daring Marta to sing the verse concerning the coffee pot, or a "kaffee kopf," by pantomiming the pouring of coffee into a cup to her. At once with the next verse, Marta nudged Grünwalda, then Griselda as she waited her turn. The chorus of women and some few of the nearest men started out with,

"Ach du lieber Augustine, Augustine, Augustine, ach du Lieber Augustine, Ich liebe dich so(pronounced as "zo")."

Then Marta jumped into the verse, gesturing as she did so in pantomime,

"Schiesse im der kaffee topf, hiesse wasser an der kopf."

There were shouts of laughter and disbelief that she had said those words. Marybelle MacPherson and Clara Nell Sanders could not appreciate it, not being German, until Griselda tried to tell them through her laughter. Then the chorus finished the song with the final line,

"Ach du lieber Augustine, *wir* liebe dich so." (They used *we* instead of *I*.)

Charley Peppleman, along with Hermann, Ben, Henry Backhaus and the other men who belonged to the *Brothers of the Stein Society*, could not stand back any longer. They had to show off their voices as they did at their weekly meeting at the brewery. They even had special jackets that they wore when marching in parades, sang in the church pulpit, or sang for other public affairs. Now was the turn of the *Stein Bruderen* to shine and show off their expert quartet and choral renditions. The women went over to the side of the depot near the granary. They were still devastated by Marta's bold song.

When Augusta Kattmann and Anna Steinhoge reached home, they found that the housekeeper and nurse they had left in charge of the small boys were keeping a careful watch over the household, and that everything was in order. Since the evening was so peaceful, Augusta suggested to Anna that they wander back Plum Street to Washington Street, past the brewery, take a look at the *Blue Swan* resting there in her slip by the brewery, and then perhaps just walk on over to the short Canal Street. The short Canal Street could take them up to the other street side of the grain depot. Anna paused at first, but when she saw that Augusta was going without her, she joined her at the side gate.

There was restlessness about Augusta that Anna could detect. What was going on in that busy mind of hers? Augusta had not out and out disapproved of the meeting at the depot, nor did she disapprove entirely of the songfest that had developed. Yet, she could not come out and heartily approve of it. Finally, as they neared the depot and stood well back in the shadows of some large tree trunks on Canal Street, the forces of the women (*Kanal Damen Musik Verein*) brought Augusta to a decision. Yes, that was it. There was no use wasting all their energy, good voices, and good spirits just for their own mere entertainment. It should be channeled into more productive avenues with profitable returns.

"You know, Anna," Augusta began somewhat cautiously, "all dot good talent is chust going to waste. Oh, not waste exactly. Happiness is nevair wasted. This could all bring so much happiness to so many more of der new scheme of hotels, inns, and packet boats on my *Blue Swan Line.*"

"Augusta, I am sure you do, but I don't think I can see. . . "

"But of course you'll see, mein Anna," Augusta interrupted her.

"Do you not remember the old folk tale handed down by our forbears from Bremen, over in Germany's Hanover and Oldenburg provinces?"

"I remember many, but more from my Brandenburg and Prussia," Anna told her with a slight tone of edification, and perhaps arrogance.

"What I am saying, Anna," Augusta said, ignoring her friend's hint of haughtiness of Prussia over the "low country" of Bremen and coastal Bremerhaven, is that dot same characteristic of putting on der show. Entertainment is ingrained in dese, our peoples. I am referring to the old tale of the Brementown Musicians, and the farcical situations they got into. We have these same comedians right here, Anna, and we can capitalize on them, make moneys for them and for *The Blue Swan Company* and make much happiness for everybodies. Ve giff chance to make some moneys for some of dose wimmens in dere who hardly know from vair de next meal iss coming from."

"I should have known, Augusta, that money or making money was at the bottom of all of this lengthy exposition," Anna answered. She could hardly help noticing that Augusta's English was better when she was in a relaxed, pleasant mood. There was not so much broken incorrect German sprinkled in with her pigeon English. She knew that Augusta had been very young when she left Germany, not old enough to have become skilled in that language. She never was disciplined enough here in the new home in the United States to make her learn correct English. She did not have to learn it, and as long as she could get by, she didn't. In later years this poor English and poorer German was a source of disappointment to her, but she was not cowed by it. No one would dare correct Augusta Keller Kattmann - not even "Papa."

The two women could look up the slight incline of the driveway from Canal Street to the crowd in the center floor of the depot. No one from the large grain elevator would notice them down there in the shadows. The driveway from the street side gave access to the granaries on either side of the center depot driveway. Inside, the wagoners could unload their grain. The wide doors to the granaries were boarded up as the grain rose higher. Power from the water wheel from the canal water flume ran the "elevators" in wooden chutes. The chutes carried the grain up into the higher storage granaries from which chutes, when opened, would let the grain flow down into canal barges, or into wagons for shipment "down north" to Toledo.

Anna remained silent as Augusta's mind raced on while summarizing all the possibilities she saw stretched out before her. Anna began to realize how much Lou-Lou, or Louise, resembled the Augusta Keller of those years of long ago. Augusta had been reared with her sister Fredericka in a strict military home of the Prussian tradition. She had rebelled just as Lou-Lou had. Her father was of the military hierarchy. He was from a near noble family and had left considerable wealth to his two daughters. Their mother had died when they were young. Governesses could not discipline the headstrong Augusta, nor could her father's riding crop subdue her will. Tutors despaired of teaching her anything, especially German grammar. English tutors did a little better in America in trying to teach her English. Augusta's rebellious revenge had been overeating in her loneliness, and refusal to conform to her father's dictatorial brutal establishment. She took it out on her English grammar and composition. Her only love became money and her inherited wealth, her devotion to medicine, and her thwarted ambition to become a medical doctor.

The miraculous thing was, in everyone's mind that knew them, the strange influence "Papa" Heinrich Kattmann had on Augusta. He did not interfere often or speak often, but when he did, she listened.

Augusta had succeeded in medicine such as nursing, as well as in business with the brewery. She left the running of the vast acreage at <u>Willow Haven</u> to Heinrich, for the land came from his family. True, they had bought some jointly, but she left those "peasant" details to him and to the country yeomanry. She maintained her townhouse as many European nobles had done, even though they owned feudal manors in the country.

She probably compensated for her wayward earlier years by her vociferous devotion to the church. Without knowing it, she had disciplined her children rather vigorously, perhaps subconsciously giving them the discipline that she had rebelled against, but in later life realized that she had needed.

Now, Anna reasoned, in the silence of the shadows of the large cottonwood trees at the depot's Canal Street driveway that this new idea of the *Swan* barge, the *Swan Line* of packets, hotels, and inns was just another notch in her desire to achieve and excel on her own. She did not need to live out here in the backwoods and wilderness of western Ohio with these "underling" people, when she could live a life of ease and cultural refinement on her ancestral estates, or those of her father's father back in Prussia.

In the meantime, Lou-Lou, Josie, Charley, and the others inched on up the towpath to the south toward the lock. They could hear the high laughter, the high soaring sopranos of the women of the Music Society and the tenors of the *Brothers of the Stein*. All the young people marveled at the sight they saw across the canal from the towpath on the other side.

"Oh, if only I had my elderberry cane pea shooter," Lou exclaimed.

"Boy, couldn't we really sting some of those large fat bottoms over there?" Charley laughed with Fritzy and Albrecht. The boys had made shooters out of the canes of elderberry bushes by pushing out the pulpy pith with long wires. The shooter tubes were too small in diameter for peas or small beans. Instead, the mischievous Jakey Backhaus, almost as mischievous as his father Henry, had devised a plan of using small shot. The small shot taken from his father's shot pouch that was intended for small game and birds, found a far different use. The small shot was propelled from the reed of elderberry with enough force to sting unsuspecting bystanders or passersby on the street by the mill. When they could not see their tormentors, they supposed that they had been stung by some insect. Johnny, or "Schani," Schlesselman had made a "y" shaped fork out of a forked small bough of strong redbud, and upon this fork he had attached a slingshot. The thongs were attached to the fork with an elastic gum cloth used in some of the machinery at the mill, and when the sling was loaded with the minute ball of shot, and the sling's elastic lines were pulled back in tension, the shot was propelled forward with a murderous sting. The boys had rolled with laughter many times when their shots had hit home on the old Irish codger or Uriah Hornback when they came through town on their barges or log rafts. They had always been afraid to try it on the swarthy faced Russian men on Big Berthy's barge.

The men's choral group of the *Brothers of the Stein* took the floor, standing in the full light of the beam from the *Blue Swan's* bow lantern. Now, all of a sudden, they became more serious and their laughs disappeared, as they huddled in conference before they began to sing. They got their pitch from

Elihu's small mouth harp, and then they began their first harmonized ballad. The quarter led first, but the entire choral group came full on the refrain,

"Our work is done, pass the keg again.
The fun's begun, so never let it end.
There'll be toil enough, in the days ahead.
Put your work down, on your feet now,
Steady, now let's begin."

The next verse became more serious as they reminisced about days of youth, how they laughed and played, and never knew that age and life's problems would catch up with them, but how as a brotherhood, they had raised their steins in a pledge of eternal comradeship.

Some of the women, who a few moments earlier had been almost in hysterical laughter, were now wiping their eyes with their aprons.

"Just look at them over there. One minute swilling down the ale like old sots, and singing out in the night like some possessed old harpies. Now they are blubbering like Irish washer wimmen of County Cork over some trivial happening of everyday life," Lou-Lou exploded.

"They allus tell us to behave like little gentlemen or little ladies," Josie protested. Gertrude Langhorst agreed.

"Dot Louveese," Lou-Lou started to mimic her grandmother, "she chud be paddled more to make der lady, Bairn-har-dee-nah!" And with that, she paddled herself vigorously.

"Why they are on the verge of a cryin jag," Dorothea Waterman observed, "singing like wild Valkyries one minute, swigging down ale the next, and now bawling like weaned calves."

"Oh for the joys of bein' growed up," Benjie Gast laughed.

"Come on, let's go back to the tile works," Schani proposed.

"New, it would be more fun to go back across the bridge, come up on the Canal Street side, and see what's goin' on from the other side," Charley Gast said. His brother, Lou, agreed.

When the group got back down to First Street, they started to sing again. First one of the girls would lead, and then another one would take over the lead.

The rapid youthful singing of the school day songs, familiar to all of them, came easily for it took no special ability. They sang rounds, humorous ditties, and some of the old tunes of the canalers who dug the "mighty ditch." Then they sang some that had words they had to avoid or change. They sang some of the songs of the legendary "Forty-niners" who just a few years ago had trudged west to the elusive gold fields of California while singing "O Susannah," and "My Darlin' Clementine."

Their voices carried up Washington Street from the lock. The group then started back south toward Front Street, while they sang and laughed.

"Vell, would you chust listen, Anna?" Augusta Kattmann exclaimed. "It seems ve haf more of der Brementown Musicians serenading de town."

"Yes-s, precisely, Augusta," Anna Steinhoge admitted stiffly, "but what is to be expected? If the ducks lay duck eggs, is it so surprising that some ugly ducklings are hatched? What did you expect?"

"You mean that like begets, Anna?" Augusta questioned her with mock seriousness.

"Yess-s-s, precisely, Augusta," Anna said very erect and arch.

"But you forget, Anna. Sometimes the unexpected happens. Maybe the eggs were swan eggs, and the ugly ducklinks turned out to be lovely blue swans, *Ja*?" Augusta joked. She laughed at her own joke. Then she became more serious when she heard the voices of the young people as they came nearer.

"*Dot Louveese*, she is der ringleader in all the mischief in this town! *Gott in Himmel*," Augusta said almost inaudibly. The two women hid themselves behind the two large cottonwood trees.

"Yes-s-s, precisely. I remember another rebellious girl back in Prussia who was very much like her," Anna observed cautiously.

The men's choral group held their silent audience spellbound. Gone were all the laughter, calling out, and witty wisecracks. The Men's *Choral Society* was now in a serious vein, even caught up themselves in the sentimentality of the olden days, of youth and youthful aspirations. They were the serious *Choral Society* now, not the easy-going *Brothers of the Stein*. Then they took a step forward and formed a tighter group as they soared into the pledge of eternal fellowship and friendship. Each had taken up a stein, but most of them were empty. The gesture they were about to make was the most important thing. It did not require ale. They had rehearsed this Stein song (the pledge song) so well that they didn't need the small band. Only the zither led them, but they sang in such perfect harmony while singing acappella that no accompaniment was needed. Their voices became liquid with golden and silver tones. Anna Steinhoge was taken by surprise and Augusta Kattmann was speechless for once in her life.

> "Raise your stein, for that's the sign to DRINK,
> DRINK, DRINK that golden ale, while the moon shines high-h-h.
> DRINK, DRINK, DRINK, pledge friendship

from the horn what won't run dry.
Bend your arm, for there's no harm, and DRINK,
DRINK, DRINK, with fondness and laughter, right from
the heart.
Grasp that hand in friendship.
Pledge eternal kinship.
Brothers of the Stein, we're the same one kind.
Never let true friendship part."

The men held their steins high for a moment, then turned to his neighbor and clasped his hand and gave their fraternal sign.

"Anna," Augusta gasped. "Did you hear? Now dat was almost, vell, almost opera. Now dose scoundrels nevair sounded like dat in church. Vot goes on at those meetings at the brewery? Chust tell me."

"It seems that quite a good deal has gone on," Anna replied.

"Did you chust hear dat Henry Backhaus? His tenor was soaring up there in the thin air, almost like the Dresden Opera, flawless, Anna, and was that other one Waterman, or Wiemeyer, almost as good?"

"I couldn't tell, but we have overlooked the fine voices of Herman and Ben Gast. They were right in there and close behind the others," Anna said.

"Ja, and dat lazy Henry Bushman, that night constaples; he even found new energy we nevair knew he had," Augusta observed.

"It is all very perplexing and revealing," Anna admitted.

"Vell, if this has not been one night of strange revelations. I nevair have seen mein Bertha and mein Bairnhardina, vell, let their voices and themselves out like that before," Augusta said, while searching for the word she wanted. Then Augusta continued, "It would do her good if mein Ernestine could just let loose a little and not be so brittle. If der stick can bend a little, dot is goot; if it is too brittle, kaputt, it breaks."

"I have observed this, Augusta," Anna Steinhoge said quietly. In their surprise with the men's choral group and the timbre of the voices they heard, Anna and Augusta forgot about their clandestine secrecy behind the boughs of the large cottonwood trees. They had inched forward toward the driveway into the depot to hear better.

As Lou-Lou, Josie, and the others drew nearer, Lou-Lou, who was in the lead, spotted her grandmother from a distance. Not able to believe her eyes, she made a sign to the others, and then stole up silently on the other side of the street to get a better view. She came racing back with her skirts gathered up to her knees and gestured the others to make a hasty getaway. They all fled into the night. Leo Wiemeyer complained that he wouldn't get to get a good shot in with his "shot reed" or with the slingshot.

"Ja, and you're just askin for the board again, Wiemeyer."

When they reached the safety of Josie's porch that overlooked the canal, they all stopped for breath.

"Now something is up, and up big," Lou-Lou told the others.

"Else, why would Grandma Kattmann be out there snoopin' with old lady Steinhoge? Why weren't they at the meeting, if it was to plan for raising money for the church stands at the circus fair that's coming?" After they got their breath and their courage, they all went back up the towpath on the other side of the canal, and across from the depot, to see how the meeting would turn out. Would Grandma Kattmann close in and break up the meeting? What was she mad about?

There was more singing from the floor of the grain depot, but the tone was not one of hysterical laughter, and Marta was not the dominant figure in the lead now. It seemed to be Grünwalda.

The small band took up a waltz tune and indiscriminate couples bowed to each other. It was a rather lively tune. Mr. Schlesselman bowed his large bass fiddle expertly. The sobbing violins must have belonged to Mr. Schweitermann and Mr. Vogelsang, but the young people could not see well enough to tell. The waltz rolled and swirled on. Jakey, Charley, Schani and Benjie attempted to do the German Schuhplatter there on the gravel of the towpath, where they slapped the soles of their shoes, and then slapped each other on the cheeks in time with the music, but their performance was hardly graceful. The others laughed at their antics. Then the music stopped and the tempo changed. The zither started out with the tempo of the Landler, almost the time of the Varsevienne; then the small orchestra began the Landler slow waltz beat. Some of the couples attempted to lead, but others were hesitant. They were not as familiar with the Landler steps as they had been with the more familiar, more rapid waltz.

"Ach, nein, nein, dot iss not right!" Augusta exploded as she saw the faltering steps on the depot floor up the driveway.

"Come Anna, ve show them. They must not botch up, nor forget the art, the kunst of our race, and our culture."

"But Augusta, really. We can't. We shouldn't be seen..."

"Nonsense, Anna. As you said, dis is a night of surprises," Augusta said. She took Anna by the arm and propelled her along up the slight incline to the entrance of the grain elevator.

The dancers were taken by surprise, but kept up their time with the orchestra. When the music seemed to falter, Augusta almost commanded the players to continue as if their lives depended upon it. Anna Steinhoge was aghast when Augusta pushed her into the dance. She found herself dancing with Jake Hemel when the time came for the exchange of dancers, rather than an exchange of every other partner. The idea, she thought to herself, dancing with the uncouth blacksmith of the town! However, he was surprisingly light on his feet. She felt as if those large beefy paws he used for his hands could crush her hand or even her arm, if he forgot his strength for a minute.

Augusta waved with her hands for everyone to join in the dance, calling over the orchestra that "they must learn it right" before the time of the fair and carnival. Augusta was surprisingly light on her feet for one so heavy as she. Marta Schweitermann was so flabbergasted that she forgot the steps of the dance and had to be pushed into her next position by the couple next to her.

Lou-Lou, Josie and the others across the canal could not believe their eyes. They stopped talking at first, and to make sure they were seeing correctly. What was the meaning of this new turn? Lou-Lou started to clown, and began to paddle herself and exclaim,

"Bairn-hard-deen-nah, dot Louveese chuld be paddled more to make der lady. Wal dog my cats, if this don't beat all. I think we have all had too much of the tile warehouse, but I also think I need more!"

Bertha Gast was delighted for once to see her mother make an appearance at the depot. She urged her husband, Ben, onto his feet, and saw that Hermann and Bernhardina also joined the stately Landler. When the music stopped with the end of the dance, Augusta commanded that they do it again. They all needed practice, and these things of the old culture should not be neglected so long again. She showed them some of the steps and told them what they were doing wrong. She used her son, Ludwig Kattmann, as her partner to show some of the steps, and then she had the orchestra to try a short portion of it again. She surprised her audience as she did the light skipping side step when the partners dance side by side instead of face-to-face. She was light on her feet and moved with agility. Weight and age did not seem to affect her performance. Anna Steinhoge felt ridiculous and out of place.

After a few rehearsals, Augusta told them that they should plan on a dance floor at the fair, charge admissions for each dance, and then the group here, or at least some of the ones who would rehearse, should put on demonstration dances of the Landler, the Tanz, and others.

Grünwalda Peppleman's mouth was open with surprise. Griselda Gertslaecker could not find words to express herself, nor to praise Augusta Kattmann. She would have to admit the large woman had spirit.

Augusta strode about the floor watching the progress, and then without warning, she grasped the unsuspecting Henry Backhaus by the lapels and steered him in front of her onto the dance floor. Then she grasped him, and made him assume the proper position for the Landler and follow through.

Henry was too startled to protest or to say anything. When they passed Marta and Charley Peppleman, Augusta said in a low but very distinct voice,

"Now Marta Schweitermann, ve show you how to do der kronsbeere step. Vell come on, kommen sie, Henry, show her how to step out and do the cranberry step you know so well at my expense."

When Henry seemed to falter and stumble, Augusta buoyed him up.

"Vell Henry, you are not in such fine voice now, Ja? Come on, ve need to get dat Wiemeyer and Waterman und giff dem some of der kronsbeere, Ja?"

Henry looked around him in vain for a way to escape, but one did not shake off easily the avoirdupois of Augusta Kattmann. When the time came in the dance where they broke away to dance side by side, Augusta managed to bump him in the rear with her ample knee and commanded,

"Wo Wachsen Sie? Now where do they grow? Perhaps ve need to get der Schwede brothers' coffee pot, Ja? Forward, IM Arsch!"

Marta and the others nearby saw Augusta's charade but noticed a twinkle in her eye instead of the expected wrath of Jove. Marta stumbled through the rest of the dance while heaving inwardly with laughter.

The first shock of Augusta's presence soon passed, and when they saw her good intentions, all joined in the spirit of the dance. Then it was time for the last dance and last songs. Augusta asked the men's *Choral Brotherhood of the Stein* to sing their song of Eternal Friendship, the pledge that many called the "*Stein Song.*"

When the song was finished, the orchestra, at Marta's bidding, began the rather slow heavy tempo of an old folk waltz called "The Light Heart." The men pulled Grünwalda to her feet in spite of her protest. They told her this dance was for her, but she protested that she could not dance and would be a spectacle out there trying to do it. The woman's chorus, along with the men, began the words of the Licht Herz, the Light Heart Waltz. Grünwalda was as shy as a young schoolgirl, but the men on each side propelled her through the slow waltz steps. Charley and Jake knew they could handle her better, so they cut in and took command of the instruction as the others sang:

"With your light foot, that's your right foot, put it coyly out front;
Follow up now, that's the way, gal, easy, round now, don't grunt.
Once again whirl, bow and dip, swirl, side step, lilt with the beat.
It doesn't matter what your weight is, if you're light on your feet."

By now Grünwalda knew that they were making up words, or at least adding some and changing others. She was enjoying it all in spite of her misgivings, and she sang along with them as she danced in the slow, heavy circling and almost elephantine dance.

"One again whirl, waltz and tanz swirl, let your huge soul take flight.
It doesn't matter what your weight is, if you keep your heart light."

Grünwalda obviously was enjoying the attention she was receiving, but
pretended slightly that she didn't, and made false feints at slaps toward Elihu,
Charley, and even Jake. She shrieked with laughter in her deep alto voice, but
the others drowned her out as the tempo increased. The orchestra finished
the dance but swept immediately into the dance rhythm of the *Women's Music
Circle* (*Kanal Damen Musik Verein*) - the so-called "Song of Thanksgiving."
   "Let us sing girls, throw your head back, lift high those full steins." Then
the orchestra switched into the men's Pledge of Eternal Friendship with the
stein Pledge Song, and Henry Backhaus, having recovered from his shock,
out did himself. Grünwalda rocked and reeled almost as if in a drunken
stupor. Never had she been so happy. Then the dance ended, and the music
faded, and at last they all went home.
   "It was as I said, Anna," Augusta apologized on the way home. "It has
been an evening full of der surprises." Then she chuckled to herself, "<u>Wo
wachsen Sie</u>? Where do they grow indeed?"

CHAPTER 23

As the summer wore on, the rush and hurried nature of emergency and tension gave way to a feeling of lazy holiday. True, work went on as usual, but not with the same driving urge as in early June. There were no more floods or berm cave-ins on the canal. The high tension of the case of Silvermann was over. Now there only remained the final rounding up of all the accomplices; soon the whole affair would be moved out of the small community and off to Columbus, or on to Washington D.C.

The fate of the four small boys was at last announced, much to the relief of most of the townspeople. The boys were declared wards of the court and bound over to Mrs. Kattmann. Now that Mrs. Kattmann had at last unleashed her decisions, most of them had been readily accepted after the initial shock was over.

Work was started on her carriage house to convert it into a school, rather of a dormitory or pension type, as were common schools in Europe. To the astonishment of the community, word was spread that footers and foundations were being laid for some sort of a rambling brick building out in the meadow of Kattmann's huge country estate, Weidenhimmel (roughly translated as Willow Haven). After das Frau ("that woman"), meaning Mrs. Kattmann, had come back from a hearing in Columbus concerning the Silvermann affair and all its side issues: Kidnapping, White Slavery, and the Underground Railroad for slaves. It seemed that groups of commissioners came at different times and talked with her. The first thing anyone knew was that the hospital/sanatorium so dear to the heart of Augusta Kattmann and to Anna Steinhoge, had become a reality, and now the ground was broken for the new buildings.

The doctors of New Bremen, Minster and Fort Loramie objected to the hospital being so far out in the country. They were in favor of its being near the highway, and especially the canal. They also thought the hospital should be in one of the towns for convenience. With a sly smile, Mrs. Kattmann pointed out that the sanatorium needed to be out in the open where the air was fresh, and away from town noise from traffic, mills and other industry. That was her plan for the rest home or sanatorium, which she planned to call Willow Home (Weideheim) after her own large rambling Weidenhimmel, (Willow Haven).

The natural pond along the meandering willow lined creek was scooped out for fill dirt so that the sanatorium would appear to be situated on a low rising knoll. Willow Lake was also created.

Back in town, plans for the new school had made the townspeople enthusiastic with anticipation of a school at last for their children. Many of the basic things were still to be taught in the homes. However, other fundamentals of arithmetic, grammar, writing, and geography, as well as music and Bible study were to be included in the school's curriculum. It would be a fine academy in time.

The children living in town could walk to school as well as those country children living within walking or driving distance. However, Mrs. Kattmann was thinking ahead. She was thinking of the needs of the communities along the canal. If she could secure teachers who were competent enough to teach the children, then she was in favor of having a large school. It would be cheaper tuition-wise, to have a large enrollment, for one teacher could teach twenty or twenty-five students as well as five or ten and it wouldn't take any more time or space.

It was for these commuting pupils that the dormitory type school was to be built. The living quarters would be upstairs.

For the time being, the four boys would live in the rooms provided in Mrs. Kattmann's town house. Perhaps later they could have permanent rooms in the school dormitory and act as boy proctors, or at least assist as room captains.

As if all of this wasn't enough, Mrs. Kattmann told Ernestine and Heinrich Hofermeyer that she was engaging them to help with the inns and passenger service on *The Blue Swan Packet Line*. Ernestine was somewhat flabbergasted, but her mother very tactfully smoothed her misgivings by painting a picture of all the money that was going to roll in. Her husband, Heinrich, could finally hold his head up and be independent. Likewise, Bernhardina Gast was told of her expected duties in helping with the school. She and Ernestine and could teach, not only grammar, spelling, and fine arts, but vocal and piano music as well.

Little by little, plans began working out. The community found itself engrossed in the plans for self-improvement. Members of the community were almost as excited about the plans as the founder was.

When the doctors talked with Mrs. Kattmann again and voiced their disappointment with having the much needed hospital and sanatorium so far from their practice, Mrs. Kattmann dropped another surprise. The clinic and emergency hospital was to be much smaller but it would be efficient. They could not believe their ears. Was there really going to be another hospital? It was then that they learned that this unbelievable energetic woman had secured state funds and bought the unused brick warehouse just off the canal at the south end of town. The Backhaus mill people were very glad to sell their investment because their other mill at the north end of town was ample for this small community.

The brick was painted white as was the woodwork trim. With a few outside modifications, the long warehouse soon took on the look of a mountain spring resort hotel. A few evergreen trees and willows gave its lawn a mellow look. With drawn plans and advice from the three or four doctors who would use the hospital, Mrs. Kattmann and Anna Steinhoge soon had the volunteer carpenters busy putting in partitions, making doors, and changing stairs.

Work soon got underway within the Kattmann and Gast families for the expansion of the passenger packet service as well as the freight service. Just as Bertha Gast predicted, one evening a string of carousel-like animals surmounting the prows of barges were towed through the locks south to the boat docks at Minster and Lockington. There they would undergo extensive examination before being refitted and furnished out for passenger service.

To Lou-Lou, Josie and the boys, it seemed like a new world had come into the one they had known. With excitement and anticipation, they looked forward to that new horizon down the towpath to the south, to the big side-wheeler steamers bound for the Mississippi, and the romance of the Old South.

When the word came up the canal from the south on several of the packets that the governor's passenger packet, with all the senators and dignitaries, was coming back through in two days and was heading for Toledo, the townspeople were excited. Then the word leaked out that Mrs. Kattmann was to be honored for outstanding work in the hospitalization of invalids and for social reform. The delegation of dignitaries was to inspect the sanatorium site out at The Willows and perhaps turn over a shovelful or two of dirt in a ceremony.

Next, they would visit the site in New Bremen, the remodeled old warehouse that was to be a county supported local hospital.

The larger sanatorium out at <u>The Willows</u> near Maria Stein was to be supported by state funds. Old Angus MacClintock saw to it, as he promised, that the town hospital would be named Kattmann Hospital in honor of its founder.

Augusta Kattmann had lost some of her preoccupied determined aloofness. She was floating on the clouds and was at last enjoying some of the things she had dreamed about all her life. She exclaimed to her church groups that "how sweet it was, almost <u>himmlisch</u>, to enjoy her funeral flowers during her lifetime, to see things come to pass during her last years, and not have to be postponed and done in her memory after she had passed on."

Lou-Lou began to have some misgivings. She had completely underrated her grandmother. She did not criticize her so much as she did at one time, and she often fell silent when others were discussing the remarkable woman. Bertha noticed this and smiled pleasantly to herself.

Now with all the attention that would be focused on the village in the next few days, all the townspeople began a frenzied cleanup of the streets, the canal front, and the towpath and docks.

The rain soaked bunting was hunted down, ironed and pressed and hung in festoons across the streets and the canal. Signs of welcome appeared over the shop fronts. Mrs. Hemel shocked even her husband with her energy when she decorated her overhanging porch above the blacksmith shop with greenbrier and other boughs from the woods that morning before the packet arrived.

The night before the arrival of the dignitaries, Bertha, Ben, and Hermann managed to steal out of the town on the routine run of the *Blue Swan* down to Minster and on out to the sawmill below Loramie Creek. The polished calliope was given a good workout while Jake and Elihu stood constant attendance on the brass steam organ to make sure its golden throats poured out its heavenly melody. The Russians in their hidden settlement heard it coming, and were on the millpond dock of the sawmill to greet the *Blue Swan*.

The girls took turns relieving Bertha at the keyboard for they needed all the practice they could get. Bertha made it a point to talk with Big Bertha and to make sure she knew about the state capitol dignitaries and senators that would be coming for the dedication of the new state hospital and the county hospital. Then Ben and Hermann told the Russian men, through Johnny Ivan as interpreter, about the showboats and circus coming in just a few days. They would probably see it in Minster first before it came on up to New Bremen but a lively time was expected. They could all tell by the white teeth and gleaming black eyes that Johnny had made the others understand that a big holiday time was coming, and that all of them were invited. Bertha

Gast did not want to bring up the Silvermann case with Big Bertha, but saw to it that Ben got the message across to Johnny, the "Mad Rooshin," that Silvermann and his accomplices were in Columbus in a state prison and would be tried in a federal court.

It was Bertha's turn to be amazed when the huge Russian woman came to her, took her by the arm and motioned for Johnny Ivan to come to them. Through the irrepressible Johnny, Big Bertha made it clear to her listeners how appreciative she was. She went on and praised Mrs. Kattmann.

"Good, good woman! Gets theengs done. Bossy, but get theengs done. I thing mibby she and thot Schoch Mann save all our life out here. We become citizen like you but thank her!"

It was then that Bertha learned that Angus MacClintock and Mrs. Kattmann had gained the respect and trust of these people, and they would make the trip to court in Columbus, hard as that would be, to testify against Silvermann and others of his gang of thieves and kidnappers.

"Bot wan theeng," Big Bertha said, nodding her head and slowly narrowing her eyes, "eef your government doan vant hang heem, then to get heem to talk, start to, how you say, Johnny, . . . start to deport heem. He rather die here and confess thousand times than be sent back Germany, and 'specially' Russia."

The others, notably big Gregori, nodded their heads, saying something affirmative in low bass tones in unison.

It was dark when the barge pulled back into town. A huge wood fire danced on the canal berm. Its reflection could be seen flickering over the smooth water a good distance down the canal. Grünwalda Peppleman and Mrs. Gertslaecker were having an outdoor party for the four little boys along with several other little neighborhood boys and girls. The delicious aroma of outdoor cooked meats on an open fire filled the summer night. It was good to see those little strained faces smiling and joining in on the fun. Grünwalda called out different orders in the games she was supervising, giving advice to this one and that one, as the children ran calling with laughter in circles in the various games.

Bertha and the girls went down into the hold of the barge until it was berthed in its slip. Then they left on the dark platform unnoticed and went home. There was no use to cause any suspicion yet. Everyone supposed the barge was returning from a delivery.

Upon the advice of Hermann and Ben, Bertha decided that perhaps they should save the calliope surprise until the circus came up the canal with the showboats. It would be more in keeping and besides the girls, reluctant as they were to postpone the musical surprise, wanted to have the undivided attention of their audiences. It would not do to steal some of the attention away from Grandma, <u>das Gnädig Frau</u>, on this day of dedication and honor, for which she had planned her whole life. No, it would be better to spring it when there was more of a carnival spirit, a spirit of careless holiday.

Besides, Bertha explained to her husband, if all went well and the calliope attracted attention, perhaps they could work out some sort of small variety attraction to make money and call it a "benefit show" to raise money for the new school, supplies and furnishings. She was careful to watch lest the girls give away the secret about the costumes. Mrs. MacPherson had already asked if the material, the calico and muslins, had made up well with the patterns they already had, and Bertha had to turn her question aside with an evasive answer. She ended up by saying she didn't quite have them all finished, but that they did look different from what she had first expected. Mrs. MacPherson looked puzzled.

The morning barge from the north, the first small packet through the lock, brought Mrs. McKeeters down from St. Marys for the dedication ceremonies. She mounted Gerta Hemel's long wooden stairs to her covered porch above the blacksmith shop while carrying a picnic basket filled with some of her special treats. She didn't quite understand the festoons of greenery on the railing.

Before long, Mrs. Hemel hurried down the towpath and brought Bertha Gast a little parcel. It was a special gift from Mrs. McKeeters.

Lou-Lou came skipping along the street, crossed the footbridge over the canal above the lock, and came running down the towpath to tell Josie some news from the Kattmann and Gast households, when she was stopped by a humorous incident at the blacksmith shop.

Grünwalda Peppleman was in a high temper and had come with her long club to the blacksmith shop hunting the elusive Charley. She banged on the large hogshead to flush him out of his hiding place, but unable to catch up with him, she hurled a wooden bucketful of water after him, and drenched him to the skin. Then she said,

"Loafer! Devil the life out'n me this morning, will you? Busy as I be, and tryn' to get der pies done before the outdoor picnic." Charley ran the best he could out through the open driveway of the grain depot, laughing and gasping for breath as he ran.

"Dot fat, lazy loafer haffing der nerve tellin' all up and down the canal how dot large hippo barge of der Frau Kattmann's iss to be named for me, saying it <u>looks</u> like me in der face," Grünwalda fumed to Jake Hemel. She followed Charley on into the depot and asked Ben and Hermann,

"Iss dis true? Iss dot ugly large hippo packet barge to be named "Grünwalda, der Hippo" after me?"

When Ben and Hermann assured her that no such thing was even mentioned, she became somewhat pacified and went toward her shop calling back,

"Und it's time you two closed up shop there and got ready fer der ceremonies. Ve ladies of the church society are planning a large outdoor dinner on der outdoor tables in the church lawn. Ach, mein pies! Dey be burned brown. Dat Charley!"

Lou-Lou giggled as she ran back up the towpath to catch Charley. At all costs, he must never tell that it was she and Josie who started the rumor among the other playmates for a joke, and now it had gotten back to Charley. He must keep their secret. Grünwalda Peppleman could be a formidable foe. On the pleasant days that promised to be ahead, Lou-Lou didn't want any ill feelings to mar the fun.

Lou-Lou came running up the steps to the side porch when she heard Bertha Gast exclaiming to Mrs. Hemel how thoughtful it was of Mrs. McKeeters to remember them with her parcel.

The minute Lou-Lou entered the kitchen and saw Josie's amused expression, she knew what the gift was. With one quick sniff, she caught the rancid aroma of the St. Marys cheese, which she detested. Lou-Lou held her nose and made an attempt to dash back out of the kitchen.

"Ye-o-w, Aunt Bert, get the shovel quick and bury that!"

"Ach! Louise Gast, you chust don't know vot iss good! Your Grandfrau Kattmann iss right! You chuld be paddled more," Bertha said.

Gerta Hemel laughed and said,

"and on your Birthday vich is soon comink up, ve might chust catch you and give you thirteen good whacks!"

"You'll never catch me," Lou-Lou called as she ran out to the canal bank while fanning herself to dispel the malodorant cheese fumes.

The dedication ceremonies were to be held in the auditorium of the Lutheran Church. It would have been fitting to have the services at the site of the hospital at the warehouse but lumber and other building materials cluttered up the grounds. Work was not far enough along there yet for a public meeting.

The Catholic Church also planned a service to honor Augusta Kattmann since she was a heavily contributing donor to the church funds, and was considered their "part-time" member since she attended mass and meetings there on a rather irregular basis.

The townswomen were busy going back and forth with baskets of food they had prepared for the dinner. Men and boys had set up boards on trestles. They were used for tables out under the trees. All sorts of kitchen chairs and benches were carried there, and were put up to the tables. White linen tablecloths covered the tables as the noon hour approached.

Everyone was ready when the large bell in the church clock steeple began to ring eleven o'clock. The passenger packet had arrived a half-hour before, and the dignitaries were being shown the site of the hospital, and were inspecting the inside of the brick warehouse. After a short while, they were ushered the short few blocks to the church and given seats of honor in the choir.

Several short speeches were given in which the need for the hospital was stressed, and then honor was given to the town for making the hospital a reality. It was then the minister stood and gave the wonderful tribute to Augusta Kattmann, and paid complimentary honors to Anna Steinhoge. Mrs. Kattmann wiped her eyes during the eulogy when her past deeds were recounted to the visitors and to the audience.

Angus MacClintock cleared his throat very slowly, took what seemed to be several minutes to wipe his glasses and took the lectern next. He gave an account of the new sanatorium and hospital rest home being built out at Maria Stein on the ground given by the Kattmann's at <u>Willow Haven</u>. He read facts and figures, giving heavy emphasis on the long need in this part of the state for such a thing. He also gave distinct honor to Mrs. Kattmann, saying she was an unusually remarkable woman with "insight years ahead of her own time."

He touched briefly on the recent tragic events; then begging the pardon of the audience for mentioning such a subject in the sanctuary of the church, he announced very tersely that the case against "the criminal and his associate criminals" was nearly closed. Lengthy trials by this "degenerate band of inhuman criminals" had been uncovered in many other places. Now it was of federal dimension. In some instances the law had not been so fortunate as here, nor in time to prevent death of the victims. He thanked the community for their help and cooperation in helping track down the criminals. He nodded toward Big Bertha.

Just as the service started, a group of latecomers had attracted attention as they were ushered to seats to one side near the center. While taking small steps, Elvira Brenner came tripping down the aisle. She was followed by a strange retinue of some of the Russian people from the sawmill. Big Bertha was hardly recognizable with her peasant holiday dress embroidered with bright colors and beads, and some sort of a gay native headdress. It was a round pillbox arrangement surmounting her raven black hair, which was parted and then drawn back into a huge coiled braid at the back of her head. The Russian men were wearing light tunics with polished leather boots.

Lou-Lou whispered to her Aunt Bertha,

"Now I have seen it all. Why I'll bet old Uriah Hornback and Sheba will show up. He will probably have his hat on . . .!"

"Sh-h-h, Louise!" Bernhardina Gast frowned at her daughter.

Ernestine Hofermeyer played a few numbers on the organ at the beginning of the services. When their vocal numbers with the organ were finished, the dedication ceremony began. Grünwalda Peppleman, Mrs. Hemel, and Mrs. Gertslaecker could be heard above the other women in the choir.

When the solemn services were over it was high noon. The deep throated bell, high up in the clock tower, began striking during Angus MacClintock's last words. The ladies' choir spared no effort on their last number which was a hymn of praise. There was a short prayer of dismissal and then the organ began playing what Josie and her brothers termed the "let-out music."

The crowd pouring out of the church onto the lawn soon filled the tables. A festive spirit replaced the solemn one of respect. The many women who were waiting tables stood ready for the crowd to descend upon them. They stood ready and soon had dishes and plates of food heaped upon the tables. Other women fanned the tables with long branches to keep the flies away. Mrs. Schweitermann and Mrs. Zinndorfer helped Grünwalda with her pies.

Elvira and the Russian people could not be induced to stay for dinner. They hurried to the *Wabash Loon* that was tied up in the basin. They spread out their own picnic dinner on the top deck. The bubbling samovar seemed to be the main center of interest to the Russians while Elvira skittered around getting dinner on the plates.

After a leisurely dinner hour, the guests departed back south to Minster where carriages waited to take the group out to Maria Stein to see the progress at the country rest home and sanatorium at The Willows. There was to be no formal ceremony there except the turning of a ceremonial shovelful of dirt by both state commissioners and by Augusta Kattmann. At last it was all over. Mrs. Kattmann entertained her guests overnight out at The Willows, or her Weidenhimmel, as she called it in German. They departed the next morning on the sleek black and white packet "North" to Toledo.

In a few days the report came up the canal to New Bremen that the circus and showboats were having a great run in Minster, but their time there was about over. They would soon dock in New Bremen.

Preparations were made for the holiday. It was to be a combination of a local fair that would be combined with the traveling show. In fact, the town council had booked the show to have it coincide with the local fair.

The church women had booths built for their food bazaar. There would be eating stands and a small restaurant with trestle tables on the street. There were clothing bazaars and displays of canned goods. Off at the edge of town several farmers had set up display pens for their prize animals. Young boys thought it was a lark to sleep all night at the fair on bales of hay and straw to take care of the animals.

The circus tents spread out on vacant lots and on the streets. Traffic was rerouted and a carnival spirit took over the town as bands of people walked in the street. Aunt Ernestine, and her Aunt Fredericka, even got into the spirit of the fair and said, "it was just like Mardi Gras in New Orleans." Lou-Lou scoffed and turned to her Aunt Bertha, and demanded,

"Now when were *they* ever there?" Bertha Gast could only smile and reply, "Who knows?"

"That's one I hope I live to go see, down the Mississippi on one of those glorious paddle-wheel steam boats. Oh, Mardi Gras."

Many of the smaller showboats were berthed around the canal basin out of the main artery of traffic of the canal. Smaller booths spread out into the town on the sidewalk fronts. It was one of the largest shows to hit town. Gerta Hemel warned everyone not to leave their houses open, day or night, with all these strangers in town, and to leave lights burning. Better yet, there should be someone at home most of the time at night. They could take turns at the fair.

The big moment came when the mayor was going to give an official opening to the fair and the carnival. Bertha and the girls were able to secret their costumes aboard the *Blue Swan* so that not even Ben, Hermann, nor the boys ever became suspicious. Jake Hemel and Elihu had the steam calliope at full pressure and ready to go at the appointed time. Ian MacPherson cursed because with the through traffic, he could not neglect the tolls or the lock gates, and he could not join in on the fun on the *Blue Swan*.

The Blue Swan was towed slowly by the stern to the south end of town where she waited at the wide turn basin for her cue to bring the mayor into Lock 2 and descend the lock where he could make the formal opening speech, cut the ribbon for entrance to the fair, and welcome all the merrymaking.

At five o'clock, the appointed time agreed upon for the opening, all was in readiness. All the circus and show people had their tents and booths ready. The showboat barges had their gangplanks over on the towpath ready to charge admissions.

The clock struck the hour. The small German band began its "oom-tah-tah" rhythm time in front of the grain depot, and *The Blue Swan*, with its high-stepping horses in flashy belled harnesses began its royal approach.

Ben called frantically down into the passenger cabin of the packet for Bertha to get up there on deck quickly, and get the calliope going loud and strong. When Bertha and the girls paraded up the gang stairs to their posts at the calliope, Hermann Gast nearly let loose of the rudder-tiller in his speechless surprise. Ben and the mayor stood with their mouths open at the gaily-costumed figures he saw pirouetting around on the deck as Bertha started the opening bars on the steam organ.

(Simple Calliope melody
heard first at Junction)

*"Hear that mel-o-dee-e
from the Cal-li-o-p-ee.
How it sings to me-ee."*

Jake Hemel was so startled by all the colorful oriental display in front of him, that he forgot his gauges. Elihu was quick to recover, and cackled out in high boyish laughter, "Mind your fires, Jake! Keep an eye on them gauges. I kin keep you in firewood!"

Bertha was in a fine mood as she swayed back and forth on the stool at the keyboard. Her purple and orchid Turkish harem costume set off the two girls' costumes. Lou-Lou pranced and twirled in her costume with the high Spanish mantilla as she snapped wooden castanets, made of large black buttons, and saying through her teeth,

"I'm a dancing señorita from gay old Madreed-ah!" Josie laughed as she remembered Lou-Lou's favorite line from the señorita at the showboat that was at Junction on the way to Toledo. Elihu "rat-tat-tatted" on a snare drum.

Josie, in her Fatima fortuneteller outfit, went into her routine of twirling her right hand above a glass colored ball in her left. It was the best she could do for a crystal globe, but Elihu had found it for her. It was a colored ball off some lightning rod weather vanes from the church, but it served the purpose. Since all three had half of their faces covered, the townspeople didn't know who the musician or dancers were at first. Everyone thronged to the canal berm, lined the streets, and rushed onto the docks surrounding the basin when they heard the ecstatic pipes of the steam calliope, castanets, tambourines and drums.

Ernestine and Bernhardina gasped in mock horror when at last they recognized their sister, Bertha, in that outrageous costume. Fearing an outburst of indignation, their Aunt Fredericka quietly sniffed her smelling salts, which she took from her poke bag.

With a final flourish on the calliope, Bertha led up to a fan-fare for the mayor. The applause was overwhelming from all sides, and the crowd yelled for more. Bertha got up from her stool at the keyboard, and took a bow, being careful to take several steps in a circle to show off after doing so.

When the townswomen recognized "their own Bertha" in those shocking, rather gauzy Turkish harem bloomers, the first initial shock gave way to loud applause. Augusta Kattmann sat fanning herself, but stopped short when she recognized her daughter, Bertha Gast, as the rather flamboyant "show woman" up on the deck of the *Blue Swan* of all things! Through her stem glasses, she inspected the costume, and drew a deep breath when she saw Bertha's bare ankle below the ballooning Turkish bloomers where they gathered into a gold band. Bernhardina Gast and Ernestine Hofermeyer rushed over to tell their mother that the other girls were Lou-Lou and Josie, in those "show-hussy" obscene costumes. *The idea!* They thought that Hermann and Ben in their wild promotion schemes were behind this.

Then for some unforeseen reason, Augusta Kattmann saw the humor in the ridiculous show. She began to see the makings of benefit shows for money. Yes! People were wild about the calliope and the show the girls were putting on. This could be a money-maker for a charitable cause, say for the school or the hospital. As Aunt Fredericka prepared for one of her faints, Augusta Kattmann nudged her sister and allowed herself the treat of a good laugh while she folded her stem glasses and applauded. At first Fredericka was bewildered, but soon took her cue from her dominating sister, Augusta Kattmann, and began smiling as she also applauded.

After the bedlam died down, Ben Gast gave a showman's spiel by waving his top hat for effect and holding his arms outstretched so that his colorful blue cutaway frock coat hung open showing a shining gold chain across his waistcoat.

As soon as the mayor finished his short speech to welcome everyone to the great "Brementown Fair and Circus," Bertha was ready at the keyboard. Lou-Lou had seen her grandmother's reaction to their show and told Bertha and Josie. "As for the other two, Bernhardina and Aunt Ernestine, watch out. Bad weather was ahead and no doubt," Lou-Lou giggled, "Uncle Ben and Papa will catch 'Hail Columbia'."

"Don't worry, Lou-Lou," her Aunt Bertha consoled her, "if your Grandma-Má and Aunt Fredericka are laughing, those other two will soon follow her. Why I believe that even Heinrich Hofermeyer is amused by this..."

Ben tapped Bertha to get ready; then without warning he gave her and the girls a big spiel,

"And now, ladees and gentlemen, it gives me great pleasure to present one of our newest and greatest attractions to the fair. . . our Lady Fatima. . . that Turkish wizard of the steam key. . . and her two accomplices. Pardon me, I mean to say 'assistants.'"

Mayor Zinndorfer stepped down the gangway onto the berm and going to the ceremonial wide ribbon that blocked entrance to the street leading up to the fair booths, he took wide shears and cut the ribbon. Shouts of glee filled the air, and the calliope drowned out their wildest calls and whistles. As soon as the mayor had left, Hermann and Jake pulled the gangplank back aboard to keep curious fairgoers from coming aboard. Bertha let the girls take turns at playing since this was their debut. Each time they stopped, the audience applauded for more.

In a short time, Augusta Kattmann excused herself from the others and commanded them to stay where they were. She and Anna Steinhoge marched up the berm and motioned for Hermann to put the gang over for them.

"Here it comes, Aunt Bert," Lou-Lou warned. "It's the charge of the Prussian artillery. Shall we duck for cover?"

"Indeed not! Keep on playing, Josie, and play loud!" Bertha commanded.

Mrs. Kattmann came over to the calliope, but to Bertha's surprise, she began swaying her head from side to side with the old Waltz, "Auf Wiedersehen." Mrs. Steinhoge's piercing blue eyes were smiling as she too became entranced by the exciting, but barbarous tones of the organ.

"Ach, mein Bairtha, aren't chew all chust full of der surprises? Eh? Anna, vot you make of all of dis showings-off?"

"Augusta, it's wunderbar, chust wunderbar! I like. I like." Then turning to Bertha, her mother demanded,

"And vair, mein Bairtha, did you ever learn to play one of dese contraptions... vot you call... der ca-li-o-pee?"

"Why I learned on this. It's just like playing the organ," Bertha said.

Hermann came up smiling, and shouted over the organ,

"You can't beat this, Mother Kattmann. Don't you imagine Bernhardina and Ernestine will want to try learning on this next?"

"You imagine! Nein, I cannot. Not those two," she answered in a loud voice.

Ben came over to the group when the organ stopped. The crowd clamored for more.

Mrs. Kattmann, always with an eye for good business, advised Ben and Hermann,

"De crowd will not leave and do business with the other concessions as long as you entertain them here. You better taper dis off with vun more and then retire. Announce that there will be a concert tomorrow at noon, and again at different times to get your crowd here."

"I suspect you are right, Ma," Bertha slipped. She never called her "Ma" to her face.

"Ach, 'Ma' is it, mein Bairtha?" Anna, haf you evair heard such disrespect, and vot with me now a celebrity?" Mrs. Kattmann asked in mock offense.

Then when Anna Steinhoge burst out laughing, Mrs. Kattmann joined her. Then she turned and slapped Bertha lightly across the back. Bertha waited until Ben made the announcement about the calliope concert later that night, perhaps at nine or nine-thirty, and again at various times the next day. *The Blue Swan* was pulled by the stern out of the right of way of the canal and back into the dock basin from which place she would give her next calliope performance. After the men moored it fast the white show horses were unhitched from their tow. Then they were taken to their livery stable.

When Bertha had finished her last selection, Jake allowed the fire to die low under the boiler. It would not take long to get pressure up again for the evening concert at nine o'clock.

While Bertha and the girls were removing their costumes in the little dressing room off the packet cabin parlor, Mrs. Kattmann inquired through the closed door,

"And vair, Bairtha, did Ben and Hermann find this steam instrument?" Before Bertha could answer, Ben and Hermann came down into the cabin and sat down.

"This was part of your good bargain, Mother Kattmann. This was down in that back hold. Jake and Elihu and all of us had to do some fixing up, but we had a good time doing it."

"Ja! I can bet you did chust that. I'll have to ask mein son, Ludwig, how many kegs of der ale haff disappeared from der ice house in the meantime," she countered. "And now mein Benjie and Hermann, what have you heard about the condition of de other barges down in drydock? Vot condition?"

"They are coming along nicely and they are in good shape. We'll soon have the bottoms redone and waterproofed. They will get new paint after the necessary remodeling is done in Dayton and Cincinnati's Lockland."

"Den I didn't make a bad bargain? Didn't get skinned?"

Ben shook his head and answered her. "Of course it is a pretty large investment to all of those barges at once," he advised.

"Ach, mein Benjie, it was a steal! A steal! Vy dot owner of the show vanted money so bad he almost gave them away. You see! Ve all see! Dey make money and repay der investment in no time. Vy I got the lot of them for almost the cost of one new one. I suspected a bad bargain, der cheat, but it seems not to be so. Ja?"

Ben and Hermann assured her that the experts at the drydock had helped them inspect all the barges carefully, and they were all in good shape. Apparently, they were fairly new and had solid keel beams and solid decks.

CHAPTER 24

THE CROWD GREW LARGER at the air and circus carnival after the formal opening by Mayor Zinndorfer. People from the country and surrounding villages
came into town until the hitch racks along the streets were filled with carriages, buggies and spring wagons. The town board rented the vacant three
acres of pastureland belonging to John Polsdorfer, which lay to the east of
Walnut Street and back of the German Catholic Church. In this lot, they
erected temporary hitch racks for the over-flow crowds of horse-drawn ve-
hicles. The shade trees in the lot and along the sides by the fences made it
ideal for hitch-rack purposes.

Charley, Ben and Lou, and most of the young boys their ages, such as
Jakey Backhaus, Albert Wiemeyer, Schani Schlesselman and others found fair
time jobs to make themselves some money. Jakey along with the others soon
lost his sense of humor and outrageous talk when the job of digging postholes
for the hitch racks became a rather hot, laborious job in the sun.

Every packet boat that Mr. MacPherson met and collected tolls from
brought passengers to the dock platform. A few of the packets that had no
pressing schedule were kept tied up out of the canal right of way in the wide
basin, while the passengers amused themselves at the fair. Large farm wagons,
some even drawn by oxen, were directed into Polsdorfer's pasture lot. Some
country people who had come long distances unhitched their animals from
the wagons and tied them in the shade where they were watered and fed. The
families stayed overnight in their wagons and slept on the hay with coverlets.
Some slept on the ground under their wagons.

Gerta Hemel and Mrs. McKeeters sat up on the bough decked balcony
porch above the smithy while fanning and watching the scene below. They
spoke of many things, but the subject of the Gast performance on the *Blue
Swan* and of all things that steam calliope, and the shocking costumes of

335

Bertha Gast and those young girls. Then they spoke of the crowds. They kept a watchful eye in both directions of the canal from the south on to the lock at the north and beyond. They were apprehensive lest that old nuisance, the old Irish codger, would show up now in this crowd, and spoil the fair with his abusive mouth, fights, and fracas his presence could cause.

The town board had persuaded Henry Wiederman and the Wiemeyers to rent or lease their two large pasture lots to the board for the duration of the fair. They were to be used for the larger displays, such as animal tents, booths and other concessions. It was here that Mary Hogan, the well-known "Hog-back Mary," had her animal acts. These two lots were just north of Polsdorfer's hitch yard lots across Plum Street, and ran the entire block from Front Street at the north to Plum Street at the south. The lots did not front on Walnut Street because nearly half of the block had houses and properties the entire length along Walnut Street.

Across the canal and the small creek to the west, the town had leased the large empty pasture lot of Franz Vogelsang to be used for additional fair tent space.

Zelda Zinndorfer was not to be outdone by Grünwalda, Griselda, and the others of the Lutheran Church. She and some of her fellow parishioners of the German Catholic Church made plans and erected bazaar and food booths right there on the church lawn. The German Catholic church faced Walnut Street, and the back of the church property adjoined Polsdorfer's hitch yard lot.

Even though Grünwalda Peppleman was one of the mainstays in the preparation of food for the Lutheran Church bazaar and its food booth, she managed to decorate the front of her pie shop and erect advertising signs that Charley had painted for her on pine planks. She had small tables out in front of her shop that were loaded with pies, cakes, crullers and donuts, over which she had spread light curtain materials and dishtowels to keep the flies off her wares.

Schlesselmann's brewery booths did a large business as did their competitor, the *Wooden Shoe*, but the bulk of the business went to the *Blue Swan Ale* stands because of their unusual advertising. Huge swans cut out of planks and painted to look like the bow of the *Blue Swan* barge surmounted the front of the stands. Ludwig Kattmann supervised all the stands, but Hermann and Ben Gast helped him out. Augusta Kattmann had ordered that all the brewery hands that were helping at the booths be immaculately clean, with clean hands washed often, and that all of them wear white shirts and white aprons. Heinrich Hofermeyer and Ernestine were shocked when told to tailor some lightweight white jackets for the helpers at the booths to wear. They were also to devise some sort of white caps to be worn with the jackets. Ernestine was somewhat miffed at having to turn the tailor shop at Minster into a production line of *Blue Swan* costumes. She and Henry had to hire some extra women in Minster to help stitch the name of the *Blue Swan* on the front of the jackets. The tedious part was sewing, by appliqué, the small swan with white wings onto the headbands of the white caps that looked like baker's caps. Her ire turned to smiles when her mother reimbursed her bountifully for all the needlework.

Since Mrs. Kattmann was in such an unusual carefree mood during this week of carnival spirit, Bertha and the rest of the family did all they could to encourage her generous out-going mood.

When Augusta made the offer, Bertha and the girls accepted the generous gesture to accompany her and Anna to eat their evening meal at the church bazaar tables. Some of the other women who had been cooking over hot stoves and open fires the entire day to prepare the food, and those who had been on their feet all day serving at the counter and at the tables, mumbled their displeasure at seeing Augusta Kattmann and Anna Steinhoge sitting at the tables to be waited upon. After all, they reasoned that it was Augusta herself who had insisted they have the food booth to make money for the church. Why didn't she don an apron and get her hands in the tub of hot suds dishwater? It kept two women busy most of the time just washing dishes.

Charley, Lou, and young Ben had the four little boys, "the new little cousins," in tow and took them all over the fair grounds, up and down the street and basin dock platforms to see all the strange sights. On one moored barge there were circus animal cages (the menagerie). Another barge offered various small arcades and side shows aimed toward the interests of children.

Lou-Lou and Josie went with the boys to see Hogback Mary's animal acts over in Wiedermann's pasture lot. She had rides for children on the backs of her fat tame donkeys, but inside of her makeshift tent, she and her helpers put the small dogs through many clever tricks - such as riding on the backs of ponies. One pony could take a few steps on his back legs when he reared up. Another white show horse performed many tricks, but the crowd inside the tent applauded most when Mary would approach him with outstretched arms. When she embraced him around the neck, he would balance himself and then raise one front leg and try to embrace Mary. The boys told Mary Hogan that since she was almost a block and a half from the water of the canal, they would help her carry water for her animals that evening. She told them that she would not have too much to carry for her attendants would take the horses, ponies, and donkeys to the canal, and take buckets along and water them there. She thanked them kindly and talked with them. She remembered them from Toledo, but also from summers past when she had played in their town.

For once Marta Schweitermann failed to see the humor in a prank some of the mill hands and rougher men played on the teen-aged boys. She became angry over it and talked pretty plainly to the men involved. Schani Schlesselman and Albert Wiemeyer were older than Charley, Ben and Lou. They were more mature for their ages than the other boys, but Jakey Backhaus wanted to be considered to be "in their league," and go in their company as much as he was considered in the company of the younger boys, such as Charley, Ben, and Lou Gast and Leo Wiemeyer. These older boys were bragging about one picture arcade on one of the barges which was marked "for adults only" and "for men only." This piqued the curiosity of the older boys. They managed to lie about their ages and paid admission to see some of the slides, lantern slides, and postcard pictures that were supposedly from France.

They couldn't wait to show their male superiority over the younger boys, and bragged about what they had seen: the wimmen, cards, and slides. They exaggerated outrageously of course. They spoke slyly of seeing Mayor Zinndorfer in there with Henry Bushman, the constable. Of course, their excuse had been that they had to inspect all the shows regularly, as well as the games, to keep them all "fit."

Some of the older mill hands at Wiemeyer's flax mill and the Backhaus flour mill heard the braggart youths and set them up.

These men knew of a nondescript barge moored way to the south of the basin. It was in out of the way wide water that used to lead to a warehouse. However, it was now abandoned and in a state of decay. Hardly anyone knew it was there, for it was not a part of the company of showboats that were with the circus and carnival. These older men knew what it was behind its facade of selling tin-ware, copperware, whetstones, scissors and cutlery. The barge also advertised that they would sharpen all kinds of cutlery. The men told the boys that they could see some "real" pictures there if they knew the right person, and if they gave the password to the large Indian or Mexican woman at the gangplank who guarded her wares of pots and tin-ware out on the canal berm. They were to tell her that "they knew Jim," and they would be admitted to the real show inside.

Schani, Albert and Jakey approached the large Indian gypsy woman and pretended to inspect her tin and coppers. They got their courage up when they saw, of all things, some bearded Amish men in large black felt hats emerge from the barge's interior. They paused to speak to the large Indian squaw gypsy. She blocked their way and very stoically held out her cupped hand, and kept repeating:

"Fifty-cent! Fifty-cent!"

The men grudgingly paid her the coins while mumbling something in Swiss German Amish about the agreed price had been "two bits" or a quarter (twenty-five cents).

The boys screwed up their nerve and went aboard when the large squaw urged them to do so, beckoning them with her large hand. When the boys went inside the cabin, they did not see any array of cards or pictures on the walls or stands. They went back out on the deck and told another dark woman that "they knew Jim." The woman only nodded and started to take them back inside. Schani and the other boys pooled their coins. They had only a few nickels and dimes. They told the dark woman, maybe part Negro, or maybe just a dark Mexican Indian, that they only had a dime apiece and that they only wanted "a dime's worth" of whatever those other Amish men had bought. The dark woman did not change her expression but immediately pushed them out to the canal berm to the large squaw and whispered something to her. Immediately the large squaw sized them up. She held out her hand for their dimes, and upon receiving the coins and putting them into her pocket, she seized the unsuspecting boys, slapped them soundly, knocked their heads together, then sent them sprawling out onto the graveled berm. Even though the boys thought they were quite grown up, they had tears in their eyes from the pain and fright. When the old squaw threatened them with a club, they got up quickly, barely missing stepping off into the canal, and scrambled up the berm path. After they had gone a safe distance, Jakey Backhaus began cursing his luck, complaining that he had spent his last dime, and that he had worked so hard to make digging postholes for the improvised hitch yard. He then added,

"You know, I'm sure glad that we only had ten cents on us."

Schani, rubbing his bruised face, asked in bewilderment,

"Why? Why are you glad about that?"

"Because," Jakey explained with a sigh, "I don't think we could have stood a whole quarter's worth of that. Them Amish sure are tough."

They overtook Marta Schweitermann at the large Cherry Street basin. She had delivered some cake and other food to some elderly ladies who were not able to come uptown to the fair. She immediately sensed that something was terribly wrong with the boys; she could see the tears in their eyes and the fright and anger upon their faces. She wasted no time in hounding the truth out of them. She warned them to say nothing about the incident, especially not to their fathers, or they would all get the "board" and a sound thrashing for going into such a place as that barge. Marta spoke in a low voice and tried to tell the boys what sort of a "bad wimmen" place it was. She found out from Jakey and Schani who had given them the password.

It didn't take Marta long to search out Zelda Zinndorfer, Hedy Schlossel and Grünwalda Peppleman. She told them what had happened. All three women looked at each other and nodded their heads in agreement. There was more cleaning up to do - like that night at the grain depot and the affair with Silvermann. Zelda was particularly irate. She knew that her husband, the mayor, and that shiftless Constable Bushman surely knew what that barge was, and why it was tied up way down there in the dark. The barge was to have copper and tin-wares. "Bah humbug," she thought!

Mayor Zinndorfer and Constable Bushman left the carnival and the shows up near the lock, and walked with direct steps down Canal Street. Then they crossed over to the berm below the Cherry Street basin and went directly to the squaw at her gangplank. They fumbled for some coins and said that they "knew Jim" and then went aboard. This act infuriated Zelda and she exclaimed to the other women who had followed her at a short distance behind the constable and the mayor.

"Iss good we found this out. Had we flushed out this rat's den, dis wild boar's hutch, we might have found dem two in there. You never know," Zelda fumed.

"Now we go into der action, girls," Grünwalda said simply. She picked up a club and approached the large squaw, while Marta and Zelda kicked all the tin and copper ware into the canal. The Indian woman could tell real trouble when she saw it and retreated in haste back aboard her barge while shouting some Spanish gibberish. The mayor and Henry Bushman rushed back out on deck in time to see the commotion. They forced the Indian woman to give back the coins and then told her who they were. She quickly returned the money. The mayor told her to close up her barge immediately. Otherwise, she, all her women, and a few men would be put under arrest and placed in jail, and their barge would be impounded. They gave them an alternative: they must leave the vicinity at the break of first daylight, or they would all be arrested.

Some younger women and boys waded out into the canal and tried to retrieve some of the floating copper pots and tin pans. Others put out the lights inside the barge and began closing up the "copper and tinsmith shop" for the night.

As the group walked back toward town, Grünwalda scolded the lazy Henry Bushman. He could only retort that "he was the law here, Mrs. Peppleman," but he kept well out of her arm's reach.

Zelda upbraided her husband, the mayor,

"Und why, just tell me why, when you smart men who are running the fair, selling der concessions, und selling der booths, vy, for vy did you allow such a disgrace as that barge in town? You and dem Gast boys, Henry Backhaus, Waterman, and Langhorst are really the smart ones."

"Zelda," Albert Zinndorfer exploded at last, "we didn't allow that barge in town. It wasn't part of the carnival. We didn't even know it was back up the canal there."

"<u>Hölle</u>!" Zelda said acidly, "<u>Der Teufel</u>! I'll chust bet you didn't. Why them kind of wimmen, and places couldn't exist if it weren't fer de townsmen, der good burghers, men who run businesses, churchmen, and even the Amish who support them. It takes two. Think about dat."

Zelda made a comic figure with her hair skewered tight on top of her head in a braided small knot, her wry face, and skinny body in contrast with the two huge women, Grünwalda and Marta, between whom she was walking. It was unusual not to hear Marta joking or engaging in some sort of humorous nonsense. Grünwalda complained and grunted as she shuffled along in her elephantine loping gait. Her humor changed when she got to her pie shop and found that Charley had nearly sold out all the cakes and pies. Many of the families who were staying overnight in their wagons at the hitch yard had bought pies and cakes to go with their own basket fare that had become depleted. Grünwalda at once fell into a good humor as she and Marta Schweitermann went to the church bazaar booth to assume their duties there. Grünwalda pretended to grumble at Charley that his good salesmanship would cause her to have to get up at dawn and start baking all over again.

After a few acid remarks, Zelda left the group to join her church ladies at the German Catholic Church stand in the courtyard of the church lawn.

Henry Backhaus had been instrumental, along with Ludwig Waterman and Leo Wiemeyer, in getting the *Brothers of the Stein* fraternity together for practices, as well as the brewery men from *The Ale Brewery*. Rather than build a dance pavilion for the song and Landler dance show numbers, they decided to use the warehouse of the Backhaus flour mill that was almost empty. The remaining sacks of wheat and the ground flour were stacked to one side.

The flour warehouse floor was much smoother than the floor of Gast's grain depot or the granary floors. The ash floor was almost as smooth as a ballroom floor from the years of being polished by cloth sacks of flour and wheat. There was a thin powder of flour that made the ash floor planks more white and smooth.

The carpenters had built a small platform at one end for the stage upon which the Men's *Choral Society*, better known at the brewery and flour mill as *Brothers of the Stein*, could perform. They alternated with the ballroom dances, giving their concerts in the afternoons and early evening. After that, the ballroom dances began.

As Lou-Lou and Josie, along with the other girls, Gerta and Ludmilla, strolled by the flour warehouse, they could hear the voices of the choral group with Henry Backhaus' high tenor above the rest. Then there was applause, after which the gate was opened, as were the warehouse doors, and the crowd inside poured out. It was the last concert. Next Heinrich Hofermeyer, as ballmeister host, started ushering patrons into the warehouse to the seats reserved for the spectators. Those who were going to dance stood in line behind a roped-off section where Ernestine Hofermeyer greeted them with all the grace of a large city concert hall's patroness.

While the orchestra was tuning up, Uncle Henry swept Josie into a few swooping turns of a waltz across the smooth floured floor. The lamp shades were covered with light pastel colored cloth and paper to give a soft glow to the cavernous interior. A few bats swooped down from the rafters from time to time and "flittered" above the heads of squealing women. Heinrich next instructed Lou-Lou in a few steps, while explaining to her not to step like a "goose," (like a *dumm stumm gans*) that was trying to extricate itself from thick mud. He told her to step more in a sliding light glide between the downbeats of the waltz cadence - more like a dandelion umbrella across the floor in the breeze. Lou-Lou compressed her lips at being called a *stumm gans* (dumb goose), but followed her Uncle Henry through the steps.

Augusta Kattmann had been strolling from show to show and booth to booth almost imperiously. She nodded her approval or shook her head and frowned in disproval at some. She came into the warehouse ballroom just as Henry was instructing Lou-Lou in the dance step.

"Ja, now dot is more graceful. Dot is it, glide on der ball of der foot," Augusta told her granddaughter. "Dance more like a Dresden china *blume* and not der Dusseldorf *sausage*." Then she left Anna and did a stately turn of a few waltz swirls. Graceful as she was and light on her feet, Augusta was rather top heavy in spite of her tightly laced bosom. She gave the appearance of a battleship whose prow was cutting through the lesser vessels surrounding her.

The seats were almost all sold out for the spectators, and the dancers who had paid admission almost filled the ballroom space. Lou-Lou and Josie sat with their grandmother to watch a few dances. The dancers had to purchase a ticket each time they danced, but the spectators could remain seated for five dances before they were required to pay for another admission.

Josie, Lou-Lou and the girls left to go to the main attraction of the showboats on the canal. They saw the outstanding Spanish Flamenco Dancers' Showboat and the small show they gave on the top deck. The girls decided they would go to the light play, or operetta show, over in the town hall first; then they would come back to the Spanish Señorita after that.

The showboat next to the Spanish Flamenco gave minstrel shows with song and dance, "Negro Soft Shoe" and "Shuffle Dances" right off the docks of Memphis and New Orleans. Lou-Lou scoffed that they probably originated not anyways close to New Orleans, but more likely in Toledo, Cincinnati or even Dayton.

The town hall was a converted lumber shed or warehouse, which had a platform stage for the mayor and the town aldermen. This oblong hall was easily made into an auditorium for the operetta. The traveling light opera company had recruited some local talent to help with the choral numbers and dance routines. Ernestine and Henry would much rather have helped with this show rather than the one in the flour mill warehouse. At any rate, they did help with the costumes. Bernhardina and the musical Mrs. Vogelsang helped with the production.

Josie and Lou-Lou fell immediately in love with the couple who sang a romantic love duet - he in a planter's white frock coat and she in the loveliest, largest hoop skirt that the girls had ever seen in that western Ohio back country. They marveled at the way the man who ran the large oil lantern could manage the lens with colored glass over it for various effects. For the last number, he placed some sort of light pale green gauze or curtain material over the front of the lamp's lens to give a delightful moonlight effect.

Then back at the Spanish Flamenco Dancer barge, Lou-Lou sat enthralled as she listened again to the slow sensuous words of the male chorus as they led up to the almost lightning rapid refrain. Then all the dancing girls flounced onto the stage and surrounded the star - the Señorita from Madrid. The chorus first sang of old Grenada, Andalusia and Seville. Deep bass guitars, some mourning bass viols and cellos, and some other chords accompanied them from some deep toned keyboard instrument the girls did not recognize.

It began after the Spanish Flamenco's almost operatic fanfare introduction; then toned down to the minor key in seven sharps.

"From your gypsy camp near old Granada,
from those grottoes where the smugglers hid.
One day your band left from Andalusia,
and from Seville you came into Madrid."

A second chorus of men's voices sang the next verse, but the voice arrangement was different. Perhaps there were fewer voices.

"Starlight in your eyes reflects the campfire;
lips sweet with the wine of Malagua betray desire."

The next short verse changed its key to that of five sharps, but was sung by two señoritas, who were accompanied by two baritones. They wore hats of Cordoba with ball fringe all around the rim. A subdued rattle of tambourines and castanets joined in the next short verse,

> "Castanets tell how your heart feels;
> tambourines and drums makes the sound of quick staccato heels."

Then the key changed back to a lower tone, to D in two sharps, as a mixed women's chorus of señoritas in lace mantillas sang,

> "Nights are filled with memories of you,
> and of a fickle heart that was not true."

The tone of the music gave an intimation of some expectancy, of a climax that was to come as the women faded into the background. Then the entire male chorus made a semi-circle, while stamping their heels and clapping their hands to the moderately slow time. The depth of their tone was a sharp contrast to the verse preceding it, in C sharp,

> "Gypsy life has taught you to love and to yearn.
> Yet you left us with searing kisses,"

The accompaniment ascended into a higher key - that of D in two sharps, as the tempo quickened with more force of volume.

> "that will ever on our lips and mem-ries burn."

All at once, the stage was a whirling blur of flashing Flamenco skirts, stamping heels of men's boots, tambourines and castanets. The orchestra built up the fanfare into a crescendo, its volume was fortissimo and the tempo was an extremely rapid presto. Then the star, the Señorita from Madrid, whirled into their midst while they danced about her; but they kept their semi-circle so that she (the star) could always be seen. They sang to her and with her, but her operatic soprano could be heard above all the others.

> "Dancing Señorita, when first you came from old Madrid,
> with high combs and lace mantilla, from us a while
> your face you hid.

> With castanets ringing, and tambourines singing,

as you whirled on through your dance.
Flamenco heels flying, gypsy eyes lying.
For a time you brought us rapture, undying intrigue,
and breathless romance.

Dance on, dance on, Flamenco gypsy, rapture to the wild guitars.
Then your barge locks on down to your camp beneath the stars."
"All at once, you're gone; yet your dance lives on, whirling on and on.
Please, just stay a while. Encore and Olé."

There were several bars of frenzied rapid music of the finale that came to
a crashing sudden end with spasmodic triplets.

Lou-Lou and Josie sat spellbound at the finale. Even Charley, Ben, and
Lou at the back of the barge cabin hall were surprised. Then they joined with
the others in deafening applause. It was by far the best and most polished
of all the shows at the fair, but then the girls knew now that it was not just a
traveling carnival showboat. They knew that it was an operatic troupe doing
the back-country. The girls wasted no time in going to tell their grandmother
and Aunt Ernestine that they simply must see this Spanish show because it
was opera, and almost ballet. Uncle Henry was amused with their enthusiasm
and took pride in his protégées. Maybe they were finally waking up to culture
and the arts. Anna Steinhoge hurried on ahead from the flour warehouse to
the showboat on the canal to get tickets for the next show. It took Augusta so
long to maneuver her way through the crowd when she had too much to say
to so many people about so many and diverse things.

The girls left the others and went to join Bertha, at the *Blue Swan* and to
change into their costumes inside the cabin. It would soon be time for the
last evening calliope number.

As luck would have it, the old Irish O'Hooligan did make his appearance
on the towpath at a late hour and began cursing all the bottleneck of traffic and
congestion of the "infernal carnival scows of human refuse." Ian MacPherson
heard him coming up the canal from the north and closed the lock gate so that
he could not enter the slip to wait being lifted or ascend the lock. Ian sent
one of his men who usually helped man the heavy gates and balance beams to
locate the Gasts, Henry Bushman, and the mayor. A drunken nuisance like
the old codger could spark the whole carnival into a riot, cause ethnic and
class wars between all the hodgepodge of race mixtures in the carnival, fair
and the patrons.

The old codger's abusive speech did not get him very far, for the lockmaster,
constable, mayor and Gasts, along with the other aldermen, harried him right

through town and out through the upper Cherry Street basin with a warning not to come back while the carnival circus was in progress.

The temptation was too great for Charley, Lou, Ben and Jakey, along with a group of other of the town's boys their age. They wasted no time in going home or to hidden places at the flour mill and getting their reed shot shooters and their wooden yoked slingshots. Schani did not waste time on small lead shot, but used his larger sling that he called his "nicker flipper," and lambasted the old foul-mouthed man with dried mud pellets and small stones. A horde of smaller boys ran along the towpath picking up dried horse manure, of which there was seldom a scarcity, and peppered the Irish barge as it was trying to make a rapid getaway. The horses were almost to a trot.

As O'Hooligan sped beneath Gerta Hemel's balcony, he kept his foul mouth shut but could not resist shaking his fist at them. When he saw Mrs. McKeeters pick up one of Gerta's potted geraniums, and Gerta raise her white porcelain night jar, he jumped back into the comparative safety of his barge cabin, and peered cautiously out on deck until he was safely beyond their reach.

To confound matters worse after the confusion of the old Irish codger had passed, another disturbance arose which posed another problem for Mayor Zinndorfer, the constable and the alderman. From the south, they heard some other music above the music of the showboat, and the organ of the carousel. It was evangelical shouting and hymn singing. The boys had kept their weapons and ammunition close by in case they needed it again. They had to shoot their victims from the darkened windows of either the flax mill or the flour mill on the canal to escape detection. However, it didn't matter; they were ready when Jakey Backhaus passed the word that the old barefoot preacher was croaking out his Swedenborgian scripture to the south of them.

In a short time, Uriah Hornback appeared on the towpath across from the main part of the circus on the Canal and Washington Street side. His wife Sheba sat nodding her head. She didn't know what to make of the scenes of carnal pleasure all around her: the music, the lights, the dancing, the smell of cooking food and baked goods, to say nothing of the beer and ale. Oh, it was the fleshpot of Babylon! Ian MacPherson was provoked with him for hauling a raft of logs to the sawmill that was downstream to the north at that hour of the night. Ian cursed him when old Uriah started quoting scripture out of context. It was then that old Uriah refused to move on through the lock, and be lowered down, so that he could be hurried on through town to the sawmill at Lock 2. He took off his low crowned tattered straw hat, and walked back and forth on the graveled towpath. His grubby bare feet were calloused to the cruel gravels from years of going without shoes. Then he called Jehovah down to witness his being tried before his enemies and to witness his torment.

"Oh see this, oh Lord. See this Babylon and it's fleshpot of carnal sin, and all these writhing sinners that are weak in the flesh," he cried.

"Come on, old man - you can preach tomorrow. Get on into the lock and get on out of the way. Why didn't you tie up down at Minster or Loramie and wait until daylight for this trip?" Mayor Zinndorfer asked him with waning patience.

"The Lord's message and his ministers can't wait until tomorrow. Tomorrow may be too late," Uriah shouted with religious zeal.

"And it is your mission in life to minister to all of us? Now get on through the lock and preach out there in the country," Henry Bushman warned him. Some of his deputies came up onto the towpath after crossing the bridge down on Front Street to the towpath side to the west.

"This is state and federal property. You people of New Bremen don't own this canal. It is a federal and state thoroughfare," Uriah said.

"Then you are violating federal and state laws by congesting the canal, tying up the lock and disobeying canal procedure laws."

"Oh hear me, oh ye in sin. The time is at hand," Uriah shouted. "Mine enemies persecute me, but my God is not sleeping."

"You can do all this ranting out in the country. We can't wait," Mayor Zinndorfer said. He nodded to the constable, the deputies, and the assisting town alderman to pole the log raft into the lock.

"O Centurion of the law. You say you can't wait. Do you think the good Lord can wait? Is he just going to open those white gates up yonder when it is convenient for him? Will he wait and dispense judgment and salvation only when he has the leisure and at your convenience? Nay, he will not." Uriah ranted on and became incoherent.

The smaller boys were enjoying the show and began mimicking old Uriah. They got on their knees, their hands were clasped together, and they took their upper bodies back and forth and up and down with their clasped hands as they made a show of mock religious fervor while mumbling,

"Goin' to Hell ... Jonah's whale ... the Lion's den ... Noey's ark."

"Suffer little children," Uriah exclaimed; then he became confused and said, "Wisdom from the mouths of babes."

When Mayor Zinndorfer, the constable and the alderman saw what a commotion the fanatic old man was making, and how it was disturbing the spending of the crowd at the fair, they knew they had to make a quick decision. They clapped their hands at the small boys and cleared them from the towpath. The deputies led the oxen down the sluice incline of the lock to the lower level, headed them toward Front Street a few yards to the north, and tied them there.

The log raft was poled into the lock and the gate closed behind it; then the wicket in the front gate's sluice was opened. The water began to rush out in a leaping torrent. The raft began to lower. It would take about ten minutes for the water level to go down the ten feet to the level of the lower canal so that the front gate could be opened. The constable and the deputies threatened to tie up the stubborn old man and tie him to his raft, and start his oxen walking down the canal to the north with the raft in tow. They told him that if he traveled without a lantern at night, and another barge collided with him, he would be liable and the law could ban his using the canal altogether. When he was locked through, the deputies attached his oxen in tow and led the raft to the edge of town. The boys in the windows of the grain depot, the flour mill, and flax mill tormented the old man with shots of lead pellets from their slings and reed shooters. They could hear the old preacher calling upon Zion to witness his "being scourged," but to forgive them for they knew not what they did.

CHAPTER 25

IT WAS NEARING TIME for the last calliope concert on board the *Blue Swan*. Rather than hitch the showy white Percheron to the towline to move the barge from her slip at the brewery, the crew and some brewery workers helped Ben and Hermann Gast pole the barge from her slip out into the canal. It would be only a few yards from the slip to the place above the lock where the *Blue Swan* would be moored for the calliope concert. There surely would be no more traffic on the canal at that hour of the night. The unruly old Irish Hooligan had been summarily disposed of and hurried out of town to the south. Then the fanatic old evangelist, Uriah Hornback, had been put through the lock, lowered down to the north and forcibly ejected from the town. He was warned to get beyond the town limits in a hurry or face being arrested and locked up in jail for violating canal traffic rules.

Bertha Gast, Josie, and Lou-Lou put their costumes on at home. It was only a short walk up the towpath to the lock and to the *Blue Swan*, which was moored just above it to the south. Elihu Sanders was like a small boy in his glee to appear on deck and to accompany some of Bertha's numbers with his snare drum and tambourines. Jake Hemel even took delight in his intermittent accompaniment with the hollow piece of hardwood that he "whacked" upon to give a staccato Latin American band sound. Gerta Hemel sniffed her contempt saying that it sounded more like a woodpecker on the roof.

Jake and Elihu had gone aboard the barge earlier to fire the boilers, make sure the steam head was up and the gauge was showing enough pressure for playing the steam pipes.

The other girls had almost overwhelmed Lou-Lou and Josie with admiration and envy. Gerta Langhorst was a little offended at first because Lou-Lou had not confided the calliope and costume tricks to her. She considered herself to be Lou-Lou's closest confidante, except for Lou-Lou's cousin Josie. Ludmilla and Dort, who were part of the close circle and some of the others were delighted with the act. They crowded around Josie and Lou-Lou to inspect the costumes and the daring "harem" bloomers. Ludmilla blurted out her envy and let it be known that she would love to be included in some sort of an act with her zither-harp. Maybe some of the girls could accompany her with a trio or sextet.

The boys, Lou, Ben, and Charley were surprised and flabbergasted that the girls had the nerve to appear in such costumes. They were more surprised that Bertha Gast had permitted it. They knew about the calliope from loafing around Elihu's tinker shop and seeing the instrument being repaired.

The other boys that were friends of Lou, Ben, and Charley were greatly impressed by the daring costumes and the calliope. "Think of it," they told each other, "We have our own calliope right here in town." They went on to say that there was no reason on earth why Jake and Elihu couldn't make some sort of a carousel for the little park near the Cherry Street turn-around basin. They could use the calliope for music now and then - maybe for evenings or on Saturday afternoons. Instead of having the usual horse powered carousel merry-go-round, old Elihu, along with Jake Hemel, and Ian McPherson could devise a way to use a water wheel for power. They could use water from the spillway overflow sluice just as the flax, woolen, and flour mills did.

Both Josie and Lou-Lou were flattered by the new attention, not only from their girl friends, but also from those other mischievous boys.

The girls had whispered confidences among themselves but they would "just die" before they would come out and say it or show it. They were at the age where they were beginning to notice Jakey, Lou, Ben and Charley. Gertie Langhorst wanted to be noticed by the tall Schani Schlesselman but didn't have the faintest idea how to accomplish such a thing. She had thought that he had paid her some interest that night at the tryst at the tile works. They could not understand the biological facts beyond their knowledge that girls mature faster than boys, but they were certainly feeling these urges. Dort Waterman complained that those "dumb little old boys were still kids and all they thought about was them pipes, slingshots, pea shooters and marbles." She thought it was worse that they liked going fishing with odious wriggling worms for bait.

Ludmilla Vogelsang who was called "Milly" by the other girls, was more outspoken. She was "sweet" on rather scrubby and freckle-faced Fritzy Witte in spite of his reputation of being foul-mouthed and just "plumb full of orneriness."

Ludmilla was always cheerful and at times was downright "giggly." Her wild cackles could be heard up and down the towpath and on the streets in spite of her rather strict and musical mother's constant admonition and correction. Ludmilla could not be suppressed much more than Lou-Lou Gast. When she got the giggles in church, her mother took her by the arm and ushered her out into the cloakroom where she lectured her until she recovered. She even cackled in a higher note with louder volume when she was paddled at home.

Mrs. Vogelsang was an accomplished musician but she was more vocal than instrumental. She and Ernestine Hofermeyer were in disagreement over the interpretation of many of the classics. Mrs. Vogelsang was not German, nor was she of any sort of Germanic stock. She was descended from the French speaking communities a few miles to the south at Frenchtown and Versailles that were not far from the Russian community. She enlightened all those around her that the pronunciation was "Vair-sai" and not the local bumpkin pronunciation of "Ver-sails." There were those who said that she gave herself airs and considered herself much above her husband's German farmer relatives. She was a Voisard, which she pronounced as "Vwa-Saar" in French.

Mrs. Vogelsang tried hard to bring out the best in Ludmilla, and certainly gave her the very best of musical training that she could. Her training had paid off in some small returns, for Ludmilla did have the best singing voice of any of the girls, and she was rather good on her harp-zither, but she was better on the square piano at home. However, Ludmilla longed for the "fun times" - the circus and the companionship of her girl friends, and an occasional try at winning over Fritzy Witte. He was just adorable when he cussed. She even liked to see him spit coffee grounds, which he thought resembled grown-up tobacco juice.

The whole gang of girls and boys had congregated on Gast's side porch facing the canal. It was only a short distance to First Street and the lock beyond it. The group could see all that was going on at the carnival on First Street from the porch. They could also see the area around the lock to the south.

The boys were laughing and enjoying telling the girls how they had peppered the old Irish codger and old Uriah, the preacher, with their pea and shot shooters and small-yoked slingshots. Then they fell to devising a play whereby they could get some good shots in at the unsuspecting carnival people. They could get some good aims from the darkened windows of the flour mill, and from the flax and woolen mills. Jakey and Fritzy were anxious to find a way to hide in the upper shadows and rafters of the dance floor there in the granary. The boys realized that if they could, they would sneak past "Old Lady Hofermeyer" at the door, or from "Old Lady Kattmann" and them other "old walruses" on the committee.

"What good would it do?" Ludmilla asked, while trying to open a conversation with Fritzy. "They have on so many petticoats and are all fluffed out with their hoops. You can never get a good shot where it will really sting."

"Hell no," Fritz exploded, "and with all them plump, fat bottoms just itching fer it. There's no use to try fer a leg with all them skirts neither."

"We'll just hafta try fer some good shots on the bare arms and bare necks," Alby Lehmluhl assured him. "No use to try for the back with all them corsets and steel stays. They couldn't feel nuthin - not even a whale's harpoon."

They all fell to discussing how they could get some good shots in on the unsuspecting carnival-goers. They were eager to get some good shots in at the baldheads of some of the musicians in the dance orchestra. Jakey warned that they needed to use a fine bird shot of lead so that it would feel to the victims like it was a sting of a mosquito or a sweat bee.

It was time for the calliope concert, and when Bertha Gast came out of the house, the girls accompanied her to the barge. The boys all left with plans for their bird shot on choice victims. Fritzy scored a bold shot and caught Augusta Kattmann on the back of the neck. She complained as she swatted at an imaginary mosquito that the canal brought mosquitoes the size of horseflies.

Bernhardina and Ernestine came on board and inspected the strange instrument. Ernestine poked at the keys with misgiving as if the calliope were something unclean. Bernhardina played a short ditty on it and laughed with detached amazement at her own audacity. It was a great joke to their trained musical ears to hear this ugly duckling attempting to gargle out the pure melodies of the masters. Ernestine stopped her sister, Bernhardina, from continuing a Mozart melody by saying such a travesty profaned the art of the great master.

Bertha Gast grunted with disgust, then had the colored lights turned up and angrily put the steam organ through such loud passages that the steam curled up in the colored lights in the cool night air. Lou-Lou laughed and told Josie that her mother looked like something out of the Arabian Nights – like the genie from Aladdin's lamp forming out of the vaporous mist.

Charley Peppleman was particularly intrigued by the fortuneteller, the gypsy woman on one of the barges who was swathed in beads and bangles as she performed her art. She was also quite adept with the sleight of hand - so much so that Charley was missing his handsome old watch and chain. He set up a bellow of protest and the gypsy woman closed up her booth door.

When Grünwalda heard of the outrage, she first thought of getting her huge broom and the town constable and going into the gypsy camp to clean out the din of iniquity. Her mother's wedding ring was on that watch-fob!

Gerta Hemel had a better idea, in spite of Jake's warning for her to mind her own business. It was dangerous business.

Grünwalda, with Gerta and Griselda's help, was able to stuff herself into some of Charley's clothing. With hair done up tight under a huge beaver hat, she waited until she saw the gypsy fortuneteller open her booth again. When the old thief didn't see Charley Peppleman or the law waiting outside her door, she started enticing passers-by into her booth. Word spread from Gerta Hemel and Griselda Gertslaecker about the good show that was about to take place. Mr. Bushman was ready behind the fortuneteller's barge in the shadows back on the towpath. Elvira Brenner whispered the word to Big Bertha and her Russians, who were going through the circus animal barge that was just a few yards astern of the gypsy Romany barge.

Pretending to be a half intoxicated huge man that was loose on the town for an evening of fun, Grünwalda put on a show in front of the fortuneteller. In no time the fortuneteller was enticing the huge man to come into her booth for what she felt would be an easy touch. Grünwalda played interested but timid until the gypsy woman left her little table and came up to tug Grünwalda by the arm. Grünwalda's deep voice sounded like a man.

Big Bertha came up on the towpath in time to see her large friend go inside the booth, and the colored flap come down over the doorway. She whistled through her teeth to Elvira that Grünwalda did not know what she was doing, for these people were real Romany gypsies and they knew how to use a knife. They had a bad name and had some trouble down in Troy. Turning to her Russian men, Bertha spoke quickly in her native tongue, and they took up places near the fortuneteller's doorway while pretending to be watching other attractions. Big Bertha had difficulty in getting Elvira to leave the deck, but she whispered for her to run and tell Jake Hemel what was about to take place, and to warn Ben and Hermann Gast. There might be a circus riot, or a big fight might ensue from what appeared at first as a little score to settle between Grünwalda and her unsuspecting gypsy fortuneteller. Big Vassily put his hand inside his sash and felt of his curved knife. Vladimir went to the back of the gypsies' colored tent on the main deck. Grünwalda played along with her hostess, mumbled in her deep voice and flashed some money bills from pocket to pocket. In a short time, the wily gypsy was fumbling over Grünwalda's clothing and took the bait planted for her. As she attempted to distract Grünwalda's attention, the gypsy hastily undid the large watch fob and chain across her intended victim's chest. However, to her dismay there was no gold watch at the end of the chain. There was only a mousetrap, which snapped onto her finger. Quick as a panther, Grünwalda grasped the thieving hand and gave the wretched woman a severe sidewise wrench on her offending hand that made her drop the chain and trap.

The gypsy woman tried to get away from Grünwalda's grasp. All of a sudden she realized that Grünwalda was an infuriated woman. She began shrieking for her gypsy men on the barge when Grünwalda slapped her soundly into silence.

"Give me mine hoosband's gold watch and chain, you gypsy witch, and mine mother's diamond wedding ring if you don't want hafing yer arm ger-broken," Grünwalda bellowed.

Immediately the other gypsies ran to the fortuneteller's rescue but found their way blocked by strange Russian men who seemed to appear from everywhere. There were only four gypsy men and three women. As big Vassily and Gregori towered above the swarthy oily gypsy men, one of the gypsies brandished a knife. Immediately the Russians showed larger knives. The gypsies saw that they were greatly out numbered, and put their knives back in their sashes as the Russians smiled large open smiles as their white teeth shown. The Russian men backed the gypsy men to the back of the barge. Johnny Ivan and others stood at the gunwales on the towpath. They were ready to catch any fleeing vandals from Romany who might try to make off with their stolen goods. One of the gypsy women tried to escape, but one of the older Russian women caught her by the hair. Then she took her swiftly by the wrists and swung her back up onto the gypsy barge with a Slavic oath. It happened so quickly that Elvira could hardly follow all of it. Gerta Hemel saw Jake hurry to the barge - followed by the constables and deputies. Soon Ben and Hermann Gast came down the street and went up the towpath to the offending barge. No one on the streets or other barges seemed to notice what was going on so smoothly did the Russians carry out their planned rescue operation.

The gypsy woman pretended ignorance of Charley's watch while trying to get free from the overpowering Grünwalda. She made the mistake of using vile gypsy language toward her captor when Big Bertha tore down the colored flimsy sheet of silk cloth over the doorway into the tent, and said something to the gypsy woman in her Slavic tongue. Then she apologized to Grünwalda and smiled.

"That veery bad language you use, Rumanian she-dog. All Rumanians thieves - thot's your profession." Then she spat out some unpronounceable Slavic term into the gypsy's face as she put her face down close to the other woman's.

"Apologize, Rumanian trouble-maker! Apologize to the nice woman whose hoosband's watch and chain you stole," Bertha hissed. The gypsy pretended she did not understand her, and Grünwalda twisted her arm again. The gypsy shrieked her innocence. The gypsy men started to her rescue again when the Russian men stepped closer to them with their hands inside their sashes and under their tunics. This time they did not smile, and the gypsies retreated like docile jackals.

"Bulgarian wart-hog," Big Bertha said in a low voice edged with anger. "Slovene rock coyote, produce the watch!"

Still the woman hesitated, but now she turned fearful eyes to Bertha when she said something in Slavic that seemed to fill the gypsy with a new meaning of fear. While Grünwalda held the furiously fighting gypsy woman securely, Big Bertha gave the little booth a thorough search for the watch by going through every box and drawer she could find and emptying the contents on the deck. When she found nothing except coins and trinkets in each small drawer, Bertha grunted a disgusted "Bah," and continued her search as she dumped the contents on the deck - much to the dismay of the gypsy woman.

"Gypsy thief, we set the whole tent on fire - burn you out. Produce the watch or burn out!" With this threat, Bertha took her cigar from her glowering lips and burned the woman on her backsides with it. Again, she shrieked with pain, and Bertha covered her mouth with her large hand because she didn't want the complete fair grounds to become alerted. When she had silenced the woman, Bertha took her by the hair and forced her to look out on deck.

"See you lying Moldavian oil-bag? Your men are pinned down, and my Russian men outnumber them. One move from your greasy Balkan jackals, and 'pssft-zt-t,' we breaka da necks, und trow your men into canal. Vell, be smart now und gives with the watch and diamond ring, nyet?"

The terrified woman shook her head and pretended innocence. While Grünwalda was shaking her much as a terrier would a rag doll, the gypsy woman bit her. Then Grünwalda started to get really rough and pummeled the smaller gypsy woman. Bertha stopped her.

"Mrs. Pepples! This calls for somethings, ah, more refined." In a quick dive inside her blouse, the gypsy woman produced a long stiletto knife, but just as quickly Bertha grabbed her hand and wrenched her wrist sidewise. Then she gave it a blow with her other hand, and caused the stiletto to drop to the deck. Bertha kicked it back under the fortuneteller's couch. Bertha's large face got dark with rage as she leaned down in the face of the gypsy, while Grünwalda pinioned both of the woman's arms behind her back. Big Bertha drew back with a gasp,

"Phew-w! Bah! Gypsy witch, you stink!" Grünwalda gasped. "Greasy thief, what do you use on your head and body - bear grease?" The gypsy woman swore at her while trying to bite the strong arms that held her.

Johnny Ivan called from outside the tent to Big Bertha,

"Katyna, have you found it? Hurry with it! The law will be on us in a minute." The carousel organ continued its loud music.

"Bah on the law. We find it. They nevair will," Big Bertha answered. Then turning on the gypsy woman who was kicking and still trying to bite, Bertha asked with sarcasm,

"Yu want to play it dirty, Rumanian pick-pocket queen?" Quickly as she spoke, Bertha began ripping the woman's clothing off in shreds with great long sweeps as Grünwalda held her. Then as an after thought, Bertha gave her a systematic search and found the watch with the diamond ring on the fob inside the woman's stayed bodice. Then she called to Johnny Ivan, and gave him the watch and chain for safekeeping. After that Bertha turned to Grünwalda and exclaimed,

"Next to the Swedish massage, there is nossing like the Russian cold bath," she rolled out "Russian" with the burred "r's." Grünwalda growled her willing consent.

"Ja, mein friend, you bathe and I massage," she said as she jerked the struggling gypsy woman upright when she tried to bite again. "But this heathen stinks so. I think ve haf to get rid of the sour grease smell. Ach himmel! Vot a sour rank smell and you a gypsy queen," Grünwalda complained. "I tank dis one iss likes, or needs der scalding barrel like ve do for hawgs at butchering time."

"Nyet, nyet," Bertha shook her head, and repeated the Russian for "no," as she continued to strip the clothes from the screaming woman. "This Croatian-Serb freak, I theenks she excretes from der bowels through the pores of the skin. Ve teach lesson. Ve clean good, maybe clean out mouth too. Maybe clean her of dirty habit of thievery and whatever else she does in this filthy swine's booth - this Romany pantry of drapes and whore's couch," Bertha said with determination as she finished stripping the outraged gypsy woman.

Wasting no time, Big Bertha bound the struggling woman hand and foot with the remnants of her torn gypsy shreds, and taking her up like a bag of meal, Bertha rushed to the side of the barge. With Grünwalda helping her, Bertha doused the woman up and down in the cold canal while reaching down to the water level with her long arms.

Since the bathing act was performed on the canal side of the barge and away from the towpath, not too many people saw the spectacle, but they soon heard the shrieking gypsy woman's cries as the cold water covered her. The crowd gathered. Someone yelled, "Fight!"

Jake Hemel interrupted the party just as Ben and Hermann Gast came up on board. When he saw that the others knew what was going on, Mr. Bushman (the constable) came aboard to try to restore law and order. Jake saw in a moment that the Russian men had the situation under control. Mr. Bushman spoke up and told the others what had happened to Charley Peppleman's watch.

Big Bertha and Grünwalda unbound the gypsy woman, and then let the half-drowned woman scramble out of the canal and get back on board and into her tent. Big Bertha grabbed her before she let her pass and told her,

"The next time ve gives the massage and the real cure. If ve just had a snow bank, ve gives you the Siberian Ice Baths. Good for muscles. Gives nerves of steel. Now you get!" Big Bertha commanded and gave the disappearing woman a resounding slap across her wet, naked buttocks. The crowd on the banks of the canal laughed in unison. Lou-Lou, Josie, and the boys all jumped up and down with excited glee.

Elihu and the lockmaster came aboard with the mayor, who upon hearing of the theft of the watch, ordered the gypsy barge to get underway and leave town, or all of them would be locked up and prosecuted for theft.

Elvira rushed up to Big Bertha and shook her hand. Mrs. Kattmann and Anna Steinhoge came in time to see the naked gypsy woman climb out of the water and scamper into her burrow of disheveled drapes. Bertha Gast watched the commotion from the *Blue Swan*, but she was too far from the gypsy barge to see exactly what happened.

Charley Peppleman was overjoyed when Johnny Ivan gave his watch to him. Grünwalda demanded to know just how it all happened.

"Well, Elihu here, and Ian MacPherson vas telling everybody how dis fortuneteller womans could tell such strange things - like nobody could tell - things that only you yourself could know...and...and..."

"Go on Charley, tell us. Just what did Elihu say?" Mrs. Sanders demanded. Mrs. MacPherson closed in too when she heard her husband's name mentioned.

"Blabbermouth," Ian MacPherson accused Charley angrily. Mrs. Hemel got up from her chair above them on the smithy porch.

"Jake Hemel! Were you in there too, holdin' hands with that hussy and having your big paws read?" Gerta called down in her best brassy voice.

"Whist, Woman!" Jake growled back up to her. "Hold your tongue." As he continued to scowl at her, she quickly sat back down whimpering,

"Mercy, I only meant...wal, pity sakes!"

Mrs. McKeeters, not knowing what to make of the unusual turn of events, sat making strange "tst-tst" sounds through her teeth.

"All we need to make this fair a real success, Gerta Hemel, is to have that old Irish cuss come through here tonight. You heared, I suppose, of the turrible fracas we had when he was in St. Marys. I'm going to try my best to have him arrested."

"Why, it's turrible," Mrs. McKeeters complained. The carousel organ drowned out their small talk.

The mayor and Mr. Bushman dispersed the crowd from in front of the gypsy barge, which was making hasty preparations to get out of town. Mrs. Kattmann told Ben and Hermann to get the music going loud to distract the crowd.

Bertha Gast and the girls were ready for the nine o'clock musical performance on the calliope but waited for word from Ben.

Grünwalda Peppleman was not one to be put off. She cornered Charley down on the street by the canal and demanded,

"She would tell you things dot only you could know vas true. Humph! Vot did she tell you? Vot did _you_ tell her, you elephantine Lothario?" Charley tried to beat a hasty retreat, but she grabbed for his coattails.

"Now Grünwalda, love, she was _chust_ a fortuneteller." Charley tried to explain as he started running down through the crowd. Grünwalda bellowed after him while trying to catch him,

"_Vot vair_ you doing in there in the first place, in dat perfumed, dirty gypsy hole behind closed flap? Answer me!" Everyone turned and laughed as they watched the huge woman dressed in a too-tight fitting man's suit trying to run after the gasping Charley. Mrs. Sanders turned on Elihu fiercely, as did Mrs. MacPherson.

"All of you old has-been Tom Cats," Mrs. Sanders said as she almost hissed. "It wouldn't be quite so bad if she were young, pretty, and clean!"

"Wal, she's clean now," Elvira Brenner put in while cackling in high mirth. She pointed out to the other ladies an imaginary oil slick on the surface of the water.

"See, she left her high water mark of gypsy grease on our canal, thanks to Berthy here."

The steam calliope began again with a loud introduction so that all voices were drowned out. People soon forgot the incident of the gypsy barge and crowded around the dock basin to watch the performance on the _Blue Swan_. Augusta Kattmann and Mrs. Steinhoge had come aboard to rest, and were sitting down in the passenger cabin when the discordant skirling music started. Mrs. Kattmann urged Josie and Lou-Lou to go up on deck to put on a little show, and dance around a little in order to attract attention.

"Keep your crowd in holiday mood so they will spend," she advised the others. "Keep it moving. Louveese, do your dance. It was rather good, _you know_, this afternoon. You do dot Spanish Señorita britty goot! Ja, britty goot! Make der mawney, too."

The sweet waltz of the carousel drew swarms of people to listen and watch the delight on the faces of the young people riding the carousel animals as they were whirled and lifted in circulating gallops.

Lou-Lou nearly fell over upon hearing a compliment from her grandmother. Both girls went up on deck and improvised a dance and pantomime number. Then they took their turns at the keyboard while Bertha pantomimed. When she saw Johnny Ivan, his eyes were drawn into slits as he laughed with the music. Bertha motioned him to come aboard the *Blue Swan*. She asked him if he would do some of those Russian dances he did out at the sawmill dock when she attempted to play some of the Russian folk songs. He readily consented, so Bertha took the keyboard and started out slowly with an old folk tune.

Johnny followed her tempo, but the calliope was no match for the Russian folk dance tempo Johnny was used to following when his people played their native instruments at their folk gatherings back at the sawmill, or over west at the Russian settlement in the woods which people called Russiaville.

The crowd clapped for more when Johnny finished his whirling dance with the strange kicking out of the legs from almost a kneeling position. He danced with pure enjoyment, and it was almost as if he defied gravity, and as if he were dancing from the end of an invisible puppet's string while being catapulted out in space. Augusta Kattmann and Mrs. Steinhoge heard all the strange rapid boot-heeled clatter above them and came up on deck to witness the wild, but expert performance.

"Vy dot is perfection, dot's ballet," Augusta exclaimed with awe.

The first night of the fair and showboat was a great success, but the second day promised to be better once word of the calliope, and dancers spread by word of mouth up and down the canal, out into the country, and in surrounding small villages.

CHAPTER 26

WORD OF THE WONDERFUL calliope and its costumed performers spread all over the immediate countryside. People wanted to see the horse-powered carousel and its organ with drums, cymbals, bells and tambourines, as well as the Russian dancers. Lou-Lou, Josie, and the boys could not tell whether the carousel was the same one they had loved in Toledo at the Swan Creek Park.

Augusta Kattmann could not contain her wonder at the agility and expert dance of Johnny Ivan. The same was true of the other Russian woodcutter performers, musicians, and those strange wonderful instruments.

Augusta immediately started to make inquiries, and plans to have this wonderful ballet included somehow in the shows at the fair – "her fair." Bertha Gast and her sister, Ernestine, tried to explain to their mother that perhaps it would not be appropriate. These woodcutters and lock carpenters did not belong to any of the churches. They would not be interested in contributing their time and effort to shows and bazaars to make money for these churches. One could hardly expect them to perform out of charity. After all, what would have the community done for these little-known foreign people who had come from the east with the coming of the canal to help construct the wooden locks, the huge balance beams, and the wooden lock gates, to say nothing of the huge hand-hewn piling logs and dock puncheon flooring?

"But their art, their ethnic <u>kunst</u> should not be lost out here. Ach, ist so <u>wunderbar</u>. Such expert dancing. Dat Jonee, dat Schani Evon, he defy gravity. Peoples <u>chud</u> see it."

The carousel's mechanical organ filled the night when Bertha Gast's playing of the calliope let up for a reprieve. However, Augusta Kattmann's busy efficient mind did not let up.

"I know, Anna, der has to be a way. Did you see how that Schani E-vawn leaped and whirled, and did you notice, eh, mein Anna, how he seemed to luff every minute of it? Ja, he chust loves the dance. Nein, he iss not chust showing off out of der conceit. He luffs the dance - he is the dance. He becomes a part of it. Ve must do something here, Anna. He needs to be seen, and he needs to be able to dance in order to grow in der dance."

"Augusta, I do indeed see what you mean. How should we do all of this? Can't you let your mind rest and just enjoy the present for what it is? Maybe he is satisfied just the way he is."

"Vell, ve see, Anna, ve see," Augusta said with deep thought. The group with Johnny did not know how to answer graciously in English when Augusta, Anna, along with Ernestine Hofermeyer, went to each and every one of the musicians and dancers, and then to Johnny Ivan and expressed their appreciation of their music and dance. Bertha Gast was pleased, and then she quietly thanked the entire troupe, but clasped Johnny's hand in gratitude. Big Bertha (Katyna) was standing near by and let her face relax into a smile. It was good to find trusted friends after years of lonely wandering.

Hermann and Ben Gast stepped up to Big Bertha, Big Gregori, and Vassili who were near her and said,

"We were in such hurrys we forgot to thank you, Bertha and you others, for helping us clean out that fortuneteller barge. Thank you now, even if it's a little late."

"Dey thieves!" Big Bertha said with contempt. Then she turned and translated to the other Russians what Ben and Hermann had said. The men nodded as did the musicians. Then white teeth shone beneath dark walrus-like moustaches when they broke into smiles. One of them said something in their native tongue to Big Bertha who hesitated at first, and then said aside to Bertha Gast,

"De men here say I should tell you something else. Dey not only thieves. Dat fortune telling, card tricks, disappearing magic,. . . dat all a, how you say, a front to keep cover up."

"A cover-up?" Bertha Gast asked quietly. "I think I can guess."

"Nyet, not da guess. Is true. Dat barge a bad wimmen barge and all dem oily men bring in der...der men business. Ve know dem from back east on der Big Erie. Vairy bad, all along slum waterfronts in large cit-tee," Big Bertha explained to Bertha Gast.

Bertha in turn told her husband, Ben, what she had just been told. The Russian men said something else to Big Bertha, who in turn translated it into English for Bertha Gast.

"Dey been for past few yairs stalking, sneaking dat stink fortune barge in out of way places along older slum docks down in Cincinnati and along stock yard docks and the riverfront."

Big Gregori said something else to Big Bertha in his deep bass voice. Augusta Kattmann, even though she was standing with Anna and Ernestine a short distance away, did not miss a word. She marveled at the voices of those foreign men. What she wouldn't have given to have their voices in her church choir. They would certainly show up Henry Backhaus, Ludwig Waterman, and Johann Schlesselman, fine as they were.

Big Bertha (Katyna) told Bertha Gast what Gregori had said,

"*Da*, there is one other filthy barge on the canal. You need keep de eye open for it. Big squaw woman run it but she pretend to tell fortunes too. She also sell copperwares, you know, de pails, pans and tin. Bah, it only cover for the bad theengs and bad wimmen."

Hermann Gast answered before Bertha could tell him, for he heard what Big Bertha had said.

"We have already met them, closed them up and run them out."

Bertha Gast was aghast, and put her hands to her face when Ben and Hermann told them what Marta Schweitermann and Grünwalda Peppleman had told them.

"That copperware barge was tied up almost at the south edge of town, down there in the dark, and way below the basin. Those hags had enticed some of the young boys aboard, and that old squaw, as Bertha here calls her, robbed them and slapped them around before kicking them out onto the towpath."

"Ben Gast," Bertha Gast demanded, "are you going to tell me that our boys, Ben, Charley and Lou were in that bunch?" Lou-Lou, Josie, and Dort had been talking with Ludmilla at one side. Ludmilla could not contain her cackling at some of Lou-Lou's mimicry, or the things she had said.

"I for one am not so convinced that Grandma Kattmann's interest in Johnny Ivan's dance is for the sake of art, and for his getting on up in the dance world," Lou-Lou scoffed. Then she clasped her hands together, and started nodding her head and batting her eyes in imitation of her Grandmother Kattmann.

"*Ja*, mein Anna, peoples *chud* see him dance. It make sooch goot moneys. Ve need to start such a show. Make goot moneys."

Ludmilla started an irrepressible trill of cackling high laughter, hardly stopping for breath. The other girls could not quiet her, for any attempt to do so only made her cackle louder.

The older people looked not with amusement, but with vexation at the group of girls. Ernestine Hofermeyer cleared her throat and shook her head at them.

"Aunt Ernestine's choked on a copper pot," Lou-Lou said in a low voice, "and she can't shake it out."

Ludmilla went into convulsions of even higher cackling laughter so that she collapsed on to the deck of the *Blue Swan*, slapping the planks of the deck as she tried to talk incoherently,

"Oh, Lou-Lou, I love it. . . I love it!"

Augusta Kattmann had not missed any of the charade. She said with vexation as she half closed her eyes and nodded,

"Dot Louveese! Now wouldn't chew chust know dot Louveese vud be at the bottom of it?"

Ben and Hermann were quick to assure Bertha Gast that their boys were not among the group who were enticed aboard the copperware barge.

"Then who were the boys, Ben?" Bertha Gast asked with concern.

"I think it was Jakey, Schani, the oldest Wiemeyer boy, and I think, oh yes, that Witte boy...the mouthy one...Fritzy Witte."

Ludmilla soon regained her composure when she heard Fritzy's name mentioned. Now this was something else, and it was more serious. Just then the gang of boys passed by the barge. Fritzy was with them. They all started applauding and calling for more numbers from the calliope and the costumed performers.

Augusta Kattmann stepped up to Ben and Hermann and said crisply,

"Chust what did take place? How far, how serious was it - the boys?"

"Oh, I am sure nothing happened," Hermann told his mother-in-law, while trying to be discreet and diplomatic. "They only had ten cents."

"Nevertheless, I chudn't wonder, chud ve tell their fathers? Maybes the village doctor chud look to them. No tellings vot dem kinds of vimmen might have that could be even worse than the cholera and typhus," Augusta said as she assumed her best pose as a nurse and surgical assistant.

"Ten cents!" Ludmilla cackled shrilly. "Ten cents! I always heard it whispered that it was two-bits."

The other girls let out screams of laughter with Ludmilla's sudden words that shocked them with delighted surprise. Ernestine Hofermeyer started toward the girls to discipline them and make them behave like little ladies. The strong ample arm of Augusta Kattmann detained her as she said,

"Wisdom from der mouths of babes. Best not interfere, mein Ernestina. Dey not all our own family, dat Vogelsang and Waterman." Then Augusta turned to her daughter, Bertha Gast, and commanded,

"Best to get der caliomee music ger-started again. Ve could lose der crowd. Dey have come for der last concert, and dot is vat dey chud get to hair. Play a few numbers, den lat go. Ve want dem to get to the other booths und spend der moneys."

Lou-Lou mimicked her grandmother behind her back to the other girls, while clasping her hands and nodding her head and said,

"Sooch goot moneys. *Ja*, make sooch goot moneys."

When Ernestine Hofermeyer took Ludmilla by the arm to help her up from the deck, she could scarcely resist shaking her a little. She also tersely told Ludmilla to act like a lady. As Ernestine shook her, Ludmilla's little flat crowned straw hat with the daisy headband fell from her head. It flew off in the breeze and landed in the water near the front white wings of the *Blue Swan*. Ludmilla could only cackle all the louder with Ernestine's reprimand. Her laugh that came in arpeggios and cadenzas was infectious, and others started laughing as the calliope's steam pipes started their skirling melody.

The boys standing on the dock grabbed for the hat but missed it. Schani Schlesselman held Fritzy's hand as Fritzy leaned out into the placid canal to retrieve the hat. When Ludmilla saw him with the hat, she ran to him. He gave her the hat and she lost her laughter and melted into an act of heartfelt gratitude. She tried to make conversation, but neither she nor Fritzy could find words to say. When he joined the other boys, Ludmilla clasped the wet hat in front of her. She had a moon-gaze on her face as she went skipping through the crowd in that rapid patter step, which was so common to her. The girls all said that she never walked; she ran in sort of a dogtrot.

"Now I suppose she will cherish that wet daisy straw hat of hers since Fritzy has handled it," Josie whispered to Lou-Lou as they went through their dance pantomime.

"Cherish? Why she'll put that hat under her pillow thinking it's something special now that Fritzy Witte has had his grimy paws on it," Lou-Lou answered when she circled back past Josie in her dance routine.

The calliope number ended, and Augusta Kattmann lost no time in boldly going up to Johnny Ivan and the other Russians to ask them to do another number. She condescended to be humble, and almost pleaded with him while telling him that it would be a special honor to see him dance.

"The Czarist Court should be honored with your art," she assured him. She did not see the shudder of disdain that came over Bertha's (Katyna's) body, nor the cold look out of her eyes. Augusta meant her words as words of supreme honor and as a compliment.

The dance was over as was the calliope number. Lou-Lou and Josie ran home to change from their costumes, and then go join Ludmilla, Gerta and Dort.

The carousel's great mechanical organ filled the night again. Also, the sound of the orchestra could be heard coming from the flour mill dance floor.

In a short time, all of the girls were walking through all the streets, and viewing the bazaar stalls before going back to the carousel. They sang the words to the old carousel waltz, "Ride the Carousel. . . feel its magic spell."

How many times they had sung that old song in the little brick school there by the church, at parties, and even while walking the streets and towpath. It was a game to see who could improvise new words to the old simple waltz melody. There were five different waltz melodies included; then it usually ended with a repeat or reprise of the first waltz that they all called, "Ride the Carousel" or "The Carousel's Waltz."

They loved the second waltz that had a rolling, undulating time, the rhythm and words being in eighth notes instead of the quarter notes of the accompanying bass clef's time. They sang this selection. Then they all sang, "Ride the Carousel" in time with the slow music that all but drowned out their childish voices with its accompaniment of cymbals, drums, tinkling bells and ringing xylophones.

The carousel started slowing as the music also became slower in its tempo. The organ waltz came to a close with a few drawn out closing runs, as the great circular platform with its riders came to a slow halt.

The four horses that were attached by traces and tugs to the outside of the circular platform of the carousel kept a steady walk. They were so accustomed to their well-trod path that they did not need a rider. The driver gave them commands to start and to stop. When the carousel started up slowly, the music from the mechanical organ was slower and somehow off-key. However, when the horses fell into their accustomed faster gait, the music reached its true pitch and volume.

Most of the young boys and girls were able to pay their fares for the carousel by pooling their coins. They shouted and laughed with glee as they found their respective mounts to ride. Lou-Lou raced to a pink horse but found that it was for boys and had no sidesaddle. The other girls had taken most of the side saddled horses. It did not matter to Lou-Lou. She gathered up her voluminous skirts and mounted the saddle of her horse just as the boys did. Her pantalets were in full view almost to her knees. Her skirts covered her knees and upper legs. She did not care. She was happy and sang out with the music.

"Lou-Lou, your mother or Aunt Ernestine will see you," Josie admonished..

"Do I care?" Lou-Lou called back. "I'll be plagued if I'm going to get the cramps in my leg from riding that silly old sidesaddle stuff."

The music reached its full volume and pitch when the carousel reached its accustomed speed of rotation. Gerta Langhorst was astride the sidesaddle of a red rooster. She had managed to ride beside Schani Schlesselman and she was so pleased that she had trouble in hiding the fact. Dort Waterman had a quick sense of wit and humor. She pointed out Gerta's heavenly ride beside the tall Schani. She leaned over to Ludmilla,

"Milly, do you s'pose Gert's going to ride off up yonder in the clouds? I think she is almost in heaven now!"

Ludmilla could not suppress her cackling laughter as she swayed back and forth on the spotted galloping pig. Josie had mounted the ostrich and Dort was beside her on a gander. The attendant would let only older boys ride the leaping kangaroo, for it not only leaped up and down in the undulating waltz time, but it also rocked back and forth at the same time. Fritzy Witte managed to get the kangaroo and he rode it for dear life. Off color phrases escaped his lips now and then, but when Ludmilla heard him, she only cackled all the louder. The other girls were being very lady-like and pretended to ignore his bid for attention.

There was a large lavender hippopotamus that commanded a single space because of its size, and because it turned on a pivot whirl as it undulated up and down. Then it turned back the other way. Two riders sat facing each other on seats carved out from the inside of the huge body. As the hippo pivoted first one way and then the other, the occupants were thrown back into their backrests by the centrifugal force. The boy occupants laughed out crazily in their high glee.

The girls sang out the words of the second waltz tune. Then the organ went into the third and fourth tunes, which had a ponderous bass rhythm with deep horns and bass drums. These tunes described the ponderous lumbering walk of Bruno, the large black bear. Two of these, side by side, circled by in their rising and falling in rather of a lurching gait. Then the heavier bass drums and horns sounded as the large gray elephant rocked by. The elephant did not rise so high in the undulations but instead it rocked forward and backward. There were four riders sitting up on top in the *howdah* and were as regal as Indian Maharajahs. Alby managed to hit home with his fine shot bean shooter. He did not have to hold to any reins as the others did to hold on to their mounts. Alby and Albert had their hands free, and they scored many hits on innocent riders from their lofty *howdah perch*.

The girls sang the words about the great lumbering bear and the verse about the ponderous elephant. There was a sprightly organ passage about the kangaroo. The music was of a rather jumpy *hippety-hoppety* type, even though it was in broken waltz time. It made the kangaroo ride seem very real to life and to Fritzy, who cussed in his delight.

There was a short repeat of the eighth notes in the second waltz tune. Then the girls sang of the rising, falling, whirling and pleasant undulations that made the heights of their leaps seem higher than they really were. It was also the centrifugal force of the revolving circular platform of the carousel, along with the rising and falling mounts, that gave it all the feeling of abandon and carefree happiness. They sang on.

Then the organ came back to the original waltz and all the riders knew that the carousel would stop at the end of this selection. They all sang, "Ride the Carousel" in time with the slow music that all but drowned out their childish voices with its accompaniment of cymbals, drums, tinkling bells and ringing xylophones.

The carousel started slowing as the music also became slower in its tempo. The organ waltz came to a close with a few drawn out closing runs as the great circular platform, with its riders, came to a slow halt.

The boys and girls all complained that the ride came to a stop all too soon, but they were not to be dismayed. They soon thought of other things to do, and other places to go. Ludmilla presented a comic spectacle as she skipped and trotted along in her short quick patter of steps. Her daisy banded straw hat had lost some of its shape since the brim had gotten wet in the canal. It had started to droop in places. It did not matter to Ludmilla for she was happy as a lark, and she ran back to thank Fritzy for riding with her. Fritzy in turn was dumbfounded for he had not paid for her ride. In fact, he had nothing to do with her choice of seat on the galloping pig of the nursery rhyme. He was further nonplused when Dort began teasing,

"The pig got loose and bit the goose, and Fritz got put in the callaboose."

Josie teased her along with Lou-Lou, that if Fritzy got out of the callaboose, he would have a ball and chain waiting.

"*Ja, Ja, Milly,*" Dort teased, keeping her voice low so that Fritzy or the other boys could not hear her. "Are you spinning that spider's web good and strong for little old Fritzy?"

"What about Gert? How come *y'don't* say something to her? Didn't you see her making 'mooneyes' to that Lanky Schani? Why it's a wonder she didn't fall off her red rooster side saddle!"

Gertrude pretended to slap at Dort and Milly but giggled as she did so, as she scarcely hid her elation at being teased about Schani.

The group stopped first at one show or at another display. At Lou-Lou's insistence, they all went to the Spanish Señorita show barge. To their surprise, they learned from the large sign that the show by the Spanish Flamenco Dancers was transferred to another warehouse along the canal. Augusta Kattmann had seen to it that the Spanish dancers and singers had been transferred to a larger performing stage. The warehouse could accommodate a much larger audience of paying customers. This was almost opera, with all of its beautiful costumes and instruments, as Augusta told all her family. These back hinterlands should be given the opportunity to see and hear good music.

The group got to the warehouse in time to see the small show and fanfare that the dancers put on out in front to draw ticket buyers inside. Lou-Lou immediately whirled and clapped her hands to imitate the Señorita from Madrid whom she so much admired.

"I'll be plagued if I ain't as hungry as a dog," Lou-Lou exclaimed, "but I ain't got a red cent."

Jakey and some of the boys suggested that they all sneak back down to the tile works for "some refreshment." No one would ever miss them in this crowd. Charlie and Lou advised against it.

"New, no we don't - not at this late hour. It's too far down the towpath, and it might be dangerous with all these strange people and strange side show freaks in town."

"Well we can't go to the church bazaar food booth. Ma says we are not to eat them out of all the profits. She told us to eat a good supper before coming to the fair," Josie told the boys.

The more they thought of food and lemonade, the more desperate all of them became. Jakey, Alby and Schani went by Marta Schweitermann out in front of the church booth. They won her good will and appealed to her generosity when they told her that if she would sneak all of them some of the left-over food, they would all pitch in and help clean up that night, and would help tear down the booth and move the tables when it was all over. Marta had a few words with Grünwalda and Griselda Gertslaecker. The three women managed to fix some food in a basket without the other church women noticing, and secreted it out the back of the large tent to the waiting hands of the group.

"Now run over and giff some of der sweet-talk to Zelda Zinndorfer and sweeten her up. She might chust giff you of der pink lemonade," Marta advised them. Grünwalda called out to them from behind her raised palm as if to cushion her deep voice,

"But carefuls of der sweet summer cider. Too much, and it giffs der cramping bellyaches and der goose squirts!"

All of the group laughed at Grünwalda but wasted no time in making off with their secret cache to a place where they could all eat. In a short time Charley, Lou, and Ben came from Zelda's Catholic Church booth with a pitcher of lemonade. Fritzy and Alby came along behind with a metal tin pitcher full of summer cider. They had but two tin cups for the whole group, but it did not matter.

With their spirits boosted with the food and drink, the group turned their attention to other prospects of interest. They lingered a while in front of the flour mill dance pavilion.

It was then that Dort Waterman gave them all a surprise. She pulled from her knit poke bag a slender metal cylinder, about the size and diameter of a wheat straw. She had found it in the junk outside the door of Elihu Sanders' tinker shop. Jakey and Schani had examined it and all of them found that it was just ideal for a "shot shooter" and could propel small buckshot or smaller lead shot with stinging impact and accuracy.

"Dort Waterman!" The other girls exclaimed as they examined the lethal weapon. "You may appear to be quiet, but you are just full of all kinds of tricks, humor and deviltry," Gert Langhorst said.

"Just you watch." Dort told them. "This is the ideal place to get in some good shots. When they come out here from the dance a puffin' and fannin', we can get them on the arms and neck or the back of the head."

Fritzy complained that there was no way to get at all those choice fat bottoms with all the petticoats and skirts padding them. The first victim was Augusta Kattmann who came out of the dance with some of the other ladies to get a breath of cool night air. Fritzy told the others in the group to stand closer and shield him, but to give him a space where he could take aim. He borrowed Dort's shooter and loaded it. When all was right, he took aim and the propelled small shot gave Augusta a murderous sting on the back of her neck below her huge rolls and braids of hair.

"*Gott verdammt!*" Augusta bellowed out, swearing in German and then caught herself apologetically and said to the astonished ladies, "I mean ter say, *Ach himmel.* Anna, see if dair is a horse fly, or maybes a bumble bee on the back of my neck."

The boys and girls in the group hurried out into the crowd as they tried to suppress yelps of laughter before they were caught.

"Not so quick," Dort told them bravely. "There is one more choice shot I have just got to get in. Oh, this should be priceless and out of this world."

"Who on earth do you have on your list?" Josie asked her.

"Now no hard feelin's, but I have just got to see how your Aunt, I mean your great Aunt Fredericka, takes a shot. Oh, you know, your grandmother's sister," Dort explained.

"Oh, she's the one with all the smiles. She smiles all the time - even in church," Schani told them.

"I'd bet that she even smiles and smiles in her sleep," Charley told them. With that, Lou-Lou started imitating her great aunt and nodded to each and all of them as she opened her eyes in wide childlike wonder, and opened her mouth wide into a "slice of watermelon" grin. It was but a short time until Fredericka came to the door of the flour mill dance pavilion in the company with her nieces: Bertha Gast, Bernhardina Gast, and Ernestine Hofermeyer.

"This won't be easy, Dort," Lou-Lou advised her. "Look who all is with her. We'll all get caught."

"Hell yes," Fritzy warned. "She's got the troops of the guard surrounding her, and old lady Kattmann too. Be careful."

When the chance was right, Josie and Lou-Lou, acting as decoys, went up and spoke to their aunt from behind causing her to turn slightly so that her back was toward Dort and the boys.

Dort took a good aim and scored home with her lethal shot. Fredericka shrieked and slapped at the back of her neck for the imaginary insect. Then she turned apologetically to those around her and seemed to bow and smile to cover up her embarrassment at having made a scene. Augusta immediately examined her sister's neck but found nothing but a small red spot.

The group of boys and girls did not tarry. Dort and Lou-Lou looked back as they hurried away.

"Well I'll be...." Lou-Lou gasped," she's still smiling."

CHAPTER 27

THE REST OF THE week of the circus and shows continued to be one of excitement for Josie and Lou-Lou, as well as the rest of their young people's group. Grünwalda and Gerta, along with Zelda, had no children of their own. For that reason they regarded this group of youngsters as something special, as if they (the elders) were self-appointed godmothers. It was not hard for the boys and girls to wheedle favors out of the women; nor was it hard for the boys and girls to coax food from the church bazaar booth all during the fair.

"And vot iss a few pieces of der pies for dese growing boys and girls?" Grünwalda asked.

"They're like wolves at that age, Zelda Zinndorfer sniffed. "They are 'holler' all the way down and there is no use ter try for the filling up!" She let her acid expression soften into a smile as she added, "However, we can try."

"Yah, we try." Gerta Hemel chuckled, "but we haf to be dee-screet and not let the other church ladies see us spiriting food out through the back folds of the bazaar tent. Old lady Kattmann will accuse us of stealing the food to take home for ourselves."

"Now dese are goot boys and girls. Dey help me deliver my pies on hot days when my feet are tired and sore. When dat lazy loafer, dat Charley, slips out and is fergitting my split kindling fer de stove oven, it is Benjie, Charley and Lou Gast what helps me out, but dot Fritzy's mouth. Where does he learn all de bad words? He is der caution but he is a goot boy. Not much home life."

"Now it is different story with some of der elders, even some of der parents in dis town und some of der business mens. I'm not giving some of dem the scraps of der bread I bake. Dot lazy Bushman, the constable and your brother, Zelda."

The women got into a light argument over the merits of Constable Bushman and some of his deputies, but Gerta Hemel broke into the conversation and broke up their differences of opinion. Zelda started finding fault with her husband, the mayor, as usual. Mrs. McKeeters got them all into a good humor with some of her malodorant cheese. Somehow, a good slug of beer or ale seemed to drown out the rank smell of the evil cheese, and they all fell into good humor again so that their shrieks of laughter filled the back of the bazaar tent when Griselda Gertslaeker joined them.

Charley and Lou Gast made some extra money by helping with odd jobs with the circus, the fair and other concessions. Benjie and Alby helped Jakey take care of watering the carousel horses, but Fritzy got the job of cleaning up the horse manure from the circular towpath around the outside of the carousel. He hauled it in a wooden wheelbarrow to the back of Mrs. Zinndorfer's garden for her raspberries.

"Didja ever notice, Schani, that there is always a great rank bunch of rhubarb and wild blackberry vines in the back alley growing the thickest behind a well used backhouse privy? Something sure makes it rank," Fritzy said, and then launched into some rough language of four letter words as to the reason it.

Young Benjie was fascinated with the steam boiler of the calliope and learned to keep the right amount of fire for the steam for the gauge. If he got too much a steam pressure up, the hissing release valve ruined the music from the pipes.

The other boys found various odds and ends jobs. However, all of them remembered their promise to Marta and the other ladies at the church bazaar. They helped clean up at night after the food booth closed.

Lou-Lou, Josie, and Bertha learned that they were expected to give calliope performances every afternoon and night. There was always a crowd gathered around the *Blue Swan* at concert time, and they started applauding when they saw the players and dancers coming up on deck.

The girls paid admissions several times to the romantic musical shows and melodramas on the main showboat. They liked best the musical costume play on the lumberyard warehouse stage. Josie, with Ludmilla's help, was able to pick out the moonlight duet melody on the piano at home. Then she and all the other girls sang the words.

When the boys teased them for their moonstruck sentimentality, Bertha hushed them and sent them outdoors. She remarked to Ben and Hermann that before they knew it, (just any day now) their young girls would turn into young women overnight. They had both celebrated their thirteenth birthdays.

Bertha did not mention it to her sisters Bernhardina and Ernestine, but it seemed to her that the group of young girls was seen more and more in the company with that group of young boys who were their own age. It used to be that they were almost hostile to one another. The girls preferred girl talk and dolls, and the boys only liked marbles, fishing, crawdads or whittling. They had broken down that barrier and all seemed to be the greatest of friends. She noticed that they could talk easily together without any awkwardness. They played games together, walked together of evenings on the towpath, and of all things, the boys would join voices and sing in unison with the girls. Bertha dreaded the coming years when their adolescence would change into young adulthood. She dreaded the thoughts of the girls getting to the age where they would be receiving attention from young men; yet she knew it was inevitable. She herself had married at eighteen.

At least for the time being, Bertha reasoned she was safe but she knew that moment of first teenage crush was just around the corner. Also, at least for the time being, she told herself that she had not noticed any two of them pairing off. She had not heard Lou-Lou or Josie mention any special young boy, nor had she heard any of the girls teasing the others about any of the young boys.

Zelda Zinndorfer, with her dour outlook, was more skeptical. She had seen the group of young boys and girls walking around over town together and up and down the towpath. Even though she had not seen anything out of the way such as holding hands, she remarked to Grünwalda and Gerta Hemel:

"Hmpf, they are all getting awfully turrible thick, it seems to me. We'd better watch them. First thing you know, they will get curious and start playing house with their dolls. Then the first next thing you know, they will start playing 'Mister and Mrs.' with the boys. "

"Zelda, you're just sour on the world," Grünwalda scoffed. "Sour as you were, I doan see how you evair got married."

"Yah," Gerta Hemel put in, "and I don't suppose you ever played 'Mr. and Mrs.' many times - even after yew wair married."

"And who's talking, Gerta Hemel? At least I wear the pants, and I don't have any big muscled blacksmith bruiser pawing over me with big beefy hands, and banging my head against the bed post if I don't just please him," Zelda spit out spitefully.

Grünwalda and Marta shrieked with laughter. They had not noticed Lou-Lou, Josie, and some of the boys standing just behind the tent flap of the bazaar, nor did they realize that they had heard all that was said. When one of the other church ladies did notice the boys and girls, she tapped Marta and pointed to the back side of the bazaar and pulled aside the tent flap and said,

"Little pitchers have big ears, ladies."

When Marta and Grünwalda did pull back the tent flap even wider, Lou-Lou, Josie, and the boys left quickly, laughing in high voices at what they had heard. Marta stood with her hands over her mouth as if to stop the words that had been said.

Gerta and Zelda kept up their banter in a lower voice, but traces of anger began to edge their words. Lou-Lou whispered mischievously to Josie and to the boys; then announced,

"Let's give em something to gossip about," and whispered her plan.

As the group of young people went back and circled the bazaar, they paired off, boy with girl, and held hands. They skipped down the towpath and crossed the footbridge across the canal to the other side. All of their voices rang with musical high laughter. Grünwalda and Marta shook their heads at the sight before them; then Grünwalda turned and said tartly,

"I tinks, Gerta, you and Zelda need to take der physic of der mouths in order to clean out der backed up constipation of vords. Der iss too much of der goose squirts comink backwards from der mouth."

Zelda and Gerta kept up their banter with each other but they were not smiling. Marta Schweitermann attempted to break in and make conversation to divert the sharp banter. It was Griselda Gertslaecker, however, who was the savior in times of crisis. It was always her cheery words, high musical laughter, and laugh lines around the wrinkles of her eyes that saved the day when any of the women of this circle got into an argument.

Griselda made much small talk with her high laughter, and found jobs for all the women to do to get ready for the opening of the tent flaps and to welcome the first customers at the counter and tables. Marta had a few new choice stories to tell to put everyone in good spirits. The storm passed but only for a while.

Fritzy Witte was faithful at his unpleasant job at the carousel. He knew he had to keep the grounds clean where the horses walked in circles to propel the carousel or people would not walk near. Parents would not allow young children to walk near it, then no spectators, and finally there would be very few paying customers.

Ludmilla had broken away from the group of boys and girls. It was no fun, even if it was make-believe, to hold hands with Alby Lehmkuhl in that procession. She saw Fritzy and ran up to talk with him. Mrs. Vogelsang saw her daughter from a distance. She was horrified when she saw her standing near Fritzy Witte with his grimy hands, and who was probably chewing tobacco and cussing. Of all things, her daughter was standing and talking with a "stable boy." She saw the job Fritzy was doing, the granary broom, the wooden scoop shovel, and the wheelbarrow already half full of manure.

She swooped down on Ludmilla fiercely as a hawk, took her by the arm and hurried her away from the carousel. With a few well-chosen words, she raised up the fluffy petticoats of Ludmilla's and gave her a few good slaps on her pantalets.

Ludmilla could not be dismayed and when she could break free from her mother, she ran skipping down through the carnival crowd cackling shrilly and holding on to her daisy banded straw hat.

"Milly, Milly," Lou-Lou and the others called to her as her mother glared at them. "What's that perfume you're wearing today, some special Carousel Cologne?"

When the group was well out of hearing of Mrs. Vogelsang, Dort Waterman teased Milly with,

"Bet you got your fill of horses. What animal are you going to ride on the carousel today?"

"Wanta bet?" Milly retorted, then imitating Ernestine Hofermeyer, she said very archly with academic precision, "We find in life that horses will be horses, just as humans will be humans. We have to accept, don't you see, and make choices accordingly."

When the others looked questioningly at her, she continued,

"Well, I've made mine, for better or for worse;" then she nodded her head apologetically and gave them the wide smiling grin of Josie's and Lou-Lou's Aunt Fredericka Keller. With this, she resumed her cackling high laughter.

When there was a lull with the preparation of the noon meal at the church bazaar and the rush of the noon serving was over, Grünwalda and Marta followed the quarreling voices of Gerta Hemel and Zelda Zinndorfer down the towpath, past the grain depot, and on to Grünwalda's small cottage to help her with the afternoon pie baking. After a few mugs of beer and ale, the pies were in the oven, and the ladies were once more in jovial spirits. High laughter came from the hot kitchen by the towpath. Griselda Gertslaecker could hear them, and she managed to find a way to leave the ladies of the church bazaar for the more interesting kitchen of Grünwalda's, to say nothing of the cold thirst-quenching beer.

Fritzy had noticed that the back privies seemed to be meeting places of some of the women who would congregate there, and even go together in parties of two and three of all things. He was an authority on privies, out-houses and back houses now that he had this elevated carnival job. Zelda and Mayor Zinndorfer felt that they had a large enough supply of "mulch" as they politely called the horse manure. Fritzy was obliged to find other places to stack his surplus. He was determined that he was not going to haul that wheelbarrow all the way out of town to some farmer's field where the "mulch" could be plowed under.

He had offered to haul a few loads for Grünwalda for her garden. He soon learned that by soliciting, he could charge a few coins from the property owner for hauling it. He was making a double wage but he did not tell the owners of the carousel.

He had talked Albert Wiemeyer into helping him since there was enough business for the two of them. He told Albert what he had observed about the women visiting in groups in the outhouses, and that they would sit out there to talk, gossip, and laugh.

The plot was hatched. Jakey Backhaus helped them plan it. He had heard his father, Henry, tell about some of his boyhood pranks with a water pump made much like a sliding basswood whistle. This pump, when suddenly compressed, and if it had good pressure could shoot a cold stream of water at least ten feet. The boys tried to make one but it wouldn't work too well. Fritzy vowed,

"We'll get some of them choice fat bottoms yet, if we can just find a hiding place to take cover in."

They knew the blow guns with small shot would take too long. They settled on the idea of fastening the brush tail of either a coon or a fox to a broom handle or long stick. A skunk's tail would have been preferable but too difficult to get. They liked the idea of the skunk because it would be believable. The "honey dippers" of the town had reported finding skunks inside the privies, back underneath the seats and down in the "honey pits." The boys said that skunks were scavengers and that they would eat anything. The name "honey dipper" was the euphemism that the polite society called the men who came before daylight with lighted lanterns to clean out the outhouses that lined each back alley. They were to come before daylight so that the neighbors wouldn't see such a common, embarrassing thing.

The boys kept a watchful eye and alerted the other boys to help spot a privy that seemed to be the center of group congregating. Fritzy knew that Grünwalda's and Griselda's outhouses seemed to be the favorite gathering place and he was ready. He had delivered a few loads of "mulch" back of Grünwalda's privy in a pile at the foot of her garden. He had already inspected the back of the little frame privy and had removed the sliding rough board door a short distance to the side.

That afternoon the ladies at Grünwalda's were having such a good time with their beer and laughter. Zelda and Gerta had forgotten their sharp words. It became necessary for some of the women (Grünwalda, Gerta, and Griselda) to start down the hollyhock path, which was beneath the long grape arbor to the privy on the alley.

Schani noticed them first from his vantage point at one of the animal tents, and then alerted Jakey who was free to help. Jakey immediately started giving the bird call of a cardinal - as was prearranged.

Fritzy, Alby, and Jakey immediately left their jobs and rushed to the protective cover of plum sprouts and trumpet vines at the back of the garden. When they were sure their quarries were in place, they approached the back of the privy. They could hear the women in conversation that was punctuated by gales of high laughter from time to time, and then all three of them (Grünwalda, Gerta, and Griselda) would try to talk at once. They never heard the slight noise as Jakey and Fritzy slid the back covering from the opening at the back.

The outhouse was unusual in that it had three seats, and was called a "three holer" instead of the usual "two holer."

"This is perfect!" Fritzy whispered, while scarcely able to contain his laughter and excitement as he peered up inside the back under the filled seats. As Jakey and Alby handed him the stick with the bush tail on the end, Fritzy whispered to them,

"Perfect! It's just like three double-loaves of bread sticking down them three holes;" then he commented with a few off-color vulgarities before he added, "and with a whole bunch of corn silk between the double loaves."

Immediately Fritzy took the stick and brush tail and passed it along underneath the seat, making sure he touched one of the unsuspecting ladies forcibly.

The immediate shrieks of horror filled that end of the small town. The boys scarcely had time to put the cover back across the aperture, catch up their brush tail, spring down across the garden and vault the vine covered board fence.

The plum sprouts hid them from view as they ran to take cover several yards away. All the other boys had come after the cardinal's whistle from Jakey, and were standing innocently at different places in the vicinity of Grünwalda's cottage.

"Vot in hell? Der's a varmint down in dair," Grünwalda shouted in her deep voice. The other ladies began screaming that much louder, and their shrieks rent the air as they tried to climb up on to the three-holed seat. They were so crowded that they could not get their voluminous skirts pulled down, nor their elastic topped fluffy bloomers pulled up. They could only stand clutching each other and scream out their terror of the "varmint."

Some of the townspeople came running toward the vicinity of the screams. It was surely some sort of emergency or terrible accident.

The boys had to hide their almost hysterical laughter from the serious faced men and women who were hurrying toward Grünwalda Peppleman's cottage and pie shop. Lou-Lou, Josie, and the other girls had likewise been tipped off to listen for the whistle of the cardinal from Jakey. When they heard it, they passed word to the others of the group so that all could witness the fun.

With all three huge women up on the privy seat, the seat broke and gave way at one end. Immediately Grünwalda, Gerta, and Griselda lost their balances. Two of the women got down with their legs in the seat holes, and were treading in the "honey" well below.

When Jake Hemel and some of the other men got there, they began pulling the women out of the pit and out of the door. When they learned that the women had been frightened by some sort of an animal that was down inside and under the seat, many saw the humor of it and broke into laughter.

Grünwalda was deeply chagrined when she saw townspeople laughing at her condition of partial undress. She ran into the hollyhocks and tried to get her bloomers pulled up. She stumbled and then balanced herself. She could not get her bloomers pulled up over her broad pear-shaped hips and she could only call out to the other women who were having the same trouble. They tried to wipe their feet the best they could on the grass.

Fritzy stood his ground at the far end of the garden with his wheelbarrow and shovels. He scratched his head when asked if he had seen anything.

"Yes, I have been seein' some sort of brushy haired fox, er maybe a coyote, around in these shrubs and undergrowth in these gardens, but I never gave it much thought." He then went on to say as an afterthought. "Well, you know, stuff comes up in town at night fer something to eat out of them woods and swamps to the south around the reservoir."

Marta and Zelda had to keep away from the other three women for they were shaking with laughter. Marta tried to keep her trilling laughter down. Even the dour Zelda had broken out with a few deep but short "huh-huh's," and her usually poker face now was wrinkled with genuine mirth.

Some of the townswomen were helping the three victims clean up and change clothes out in the woodshed where Grünwalda usually had her bath and did her washings. Even Griselda had lost some of her good humor as she sat trying to wash her feet in the wooden tub of hot suds. When Fritzy dauntlessly came to the door to tell Grünwalda that he would bring her some more mulch when she wanted it, he mentioned absently, if not innocently,

"Now I have been afraid to rustle around in that underbrush at the garden fence. I have seen a skunk nosing around the back of the privy in them blackberry brambles."

"Der skonks!" Grünwalda shouted and the shrieking began again from the other women. Marta knew it was time for her to leave and get back to the bazaar, but she stopped by to tell Henry Backhaus what happened. The story rang a bell to Henry for he remembered that same sort of a trick from his boyhood in Brementown.

When Henry questioned Jakey about the "varmint" incident, he could only get evasive answers from his son. He tried to be strictly serious but Jakey could see the hint of laughter around his father's eyes. He stood his ground and did not give any secrets away.

Henry read enough between the lines to know that the "varmint" had been a human varmint. He told Marta Schweitermann of his opinions and they both laughed loud and long. Ludwig Waterman and Leo Wiemeyer were let in on the joke and they too relished it to the limit.

Fritzy kept his calm through it all and maintained a poker face when asked about it. He would not have been unnerved even if he had been caught and proven guilty. He would have some choice words for all of them.

Mrs. Vogelsang was careful when she reprimanded Ludmilla at the carousel not to speak to Fritzy or incur his wrath. She knew only too well about his reputation, and knew that if she had ordered him not to speak to her daughter again; he would have cussed at her with vile oaths that would have mortified her in front of the townspeople until the whole town would hear of it.

Leo and Ludwig told Henry between gulps of laughter,

"It's too bad they couldn't play the trick on old lady Kattmann. It might even loosen up that Steinhoge a little."

Augusta Kattmann heard about the afternoon's "varmint" incident but considered it very low, common, and of little interest. She remarked that health laws should be made about inspection of all the "necessary houses" lining all the back alleys in town. They should be cleaned periodically and often with a generous amount of lime used to dry up and purify the pit contents. She went on to point out that every town property out of dire necessity has to have an outhouse, or "necessary house" out back, of course. She was at her best when she could discuss medicine, health, sanitation and diseases. She then continued to point out that each property, each dwelling, had to have a dug well as well as a rain water cistern. She asked her listeners if any of them had considered that most of these wells were only a few yards (maybe ten or twenty) from the outhouses. If these necessary houses were allowed to become horrid refectories of putrefication and unspeakable pits, then of course seepage into the ground could take place, and would eventually seep into the ground water that fills the dug wells.

"Vy, Gott in Himmel, it iss der wonder we all don't die from der typhus, cholera, typhoid and der fevers," she exclaimed.

Augusta had given the case of the Russian musicians and the dancing of Johnny Ivan, deep serious thought. She knew that she couldn't expect these people to come up daily from their work at the sawmill below Loramie and Newport to sing and dance. Still, there ought to be some way. Of course they could not be expected to contribute to the church bazaar fund since they were not members.

Augusta scoured the downtown business district to find a storeroom, a warehouse, or small shop that was not in use. She knew she wanted a room large enough to seat a good-sized audience and one where she could have a strong stage floor built which would withstand the vibration of the furiously paced Russian folk dances. She harassed Schnelle's for one of their unused storerooms. She pressured Boesels, Greisingers, and Grothauses for a space. She finally bludgeoned the Gast brothers to help her son, Ludwig Kattmann, convert the driveway of *The Blue Swan Brewery* into a temporary auditorium with bench seats.

The raised unloading dock inside the driveway could act as a strong, substantial stage, but that rough splintery floor would have to have some attention. Augusta financed the quick laying down of a new hardwood floor over the old one, saying that it had been needed for a long time.

The space to the left of the driveway was cleaned out, and the boxes and barrels were carted to another warehouse for the time being. She had additional lamps and flambeaus brought in for nighttime performances.

She then asked Johnny and the others if they would consider giving a few performances if they had any afternoons free, and on as many nights that they could have free. She explained that the profits would go mostly to the performers, but that she would have to hold out some of the ticket money for the expense of lights, the bench seats and other expenses. Johnny Ivan was overjoyed at the opportunity to really dance for an audience rather than a bunch of disinterested drunks in some bar or on some canal dock.

The performers of Johnny Ivan's troupe managed several appearances during fair week. They reasoned that it would be a vacation for all of them. They brought their lumber barges up to New Bremen from the sawmill village and lived aboard them. They did most of their cooking aboard the barges, but now and then Big Bertha cooked some things on a larger fire she built out on the ground not far from the towpath.

Word soon spread about the gravity-defying dances of Johnny Ivan, whom some called "Mad Johnny and some called him "Bad Johnny." Bertha Gast and the others noticed that Big Bertha, Vassili, and Big Gregori allowed Johnny to dance only so long at a time.

The dance show of the Russian woodcutters became one of the great drawing cards at the fair. It was not only the dancing by Johnny Ivan and some of the others of his troupes; it was the singing and the colorful embroidered costumes of the performers that drew the crowds and held them spell bound.

Johnny never seemed to tire and would dance on and on with his spirals, leaps, catapults and furious folk dances. Big Bertha and Big Gregori watched him all the time he was dancing, and when Gregori nodded his head to Vassili, the latter gave the sign to the musicians to stop the dance. The dance sometimes ended abruptly and Johnny danced on for a few turns, but caught himself and came to the front of the stage for his bows.

Lou-Lou and the girls would oft times meet during the languid hot afternoons at Josie's house, and rest in the cool shade of the trees or on the porch that faced the canal.

Charley, Lou, and Benjie told them of their plan for a trick to play on Fritzy. They would see if nothing daunted him. The boys knew from swimming in the canal and in the river that Fritzy was almost hysterically afraid of snakes. He had a phobia of them but he tried not to talk about it, nor to show it.

The boys devised a trick to play on Fritzy, who was the master trickster on everyone else. They knew where he hid his secret smoking pouch up on a beam in Witte's warehouse that was used for a barn at the edge of town. They had seen him stand up on a barrelhead and reach up to pull it down before they set out for the river for fishing or swimming.

The boys had heard about enough of his bragging and self-praise about the "varmint" trick. They planned an outing for one morning before their chores and work at the fair started. Most things at the fair did not start until noon or shortly before. Farmers and people from nearby villages had to have time to get their morning work done and to drive into town.

The boys planned it well. They would take a short drive down south to where one of the small creeks joined the reservoir at Loramie; then they decided to go to one closer where a creek joined the reservoir just south of Minster. That would be good swimming.

Of course they planned to have some good smoking. Two of the older boys, Schani and Albert Wiemeyer, were able to find a long blue racer blacksnake and kill it. Just a little while before time to go, Schani being the tallest, was able to stand on the barrel and plant the dead snake on the flat beam back out of sight. The boys attached a piece of fish line around the snake back of its head then attached it to the leather pouch in which Fritzy kept his smoking supplies.

The boys, Charley, Lou, Benjie, and Jakey managed to be with Fritzy when he went to the barn to get his smoking supplies. He had to do it when he was sure the coast was clear, and that his parents weren't watching. Schani thought that he would stay out in the carriage to hold the reins in case the horse became restive when Fritzy came running out of the barn. He knew that Fritzy would surely be jumping and screaming with fear.

At the appointed moment, Fritzy jumped up on the barrel and pulled his pouch down without looking. To his horror, the snake dropped around his shoulders. Fritzy ran screaming from the barn in terror, "Get this god-damned reptile off me!"

Schani held the horse and the other boys had to calm Fritzy. They had a good laugh at his expense, but he was too angry to enjoy the swimming very much. The tables were turned and it wasn't funny. He swore at them and used special crudities and profanities the boys had not heard before. His devious quick mind was working right then at getting even. He would find a way. He would put a live snake or at least some crawdads in their beds.

CHAPTER 28

THE MIDDLE OF AUGUST rolled around before anyone knew it. Everyone had hoped that they could have the school ready by late September or by the cool weather, and the first frosts in October. Work was progressing very rapidly on both the school and on the Kattmann town hospital. The other larger hospital, or sanatorium, was a much larger project and everyone knew that it would be a year, or perhaps two, before it would be ready for occupancy.

Mrs. Kattmann wasted no time while all the building was being done. She and Anna Steinhoge were in constant consultation with authorities from Columbus, and with the local doctors. The problem of staffing the hospital and the larger sanatorium would be as complex, if not more so, than the actual building.

Traffic steadily rose as the summer drew on. Now that most of the earlier grain was harvested, barge load after barge load went both ways on the canal for shipment. The large depots for grain crowded the docks at Maumee for later shipment on the Great Lakes, and to the elevators in Chicago. Cincinnati grain warehouses were bulging as well.

The grain depot at New Bremen was bulging with summer wheat and there was more to come. Warehouses near the lock and grain elevators were full. After the bumper crop of summer hay was cured, huge barge loads of hay stacked as high as an outdoor rick of wood began to pass south on the canal. It was later learned that most of it went to Louisville and on south for the horse barns.

The South produced mostly staple money crops. Therefore, it was necessary to import a great deal of its food and manufactured goods from northern states. The Ohio and Mississippi Rivers were a natural artery of commerce from the central Atlantic and Midwestern states to the deep south.

The Miami and Erie, as well as the other Ohio and Indiana canals, shipped to the river ports where the produce was then shipped south on the riverboats.

One could still see a few flatboats coming to the Ohio River from the smaller rivers of Ohio and Indiana, for farmers in the back areas could ship easier by that pioneer method than they could travel over impossible mud roads with wagons to bring their produce to the canal docks.

With the canal boom reaching its peak, there was talk of more canals, or at least making the existing ones wider as they had up in New York State on the much traveled Erie Canal. No one in this year of 1850 could see the shadow of the railroad that was to crowd out the importance of the canals, and take over their commerce. The pressing need of quicker and cheaper transportation, which the war would bring in the next decade, would give the seal of success to the railroad, and spell extinction for the picturesque canals.

Bertha Gast had planned to have a large birthday party for both girls, since their birthdays had come so close together last month. She had doubts, however, if one large cake could serve the purpose without making either one of the girls feel slighted. Mrs. Kattmann came to the rescue and suggested that they have two smaller cakes with decorated icing and candles with "thirteen" on them; she dropped the subtle hint that perhaps some of the "iced cream custard" would tide over any slighted feelings. She also suggested that perhaps, since strawberries were no longer in season, that a few drops of the pink cake coloring would make the iced custard look like strawberries. There was even an artificial strawberry flavor that Mrs. Peppleman put in her pink tarts. Why not try this for an extra "birthday frill?"

The birthday party was in full swing. Mrs. Kattmann had a large family gathering out at <u>The Willows</u> for now, with the added "four little cousins," it took more table room. With all the Gast and Kattmann family congregated at one table, there was needed room for twenty people, or twenty-one if Anna Steinhoge was present.

The strawberry colored ice cream was a huge success. It was soon time for the opening of birthday gifts. Everyone remained seated at the long table in the huge dining room while the gifts were placed in front of the two girls who giggled nervously.

There were little trinkets, ribbons for their hair, a book, new frilled aprons and other sundry things. When the gifts were nearly all put aside, Augusta Kattmann arose from her place with Mr. Kattmann at the head of the table, and went down into her black bag to the envelopes tied with ribbons, and placed one in front of each Josie and Louise. Ernestine cast a quick knowing look at Bernhardina Gast, as much as to say, "She is going to spoil them with a gift of money."

The girls, at their grandmother's bidding, opened the envelopes carefully, expecting some sort of a joke or at most, a pamphlet on deportment. Their grandmother was always digging deep into that bottomless black bag, producing a pamphlet or brochure on every subject on human behavior, religion or temperance. To their amazement, the girls found invitations instead to a round trip excursion with their grandmother, down the canal to Cincinnati, and a boat ride on one of the river paddlewheelers.

When they read the notes and held them up so that all the rest could see the riverboat tickets that were pinned to the top of the note paper, everyone began talking at once in happy excitement. Charley, Lou and young Ben immediately set up a "howl" because they weren't included; whereupon their grandmother promised them a similar trip when their time came, and she turned to the four little boys and Daisy Baby,

"Und I take all you little cherubs, maybe across the Erie Canal to New York. Who knows, maybe ve all go down to New Orleans."

"That's a close chance," Charley complained. "Know what, Lou and Ben? We can all pitch in and help Papa and Uncle Hermann build that steam propelled barge; then we can all go down the Mississippi on our own barge."

"I know a closer one, Charley," young Ben said. "We will probably get a little steam barge made that will take us across the reservoir, from St. Marys to Celina on the other end."

While the boys lamented their ill luck, the four smaller boys laughed at all the family banter. Little Will told of seeing a small barge or launch of some sort on the lower end of the canal. It was used on the riverfront at Cincinnati, and sometimes it came up the ten locks into the canal basin to haul freight short distances. Ben and Hermann listened with interest. Steam power fascinated them, and along with Jake Hemel and the others at the dock, the thoughts of the possibility of a steam barge were not completely idle dreaming. Summer excursions on both reservoirs would be a good moneymaker, to say nothing of the fun doing them.

With everyone talking at once and the flush of the exciting surprise, both girls neglected to thank their generous grandmother. Bertha caught Josie's eye and nodded toward her mother. In a rush, Josie sprang up from her chair and went to her grandmother. She leaned down and kissed her on the cheek, a thing she had never done before in her life, and thanked her for the wonderful gift. Lou-Lou felt trapped. Why, she couldn't remember of kissing even her own mother in recent years, let alone her grandmother.

Bernhardina Gast almost stared at Lou-Lou until she followed Josie's example and kissed her grandmother. Mrs. Kattmann, who was surprised and somewhat embarrassed by the show of affection, patted Louise's hand when her granddaughter thanked her for the wonderful trip.

"Vell, mein Louveese, dis is a pleasant surprise! Now all at vonce you are grown up, more like a lady, like Mein Josephine." Everyone else laughed and teased Lou-Lou. Her brother Ben teased,

"Yah! Now she is growed up! She can wear longer skirts now and hide those chubby sausage legs."

The other boys started teasing her, but they were at the other end of the table and it wouldn't do to rough house in grandmother's dining room, especially with her own mother snapping her fingers at young Benjie, and correcting him for his manners and unseemly references. His Aunt Ernestine corrected his "growed up," and supplied the proper form of the verb. Lou-Lou hesitated a moment at her grandmother's chair. Then good soldier that she was, brave enough to face what she must, she ran out into the kitchen. She knew that there was a paddle there somewhere, perhaps sticking behind the kitchen cupboard. When she found the paddle reserved in all the Gast households for all emergencies, offspring as well as cousins, and whacking it against her bouffant short hooped skirts, she ran back in with it, and presented it to her bewildered grandmother.

"Grandma-Má Kattmann, I guess I didn't have you figured right. You're just great. Here, you are right! I should be paddled more." When Augusta Kattmann opened her mouth in astonishment, everyone else joined in a loud outburst of boisterous laughter. In a moment, Mrs. Kattmann recovered her usual aplomb, and grasping Lou-Lou by the wrists, she exclaimed as she arose from her chair,

"Ja, dot iss not a bad idea at all. Boys, grab dot Josie too. It giffs thirteen ger-whacks for each vun of them, and a few to grow on."

Josie tried to make a scramble for the door, but the boys grabbed her and held her for their grandmother. Laughing as she did so, Augusta Kattmann called young Ben to help her, and she bent Lou-Lou over the arm of the horsehair divan and gave her thirteen light whacks through all those petticoats and those whalebone short hoops. Mrs. Kattmann, with a mischievous look on her ample face, exclaimed.

"*Ve fix dot, mein Benjie,*" and shaking her head in mock pity for Louise, she added, "*Dot young Benjie, sooch gut boy, so thoughtful, eh mein Louveese?*" Quickly Augusta Kattmann pulled up Lou-Lou's hoops and petticoat and gave her a resounding whack across her embroidered white petticoat, and Lou-Lou let out an exaggerated squall much to the amusement of the on-lookers.

"And dots for the panting like a dog, embarrassing me so dot day ven die governor's barge came through, mein Louveese."

"Oh, grandma, my poor beautiful bottom hurts. I'll never...d..." Then another smart whack took Lou-Lou by surprise, almost bringing the tears to her eyes, as her grandmother said in a low voice to her,

"And dot one is for der sending the Holy Father dot money for the tithe box for foreign missionaries, wrapped in der *Blue Goose*...ach, I mean *Blue Swan* letter head paper. Little minx, were you thinking I didn't know who would be doing sech ting?"

Everyone present was laughing so hard at the surprising spectacle taking place across the divan settee that they failed to notice the hard laughter of Anna Steinhoge. Aunt Fredericka was amazed by the laughter from the severe, blue-eyed woman at her side, for she had never seen her amused by anything before. Mrs. Kattmann laughed a deep, throaty laugh, and then gave Josie her thirteen licks.

"Mein Josephine, you sooch gut girl, I giff you only one extra to grow on."

"No fair. I can tell you plenty," Lou-Lou protested. The boys began kidding their sisters, putting make-believe corncob pipes in their mouths and puffing in pantomime when they thought their parents weren't watching. Lou-Lou and Josie slapped at their hands, and called them "squealers" until Bernhardina Gast and her sister-in-law, Bertha Gast, clapped their hands for order and made the frolicking youngsters take their seats.

After another helping of the strawberry iced cream dessert, and huge wedges of cake, the children were ready to play in the spacious lawns under the weeping willows of Weide Himmel, and then all too soon the memorable birthday party was over.

The next few days were filled with pleasant anticipation for the birthday trip to Cincinnati and the exciting trip out on the Ohio River on one of the large paddle wheel riverboats. But it wasn't only a pleasure trip for Augusta Kattmann; she was going on a much needed buying trip, one of the many she would need to make before all the furnishing and outfitting of both hospitals and the school would be completed.

In the meantime, Mrs. MacPherson took time from her small shop to help Bertha and Bernhardina Gast with some much needed sewing for the girls' trip down the canal on the packet to the city. Mrs. Gertslaecker pointed out that now that the girls were a year older, they could wear their hooped dresses a little longer so that not so much of the lace-bottomed pantalets showed beneath them. Bertha was reluctant to bow to what she new was true, but she complained that they grew up so quickly and she hated to take their childhood from them. As all the women sat in a circle in Bertha's dining room sewing for the girls, Gerta Hemel announced that she would do the special embroidery and eyelet work on the undergarments for she couldn't do the fancy, expert work that Griselda Gertslaecker could on the outer garments.

In a few days, the girls had beautiful new clothes for their trip. Augusta Kattmann and Mrs. Steinhoge hired Mrs. Gertslaecker to make them some new dresses, but the other ladies came over in the afternoons to help her, for they knew she could not get such a large task done in the short time left before the trip.

One afternoon Elvira Brenner stopped by Bertha Gast's and told her about the invitation the Russian people out on the sawmill below Loramie Creek had offered her, Ben and the girls. It was some Sort of a Slavic holiday, one of their Greek Orthodox Church days honoring some saint or other. However, Elvira knew that it was to be a big day for them. There would be all sorts of Russian food, music, dancing and singing. At night there was to be a big log fire where they danced around with sticks and ribbons to commemorate something or other.

"Law, I can't tell you all what it just does mean, Miz Gast, but I know it's something special. Why all them Russians from over west in that settlement somewhur, you know, is called Russia, or is it Russiaville? Mebbe Mosskow, I dunno. It's a big doin's with fancy holiday costumes; you know how them people is..."

"Well, won't we be outsiders? Are you sure they want us to come, Elvira? Bertha Gast inquired.

"Plumb shore. Big Berthy herself asked us, and asked me to stop by and ask you folks, that is, you and yer fambly. They caint feed and entertain the whole plumb town, y'know, but she holds you and yer mother sorta special like."

"Well of course all of us will be glad to go. The children are crazy to see that place out there. But what will we fix to take? We would make a lot of extra mouths to feed, and you know kids eat like hogs when they go away from home, someone else's cooking and all of that."

"Don't I know! Don't it beat all, Miz Gast? But, now, we are not to fix a thing. It would insult them for this is a feast of some sort, and they'll fix special Roosian vittles."

"What if it's some strange sort of stuff, and the children won't eat it? Won't that be embarrassing?" Bertha asked.

"I'm game. I've et there, and I'm one to tell you, it's good."

"How many will there be, do you suppose?"

"Oh, an awful slew o'people. Them French people, they're all Catholic you know, from over west around that community they call French Village, or is it Frenchtown? They are all invited."

"French people? They aren't the same religion, are they?"

"Law, I don't know, but they are going to show some of their native costumes and do some of their dancin' and singin'. They say them French vittles, kwee-seene, or something like that, is out of this world." Elvira laughed while slapping her hands against her skirts. "All that stuff they pour brandy over and then light a fire before it's et, and them snails boiled alive and then sucked from their shells." She sucked air between her lips with a smacking sound.

"I don't know, Elvira." Bertha hesitated.

"Yass you do! Miz Gast, it would insult them and break their hearts if'n you'uns wuz not to come. Come on! Let's be game."

"Yes, I suppose you are right. I'll have to talk to Ben and Hermann. It will be hard for mother to arrange her schedule, but I'll have to tell her in time. Yes, this is a must, Elvira," Bertha added on second thought.

"If we all go on the barge, that is if you people take the *Blue Swan*, mebbe all of us can pile on. Be less bother and fewer horses out there in that narrow sawmill creek canal. Course there is room enough inside the sawmill basin. But if you take the *Blue Swan*, then we'd have that steam calliope thing," Elvira reasoned.

There was an air of excitement at theRussian village, which was down in the deep woods beyond the sawmill. When the *Blue Swan* pulled into the sawmill basin, the Russian men were on the plank docks to help them with the lines. The Gasts were treated as if they were visiting nobility from the Czar's court at Czarskoe Selo. (The name, *Czarskoe Selo*, was the country residence of the Russian Royal Family. It is different today, and has been called Pushkin since 1937. The town is made up of about 100 thousand people and is located 28 kilometers south-west from St. Petersburg in Russia.)

Great heavy tables with log legs were spread in the courtyard that all the Russian log houses faced. Elvira marveled at all the running back and forth, and all the colorful Russian peasant holiday costumes. It was much easier for the children to get acquainted and play together in spite of the language and nationality barriers; the grown-ups were awkward with each other.

Augusta Kattmann was overwhelmed by the beauty of it all. It was her diplomacy that helped break the ice of hesitancy.

The meal was ready at last; in fact, it was a banquet. An ox had been barbecued in an open pit, but there were all other kinds of meats prepared. Elvira whispered to Bertha,

"Law, there's no tellin' what all we're eatin' and don't know it - maybe bear eyes, wolf, or roast dog." Her daughter told her not to talk about it or she couldn't eat. "Eyes? Arg-rar-gh!"

"There is one thing that we are going to do today," Bertha told the others, and her mother turned toward her to listen, "and that is learn the correct

name for Big Bertha, and learn to call her by her right name, or at least
something that isn't offensive to her."

"I've heerd it many a time, but can't pronounce it, Miz Gast," Elvira
offered. "And those last names – why they'll just kill ye." When Big Bertha
came to their table with platters of barbecue, and another woman brought
heavy metal covered dishes of fowl, Bertha Gast and Elvira made an effort to
thank her and tell her what a wonderful feast it was.

Bertha Gast caught Johnny Ivan's attention at a nearby table and motioned
for him to come to her. The bright faced Russian bounded across the table
and stood beside her, nodding to Mrs. Kattmann respectfully.

Bertha had Johnny tell them Big Bertha's name repeatedly. She explained
that the time had come for all of them to know her by her right name, but
Johnny flashed white teeth when he told them that she didn't take it as an
insult when the "good" people called her 'Big Bertha.'

"Now pronounce it again Johnny. I want to write it down," Bertha said,
as she held her small pencil ready to write in her little notebook that she
always carried in her bag. Johnny saw her trying in vain to spell the names
he reeled off, so he took the pencil and pad and printed all three names: her
given name, middle, and last (family name from her father). (Patronym is
another word for last name.) Bertha stared at the printed names completely
perplexed. She realized that they were written in a Russian Cyrillic alphabet,
and the letters didn't make sense to her.

"See! I tole you," Elvira chimed in. "That's why it'll always be 'Berthy'
for me. Johnny, I'll bet that ain't yer name either."

"No," he laughed. "It's Ivan," and he pronounced it correctly as "Ee-
vaughn" for them, "but Ivan is Russian for John." (Ivan Vladmirvitch
Daglievskaya.)

"Now pronounce her name for me again. I am bound to get at least one
of them," Bertha insisted.

"It's Katyna! 'Ka-teen-ya,'" he smiled. Then he disclosed the fact that
Katyna, 'Big Bertha' to them, was his oldest sister. He smiled as he pronounced
her full name again, but told them not to worry about remembering it:
"Katyna Vladmirevna Daglievskaya." Elvira gasped, "My God."

"If you can't remember Katyna, just call her Katharine; she won't mind,"
he assured her. "Even if you call her 'Bertha,' she won't be offended."

After the heavy meal dragged on for what seemed hours, Johnny brought
a brass samovar and set it in front of Mrs. Kattmann, bowed to her, and said
something in Slavic that meant, "Respectful Madam."

The rest of the groups at the other tables waited until Johnny got the
samovar to bubbling before they took steaming thick coffee from their
samovars. Mrs. Kattmann did not quite know how to manipulate the spigot,

so Johnny did it for her. He told her that she was the guest of honor for all that she had done for them, and that they were waiting for her to draw the first cup so that they could all drink in fraternal fellowship - a pledge to their friendship. When Augusta Kattmann drew her cup, then drew some for the others at her table, she stood with her cup and drank a sip as if she were offering a toast of goodwill. Immediately all the Russians stood up, raised their cups to their lips, and the woods resounded with strange yelps of Slavic utterances, which sounded to Ben and Hermann like "Hai---nyenna all-lay yupp."

Not one to pass up a courtesy, Mrs. Kattmann addressed a few words to the group after asking Johnny if they would understand her. He told her that most of them would not, but they could tell by her tone about what she was saying. He would translate.

She thanked all of them for the kindness of their invitation and for the honor that they gave her. It was then she asked Johnny to interpret for her what she was going to say next to them. Bertha Gast nearly fell off her log puncheon seat when she heard her mother tell the Russians that she wanted all of them to endorse her school and to use her hospital when needed. She made it a strong point to tell them that one of the privileges for citizenship in this, their country, was to learn to read and write and to speak the language. School and association with other English-speaking children was the only way, and she expected all of them to live up to their obligations by sending their children to her school. She explained the tuition cost and how it could be paid for. She told them that she needed good lumbermen and carpenters, and the fathers of school age children could help with their tuition by working on the school or on the hospital. She explained to the mothers how they could help with cleaning services, laundry at the dormitory, other helpful things, and even embroidery work.

After thanking them again, Mrs. Kattmann took her seat and had another cup of the delicious thick coffee. The Russians followed her example. Then a murmur arose from among them and they all applauded her. Johnny interpreted this to Mrs. Kattmann to mean that they approved of what she said.

After the banquet was cleared away, the program began. There were some icons with ribbons marching around the group for all the Russians to gaze upon, and they touched their foreheads in religious obedience. Then to the accompaniment of strange stringed instruments, some bells on frames, another thing played with leather bound hammers, and square tambourines. The older women and men sang an old Russian anthem/hymn called "God Preserve Us, Thy People." Their voices reached organ-like quality in the purity of their tones. The male bass was unbelievable. Ernestine and Bernhardina sat entranced by the perfection they heard. They loved a folk song or lullaby, called, <u>Spi, Spi Babatko</u>.

Katyna, and the other Russian men and women sang a Russian folk lullaby in the Russian woodcutters' sawmill camp, which was off the canal in the black swamp, on the night of the festival. A mixed chorus of men and women, after Johnny Ivan's mad, delirious dance and his collapse after the folk dance called the Hopak, his own variations and his wild Cossack leaps.

<u>English Lyric::</u> <u>Sleep Sleep Little One</u> or <u>Sleep Sleep My Baby</u>

Sleep and rest Babatko, night is coming soon.
Go to sleep, Babatko, with the setting moon.
Sleep nor dream, Babatko, how the wild wolf calls.
Mourning as the moon sets, when brooding winter falls.
Soon will come the springtime.
The deep full Volga will flow.
Summer swallows' trills will rhyme.
Wild flowers will drive away the snow.
Sleep in peace and quiet, sleep but sleep Babatko.
Sleep...Sleep...Sleep.

<u>Russian Lyrics:</u> – <u>Spi, Spi, Babatko</u>

Spi a otpocavaj Babatko, noc pride naskone.
Shot spat Babatko, ket mesar rapadne.
Spi alebo snivaj Babatko, jakten drive vik vola.
Smutno as ten mesac usedne, ket ralostna zima vjde.
Naskone pride yano, hlboka volga plna tece.
Vleca ket ftak spiva shotu, drive kvietk Snahom.
Spi pokojne utichosti.
Spi a spi Babatko.
Spi...spi...spi.

There were other numbers of the same type. Then the men put on something like a pageant where the men paraded with sticks and ribbons while crossing themselves. The younger children, who sang with almost adult precision, did another part of the religious observation.

When the religious festival was over, it was time for folk dancing and contests. The party got faster and faster. The French people did some dances and some of their songs. After the French people had done some group folk singing and some rounds, they ended with everyone singing parts to the ageless old "Alouette, Gentille Alouette."

A group of tunic-clad Russian men formed a loose semi-circle and began a slow, rather sad ballad on the stringed balalaikas. Elvira was puzzled by the strange instruments, and queried,

"Whut is them strange lookin' things? Look like triangle shaped cigar boxes with long gittar necks." (The *Balalaika* family of instruments includes, from the highest-pitched to the lowest, the prima *balalaika*, sekunda *balalaika*, alto *balalaika*, bass *balalaika*.)

The balalaika introduction ended; then it was accompanied by an all male chorus who gave deep organ-like tones to the melody they voiced. Evidently, they weren't singing the words, but they were just toning with an open mouth.

Then Big Bertha, (Katyna to the Russians) and two large bearded men (big Vladimir and big Gregori) stepped into the semicircle in front of the balalaika players. Johnny translated the story.

The magic of their sorrowful and entrancing song captivated all the listeners. It was a song about a beautiful girl in the village named Sonya who came to them in the spring, but went away in the autumn. She was never seen again. Only the children in the woods saw her while picking snowdrop wildflowers, and they could hear her voice among the snowdrops. The spirit of the snow maiden lived on in the snowdrops each spring. It was a beautiful thing, and Bertha and Elvira turned to Bernhardina and Ernestine when Katyna's voice rose above the others in the solo part, the sad spirit of the departed snow maiden.

It almost brought tears to Bertha's eyes, and she could hear her mother murmuring in German: "Ach ist so schön! So schönen the musik - so beautiful!"

When the number was finished, and Katyna stood with bowed head receiving the applause from the enthusiastic group, Bertha Gast rose from her seat and hurried across the courtyard to the group.

"Thank you," she said to the huge smiling woman. "Thank you. That was most beautiful, Ka-teen-ya!" The Russian woman's eyes flashed with pleased surprise. Then Bertha went on with deliberate but hesitant pronunciation,

"Katyna...Ka-teen-ya Vlad-mir-ev-na..." but she did not attempt the last name. She turned to each man, shook hands with each and pronounced their names, "Vladimir...Gregori...Vassily."

There was immediate applause from the Russian people as Bertha took her seat.

As the afternoon grew into early evening, the shadows lengthened. The French people started home for they had a twenty mile trip over poor roads. Their French community was six or seven miles northwest of Versailles and it would take hours over dusty roads and woodland trails.

After a while there was more food passed. When Bertha Gast and her family made an attempt to leave, they were begged to stay a while longer. The Russians passed wine, and then the never failing vodka made its rounds, but the German folks from Brementown declined to take any. Ben and Hermann warned the others that it was strong enough to make their teeth come loose, or at least blister the gums.

The mischievous Johnny Ivan spiked a couple of glasses of wine with vodka, which he passed to Elvira. Not being one to be ill-mannered, Elvira tossed off the glasses a little too rapidly. Before long, she was overly talkative and even wanted to dance.

Then the huge log fire was lit and a special part of the religious festival took place at twilight. All the Russians circled the fire while chanting some hymn. Wine was poured on the fire from each brass cup. When it was over, the all-male chorus of older men sang a hymn about Mother Russia and the soul of the God of their fathers from which all strength came. At the conclusion of the soul-tearing anthem, the men took handfuls of earth and almost walked into the fire. Their beards were nearly singed as they dropped the earth into the fire, which sent up sparks from the moist earth.

"That is the Asiatic Tartar in them. Look at that. They aren't afraid of physical harm," Bertha said to her mother in a low voice. She did not see Katyna standing behind them, but the huge Russian woman whispered to Bertha that this was the most holy part of the ceremony. The presence of God was in their bodies, as was Mother Russia and the Holy Saints. She told Bertha that not the fire or even any sort of pain could reach them, for they were in a holy trance and could feel no physical pain. Augusta Kattmann sat transfixed. Even Ben, Hermann and Joel Brenner, who were not overly religiously inclined, were impressed. Elvira Brenner started sobbing out loud for some uncontrollable reason. Joel whispered for her to hush up and told her that she had just had too much wine.

There were rounds of wine and vodka. Folk singing and wild Cossack dances filled the whirling courtyard. The older people sat clapping their hands at certain places in the wild barbaric songs of the steppes. Then it was Johnny Ivan's turn to capture everyone with his special dance. He groomed himself for it, and Katyna frowned when she saw him refresh himself with a little too much vodka. He wore a special costume of flame colored trousers that were tucked into soft leather boots, and he wore an embroidered tunic with a tight waist. Then Johnny Ivan started his mad dance that had gained him the name of "the Hog Eye." No other person could put the human body through such contortions and still live.

The strange instruments with the funny hammers plunked away, and at certain places in the music, Johnny jumped into the air as all the Russian throats shouted a short "Hai" and then a "Nyenna-yup."

The balalaikas took up the rapid tempo; then the square box drums thumped and boomed. Russian gypsy violins trembled and sobbed and still Johnny whirled, leaped, shuddered, turned cartwheels, leaped over tables, turned back somersaults and landed on his wildly thrashing feet. The Russian voices took up the folk song that said something about "The Barrel," and then "Rare Old Wine." Johnny called to the players,

"Faster...faster..." and he heard Elvira Brenner half scream, half sob, "John-nee...John-nee E-von! Either the devil's in yer boots, or there's angel wings on yer shoulders."

Johnny pirouetted and circled, leaped and shouted, "Hai." As he swept around the outside of the circle, he caught up Elvira and whirled her around in a maddening vortex until she nearly lost her senses. Katyna looked at Vladimir and Gregori with alarm. Was the boy mad, or was he in a trance of religious fervor? Katyna warned the men that they should rescue Elvira and stop Johnny. He had gone far enough; he might kill himself. She knew this scene well.

When at last he put Elvira down, she shouted and kept on circling while trying to sing something, but the vodka in her wine had made her incoherent. She fell, and then Joel helped her to the table as she crawled toward him. She was half-crying and half-laughing. Katyna came to Elvira, smoothed out her clothes, and helped her arrange her flying hair.

"Little Missus! Turrible sorry. Johnny, he don't know what he is doing. Come and sit on this side of table. Bad Johnny! Mad Johnny!"

Then came the rapid finale of the dance routine, which only the most wild and the most Asiatic of the Cossack dancers could do. The extremely rapid tropism gained in momentum. Without missing a beat, Johnny's flailing legs took his body through the up and down gyrations of the dance. Next he danced on one of the heavy tables, and then he hit the wooden platform of the dance floor, and landed in that strange Cossack sitting position. His arms were folded and he kicked out his feet in front of him. It looked as though he were some sort of a toy suspended in space on an invisible string. Then he changed to the Ukrainian Hopak.

As the dance ended, Johnny cried for more and kept on dancing, but Vladimir and Gregori walked to the players and put their hands on the strings as they roared in deep voices,

"Na more!"

Johnny staggered toward the players in a frenzy of human exhaustion, and as he started to collapse, Vladimir caught him as he fell, and he and Gregori carried Johnny from the wooden platform toward Katyna's log house. Johnny was crying now, and was struggling with the two giant lumbermen. Katyna ran ahead to open the door. The musicians began another sad ballad to drown out the incoherent screams from the hysterical Johnny. Some of the other Russian women who were used to this scene, hurried to Katyna's aid. The music covered the sobs from inside, and the following recital of all the inhuman wrongs that had happened in years past. So this was how it was. Ben and Hermann told the others that they had seen this same thing happen in the taverns along the canal, but they had seen all of the Russian men get into the act. Soon they heard the low contralto voice of Katyna singing the lullaby called <u>Spi, Spi, Babatko</u>.

Katyna came to apologize to the guests, but Bertha and the others put on a good act of not noticing and made gay, small talk. The Russians clamored for her to play the "steam box" for them. It took a while for Ben and Hermann to get the gauge up to playing strength, but before long Bertha was at the keyboard. The Russians loved it, and clamored for more as they pressed closer to the *Blue Swan*.

Joel Brenner and his boys were embarrassed and disgusted with Elvira's intoxication. She moaned as they carried her on board, and put her down in the passenger cabin on one of the bunks.

Then it was time to go. The hour was growing late, and it was always easy to navigate the canal at night when there was not so much traffic. In addition, the moon was full and shone bright through the overhanging great trees.

Good-byes were said, and Augusta Kattmann, even though bewildered at what she had witnessed, was glad she had been a guest out here in this strange village of the red stained log houses in the dense forest. Lou and Charley were silent as they rode the horses down the towpath in the darkness. Young Ben and Brenner's oldest boy, Bob, walked ahead with a swinging lantern along the narrow mill creek to light the way. Bertha played the calliope in the semi-darkness until the *Blue Swan* was around the bend in the towpath, and the Russian village lights disappeared in the murky shadows of the forest. They left the sawmill side cut and entered the main canal toward Newport and Loramie. A boat from Minster met and passed them on its way to the basin at the storied Lockington of the six locks and village.

As Bertha Gast played on into the night on the steam calliope, her thoughts strayed from her sheets of music and from the keyboard. She knew now, or thought she knew why Vladimir, Vassily, and Gregori, as well as Katyna, watched so intently while Johnny did his dances, and why they kept his dances limited and stopped the music if they saw signs of his overdoing. There was something more. Was it recurring insanity or spells of some sort? Was it just "fits" as the old town midwives diagnosed many cases of children's delirium brought on by high fever? Perhaps it was much more than all of these. It was probably something that had its roots far back in the past.

Then Bertha mused over the strange case of Elvira Brenner. She knew that her malady was not recurring delirium or "fits." She strongly suspected that Elvira's malady lay in the over dose of vodka, that strange, potent liquor that the Russians made. That strange potion could sneak up on the unsuspecting novices and render them incapacitated.

Lou-Lou, Josie and the boys sat up on the top deck above the cabin for a while and made but little conversation. They too had experienced new things, as well as new relationships. They were having a little difficulty in digesting all of it. For one thing, Lou-Lou pointed out that they saw these Russian woodcutters in a different new light. They saw them not as "furriners," but as an ethnic people with their own culture, background, faith and affections. They felt the same way toward Mrs. Vogelsang's French people from Frenchtown and Versailles. How much we are all alike, once we get to know more about one another and see underneath, was the way Josie explained it to the boys in her own words.

Elvira Brenner's children, Malissy, Mirandy and Bub did not stay long up on the top deck, but checked upon their mother's condition down in the cabin. Elvira was stretched out on a pallet bunk, and for all appearances, she was either asleep or "out cold." Joel Brenner suspected that when she did come to, she would be so embarrassed and ashamed of her performance that she would pretend sleep and keep her head covered for fear of detection.

After a while, the lights of the sawmill village disappeared from around the bend of the side-cut canal. Soon the barge was out on the main canal and on its way north to Newport and Loramie. The overhead arch of the deep forest began to grow less dense, and the moon could be seen more brightly through the overhead screen of branches. When the Brenner children left the deck, the others sat and talked a short while. Their banter and mischief was gone. They were thoughtful and their words came slowly. They fell to discussing their friends of their closely-knit group and wondered what Milly would have thought of the music. The boys wondered what Jakey and Schani would have thought of the village, banquet and ceremony. They wondered about Alby, and of Dort Waterman and her surprise blowgun shot-shooter. Just in this short time of one afternoon and evening, they all admitted that they missed the group comradeship of all the kids back home.

They left the top deck and went to the back ladder steps that led down to the little poop deck, and on to the rudder area where the tiller sat while underway. They had to watch their words and speak low because Uncle Hermann was at the tiller and Ben Gast and Joel Brenner sat near by smoking their pipes.

They remembered with covered subdued laughter the blowgun incident when their "churchy" grandmother had sworn profanely with pain, even if in German.

They left the back tiller area and went up front on the bow where only three of the crewmembers 'manned' the bank "poles" and watched the towline. They could hear the two men drivers who were riding "hoggee" and talking back and forth ahead on the dark towpath. Another crew member walked ahead with a lantern.

Josie, Lou-Lou, and the boys talked in low voices among themselves, and relived all those joyous days and nights at the fair.

They laughed when they remembered Grünwalda's outhouse varmint scare, but felt pangs of some remorse. They had not figured on its going so far, or in the disastrous results of the broken down seat. They laughed when they remembered Fritzy being the butt of the smoking pouch joke. They remembered fondly the trysts at the tile mill. Could they ever forget the Fatima fortuneteller? Could they forget the musical shows, and the Spanish Dancers? Could any of them ever forget how they rode the carousel?

August was passing and it was a full moon already. This was the last month of summer. Somehow, they felt something was changing, and they didn't want it to pass away so quickly.

Lou-Lou and Josie looked ahead down the canal and at the flickering lantern of the lantern man who was the path master. Then, without words, they looked up at the head of the great swan. How proudly she arched her aristocratic neck. She looked different at night with the brass lighted lantern shining on her features. She held its bail in her beak. Was she just looking ahead into the darkness to be watchful of her charges, or was that proud countenance looking ahead into the future?

Augusta Kattmann came alone to the top deck. She wanted to sit alone up on the top deck in the peaceful night air in the moonlight. It was a relief to have quiet now, away from the conversation of the cabin below, and away from the small talk of her daughters, Ernestine and Bernhardina. She could feel Ernestine's resentment of having the sleeping form of Elvira occupying one of the bunks. She had accepted silently Anna Steinhoge's slight reference to Elvira as "strictly and precisely *Third Estate* type." Ernestine Hofermeyer had told her sister, Bernhardina, that Elvira was a pure example of true *peasant stock* - the type from the flinty Allegheny and Cumberland Plateau - whose accustomed fare was "hog innards and collard greens."

"However, she is the true salt of the earth type," Bertha Gast spoke up defiantly. Augusta Kattmann then bolstered her daughter's viewpoint with,

"Ja, even iff ignorant, she iss die meek and good of dis earth, with der goot heart and mooch of der love as in der Holy Scriptures." Then without naming them, she put her finger on her two daughters, Ernestine and Bernhardina, "und sometimes dem what cast der first stones, have to swallow dem later."

Ernestine and Bernhardina stiffened at these words and their faces became rather somber when Augusta continued,

"Und iff der stones haf ter be passed out from der kidneys and der bladder, dey sometimes sting und cut to beat *der Teufel*."

Yes, Augusta told herself, it was a relief to have quiet now, after all the music, dancing, and hysteria of the evening. It was a relief to have the loud calliope silenced at last.

She sat alone with her thoughts as she pulled her knit stole around her shoulders. She began to wonder what life really was. She wondered how she could have been so sure of so many things in the years of her past life.

The moonlight was very soothing now that the swan barge had left some of the overhanging trees of the deep forest. Augusta Kattmann wondered if her mind playing tricks on her. She had always been so sure of herself in years past, but she tried to pass it off and began thinking perhaps it was the wine and other drinks back at the village. Maybe it was that strange food. She afforded herself the luxury of imagination and fantasy. It must be the *Blue Swan*.

Yes, that could be it! It had changed all their lives. Yes, it was the mystic magic, that inexplicable something of the *Blue Swan*. However, it is not blue she told herself. Oh perhaps the body (the gunwale) was a light sky blue, but those great white snowy wings, along with her white arched neck, were surmounted by that aristocratic head was looking serenely ahead. Yes, those great white, snowy wings half raised well out of the water as if ready at a moment's notice to take flight.

Yes, Augusta mused to herself, the *Blue Swan* must know something that no mortal did. She then remembered some of the words and the melody of the Russian Lullaby, "Spi, Spi Babatko," and she winced when she thought of the incoherent Johnny Ivan. He had danced his heart out for them. Without knowing it, Augusta found herself dozing off into a peaceful sleep.

Chapter 29

The August morning was bright and pleasant, but the travelers knew that the day would grow hot by noon. Village after village slipped by as the *Blue Swan* with its cargo and passengers glided south on the canal. After Fort Loramie, the small villages of Newport and Lockington passed in the early morning. They descended the six locks and then crossed over the wooden flume over Loramie Creek. By the time they passed through Piqua and Troy, the sun was getting hot, and it soon it was noon.

Lou-Lou and Josie sat on the top deck, on their favorite seat behind the swan's neck above the pilothouse. Their grandmother called to them from time to time to be sure to keep their arms covered and their parasols up in the hot sun, or they would look like country bumpkins. If they were going to take a trip with society folks on one of the floating palaces on the river at Cincinnati, they would have to look the part and act like ladies.

The *Blue Swan* would unload its cargo of ale kegs from the holds in Tipp City, and then the greater bulk of it would be unloaded in Dayton. They should be in Dayton before dark, and perhaps tie up there for the night. The other barge laden with the *Blue Swan Ale* followed close behind and on it were fresh horses that were traded from time to time. The hay and feed were also carried on the other barge. The show horses were kept for showing off on the city towpaths.

What was first planned as a birthday trip as a gift to the girls from their grandmother somehow got changed when the time for departure came, and they prepared to travel south down the canal to Cincinnati. Much to Charley, Lou, and young Ben's delight, they learned that Hermann and August Ben Gast would take two crews from the brewery and grain depot gangs, and take the *Blue Swan* with another barge to haul cargo. The boys were not old enough to ride or drive as hoggee in the congested, boisterous traffic of the cities and heavily traveled south end of the canal. However, they could go along to help with loading and unloading, and to relieve the drivers in less congested areas in the country.

Bertha declined emphatically when asked to go, for she remembered the work involved with all the cooking on the trip up to Toledo to get the *Blue Swan*. The experience would be good for the girls to be on their own and to feel some of the responsibility. Mrs. Kattmann, while planning to combine a buying trip with a pleasure sight seeing trip, also had another plan in the back of her never idle mind. She saw to it that Ernestine and Heinrich Hofermeyer accompanied the floating *Odyssey of the Blue Swan* down to the "Queen City" to get the feel of the canal, and of the packet service. It was to be their debut to what might well become a profitable business enterprise.

Lou-Lou and Josie were indignant when they learned that their Aunt Ernestine was going along to help cook and keep house along the way. Mrs. Kattmann had one of her cooks, Mrs. Noffsinger, from The Willows to come in and accompany them to do the cooking, and another, Mag Threewits, for the washing. After all, feeding a double crew and all the family would require quite a good bit of preparation and cooking. It would save more time and be more economical to feed the crew and family on board rather than to waste time stopping at inns along the way.

Mrs. Kattmann's shrewd business sense told her that the large men of the combined German and Irish crewmen and the boys would eat like hawks, and they would swill down as much food as an army. Everything always tastes so much better when eating away from home. The boys agreed. It would be far cheaper to feed them all aboard the *Blue Swan*.

While the older people amused themselves with conversation down in the packet cabin, or watched the pleasant scenery pass by while sitting up on the top observation deck under parasols, the children scampered all over the *Blue Swan*.

Lou-Lou and Josie particularly loved their observation seat high up above the pilothouse behind the arched neck of the swan. Charley, Lou, and Ben liked to sit with the tiller on the low lazarette deck, and watch the swirl the rudder made in the backwash of passing canal water.

In these cities to the south, people stopped and stared at the astonishing *Blue Swan* with her handsome equipage. The canal was a little wider down here for it was older and had been in use for more years than the upper and middle sections. The docks in the cities were larger, and more crowded with shops, mills and taverns. Waiting crowds tried to book passage on this newcomer packet, but found it was exclusively booked for an excursion on this trip. Heinrich Hofermeyer put on his best business smile and affable manners, and was quick to advise the disappointed travelers that The Blue Swan Line would soon be in operation with a host of other new and surprisingly well-appointed packets for their service.

It was particularly galling to Lou-Lou when she noticed that her Uncle Heinrich gave the impression that he was the owner of the line and was soliciting business in a rather cavalier manner.

Overhanging trees in the country made a rather welcome arch to pass beneath while giving temporary relief from the blazing hot sun.

When the boys grew weary with inaction and sluggish from the heat, they went back down to the low lazarette deck by the tiller. They then removed their shoes and socks, let their feet and legs hang over the back of the packet, and dangle in the cool water. Hermann and Ben took turns at the rudder tiller, but when a crewman relieved them, they passed the time by playing checkers on a keg top.

Augusta Kattmann visited some of the time with Ernestine or with Anna Steinhoge. However, when a lull developed, she delved into the constant always-present black bag and brought out sheaves of pamphlets to read, or reports to check on. She wrote letters and notes, checked her buying lists, discussed materials with Anna Steinhoge, and prepared for the onslaught she would make on the unsuspecting merchants in the city. She would drive a hard bargain and get the best purchases possible for her money. "Ach, das ist *richt*."

Charley, Lou, and Ben jumped off the packet onto the dock at one small country loading dock. They ran along beside the barge, and saw a companion bridge ahead that spanned the canal. Then they ran on ahead, mounted the bridge, and when the barge slid beneath them, they dropped onto the top deck from the bridge.

The traffic was much heavier now that they were approaching Dayton at late evening. Swallows dipped low over the placid water while swooping and turning to catch insects. Bullbats that made their discordant strange calls while fluttering high overhead above the city buildings, told the travelers that night was coming.

Josie and Lou-Lou viewed the large stone aqueduct ahead with interest just as the *Blue Swan* made a large curve to cross the Mad River. From the height of the long aqueduct, they looked down the long distance into the rapidly flowing Mad River on its way to join the Miami in Dayton. When they went under the large stone bridge that spanned the canal east of Vandalia, the boys called up to the girls above the captain's pilothouse. There were several wagons crossing the bridge that had large bows supporting white canvas tops. No doubt settlers were going west in covered wagons much as they had the year before. The "49'ers" were going to a new life in the west, and to what they hoped would be fortunes laying just over the horizon toward the setting sun.

Ben pointed out to the children that the much-traveled road was the famous <u>National Road</u>, better known as the extension of the <u>Old Cumberland Road</u>, which extended west from Cumberland, Maryland across Western Virginia and through Pennsylvania. Then the road ran a straight line across Ohio and on across Indiana toward St. Louis, Missouri.

It was exciting crossing this highway, the crossroads of the nation - almost of the world! They felt that they were a part of history in the making. It was breathtaking to dream of the adventure of those covered wagons going west. After jumping off at St. Louis and crossing the river, the wild unbroken and uncivilized west lay beyond. Who knew how many would survive the ordeals of wilderness trails across the plains and deserts and through Indian infested areas? What would lure them to venture on through such hardships? How much gold would any of them find?

Lou-Lou dreamed of all of this but told the others she was glad she was on the comfortable *Blue Swan* instead of those dusty, bumpy old wagons that were going so far into the setting sun. Few, if any of them would ever live to come back. No sir, give her the soft gliding barge, the cool canal, and the green country any day!

Besides, *gold is where you find it* - whatever that meant. She had heard her mother and father say so. Josie added that nearly all the things you look for and want so badly are usually right at home in your own back yard.

Charley, Lou, and young Ben did not quite know how they were going to manage a trip on the large riverboat, but surely there would be a way. It was the girls' birthday trip, they admitted, but it would be so nice (since they were so close) if they could manage to go along without spoiling it for the girls.

It had been a long day and now the first leg of the long journey was over. They had made good time, but now the going was slower because of the increased traffic going both ways.

At one lock, as the canal level fell lower to the south, the barges were lined up for nearly an eighth of a mile while waiting their turn to go through the lock. Fortunately, down here near the city they had encountered no log rafts, but they had passed several slow barges of heavy slow freight.

With every barge they met, the people stared at the *Blue Swan* in astonishment. After the early evening meal, Augusta Kattmann and the other women dressed in their better gowns and Sunday bonnets. They went up on the promenade deck on top of the cabin to sit and watch the city of Dayton come into view. There was heavy traffic now. The quays and docks were thronged with people, both sightseers and travelers, but none missed the elegant *Blue Swan* as she passed.

The evening twilight became cooler, and it was very pleasant to sit on the top deck of the smoothly gliding packet and watch the world pass by. Each mile was bringing more of a new world into the lives of the small town folks of Old Brementown on the canal.

Just after crossing the Mad River stone aqueduct, Ben and Hermann were arrested by shouts from the boys on the top deck. They saw a strange contraption coming toward them, but there were no horses on the towpath pulling it. Then Hermann saw the smokestack of the barge that had a tent-like canopy over its top deck to shield the seated excursion passengers from the sun and smoke.

The crewmen got out and helped the hoggee drivers with the horses. They were going to meet a steam barge and there was no telling how the horses would react. The steam packet made little noise except for a soft "whump-whump" sound from the steam in the exhaust up the smokestack. The horses paid little attention to the strange packet boat. The turning paddle wheel at the back took the attention of the passengers on all the barges meeting the steam packet.

Hermann and Ben could not take their eyes from the steam barge; here was an example of the mad inventive scheme they had nurtured for a long time - a steam barge! If only Jake Hemel and the others could see it, they could examine it closely or ride on her. It would be the ideal barge for travel across the reservoirs. Would it be practical for travel on the canal? The speed would have to be cut to a minimum to keep the wash from the bow and the paddlewheels from damaging the earthen banks of the canal berms.

The *Blue Swan* was tied up in the wide basin at Dayton while the passengers went for a walk on the paved stone quay to stretch themselves, and to see some of the downtown that was near the canal. First, they walked along Patterson Avenue beside the canal. Then they walked onto Dayton Street where there were many shops.

There was some debate about tying up for the night, but Augusta Kattmann asked Ben and Hermann about the advisability of continuing after resting a while. It would be much cooler for the horses to go at night. Hermann admitted that there would be very little, if any, traffic after dark, and they could make good time. Ben was in favor of going on, because in the morning all the commercial bustle here at the Dayton docks would be tedious and very delaying. Mrs. Kattmann left it up to her sons-in-law, but advised that it would be well to get on down toward Cincinnati if only as far as Middletown. The heavy traffic that they would meet as they came into the congested area of Cincinnati the next day would keep them from making good time. The horses were in no undue strain since they were exchanged in relays from time to time. They did not have to pull too many miles before being relieved. The unanimous decision was to move on down the canal at night. They were carrying enough crewmembers to have enough hands for dogging the watch every two hours as they exchanged horses.

The crew, the boys, Ben, and Hermann unloaded the kegs of ale at the warehouse from which the order had come. After exploring the blocks of docks and adjacent streets of downtown Dayton, Mrs. Kattmann took the two girls for a walk. They found an attractive inn not far from the docks in the main part of the city where they stopped for a light supper. Mrs. Kattmann told the girls that this was part of the "birthday treat," but that she was going to take them to a real old German Burgher restaurant in downtown Cincinnati, an old well-established place that she visited when she stayed in the city in the large old hotel. It was a dress-up place and they would all have to put on their very best clothes and manners. They might see some famous people who were on their way down the Ohio River on the floating palace riverboats.

When they were all rested after having had their evening meal and darkness had set in, they were all anxious to start on toward Cincinnati. By starting at daylight, and traveling all day until almost dark, they had reached Dayton. Now at ten-thirty in the evening, they were ready to go on and travel throughout the night. Without meeting much traffic, they could make a good five or six miles an hour, and it was cooler for the horses which they exchanged in relays every two hours or so. Ben and Hermann estimated that by making an average of five miles an hour in the seven hours until sun-up, they could cover at least thirty to thirty-five miles. They could have breakfast while underway and make still another good three or four hours before the traffic became heavy near Cincinnati. Ben and Hermann knew full well that they could encounter congestion at the locks and weigh-stations. Other delays might also arise.

After the sounds of the city died away and the street lamps faded into the background, the occupants of the barge settled down to a pleasant rest as they glided through the cool night and descended through occasional locks. From time to time during the night, a boat horn called in the distance as the two barges approached each other. Then they were past and the quiet of the night enveloped them once again.

Lou-Lou and Josie were permitted to sleep out on the top deck for a while. The pole crewman stood in the prow just below the windows of the pilothouse. He used his long berm pole to keep the front of the barge away from the banks and docks in case it glided in too close while passing. The man at the rudder till maneuvered gracefully along behind her tow of handsome horses hitched in tandem.

With the silence of the night, sleep came quickly to those on board. The crew was expert in changing horses or passing a slow tow, so that little time was lost. There wasn't much noise to shatter the peace of the night.

The boys grew tired of helping the drivers, the tiller, and the prow pole man, and they succumbed to sleep at last. Their Aunt Ernestine was very particular and inspected them carefully after they had washed themselves for bed. She was not going to have any dirty feet and legs soiling the clean sheets on the bunk beds. The boys decided to take blankets and sleep back above the cargo hold. Grandma Kattmann had given strict orders that she didn't want any stamping of feet overhead on the top deck after she had gone to bed.

Little wayside hamlets passed in the night. The late moon rose now pale and gibbous, casting only a warm glimmer of its past glory when it was full, as it was just those few nights since the night of the Russian banquet at the log village in the deep woods.

The pleasant tinkle of the small bells on the horses' harnesses, combined with the muffled hoof beats on the soft earth of the towpath, had a soporific effect as the listeners aboard were lulled into pleasant sleep. The soft slap of small waves caressed the sides of the gallant swan barge as she sailed smoothly along in the pale light of the late and nearly spent moon.

They passed through Middletown before daylight; then after another exchange of horses on both barges, they started on toward Hamilton. The barges descended lower by each lock into the rich Miami valley toward the beautiful Ohio.

Ben and Hermann were pleased with their night's progress. In a short time, they would tie up in Hamilton, for the sun was high now and it would be just the right time for breakfast. They had deliveries to make in Hamilton as well as an order for several dozen barrels, plus a few dozen small ale kegs, to leave at the huge cooper mill where newly staved barrels and hogsheads were stacked outside and ready for sale and delivery.

The girls did not awaken until the bright sun shone in their eyes from the east. After they did awaken, they lay snuggled in their blankets and talked from time to time. However, for the most part they rested peacefully, and were reluctant to get up and face the tasks of the pleasant day ahead.

The boys were awake much sooner, and were ready for something to eat. In a spirit of frolic, they stole up to the girls' reserved special place behind the head of the swan, and threw some cold water on them as they lay down and pretended to sleep. In a flash, Lou-Lou jumped up and chased them back across the top deck above the passenger cabin as they laughed and shouted in high spirits at their joke. Augusta Kattmann pounded with a cane on the paneled ceiling above her for silence, and shouted a command in German, such as "Halten," for their immediate obedience. Ernestine was now fully awake, and knew it was time for preparing breakfast for there could be no sleep now on this "ark menagerie."

After a welcome breakfast prepared by the experienced cooks from The Willows, assisted by Ernestine and her mother, everyone prepared for the final miles of the journey. There were only fourteen or fifteen miles left in the journey to the Queen City on the Ohio.

This last fourteen or fifteen mile stretch of the canal journey promised to be the most exciting for all the travelers. The polemen, linemen, and hoggee drivers knew that it would take more skill and patience here because of increased barge traffic. The right of way had to be given to faster boats and schooners, and the many locks had to be manipulated. They had to go around docked schooners and barges that were tied up at the many small inlet basins, and the reported miles of extended great basins and docks. Charley, Lou, and Ben were amazed to learn that after leaving Hamilton, Ohio the canal would swerve to the east and follow the valley of Mill Creek into Cincinnati. They thought that the canal would continue along the valley of the great Miami River. The Miami River would change its course to the southwest, passing Cincinnati several miles to the west, and join the Ohio River at the Indiana and Ohio State line. Before breakfast on board the *Blue Swan*, the girls walked the length of the seven block long Hamilton Basin that paralleled High Street from the canal back to Fourth Street. It was five foot above the ground level and leaked constantly. Charley, Lou, and Ben joined them to help inspect and explore the passenger depot at the basin's west end at Fourth and Basin Streets. They learned that there was another freight basin to the north on Mill Street, and that there was a system of other feeder canals and short commercial side cut canal slips. They saw where the feeder made a turn from the north and went to the west, about a block from them; then it drained back into the Miami River between Dayton and High Streets. They did not have time to explore farther because they heard the unmistakable sweet horn of the *Blue Swan*. They hurried back to the barge to help get underway.

The boys were awake at daybreak when the barges were coming into Middletown. The series of descending locks, voices, and the slight shuddering jar of the barge against the fenders and protective bollards at the mouth of the lock slip, had awakened them. Two miles north of Middletown the canal had received its last feeder from the Great Miami River. A dam to the west of Lock 30 impounded water from the ever-swelling river, and a half-mile channel of the feeder was regulated by means of head gates. Then a guard lock of a sort, or feeder gates, let the water into the canal. Water entered the canal by means of six timber culverts built under the towpath. This was the last supply of water to take the canal on down into Cincinnati, except for a small feeder coming into it from the Old Miami River, a looping branch of the former river bed of the Miami, which was now only a smaller branch of the main river.

There was a long level stretch from Hamilton to Lock 38 at Rialto. From there on, it was just a few miles to the series of the last locks before the city at Lockland. Here were Locks 40, 41, and 42. Across the Mill Creek aqueduct was Lock 43. Paper mills, starch factories, and other mills hugged the canal to be able to use the water power falling from the eleven foot locks before it turned back into the canal. There were two basins here. Now they were entering the oldest part of the canal that had been dedicated and put into use in 1828. It gradually worked its way up to the north in sections. This lower, older division from the feeder above Middletown was forty-four miles long. It contained thirty-two locks in order to fall the 212 feet to the low water on the Ohio River.

This next stretch from Lockland's Lock 43 on south was called the "twelve mile level," for there were no more locks until the end of the level at the basins, which were right in the heart of the city. The traffic became heavier on this long level, which was one long basin in itself.

Hermann and Ben knew this lower end of the canal (the old part) only remotely, for their grain and brewery deliveries had not taken them this far south. They usually did not travel below Dayton. At the last basin, they had put the grain barge ahead of the *Blue Swan* to open the way, and as a precautionary measure for protection. The older, more experienced drivers now rode the lead horse on each tow. The polemen and linemen had to be more alert to prevent collisions and snarled lines. This twelve mile "level" section would turn sharply to the east at Eleventh, or Canal Street, and proceed for six blocks (nearly a half mile) and terminate with the Lockport Basin at Broadway Street. The last two miles of this level became one long commercial basin, for it was literally lined with boat line offices, ticket offices, warehouses, forwarders, merchants and a variety of shops, mills and factories.

The twelve mile level of the canal descended on south of Lockland through Carthage, and Cumminsville, and wound its way around the western slopes of Cincinnati's hills. After crossing the Harrison Turnpike and Hamilton Road, it curved southeast and paralleled Central Avenue. It came down the middle of Plum Street to Eleventh, or Canal Street. There it turned abruptly into the final six block long level to the east and terminated in the Lockport Basin. Another longer basin from Eleventh Street down to Eighth Street, called Cheapside Basin, joined the Lockport Basin.

These basins lay between Broadway and Sycamore Streets. The unusual engineering feat of the ten locks and the extension down into the Ohio River adjoined the Lockport Basin. Starting from that basin, it crossed Broadway, and then started its mile long descent down Eggleston Avenue. Each of the locks had an eleven foot drop to go down the 110 foot steep descent.

Ben and Hermann had received their docking orders back at Lockland. They were somewhat amazed to learn that the lower level space, and most of the basin space, was occupied. They would be obliged to descend the ten locks to the limitless space of the river level barge docks where riverboats would be docked on either side of the barge space.

The slack water of the Ohio River near the barge docks below Front Street had but little current, so the moored barges would be safe, except in time of river flooding. At such times, towed barges would not be permitted in the river unless they were towed behind a steam propelled boat.

The barge docks extended both up stream and downstream from the mouth of the canal into the river. A protective breakwater of a sort caused the slack water near the riverbank to become a placid quiet pool. Barges were towed from their berth at this long riverfront dock and poled to a position alongside a riverboat, upon which the cargo would be transferred. However, most barge captains often found this method not to be efficient. Many times cargo needed to be transferred to a warehouse, or forwarder, who would ship it on the riverboats at a later date.

They were now making their arc around the western hills and had passed St. Bernards. They would soon cross the Harrison Turnpike. Uncle Henry and Aunt Ernestine had told the younger ones about the fabled "Over the Rhine" district, at the twin basins, where the city did not sleep. The little opera house, the parks, and sometimes the carnivals and carousels were lively all summer long. If only they could leave the *Blue Swan* there, and moor the freight grain barge on down the ten locks in the riverfront basin.

The outskirts of Cincinnati came into view after another 3 hours. The traffic grew heavy as they came farther south and noon was upon them. There were delays with slow moving cargo barges ahead of them. The canal traffic coming north seemed to be one steady line of traffic. There were three passenger packets only a few yards apart, and their crewmen were yelling at each other, each belittling the other while trying to overtake and pass one another.

There were no familiar faces on the barges now. These were all strangers with faces that were not so friendly, or familiar, as those the occupants of the *Blue Swan* barge were used to seeing. There were several foreign swarthy faces, but none so as kind as the Russians they had come to know well. There was no Silvermann, nor were there heart-rending scenes like those that they had witnessed during the summer. However, there were some skimpy looking cargo barges. Their owners looked rather pinched and overworked, as if the coins of commerce came their way rather late. Everyone stopped to look at the beautiful *Blue Swan* with its snowy white wings.

When Mrs. Noffsinger, the *dutchy* cook from The Willows, learned that Ben and Hermann planned on being docked on the riverfront by early afternoon, she suggested that they delay their big meal until then. In the meantime, she sliced ham and made sandwiches with her home-made bread. She then passed them on plates with helpings of her German potato salad, deviled eggs, and sweet pickles. She urged the children to drink their milk and finish it up, for she didn't think it would keep much longer - even in its ice-packed barrel.

As the majestic *Blue Swan* entered the city, every eye along the canal's quays was upon her. After the light lunch, Ernestine, Heinrich, Mrs. Kattmann and the others put on their "dress-up clothes." They were getting ready for the grand entry into the city on the handsomest passenger packet on the canal. Mrs. Kattmann sat up on the promenade deck under her large parasol to shield her from the August sun. Others of the family sat around her much like the entourage of royal celebrity giving her the deference of her rank and age. Augusta Kattmann nodded pleasantly to all passersby, but her mind's eye was busy making evaluations of the passenger packet trade. Along the route down, she made careful notes for possible locations where inns were needed for overnight guests. If there were over two thousand weekly travelers paying fares between Dayton and Cincinnati, why not get more paying fares between Cincinnati and Toledo, up the northern trunk of the canal? With improved overnight inns, better restaurants, and a commodious new line of packets with reduced prices on fares, she intended to beckon the trade north. With the commerce along the way, to say nothing of the Indiana branch canal, the Wabash and Erie into Fort Wayne, Huntington, and on to Lafayette, there was sure to be a thriving cargo and passenger business to be built up. Augusta Kattmann meant to see that Heinrich Hofermeyer helped build up that business, to give it good taste, and to make his pocketbook swell along with his own self-importance.

Lou-Lou and Josie rode up front on their chosen bench while the others gathered on the promenade (parade) deck. It was rather embarrassing when people gathered along the sidewalks and came over to the quay and docks as the barge passed. With the barge-packet going at such a slow pace, it seemed that the eyes of the crowds of shoppers and strollers devoured them with their curious stares, friendly waves, and speechless amazed faces. None of them had ever seen such a packet before, or such high stepping and beautiful full-blooded horses. Ernestine Hofermeyer wondered how they would receive the other packets that were to follow, if the *Blue Swan Packet Line* really got into operation during the coming year. What would they make of the giraffe, elephant, rooster, and especially the large hippopotamus?

Now came the long wait in the hot sun, the careful maneuvering in the heavy traffic going both ways, the poling-off to miss pilings, barges, and the stone bulwark of the bridges and aqueducts.

"It would take hours," Ben complained when he saw the pile-up of blocked canal traffic ahead waiting for the locks. There were ten locks in a row down to the level of the docks on the Ohio River wharfs.

After the initial excitement of the city was over, tedium set in as the swan barge travelers began the long wait for their turn in the locks down to the Ohio. The heat became unpleasant in the humid city. The horses stood it well because they had only to pull from time to time. There were long minutes between each tow because they could only move up a little at a time. They had to wait until the locks opened for two more barges before they could lower to the next level.

Augusta Kattmann soon had enough of the "the grand entrance" and the show they put on up on the promenade deck. She fled down into the cooler shade of the cabin and put on a cooler cotton dress. The others followed her example. They would put on a more simple attire and get off on the dock before entering the series of ten descending locks. They could walk about the city dressed more like the everyday shoppers that were dressed sensibly for the heat, instead of being dressed for a royal presentation at court.

When the girls left the packet with their grandmother and Aunt Ernestine, the boys decided to stay on board and go down to the locks on Pearl Street.

Mrs. Kattmann assured Hermann and Ben that they would have no trouble finding the *Blue Swan* at her berth along the lower level of the docks. All they would have to do is walk the several blocks along the riverfront. Surely, no one could miss the unusual light blue swan packet with white wings wherever it was tied up.

Short tempers flared with the canal men as some of the other barges tried to get ahead of others to either ascend or descend the canal locks. Finally, the last lock was cleared, and as the lock gate opened, the *Blue Swan* glided with scarcely a ripple along the lower docks to her assigned berth. At the western end of the dock to the right, the long basin opened into another canal that followed the riverfront. Then it ascended the locks at Station 27 on Pearl Street, which went to Harrison and North Bend. After that, it joined the Whitewater Canal that came down to Cincinnati from Indiana. The Whitewater Canal connected the towns of Metamora, Brookville, Connersville, and Cambridge City to the ports of the Queen City.

Now they were docked. They were at last in the Queen City of the Ohio River, or so Cincinnati people liked to think. Ben and Hermann took a long sigh of relief, and prepared for their stay at the dock. Mrs. Noffsinger, and her helper, Meg Threewits, started preparing her heavy meal for the crewmembers of both barges, planning to make one heavy meal serve for both late dinner and early supper. The horses were unharnessed in their stalls and fed. Afterwards, they were taken to the large livery stables down the dock and up the hillside a short distance. The passenger depot was alive with people. It was situated on the docks for the convenience for both canal travelers, as well as the steamboat packets on the river. No malodorant livery stable with hundreds of horses would be tolerated in this congested area as it was in Toledo. Therefore, it was placed well up the hillside and a good half mile away from the depot. There were green pastures along the river upstream from the stables.

The boys could scarcely wait to explore up and down the docks. There was so much to see. Ben and Hermann made them wash up and then take time to eat. Mrs. Noffsinger, with the absence of the other women, took over supervising the washing and table manners of the young boys. Her firm words, even through accompanied by a smile, were obeyed without question.

Charley, Lou and Ben "hurried down their meal." Then they went out on deck to get a good look across the river. A wide expanse of paved dock lay between the canal and the actual riverfront. There were dozens of large river steamers tied up at the quay, some with smoke rising in spirals from their tall stacks, and others dozed silently at berth with no steam head up.

The boys could look over across the Ohio River to Kentucky through the open spaces between the river queens.

"Charley," Ben called from the top deck, "I'll bet it's a half mile, if not more, across the river to Kentucky." One of the crewmen on another barge told him that it was not more than a quarter of a mile wide here but that it got wider downstream. He captured their young boys' wonder when he told them how the wide Mississippi got over a mile wide before it reached New Orleans.

At last, the boys were given permission to explore up and down the riverfront, but they could not go beyond the limits of the stone paved docks in either direction. They were to come to the packet immediately when they heard the *Blue Swan's* own double-toned horn blast. They would know it for there was no other like it on the canal.

CHAPTER 30

FROM UP THE RIVER and coming around the curving bend to the east, a large steamboat gave a series of blasts on her steam whistle. In a short while, stevedores and dock crewmen made ready to help berth the steam packet.

As the boys explored up and down the docks, their interests were no longer centered on the other barges on the canal side of the dock. They were fascinated with dozens of huge steamboats tied up at the piers. Scores of well-dressed people were going aboard the steam packets. They were headed south downstream to Louisville or upstream to the northeast toward Pittsburgh.

The boys' attention was attracted by the sound of their names being called. They looked around and saw an open carriage with a colored cab driver pass by them. Lou-Lou, Josie, and Grandmother Kattmann waved to them as they passed by on the dock beside the *Blue Swan* where they descended from their hired carriage carrying boxes and packages.

After Mrs. Kattmann and Ernestine Hofermeyer had gone aboard the barge with their packages, the girls ran down the dock to join Charley, Lou, and young Ben. Heinrich Hofermeyer came strolling after them as a chaperone. After all, they were only small town children who were loose on the waterfront of a large city.

They went down the riverfront from one large steamboat to another. They could hardly wait until Grandmother Kattmann was to take them for a ride on the riverboat.

They marveled at the handsome balustrades, gleaming brass lamps, doorknobs, and handrails that were up along the decks of the passenger riverboats. They walked down the finger piers that extended out into the river harbor where some of the large paddlewheelers were berthed. Charley gasped at the size of the great paddle wheel at the stern. Why, the top of the paddle wheel extended up almost to the top deck, or at least above the second deck on some of them!

"Look at that one," Ben called. "It has to be a good thirty feet in diameter, and half of it is submerged in the water!" They all went close to the edge of the quay, and looked at the gleaming white paddle wheel at the stern of a great river queen.

Negro stevedores walked among the crowd on the quay. Porters hurried aboard the steamboat with carpetbags, valises, and bandboxes. Next a pushcart bustled them from behind as another couple of Negroes pushed it to the large cargo gangplank over the side, and then onto the deck of the steamboat. The boys watched as large booms overhead loaded barrels and boxes onto the decks. Well-dressed women wore fashionable swaying hoops that were much larger than the ones the girls saw at Toledo. They smiled at the girls, and then exchanged pleasant conversation with the men who were with them. The gentlemen were wearing top hats, and frock coats with bright colored waistcoats under them.

Josie and Lou-Lou were especially spellbound by the group of fashionably dressed people who disembarked from another steamer that came upstream from the southwest. The steamer was a side-wheeler that went forward on one wheel; then she backed down on the other as she maneuvered easily into the dock sidewise. Soon the large gangplank was lowered from chain booms onto the quay.

Charley and Lou read out her name, *The Natchez Belle*, which was written with scrolled letters along the gunwale at the forecastle. The same name was emblazoned on the pilothouse high above the top Texas promenade deck.

"Just think, Ben," Charley called, "this one has come all the way from down south at Natchez on the Mississippi." A large Negro porter who came hurrying down the gangplank smiled a large smile that showed his white pearly teeth. He told the boys that it had come from New Orleans, but had just come up that afternoon from Louisville where it had stopped over and taken on cargo the day before.

After a while some of the passengers began to disembark from the steamer and go into the depot. Other passengers began to come aboard for the return trip down river to Memphis and on south. A very pleasant lady with the most beautiful gracious voice the girls had ever heard, bent over to speak to them in a modulated soft southern voice. She asked the girls where the passenger station was. The girls, trying hard to be very grown-up and polite, offered to take them down the quay to the vicinity of the depot. The colored maids came behind carrying personal belongings of the ladies, while butlers and stevedores brought the heavy trunks.

After making acquaintance with the southern ladies, the girls were thrilled when they learned that their new friends had just come up river from Louisville, and one of the aunts was from Memphis. All of them were on their way upstream to take another steam packet.

They were going to get their tickets on a steamboat that would "carry" them up the Ohio to Point Pleasant, Virginia where they would turn south into the Kanawha and go to Charleston. From there they would take the stage across the mountain turnpike to the White Sulphur Springs.

Josie and Lou-Lou were entranced by the beautiful manners and the speech of their newly found friends. One of the older ladies was especially attracted to Josie and asked her name. She then complimented her for her courtesy and sweet nature. Upon learning that the girls were on their birthday trip, and had been promised a trip on a river packet excursion boat, the old southern woman from Memphis promised the girls that they were to go back on board with her to her stateroom, and they could see the wonderful packet on which the women had just arrived.

At this moment, Heinrich Hofermeyer interrupted the party and dipped his hat to the ladies, and then reminded the girls that their grandmother was probably waiting for them. He knew that this was not true, but he did not trust leaving his charges in the hands of these strangers. The girls then introduced him to their southern friends, and Heinrich accompanied the party up the gangplank of the *Natchez Belle*.

Lou-Lou and Josie were ushered into another world. They were given attention by the handsome well-mannered young men in top hats, bowed to as if they were grown women, and were called "Miss Louise" and "Miss Josephine" formally by the southerners. Now they had arrived into that new world just down the towpath of which they had always dreamed. They could not believe the walnut paneled staterooms, the elegant fine wood beds with satin and embroidered silken counterpanes, the gleaming white woodwork, the soft red and mauve carpet in the hallways, or "companion ways," as they were called aboard the packet. The elegance of the chandeliers in the ballroom on the middle deck took their breath away.

Lou-Lou was astonished when one of the young men asked for her hand in a dance. The other women smiled, as the musicians who were practicing at the end of the ballroom, began a slow waltz. They were thankful now that Uncle Heinrich and Aunt Ernestine had given them lessons in deportment, and had insisted that they learn to waltz and to perform other ballroom dance steps. Josie could not believe her eyes when a colored musician in a green uniform opened the top of the grand piano. She was further stupefied when she saw that the piano was decorated with inlaid ivory and golden filigree curlicue down its slender legs.

Uncle Heinrich was in the world of his liking and assumed the gracious airs of his hosts. Lou-Lou, curbed her quick tongue and assumed airs of fine breeding, thanked the young man and then asked her uncle if she might be excused and given permission for a dance. Heinrich bowed to his niece, and gave permission to the young man. After that, he carried on his conversation with the women who seemed charmed by his subject of conversation and his deferring manners.

"So this is your thirteenth birthday, my dear," the old aunt from Memphis said, while taking Josie's chin in her mitted hand. "It is such a little time from thirteen until sixteen my dear, and then suddenly the world grabs you up and you are no longer a little girl."

"Aunt Caroline, you're getting sentimental again," another young man in the group said. He smiled into Josie's eyes and said:

"Only thirteen and you look and act as if you are already grown," he sighed with that pleasant modulated drawl. Then he asked for her hand in the dance, but first he addressed himself to her uncle. Josie apologized that she did not know all the ballroom dances but said that she could waltz a little.

"Miss Josephine, you are too modest. You waltz divinely."

When the all too short dance was over, the young men escorted the girls back to the group and bowed over their hands.

Lou-Lou caught up in the romance of the moment, and could not contain herself. With a hint of mist in her eyes, she said,

"You beautiful people, if we could just go to the springs with you...just to see...the White Sulphur...a real ballroom!"

"It would be most charming, if you could, my dears," the women said as they smiled graciously.

"And you are just thirteen," one of the young men said. "You should have thirteen kisses for your birthday instead of the paddlings you said you received," he teased. The older aunt tapped him with her folded fan and pursed her lips at him. Lou-Lou blushed for the first time.

"Philip is an incurable romantic, my dear. Pay him no mind at all. He will recover once he gets to the springs and takes the waters." She laughed lightly; then bent and kissed each of the girls on the cheek. Josie loved the light fragrant scent of lemon verbena cologne from the older woman, the lace of her frilled sleeves, and the lace patterned hooped skirt that collapsed easily when pressed by the others on either side.

Charley, Lou, and Ben had been more interested in the long corridors along the outside and next to the scroll railing of the second deck, or boiler deck, as the stevedores and crewmembers called it. They wandered along the long expanse to the paddle boxes that covered the huge thirty foot paddle wheels on each side. Each wheel had buckets nearly six feet wide, and each paddle was nearly six feet deep. The paddle wheels on the *Natchez Belle* looked like they were over five or six feet wide, and the paddle buckets seemed to be submerged at least three or four feet into the water.

The pilothouse up on the Texas, or promenade deck, took their eye, but they only went up to the door and looked through the glass at all the brass instruments. To their astonished delight, they saw a large brass steam organ (calliope) just back of the pilothouse. The tall smokestacks were fluted and fringed at the top like a coronet, and were painted gleaming black. The black color made them stand out against the new coat of white paint that was trimmed with green lines.

Somehow, the boys knew that they just had to talk their fathers into a ride on one of these gorgeous floating river queens. They knew they would probably not get to go with Lou-Lou and Josie when their grandmother took them on their birthday voyage out on the river, but there had to be some way to get at least a short ride after coming all this way. They were so close that they could almost feel the lurch and sway of the huge paddle-wheeler in the current of the river when it was underway.

They came back down to the second first class deck to the double doorway of the ballroom, and got there in time to hear the end of the waltz, and see Josie and Lou-Lou waltzing with the two elegantly attired young men of the southern party.

They knew they could not tease the girls now but they would bide their time. However, something did not seem quite right to Charley or Ben. They had not thought of their sisters of being "that" grown up; they seemed out of their element with these people as well as being beyond their years. They preferred the rollicking, fun-loving tomboy sisters they had known all the time before. It was too much and too soon for the boys to take in.

After a while, Uncle Heinrich thanked the southern hosts, took the girls and his young nephews, and started the group back to the *Blue Swan*. Upon parting, he advised the southern group that if they were staying over for any length of time and were looking for a very hospitable place to eat, he recommended the elegant Holland House with its well-appointed dining room, the Maison Terrace. It is known the entire length of the river for its French cuisine, its wines, and expertly trained staff of service people.

When Lou-Lou and Josie caught sight of themselves in the tall pier glass mirrors along the side of the ballroom, all of a sudden they felt very out of place. It came home to them all of a sudden. They felt like little "Dutchy" country bumpkins dancing in an elegant ballroom with dark princes, past gold framed mirrors, and under diamond-clustered chandeliers with hundreds of prisms. They became self-conscious of their little girls' short-hooped dresses with their ruffled pantalets showing at their ankles and their low-heeled, button shoes. The simplicity of their afternoon dresses stood out like a sore thumb against the elaborate but stylish gowns of their southern hosts. They felt like Cinderellas who had ventured into a palace ballroom and had taken advantage of the polite courtesy of their well-bred hosts. Of course, they were out of place, but what an exciting and romantic thing to have to remember and take back to their little town. It was time to go because the swan would be waiting. It was all the fault of the unbelievable *Blue Swan* that had chosen to alight on their canal and make them all giddy-headed with its splendor.

Not wanting to appear too rustic and lacking for words, Lou-Lou told her hosts about their trip down, how her grandmother had been honored, and that they were selecting furnishings for the new sanatorium and hospital.

Not to be outdone, Charley and Lou spoke up and told about their *Blue Swan* and the new line of packets the family were about to establish on the canal, with their own string of inns along the way. Heinrich Hofermeyer silenced the talkative children and apologized for their self-esteem. He very tactfully explained about their business trip in a few words; then he took leave again of the southern party and herded his wards up to the dock. Heinrich scolded them for telling all the family business to strangers who were not the least bit interested.

When the opportunity presented itself, the boys began to beg their fathers to take them on an excursion trip out on the river. Ben and Hermann told the boys that they feared all the trips on the large boats were long voyages to ports up and down the river. Ben and Lou made it their business to inquire. They found that there were short excursions up and down the river of only a couple of hours. Refreshments were served on board if the passengers wanted to enjoy them.

When the boys got Lou-Lou and Josie cornered out of hearing of their grandmother and Aunt Ernestine, they teased them mercilessly about "waltzing" and putting on airs with the gentlemen and women, and about trying to impress them. Charley and Ben locked arms up on the top deck and pretended to waltz together while Lou sang in a whining voice. Instead of their usual protest and attacking their tormentors, the girls only turned away and said very little. This puzzled the boys. It was no fun to tease them if they were going to act this crazy. For a minute young Ben thought Lou-Lou was going to burst out "bawling." However, she turned it into a joke and smiled up at them while trying to be her usual self.

After the boys went back down to get washed up for the evening supper meal, Lou-Lou said simply to her cousin Josie,

"You know Jo-Jo, after our boat ride and we get all our sightseeing and shopping done, I'm sorta mixed up and crazy like!"

Josie thought she heard a hint of a sob in her voice. Something clutched at her own throat. Therefore, she did not venture an answer until the spell passed. At last she found her voice.

"But Lou-Lou, we just got here today," Josie protested. "We have all of the best things of our trip ahead of us - the ride on the river, shopping for new..."

"I know. Its' crazy, isn't it?" Lou-Lou said quickly. "I don't know. It's just something that came over me."

"Well, it's not so crazy! I have just been wondering how Mama is getting along and what they are all doing today," Josie answered.

"Your mother and mine are going to take Grandpa Kattmann down to the reservoir at Loramie and go out fishing. Uncle Ludwig is going to drive them and take them all out in a boat."

"That will be a good visit for all of them. It seems that they never get to see Grandpa Kattmann, for there is always so much going on at home with Grandma-Má and all of her goings-on."

Lou-Lou looked far away across the river to the Kentucky shoreline, and to the wooded hills beyond. Then she said to Josie, "Isn't it funny how you take things for granted? I wonder about all those crazy people at home. Sure, Mrs. Hemel is aggravatin' and Mrs. Peppleman gets on your nerves with her loud voice and bossy ways, but I even miss them in just this short time."

"I sorta miss hearing Jake Hemel clanging his hammers on the anvil in the blacksmith shop. I remember that most of all when I think of Brementown. All my life I have been used to hearing that sound early of a morning while I'm still in bed. I'm also used to hearing the whistle on the brewery stack, the bell at the lock and boat horns on the canal."

Neither girl could put into words what really made them feel so strange, suddenly longing for home and for something tangible and familiar. They were coming up against strange new feelings and their courage was failing them.

The evening came on pleasantly. After a leisurely meal on the barge, which Mrs. Noffsinger and her helper served with pride, the family was ready for a trip uptown. If they only took a walk on the main streets to see the people, the carriages, the depot, and all the exciting commotion of passengers coming in on river or canal packets who were all bound for somewhere else, it gave them quite an interesting day.

With all the strange faces and different types of people, their speech, and their facial expressions, Josie mentioned to Lou-Lou that it would be funny if they ran on to Elvira Brenner or that old Irish troublemaker from up in their neck of the canal.

The next day, Mrs. Kattmann and Mrs. Steinhoge prepared early in the cool of the morning for their first onslaught against the dry goods and bolt goods merchants. They planned to buy their bolts of ticking, sheeting, pillow casing and all the yardages of white goods first. They would get the easy things done first, and save their energy for the tedious searching for the smaller things last. The late afternoon was reserved for rest and for the planned riverboat excursion. The evening would be spent by doing more sightseeing. Perhaps one evening they would take supper in the famous, but expensive, Holland House and eat in its renowned Maison Cherie Terrace. Lou-Lou and Josie could not believe their ears. What if their southern friends were there?

Box after box was delivered to the canal deck and stored aboard the barges tied up there. Mrs. Kattmann's purchasing went more rapid than she had feared, and in a few days, she had completed her purchasing from the lists she had prepared.

It seemed odd to Charley, Lou, and young Ben that every time they went walking with their sisters for a little diversion from the busy depot and dock area during the next few days, that every trip somehow took them past the Holland House uptown, and back past the *Natchez Belle* at her berth.

When the girls tired of accompanying their tireless grandmother on her endless shopping tours, they stayed on the swan barge and wrote letters home or to their friends and neighbors. The boys chided them and made fun of their homesickness. Why would they waste time writing home when they had only been gone a few days? In a short time it would all be over, and they would be nestled aboard the homing swan with its folded wings. Josie had to turn away to hide sudden childish tears.

One morning the packet from the north brought a letter from Bertha Gast to Ben and all the rest. Josie read it over and over, then sat down and wrote a return letter to go back on the passenger packet that was going north to Brementown.

Bertha wrote about things at home - everyday, commonplace things, and told them how quiet the house seemed without all of them there. In fact, the neighbors around the locks and depot said that the whole town was quieter.

On the appointed night of the big supper at the Holland House in the Maison Cherie Terrace, Augusta Kattmann was in a high rare mood. She had completed most of the buying that she had dreaded. The heat had not been as unbearable as she had feared it would be in the comparative quiet and ease of the almost empty barge's passenger cabin lounge. Taking great care to supervise the toilet and attire of Lou-Lou and Josie, she and Mrs. Steinhoge set out with them in a hired carriage for the Holland House. The girls were flabbergasted when their grandmother called them down into the passenger packet cabin that had taken on much of the air of her own personal living room. She and Anna Steinhoge showed them two gowns they had picked out for the girls. The gowns had real lace tiers of summer weight material with pale pastel satin and watered silk (moiré) underskirts, which showed through the open lace work. The girls cried out with delight when they found that the gowns were special birthday gifts for them, and that they were to stand for alterations and fittings, because they were to wear them to the famous Holland House. The homemade frocks from back home would not do.

In no time, the two older women, with the expert help of Mrs. Noffsinger and Meg Threewits from the kitchen gallery, had tucks here and fitted the bodices a little tighter there. The gowns fit almost as if they had been tailored especially for them by an expert dressmaker. Mrs. Kattmann viewed the handiwork on the gowns with a pleased air of satisfaction. She then announced to the girls that the gowns were imports. In fact, most of the ready-to-wear gowns were imports for it was cheaper to get gowns, hats, and gloves made in Paris and Vienna than it was to hire dressmakers and modesties here in the city. The two girls were in the heights of excited happiness. These gowns were their very first "grown-up" dresses. They did not quite sweep so close to the floor as a fully-grown woman's ball gown, but at least they came to almost full length, and hid the little girl's ruffled pantalets and button shoes.

They were permitted to wear gloves and stoles the same as a sixteen year old debutante (belle), and an evening lace net snood for their hair. Augusta Kattmann and Anna Steinhoge were not much help when it came to helping the young girls to do up their hair in a formal coiffure. Theirs was a world of practicality and duty. Mrs. Noffsinger, who had daughters of her own, saved the day. She had little trouble brushing the girls' hair back into a loose curled chignon in the beaded and corded net snood.

Anna Steinhoge gave each of the girls a broach pin for the low Bertha collar of their décolletage. They were birthday gifts. Since the girls were too young to have permission to have pierced ears, they were obliged to go without ear pins. They did not mind, for they were too pleased with the nosegays of real flowers, and their new lace mitts to miss having jeweled ear pins.

When they made their appearance up on deck behind the passenger cabin, the boys put up a loud hue and cry while circling the girls and trying to believe that they were the same girls who were their sisters. Ben Gast was taken by surprise, and he had to rub his eyes to make himself believe that this blonde young lady was his own "little Josie," who was so recently of Old Brementown. Now she was as elegant as the majestic swan that had brought her to the queen city and out of her ordinary surroundings. Hermann Gast complimented Lou-Lou, but the girls could tell by their fathers' subdued words that they didn't exactly approve of all the finery.

When the supper party left the swan barge for the waiting carriage that was to carry them to the elaborate Holland House, Ben said with hesitating words to his brother,

"Those girls will never be the same little pranksters..."

"I was thinking that, Ben. Mother Kattmann means well once she gets in the swing of things, but she'll spoil them. They grow up too soon as it is," Hermann said with a tinge of regret.

"Too much too soon...and it was only yesterday that..." Ben's voice faded haltingly.

Mrs. Noffsinger calmed their fears as she served them their supper on the barge after the carriage had pulled away from the dock. She knew from raising girls of her own what a lift "new clothes" gave a woman in the dumps, even if it was only a ribbon or a handkerchief.

After the delicious meal, the boys persuaded their fathers to take them for a stroll along the docks, and maybe they could go aboard another river steamer. The walk was not without the hoped for results, for the boys had designs of finding a paddlewheel packet that would take passengers on short trips for a price they could afford.

Since Mrs. Kattmann was to take the two girls on a riverboat excursion, Ben and Hermann thought it only fitting if they were to take their sons on a short trip out on the river. Perhaps some morning they could go without telling the others, but it would have to be after the girls had their trip. Yes, the boys' trip would have to be after the girls had their trip. Otherwise, the boys would spoil it with their bragging, and take all the exciting fun out of the "first" trip for the girls on the dreamed-of river steamboats.

Charley and the other two boys had seen the large poster in the depot advertising river steamer excursions, some three and four hours long, and a short special one downstream the few miles to Aurora and back. Hermann and Ben agreed to take the boys on the short trip, but they were to say nothing to the others about it. They would wait until Grandmother Kattmann had gone uptown for her morning forays into the shops and warehouses. Besides, Ben and Hermann were anxious to view the workings of the steamboat's engines and paddlewheels. They wanted their own steamboat for the reservoirs. A smaller replica of one of these river packets with smokestacks and all would attract passengers on the reservoirs. They might even visit the famed "Over the Rhine" district up the hill.

When the carriage pulled to the landing of the Holland House, stiff-backed colored porters met them and opened the door of the open top carriage. The porters handed the girls down first onto the steps at the side, and then they handed the two older ladies down to the curb. Mrs. Kattmann handed her tickets of reservation to the concert in the ballroom to a stout head porter who met them in the foyer that led from the marble parquet floored lobby.

During the light chamber music concert, Augusta Kattmann fanned herself and made conversation with the girls during the intermissions as they perused their programs. When Mozart and Haydn gave away to the more romantic music of Lanner, Strauss and the melodious waltzes from Vienna, Lou-Lou and Josie remembered the beautiful elegance of the ballroom on the steam packet. They looked at each other, smiled, and nodded their heads in time to the music.

Then the short concert was over, there was time for loitering in the drawing rooms or in the lobby, until the Maison Cherie Terrace supper was served. Mrs. Kattmann, thinking to do her birthday treat up royally, announced to the astonished girls that they would take "tea" on the open-air terrace. The terrace overlooked the broad expanse of the river. It had a clear view up and down the river so that they could enjoy the sites.

Augusta Kattmann and Anna Steinhoge treated themselves to a small goblet of vintage wine, but ordered small demitasses of chocolate for the girls. At the last minute, Heinrich Hofermeyer and Ernestine decided to attend a summer opera presentation of operatic arias given in the city park pavilion nearby in "Over the Rhine." They might come to the ball after the opera, or at least put in an appearance in the ballroom, and see the others safely home.

After the twilight turned to near darkness on the river, the candles were lighted at the terrace tables. Mrs. Kattmann called the waiter and gave him her reservations for their table inside the Maison Cherie dining room. Lou-Lou and Josie were dazzled with the luxurious appointments of the dining room: its soft white pillars, golden chandeliers, and huge pier glass mirrors along the arches between the pillars lining the walls. Glass china cupboards were interspaced below the pier-glasses, and the glittering crystal inside of them shone in the hundreds of candlelights as though they were diamonds shining from their glass cases.

The girls watched their grandmother and Anna Steinhoge before they ate each course, and Mrs. Kattmann very tactfully whispered directions to them to put them at ease with all the silverware, goblets, and endless courses.

The girls were game; they tried to eat everything put before them, as if they were used to such elegance everyday in the week. Lou-Lou hesitated when the French snails were served in the shell. Other foreign delicacies delighted the two older women, but the girls approached each new course with intrepidness, wondering what it really was behind the high-sounding

French name. Lou-Lou whispered to Josie, who had to suppress a well-bred snort when the next course came.

"Can't you imagine Elvira Brenner here? She would exclaim,"

"Law, I didn't know that even heathen would ever have et such vittles!"

"Capon-poulet avec vin," Anna Steinhoge said as she translated the menu for the girls. "That merely means young capon, tender chicken served with wine poured over the meat while it is still hot."

The girls tried to assume very dignified and well-bred airs in order to do justice to the efforts and expense their grandmother had undergone. They tried to imagine that they were southern belles and that this was their debut, their grand soiree at the springs, and they wanted to make their chaperones proud of them. It was difficult for Lou-Lou not to clown, for she saw so many humorous things around her. However, she managed to assume adult dignity.

The evening was passing so quickly. Without putting it into words, the girls felt some strange anxiety. They stole glances around the room when it seemed proper to do so. They didn't want to appear to be gaping like country bumpkins who just arrived at the county fair. Would the coach turn into a pumpkin?

They never said it to one another, but nevertheless there was a feeling as if something was lacking, or as if something were about to happen. They hoped it wouldn't. It was hard to explain. Would the clock strike twelve o'clock?

Augusta Kattmann relented and allowed her granddaughters to have a very small goblet of champagne after the dinner. They had never tasted champagne but had heard about it. Now they had tasted it, and they were dining with the gods on the heights of Olympus. The champagne was the nectar of the gods. Lou-Lou thought that she felt her spirits soar and her head become lighter. Was it only her imagination? Anna Steinhoge admonished Lou-Lou and told her that it *was* only her imagination. Josie also felt the exalted soaring of her spirits and wanted to imagine it was the champagne. After all, why taste expensive champagne if you couldn't at least feel something grand, expensive, and forbidden to go with it? It was very bewildering, yet exciting, strangely sour - even bitter.

The orchestra that played from the alcove during the dinner hour (supper) was reserved for much later in the evening. It made the elegance of the huge dining room seem like a luxurious European spa, a resort on the Mediterranean. It could be viewed to be much like a palatial "Schloss" (castle or mansion) high in the wooded hills of the Vienna Woods that overlooked the fabled circular city on the Danube. How handsome the players were! Mrs. Steinhoge, reading from her notes on the back of the embossed menu, announced that the orchestra was indeed a Viennese orchestra engaged by the

Holland House for the summer. The orchestra was to play for the dinner hour, and then in the ballroom for the whirling balls that went on interminably into the night. The balls lasted until the mists stole up the beautiful Ohio and settled over the wharfs of the queen city nestled there.

Josie didn't notice at first, but something in the directness of Lou-Lou's stare toward the orchestra told her that maybe her cousin had found the answer to that feeling. Josie wondered if something illusive was about to happen. Perhaps the apéritif was the missing ingredient. Lou-Lou looked quickly to Josie and then to her grandmother, but said nothing as she looked at the program on the back of the menu. Then Josie looked toward the orchestra across the room in the alcove by the wide paneled windows. They had dozens of small panes. Then she could see the lights of the night appearing on the wide expanse of the river beyond. A steamboat was coming into her berth down in front of the depot. Then Josie focused her eyes on the orchestra leader who was talking with two dark complexioned young men. She saw them hand the orchestra leader a note; then they looked in the direction of the girls. It was the two young men from the riverboat. Now Josie understood why Lou-Lou suddenly found her program so engrossing. She shot Lou-Lou a quick look of understanding and began reading the program notes about the ball, the orchestra, and the other afternoon concerts scheduled for that week.

While the desserts were being served, waiters in evening attire also served champagne and other wines at various tables from silver ice containers. Now the violinists left the orchestra in pairs and seemed to serenade various tables for a while as they wandered through the room. Toasts were drunk at the tables, and then the violinists moved on.

There was no doubt about it now. Lou-Lou and Josie recognized the young men from the southern group who had been so courteous to them on the *Natchez Belle*. The girls knew that the dark young men had not seen them among the great crowd in the dining room. During the intermission, and before the next number, the orchestra leader announced,

"And now this next number, ladies and gentlemen, with your kind indulgence, is dedicated to the honor of two young ladies in our audience whose names we hold fair not to disclose, but whom we honor on their anniversary. We wish a happy anniversary to Josephine and Louise who are somewhere here in our audience. And now to our young ladies, we dedicate 'Auf Wiedersehen, But Don't Say Goodbye.'"

The old waltz began its haunting melody; then the high soaring violins throbbed with the counter-melody in sweet harmony.

"It's the same old waltz!" Lou-Lou gasped to Josie whose mouth was open with astonishment. Augusta Kattmann saw the expressions on her granddaughters' faces and smiled in surprise.

"Lou-veese, and mein Josephine, how nice dis ist, Ja? "No doubt your Papas have put a bug in der ear of the orchestra."

"I suspect, Augusta," Mrs. Steinhoge said with authority, "that Heinrich Hofermeyer would come nearer. You know, he and Ernestine said they might come to the ballroom after the opera selections."

"Ja, I mean yes, Uncle Heinrich," Lou-Lou said nervously, and Josie hurriedly added to her cousin's explanation.

"That must surely be it. Yes, it was Uncle Heinrich! That's it."

"Mein Josephine, do you feel well?" Josie answered her grandmother, but she wished Mrs. Steinhoge would not stare at her with those cold clinical eyes. Then from behind them, seemingly out of nowhere the wandering violinists stopped at their table and played the refrain of the lovely, romantic old waltz. Augusta Kattmann and Anna Steinhoge were most receptive and were transported to heights of rapture by the music, the honor of being serenaded, and the eyes of people upon them. The girls tried to smile and assume the poise of their elders but it was hard to do. They knew that their southern cavalier friends from the *Natchez Belle* had fostered the serenade, but how would they ever tell their grandmother? It was easier to remain silent unless their hand was forced by an unforeseen appearance. Both girls looked sidewise nervously from time to time, and they were halfway expecting to see the young men standing at the table beside them. How would they ever explain, at their age, two strange men much older than they, and how they met them on the dock and waltzed with them in a ballroom? Josie began to know what her great-aunt Fredericka must have experienced each time she had one of her "faint" spells coming on. She did not even have a vial of smelling salts in her reticule. No, this could not be actually happening. It was just the champagne. Before they knew it, the orchestra leader stepped aside while a male trio stepped to the side of the grand piano, and started singing the refrain as the violinists continued their serenade,

"Don't say goodbye, dear, Just say Auf Wiedersehen.

When falling tears dry, just say we'll meet again..." Lou-Lou forgot herself and clutched at Josie's mittened hand,

"Mein Gott, Jo-Jo! Heilig katzen! It's...it's that same..."

"It's that same waltz, Lou-Lou," Josie completed her thoughts. Mrs. Kattmann turned from the musicians and asked,

"Vot same song, mein Liebchen? Vot you mean?" The girls quickly turned her question aside and answered,

"Oh it's an old one we tried and tried to play at home, but somehow we can't quite get it," Josie said evasively.

"Yes...we even tried it on the steam calliope," Lou-Lou blurted out. Anna Steinhoge, annoyed with the interruption and disturbance from the beauty of the song's spell, said haughtily,

"Calliope indeed! How could you degrade such 'himmlischer' (heavenly music) by profaning it on that common road show squall-box?"

"Sh-h-h! - All of us! - <u>Halten der</u> noisy <u>geschrein, bitte</u>. Ist so schön... <u>ist so himmlischer</u>...so beautifully heavenly," Augusta Kattmann commanded them. Then she reverted to the distant Frau Kattmann, speaking regally in her native Prussian tongue.

The well-dressed people sitting at the surrounding tables began to suspect that Lou-Lou and Josie were the two young ladies being honored by their confused and embarrassed actions. When the song was over and the violinists prepared to move on, Mrs. Kattmann nodded very graciously to them and spoke a few words of thanks in German to them. They in turn answered her in soft Austrian accent with the Vienna slurred dialect, and bowed from the waist. Anna Steinhoge told her companion that undoubtedly the violinists were Hungarian gypsy violinists. What Viennese orchestra would be complete without the Hungarian violinist or the omnipresent zither from the Austrian villages and countryside?

The last courses of desserts were served and after a while, the chandeliers were lighted to a greater brilliance. Late diners lingered at the tables. The tables were slowly cleared. The orchestra played its last selections and at last drifted out of the dining room of the Maison Cherie.

In the distance, up the grand staircase to the second floor above the dining room, Lou-Lou and Josie could hear the orchestra tuning in the ballroom. It was time for the ball. How did it become nine o'clock so soon when it seemed that they had just arrived at the Holland House a short time before? It was truly a wonder world of enchantment that was just such a short distance off that towpath, and it was such a short time ago.

"No pumpkins yet, nor fat rats," Josie whispered to Lou-Lou.

"No, but the steeple clock hasn't struck twelve yet," Lou-Lou answered.

"Vot ist der pumpkin business?" Their grandmother asked.

"You know, Augusta, that nursery tale, Cinderella," Anna told her.

"Ach, dot Aschenbrodel in der cinders," Augusta laughed.

"Vell, ve chust wave der magic wand a little more hard. Watch der slippers!"

CHAPTER 31

NEARLY ALL THE GOLD lacquered upholstered chairs were occupied by the time Augusta Kattmann and Anna Steinhoge ushered the girls into the ballroom to the seats reserved for them. Mrs. Kattmann had tipped a uniformed liveryman generously for going ahead and securing chairs for a party of four, at some good vantage point, where they could watch the progress of the ball for a while. The girls knew that this was the last big night, and after their much awaited-for trip on the river steamboat, they would be heading home. How commonplace the once elegant *Blue Swan* would seem after the *Natchez Belle's* opulent interior. They had just dined with the gods on Olympus and sipped the forbidden nectar from crystal goblets. The girls entered the ballroom with as much poise and grace as they could muster. They were half eager, and half afraid to enter the ballroom. The scene was set and they could only follow their grandmother, the "Gnädig Frau," as the violinists had uttered as they had bowed to her.

"I don't think we belong here, Josie," Lou-Lou wailed in a half whisper.

"Where is that Boy Blue, who looks after the sheep? We should be under the haystack, fast asleep," Josie said in a low voice.

"Lady Swan, lady bird! Fly away home. Your house is on fire and your children will burn," Lou-Lou continued as she looked ahead.

"What nonsense are you two mouthing?" Anna Steinhoge asked with amusement in her eyes, and nonplused with their curious game.

The orchestra drowned out whatever sensible answer the girls could have made. The ball master called out the figures of the dance, and throngs of dancers followed his calls with each selection of the orchestra. There were stately quadrilles, and then a procession of the cotillion. Older people took part in the stately polonaise that opened the ball; then it gave way to schottisches, and rapid polkas with slower waltzes interspersed. The dim lights from the side sconces of candles gave everything a dim aura of unreality. The huge crystal chandeliers with their hundreds of baubles and prisms shone down on the bare shoulders of young ladies whirling in the dance with their partners.

Through the throngs of whirling dancers, gyrating like two large wheels, one circle inside of the other, Lou-Lou caught sight of Philip, the dark complexioned "prince" with whom she had waltzed on *The Natchez Belle*. When he smiled recognition to her, she smiled back, and upon catching herself, looked quickly to her grandmother and then at Anna Steinhoge. The dance went on, and he was lost in the throng. Josie had seen that smile too, and then in a few minutes she caught sight of the other young man, Lance, the young nephew from New Orleans who had accompanied his aunt from Memphis to Louisville. How foolish it felt to be sitting here along the wall. However, many other spectators were doing the same. How Lou-Lou and Josie's feet tapped in time with the music under the sedate, covering protection of their long skirts! How they longed to dance, but they could never risk taking part in a formal ball at their age. They knew only a few simple steps, and then anyone could follow an unprogrammed waltz if it were led expertly.

It was too much to expect or even hope for another dance with the handsome young gentlemen. They would never be asked to dance in this fine ballroom. How could they? The smooth granary floor of the grain depot was more their style. Those young men were with partners of their own, and it was unthinkable to go around asking for dances at random. Respectable people filled their dance programs, and polite young men came around and asked to sign the dance program book for whatever dances the lady had free. Lou-Lou and Josie moaned the fact to each other that they didn't even have a dance program.

Out of the shadows from the seated spectators at the right, a gracious matronly lady and her companion stooped and patted Josie on the arm as she spoke to her. Immediately Josie and Lou-Lou stood up out of respect to the two older ladies and greeted them warmly. Mrs. Kattmann and Mrs. Steinhoge, although pleased with the courteous actions of the girls, were rather surprised with the visit from the strange ladies. When they heard their southern voices as they were introduced, they were more bewildered. Where had the girls met these people?

Lou-Lou and Josie introduced the southern ladies, and explained that they had met them in the passenger station when they had landed from down river. Pleasant conversation filled the intermission between dances, and then Lou-Lou and Josie thanked the gracious "Aunt Caroline" for the lovely dedication song at dinner down in the Maison Cherie. The older southern women were amazed at the transformed "young thirteen year olds" who were dressed in their imported Paris ball gowns. "How perfectly lovely and grown-up you are!" Augusta Kattmann sat in wonderment. Someone should fill her in or at least give her the cues. This was a play she hadn't rehearsed. She didn't know the lines, and she was trying hard to look intelligent.

Josie explained to her grandmother that these kind people had been the ones who had sent the violinists to their table and who had had the song, "Auf Wiedersehen," dedicated to them for their birthday anniversary.

"You must thank the kind people, Mein Josephine, und Mein Louveese, she admonished her granddaughters.

"The others," Lou-Lou nodded to the southern women, "You must thank them for us," she stammered, nodding to the group of the southern people in a cluster of gold lacquered chairs that were halfway down the side of the ballroom. She avoided saying "young men."

"What others, mein Louveese?" Inquired her grandmother.

"There is a whole party of people that we met. They all had the birthday song played," Louise tried to explain.

"Then Louveese and Josephine, vair are your manners? Of course you must go yourselves and thank the kind peoples," Mrs. Kattmann commanded. Then she smiled graciously to the southern matrons and gave them a courteous slight bow and exclaimed,

"*Danke schön. Ist war so schön*, so beautiful. You do my granddaughters great honor. You please them so, and they are so young." While Josie and Lou-Lou lingered, their grandmother nodded to them to obey her wishes and convey their thanks to their benefactors, as courtesy and decor would demand of well-bred people.

While one of the Southern aunts sat to talk with Mrs. Kattmann and ask about the hospital she heard about, the other aunt took the girls back to her group where they found all the rest of the southern party waiting. Immediately the two young men, and another older man, got to their feet and gave bows of courtesy to the two young girls that were with Aunt Caroline.

Lou-Lou tried first to blurt out her heart-felt thanks for the lovely birthday gift: the violin serenade by the Viennese orchestra violinists, and the vocal serenade by the trio of foreign Austrian singers with the orchestra. They could never forget it. Josie tried her best to make small talk and pleasant conversation, and when the girls excused themselves to go back to their grandmother, the young men stepped to their sides to escort them.

Just at that moment, the waltz started again, and the orchestra swung into a frenzy of the intoxicating Viennese waltz. The way was blocked as the ballroom was filled from the dancers at the side. It seemed that everyone came to the floor to dance this dance for it was a series of waltzes. The girls felt awkward trying to find their way through the pressing crowd. Philip and Lance came to the rescue; there was an easy remedy for the blocked passage. They would join the other dancers. Not knowing how to answer, or how to refuse gracefully, the girls knew that they could not get to their grandmother to ask permission, and they knew they were not going to miss the opportunity of dancing on their birthday ball night. An experience quite like this would never come again.

Around and around they swirled with their graceful partners in the graceful but intoxicating evolutions of the Viennese waltz. It didn't seem quite real. From the great windows on the second floor ballroom they caught glimpses of the lights on the river. The lights were reflected on the river at night like a silver ribbon among the stars. They saw a swan in the mist on the river - or was it just mist in their eyes?

Lou-Lou and Josie were parted during the dance, but they caught glimpses of each other as they passed. Whirling, whirling, the world seemed to pass by them, and they were whirling out in space; then the ballroom came back. The figures before them seemed to blur; they seemed to float in time, and be propelled into space. However, they were directed by the strong arms of the dark, tall young men above them who smiled down into their faces. Josie could hardly imagine she was where she was. Who was this young man, so much older than she? Why was she here and why was she acting so grown-up in her belle gown? She knew she was little more than a child, and a country child at that, with perhaps rustic and "Dutchy" ways. There was no use pretending, but what gay fun it was! Was it pleasant for him?

After a while, Augusta Kattmann caught sight of her granddaughters being catapulted through the gyrations of the fast waltz, which had replaced the earlier one. Dance followed dance, and still the girls did not come back. Mrs. Kattmann motioned to them.

Then it was nearing midnight. They were only children and it was only a birthday special gift. Mrs. Kattmann explained to their newly found friends that the hour was late and the girls must be taken home. It was time for rest, and they had a long day lay ahead. Then the dance ended. With the waltz still swirling in their ears, the girls descended the long grand staircase with their grandmother and Mrs. Steinhoge. The chandeliers seemed to sway, the music swelled in their throbbing heads, and the marble squares of the parquet floor did tricks. It was a chessboard and they were merely players, pawns skipping from square to square, as all humans do in life. Nothing is real or solid. Nothing goes on forever. The rolling, winding, reeling waltz stopped. Had they danced out their girlhood too soon? Was the Swan calling them back in alarm? Would they ever dance again on the crown plateau of Olympus?

The night air was chilly in the carriage. The night was broken by the sound of hoof beats of the carriage horses near the Holland House. There was some activity on the docks as night workers, roustabouts, stevedores, and crewmen moved cargo to and from the waiting barges and steamboats.

In the distance, the deep broad whistle of a late-coming steamboat filled the night. Sparks from its tall stacks flew back in the trailing flumes of smoke like fireflies in a gray fog, and then died out over the water.

When the girls were finally off to bed in their bunks up in the small cabin back of the pilothouse, Augusta Kattmann said simply to Anna Steinhoge,

"Our little girls are no longer der little girls, Mein Anna. Did you see? Ach dot Louveese! She is so sure of herself."

"Ja, it is so, Augusta. They became young ladies, but fine young ladies, and they knew the lines to their roles. Don't ask me <u>how</u> they knew to dance, speak and deport themselves like that, but they were fine young ladies," Anna Steinhoge assured her.

The next afternoon Augusta Kattmann and Mrs. Steinhoge took the girls on a much and long awaited-for steamboat ride. They went east up the river in the afternoon. When they were gone, Ben and Hermann took the boys on an excursion down stream. They went toward Aurora on a smaller excursion steamer.

They had refreshments on board the steamer, and Mrs. Kattmann went from deck to deck with the girls, and pointed out all the interesting things on the huge steam packet. The girls never tired of watching the huge paddlewheel at the stern, of hearing the music of its rhythm, or of its dripping cascades of water from the paddles. When they looked back in the wake, they saw another large steamboat coming up astern that was bound for ports upriver. Perhaps it was headed to Pittsburg or down the Monongahela into Virginia.

On the noisy main deck, excursion passengers milled about going from railing to railing and looked over at the passing banks. The great piston beams extended from the steam cylinders for the entire length of the boat, and to the crank arms of the paddle wheel. Lou-Lou and Josie were fascinated by the constant back and forth, up and down motion of the great wooden Pittman beams, which were in motion at either side of the main deck. The beams were the size of barn beams or house sleepers.

There was a slow rolling, lurching sensation as the boat was caught by the current in the middle of the stream. Josie and Lou-Lou went to the railing again. They took the companion way to the upper Texas promenade deck. The leaning, swaying sensation was greater up here. Then when the girls saw the river bank turning away, they realized the great boat was turning around slowly, and was getting ready to head back downstream toward Cincinnati with the current.

The gleaming white passenger steamboat came close by as she passed them going upstream. The boats exchanged whistles. People waved and shouted.

There was no mistaking them. Josie and Lou-Lou stood looking at the party of southerners bound for Point Pleasant and for the Virginia springs. Then it seemed they were only a few feet from the rapidly churning side-wheeler as it passed them. For a few moments, Lou-Lou and Josie waved to the older southern women. Then they were looking directly at the two young men that had been their dance partners. A slow smile came over the handsome dark faces as the young men recognized them. Their tall top hats came off in a polite gesture as they tipped their hats and called out their names in that soft, accented musical voice.

"Good-bye, Miss Josephine. Good-bye, Miss Louise!" Then the ships were getting farther and farther apart. An expanse of water separated them. They could still see them waving, and they waved back even though they were unable to say a word.

The large steamboat sounded her whistle again and then she was fast disappearing up the river, while the excursion steamer took its passengers back to the landing wharf. Josie murmured to Lou-Lou that the glass slipper couldn't be seen in daylight.

Lou-Lou and Josie walked the lengths of the decks mingling with the holiday crowd. How different Josie thought it was from the polished, well-dressed crowd of last night at the elegant ballroom of the Holland House. From the high Texas deck they could look out over the rippling river to Kentucky, or over to their right to Cincinnati, which seemed to hug the wharf. As they neared the city after rounding the east bend of the river, the steam calliope up behind the pilothouse started its happy holiday music. Perhaps the music would attract other fares to the excursion steamer for the next trip up river. The girls came back to the second deck where their grandmother and Mrs. Steinhoge were sitting at the railing. They were watching the river scene, and they were evidently absorbed in the scene of pastoral quiet, and the lull of the gently swaying steamer turning across the current.

The music from the calliope above them on the top Texas hurricane deck did not exactly please the two older women, but they accepted it as the inevitable price they had to pay when traveling gregariously with the indiscriminate excursion masses of humanity that were bent on finding holiday merriment.

The girls left after exchanging a few words with the older women and went for another walk on the second boiler deck. They stood and watched with fascination, the lulling regularity of the churning back and forth of the piston stroke of the huge wheel beam rods that turned the paddlewheel. Then they went to the forward end of the deck, and descended the fluted curving stair gang that took them down to the main deck. It was more boisterous here with all the noise of firing the boilers, the deck crews, and the denser crowd of excursion pleasure seekers. The girls walked to the stern again to watch the great paddlewheel as it turned patiently and pushed the huge boat closer to the landing and to the end of the river trip.

"Well, Josie, who would ever have thought that all of this could have happened? Did last night really happen?" Lou-Lou asked.

"Yes, it happened, and more too, Lou-Lou. You know, aren't we fools? That meant the world and all to us. Wasn't it really nice for those young men to notice us?"

"They did more than that. They took time from their evening to dance with us and show us such a good time for our birthday."

"They hardly knew us. We thought we were so big and grown up in all our finery, and it was wonderful, but Lou-Lou, we have to get off here and get our feet on the ground. We have to get our bearings. We are only kids, and country kids at that; somehow it wasn't just honest or fair pretending we were so much. We were really fooling no one but ourselves, but it was such exciting and thrilling fun to think we impressed the world."

After Josie's long speech that rather cleared the air for both girls, they stood at the railing, were silent for a while, and watched the great paddlewheel continue its steady patient revolutions. They listened to the lulling sound of the dripping water, which dropped back into the current's wake from the turning wheel. The whistle blew for the landing crew on the wharf to be alert and ready for the lines. The calliope redoubled its efforts to be happy and gay.

"You know, Josie," Lou-Lou said at length, "I wonder why those people did go out of their way so much to be so polite."

"It was more than just polite courtesy. They owed us nothing. Oh, we did take them to the depot and give them directions, but anyone could have done that. No, it was something more, Lou-Lou."

"Yes, but let's not kid ourselves into thinking what we know is not the truth. We are only greenhorn country "Dutch" kids. You know no one is going to look at us twice when we aren't dry behind the ears yet. No, all those people went out of their way to bring happiness into our lives. It wasn't just well-bred courtesy. They wanted to do it, and I think they were happy just making us happy. That's all it was," Lou-Lou said.

"Well, in this world that's quite a bit. That's enough. Wasn't it heavenly of those handsome young men to make us feel like queens for a night without ever letting on that we were only green young kids? Why we didn't even know what to say," Josie said with a note of sadness. She didn't understand a thing about how she felt. "It was those expensive grown-up Paris gowns."

"I wanted to say something, but I felt like a fool. My throat just went dry when they called good-bye to us from the steamboat as they passed a while ago," Lou-Lou admitted.

As they neared the landing, they could hear the crowd on the wharf noisily calling and cheering the approaching steamboat. Many were standing behind the roped-off area waiting until the passengers had disembarked so that they could rush aboard for a choice seat along the railing. Beyond the front wharf that faced the river, the girls could see the second dock behind it, and then the canal with its docks and landings on the level with the riverboat wharf above the river's water level.

Standing higher than the other barges in the piers beside her, the *Blue Swan* stood out as the most handsome of all the packets and barges. Josie saw her Aunt Ernestine sitting up on the top deck under the awning shade getting a breath of cool air from the river.

"Do you know something else?" Lou-Lou said. "I guess I never did know Grandma Kattmann. Why, I never figured any of this. She is a different person since the *Blue Swan*. It's touched us all."

"Maybe we all are, Lou-Lou. You are right. Things certainly are different from anything we had pictured. Mama was right. You know, she has always said we didn't know or understand grandma, and that we should try to be more considerate of Aunt Ernestine, and humor great Aunt Fredericka. Grandma has sure growed up in a hurry."

"Look at that beautiful *Blue Swan* sitting up there so proudly. Look at the people who stop to look at her."

"This sounds silly - like a little girl - but do you know what, Lou-Lou Gast? I think I am going to be glad to get home, and sleep in my full size bed again. I am homesick for Mama and little Daisy Baby."

"That's not so crazy, Jo-Jo. I think I am just going to be lazy all the way home, and just ride along, catnap and sleep all the way. Grandma-Má is still going strong, but I am tired all of a sudden. Josie, it isn't just being homesick. You and I both know someone let the butterflies out of Pandora's Box."

The boat gave another whistle for the landing. Now she was coasting in slack water, slower and slower. The girls left the churning paddlewheel just in time. The pilothouse bell clanged into the engine room for the engineers to reverse the paddlewheel to back down and slow the speed of the coasting steamer. The reverse direction of the wheel's paddles threw a spray of water with a fine mist that covered the area where the girls were standing. They laughed as they danced away and went hurriedly up the curving stairs to the second deck to their grandmother.

There was a clanging of engine bells, and the lurching of the boat, as the reverse action of the giant paddlewheel slowed her drift into a slow, scarcely moving drift. There was a soft bump and shudder as the gunwales rode along on the guiding pier piles; then the forward prow came against the cushioning fenders of the dock. Immediately the booms lowered the large gangplanks as the crowd streamed off the steamer onto the landing dock.

Josie and Lou-Lou viewed the ending of their birthday trip with mixed feelings. They found it hard to believe that so many things had happened and that they had seen so much. They still had the rest of the afternoon to explore the "Over the Rhine" up the hill to the area around the two basins of Lockport and Cheapside with Charley, Lou and Ben. They viewed the end of the trip with regret - and yet there was a feeling of relief. They looked forward to the homeward trip because it would be more leisurely, and they knew that they would have time to wander the docks and streets in Hamilton and Dayton. They could give vent to the ridiculous indescribable feeling of homesickness and get that out of their systems. However, there was something else. Things were not the same.

The girls lingered along the riverfront wharf near the area where the *Blue Swan* was moored. When they were alone, they sat on a dockside bench looking out over the busy river. The boys and both fathers, Ben and Hermann, would surely finish talking sometime about the steamboat they would like to build for the canal reservoirs back home. Then they would be ready to take the group up the grade of Eggleston Street and the ten locks to that fabled place everyone talked about, "Over the Rhine."

"Josie, I don't know how to say this, or if I am right in saying it, but there is something we are blind to, something we haven't let ourselves believe or say," Lou-Lou said slowly.

"What are we blind to, Lou-Lou?" Josie asked simply.

"You know how all of us laugh a little at Gert Langhorst and little Milly Vogelsang for being secretly silly over Schani and Fritzy, and we think they are so green and silly?"

"Even little Dort Waterman likes both Jakey Backhaus and Alby Lehmkuhl, but they would never let on to us," Josie replied.

"Well, we're so sure of ourselves and can laugh at them, but do you suppose it has happened to us - just a little bit?"

Both girls were so full of surprise at the thing they had just uncovered that they remained speechless for a few minutes. After a while, Josie answered her cousin,

"So that is the way it comes. It steals up on you unsuspectingly, covered up with dreams and other fine things, so that you don't notice it."

"Until it's too late," Lou-Lou said. Then she grew uncomfortable with this peek into adulthood and immediately lapsed back into the familiar lightheartedness of her former self. She began to laugh at herself but could not think of one single thing to mimic or to pantomime. She was surprised that she had gone dry.

Just then both girls saw a rat that was coming down the slanting hawser toward the bollard on the dock. He was coming slowly and cautiously from the grain barge that was moored at the dock.

Both girls jumped from the bench and ran a few steps away, but they were glad to change their thoughts, and welcomed the rat's intrusion into their perplexed reverie. As an afterthought, Lou-Lou ran back and shook the heavy rope line but the rat hung on tenaciously. They left the bollard and the heavy rope, and from a distance, they saw the rat scurry down and disappear beneath the heavy planks of the dock.

The mood of the girls changed rapidly when they joined Charley, Lou, and Ben down the dock near the *Blue Swan* barge. When their fathers came along with Uncle Henry, they were ready. They all started walking up Eggleston Avenue past the ten locks to the Cheapside and Lockport basins. Charley, Lou, and Ben crossed over the canal on the bridge at Symmes Street, and walked on the other side of the canal on Lock Street until they got nearer the first basin. Then they crossed back over the canal at a bridge and joined the group. There was an air of carnival gaiety in the streets in the area of the basins. The quay was wide on both sides of the basin, especially on both streets that paralleled the wide canal where it turned to the west. It went for six city blocks into what was formerly 11th Street before the canal was built. Now there was North Canal Street on the north and South Canal Street on the south - all along these six blocks.

Sounds of music were coming from the organ of a carousel somewhere in the vicinity. Music from a dance parlor carried out into the street from somewhere to the south. Perhaps it was on Court Street. Josie and Lou-Lou marveled at the tall spires of a city hall and a cathedral across the tops of other buildings. They asked their Uncle Henry what the building was with the dome on it. It looked like pictures they had seen of St. Peters at the Vatican. They were fascinated by the four stories of the large Eagle Brewery. How much more dignified it looked than the breweries back home.

In the next block they passed by an "outdoor cafe" where the customers were seated at individual tables under the trees that were lining the curb. They passed by a wine garden where a small orchestra was playing pleasant waltzes. Farther on a raucous tuba band played at an outdoor *Beer Garten* where the merrymakers were more garrulous. In a small green park, there was a pond with ducks, geese, swans, and some other noisy water birds. At the end of the little park or zoo, there was a bandstand and a stage where a singing trio was presenting some classic opera aria.

On another street, they passed many beer taverns and outdoor cafes. There were shows of some sort that were charging admission. It was clear to all of them now why this entertainment area was called "Over the Rhine."

They passed another theatre near the city hall on the public square. A small opera troupe was engaged there. Farther on, they saw their old favorite, the Spanish Dancers and the Señorita from Madrid. Instead of performing on their canal barge, they were now back to their permanent theatre.

The music from an open-air concert group faded into the background as the group was drawn into a side square. It was off one of the streets that seemed to be the home of a permanent carnival group.

They did not perform in tents or makeshift buildings. These were permanent small buildings facing the small square. Out in the center was the large carousel. Charley, Ben, and Lou walked all around it trying to see how it was propelled, for there were no tow horses attached. Ben and Hermann were as excited as the boys when they found that a small steam engine supplied the energy to rotate the rather large carousel. The men had found steam engines used more and more, and they began to take hope that they could build one small enough, yet strong enough, to propel their steamboat on the reservoirs.

They listened to the carousel music for a while. The boys rode it, but for some reason Josie and Lou-Lou found their interests elsewhere. Even though there were more varied carousel animals, the girls still declined to ride.

Ben and Hermann left the young people with Henry, and went back down to the riverfront to look at more engines on the steamboats docked there.

Hermann and Ben could not get enough of inspecting the riverboat that carried them and the boys downstream and back. If only they could get the parts here and there and make their steamer. They sure could have fun on the reservoir! Of course, there was the problem of berthing her and caring for her during the winter and during storms, but there must surely be a way. They took the boys on another riverboat ride.

Later in the afternoon, the other steamboat that was coming back upstream from Aurora landed and deposited Hermann, Ben, and the talkative boys on the landing dock.

Every one of them was so tired that they were content just to visit with each other and have a leisurely supper on board the *Blue Swan*. The crew had their instructions from Ben and Hermann in order to prepare for the trip back to Brementown. They would see about extra feed for the horses, supplies for themselves, have the water barrels filled, and take care of all other details.

After supper, Ernestine Hofermeyer and her husband took the three boys and the two girls on a walk with them. They took the ferryboat across to the Kentucky side to walk around in old Newport. They wanted the children to be able to say that they had been on the actual soil of Kentucky when school started.

Mrs. Noffsinger, Meg Threewits, and some of the older crewmen were old neighbors, and they sauntered up into town to look around a little on this, the last night in the city, and take in that "Over the Rhine" district. The Carousel played "Ride the Carousel" and the girls caught their breath.

Traffic came and went through the canal basin. Packets coming from the north deposited passengers who were going on to some farther destination. Other passengers came in carriages to the station, bought tickets, and boarded canal packets for passage north to towns along the upper Miami and Erie Canal. The large steamboats came and left from the river wharf landing. The girls never seemed to grow tired of watching the boats on the river, even into the later hours of the night. After the swan barge settled down for the night, and the lights were lowered, Lou-Lou and Josie sat up on the top deck watching the lights on the river. They could look up the hill above the river to the stone cornices of the Holland House, with its serrated Netherlands style gables, and the stone facings over light brickwork.

They never tired of watching the throngs of people walking on the river wharf and along in front of them on the canal dock. They talked into the late night. Charley, Lou, and Ben talked with them for a while. They exchanged stories about all their exciting explorations aboard the steamboat. After a while the boys, who had been romping for days with hardly a let up, grew drowsy and started to nod. Their Aunt Ernestine hounded them to the washroom and made them wash up and go to bed before they had a chance to stretch out on the warm deck and fall asleep.

Ben and Hermann sat on the fantail, well back on the stern by the tiller, and had their evening pipes. Their soft voices purred with conversation. Heinrich Hofermeyer and Ernestine pored over the city newspaper and some new books they had bought at the huge Shell Lotto department emporium.

One by one, the lights went out on the barges around them. Lights were extinguished in the taverns and inns along the dock. After midnight, the bright lamps were dimmed in the passenger depot. High up above the river, bright lights gleamed from the Holland House. From the open windows in the ballroom, Lou-Lou and Josie could hear strains from the orchestra. As voices and traffic grew quieter on the canal dock, the music from the orchestra could be heard more plainly. The girls listened from time to time when there was a lull in their low conversation.

Later in the night, there was a cold breeze across from the river. Josie and Lou-Lou went into their bed in the upper cabin behind the pilothouse. From the small-paned window, they could look from their bed through the pilothouse, and see through the large glass of its front windshield to the lights blazing from the Holland House. Just as they were drifting off to sleep, they heard what must have been the orchestra's last selection. They let their hearts sing with the old sweet refrain from the Viennese orchestra; then they remembered the words "Auf Wiedersehen, but not good-bye."

Sometime shortly after that the girls drifted off to sleep, and the swan with her wings folded back nestled her sleeping brood. With her neck proudly arched, she looked down as she kept watch on the dock below.

Sometime before daylight, the prancing white horses were brought to the *Blue Swan*, and without much delay, the handsome packet glided from her berth in the cool twilight toward the locks. One by one, the swan barge and its companion barge raised the ten levels of locks to the straight level channel of the two basins, Cheapside and Lockport, and the canal that led home. A heavy fog had settled over the river and laid heavily over the riverfront wharfs. The gables of the Holland House could not be seen through the moist, gray mist. At one time Josie was partly awake, and saw the mist through the cabin window. She imagined that she was home and seeing the mist through the window as it lay over the canal in early morning back in Old Brementown. Too full of sleep to know whether she was seeing it or dreaming it, Josie moved her lips in some incoherent words. She had always loved to see the wisps of fog rise from the smooth surface of the canal. She used to imagine that she could see figures in the mist much as she did in the cloud formations. Josie thought she saw the faint outline of a majestic swan with arched neck gliding on the canal surface through the wisps of the mist, which obscured it from time to time. She felt strange tears start in her eyes.

Josie felt herself floating off with the beautiful light *Blue Swan* with the white snowy wings, and drifting off on clouds of the mist, and she was either into a deep sleep or into dreams. She imagined that she heard the rippling chords of a chorus of harps. The sound lulled her more deeply into peaceful forgetfulness with its lullaby; then she heard soft voices blended into a choral lullaby. She saw no one else, only the majestic, nearly white swan floating serenely along. Could the solo standing out from the chorus be the voice of the swan? Then she remembered the legend that the swan can sing only once - in its final flight just before death.

The words seemed to come from a distance, even from yesteryear. She was looking back into the years past, the years of happy childhood, and the words of the lullaby caught at her throat. The harp's bass chords simulated the graceful strokes of those wings.

> *Fly away, fly away, fly away home.*
> *Fly, Blue Swan, spread your wings.*
> *Cry your sweet song.*
>
> *Dry my tears, calm down all my fears,*
> *With your downy white wings.*

The lullaby became fainter as the rippling flourishes of the harps seemed to drown out the sweet song. Through the mist in the distance, she saw the swan spread its wide wings and sail off above the canal. It disappeared into the gray, silent fog, with those strong pinions in rhythmic time, and with the deep chords of the harps.

Homeward it flew - Josie didn't know how she knew - but she knew the swan of yesterday was winging its way home through the years, on a straight, true course, true as a homing pigeon. She also knew somehow that Lou-Lou was there with her, and that she was dreaming or seeing the same homing swan, and hearing that lullaby. Lou-Lou called out in her sleep, moved slightly, and then was silent.

> *Soft summer moon, we'll slumber soon.*
> *Again back home, safe beneath your white wings.*

Josie knew who she was - yet she didn't. She knew that she was Josephine Gast, didn't she? She heard Louise Gast, her cousin Lou-Lou, sigh in her sleep. She heard the faint chorus again in the distance through the mist. There were a few soothing ripples of the accompanying harps. She was conscious of those strong wings, so steady, so reassuring; then she must have fallen into deep sleep with the lullaby, for she scarcely remembered anything else.

There was only the deep contentment of peaceful oblivion, knowing that everything was in place, and that she soon would be home in her mother's arms somewhere up the canal in the distant fog, many locks ahead. Soon Josie would be back in her own familiar room and sleep in her soft featherbed. If only the sweet song of the ever-watchful swan didn't tug at her heartstrings, and if she could tell whether or not the sweet swan was crying or singing.

The pleasant slight roll of the gliding packet barge acted as a further soporific sleep inducement. Distant barge horns sounded through the fog in this twelve mile level between locks. The drivers, polemen, and the rudder man at the till proceeded with caution in the enveloping, gray shroud. It covered them and cushioned the sound of the tinkling silver bells on the horses' harnesses.

There was scarcely any travel on the towpath at this early hour, and as daylight approached, just before the sun was about to creep over the eastern misty horizon, the swan barge was well on her way, and every step of the proud white horses brought them that much closer to home.

Epilogue

Oh Blue Swan, spread your white wings.
There's joy in your song.
Perhaps tears on your breast, but
Oh Blue Swan, fly away home.

Take us safely back home.
Wing your way through the mist.
Take us back through the years.
Was there laughter with tears?

Follow the towpath, along that clear Stream.
You know the way, whether by night, or by day.
Back through the years, back through our dream.
Oh take us home, oh Blue Swan,
Fly, fly away, fly away home.

FLY AWAY HOME

A Lullaby
of
The Blue Swan

Fly away, fly away, fly away home.
Fly, Blue Swan, spread your wings.
Cry your sweet song."

Dry my tears, calm all my fears,
With your downy white wings.

Through the mist, through the years,
Laughter and tears."

Wing your way, time will not stay,
Lovely Blue Swan.

Soft summer moon, we'll slumber soon.
Again back home, safe beneath your white wings.

O WHAT DO I BRING?

This is the song of the old Irish codger, Hooligan. This is an old Irish folk tune supposedly and he has adapted it to his own use. In reality, the old tune is about an old Irish codger. The title sometimes is:

<u>O What-Leth Ya They?</u>

The common title, "What-Leth Ya They," is hard to spell for it is said in a drunken stupor to mean, "Oh what do you say?" OR "What did you say?"

<u>VERSE</u>:   Up and down and through the town,
An old Irish codger passes by.
Back and forth each way, he canals each day.
Yet no one knows where he goes or why.

At each lock he'll dock, and his whisky swig.
He'll hurl insults, and do a drunken jig.
All old women are bad; small boys are no better.
Lockmasters are evil; all gossips he'd fetter."

O what's his name? No one knows the same.
So Hooligan's the name they call.
His ribald song, he sings all day long,
And drunken insults they hear him bawl.

With barge all closed tight, no one comes on board.
With all boxes nailed shut, strange barrels to hoard.
So the mys-ter-ee, that no one can see.
Faith, the question for all, on his deaf ears does fall, is:
What on this earth does he haul?

<u>REFRAIN</u>: *Polka-gig and side-reel*

O what do I bring, the Divvil you sing!
O don't you wish you knew.
O what's in my barge? O hooch barrels so large!
Whist! Maybe it's Irish brew!

Old wimmen, yer vile with yer old toothless smile.
You rile up my bile, but that's your hag style.

445

You spend all the day, up the towpath each way.
And with gossip you say, "O whaddleth thay-y-y?"

You said from the stall, manure I haul.
Faith, and how you lie.
Why, it's now don't you know, it's stolen cargo,
With pirates and thieves I vie.

I'll lock on through, but I'll be back.
And I hope to hell, your dry lips crack."
I'll turn loose on this whole doggone ta-own-n.
A thousand or more of Leper-chaun.

Who can-awled with me, from across the sea.
All the way from I---re----- land."

The song is sung in Irish dialect, better with drunken thick lips for the parts supposedly sung by Hooligan.

Since he had few front teeth, and was supposedly drunk, the title words would have to be heard pronounced to get it correct, but it is something like, "Whadd-le yeth thay?"

LaVergne, TN USA
09 October 2009
160316LV00004B/2/P